Vodka Neat

Vodka Neat

ANNA BLUNDY

FELONY & MAYHEM PRESS • NEW YORK

All the characters and events portrayed in this novel are fictitious.

VODKA NEAT

A Felony & Mayhem Mystery

PRINTING HISTORY:
First UK edition (Sphere): 2006
First U.S. edition (St. Martin's): 2008
Felony & Mayhem edition: 2009

ISBN 978-1-934609-34-7

Manufactured in the United States of America

Library of Congress Cataloging-in-Publication Data

Blundy, Anna, 1970-
Vodka neat / Anna Blundy. -- Felony & Mayhem ed.
p. cm.
"A Felony & Mayhem mystery."
ISBN 978-1-934609-34-7
1. War correspondents--Fiction. 2. Women journalists--Fiction.
3. Russia (Federation)--Fiction. I. Title.
PR6102.L86V63 2009
823'.92--dc22
                    2009014190

For Grace.
It's so nice to have someone to share Moscow with.

The icon above says you're holding a copy of a book in the Felony & Mayhem "Foreign" category. These books may be offered in translation or may originally have been written in English, but always they will feature an intricately observed, richly atmospheric setting in a part of the world that is neither England nor the U.S.A. If you enjoy this book, you may well like other "Foreign" titles from Felony & Mayhem Press.

———◆———

For more about these books, and other Felony & Mayhem titles, or to place an order, please visit our website at:

www.FelonyAndMayhem.com

or contact us at

Felony and Mayhem Press
156 Waverly Place
New York, NY 10014

Other "Foreign" titles from

FEL♀NY⚭MAYHEM

PAUL ADAM
The Rainaldi Quartet

KARIN ALVTEGEN
Missing
Betrayal

ANNA BLUNDY
The Bad News Bible

ROBERT CULLEN
Soviet Sources
Cover Story
Dispatch from a Cold Country

NICHOLAS FREELING
Love in Amsterdam
Because of the Cats
Gun Before Butter

TIMOTHY HOLME
The Neapolitan Streak
A Funeral of Gondolas

ELIZABETH IRONSIDE
A Good Death

STUART KAMINSKY
Death of a Dissident
Black Knight in Red Square

PAUL MANN
Season of the Monsoon
The Ganja Coast

BARBARA NADEL
Belshazzar's Daughter
The Ottoman Cage
Arabesk

CLAIRE TASCHDJIAN
The Peking Man is Missing

L. R. WRIGHT
The Suspect
A Chill Rain in January

Vodka Neat

PROLOGUE

Moscow 1989

THERE WAS a do at Dom Literatov, the literary house. I remember that much. Some author, Limonov maybe, was launching his book and all the foreigners with pretensions to speaking Russian or knowing anything about anything were going. I wore a short, tight, black velvet dress with puffed sleeves that dropped off my shoulders. My landlady, Zinaida Petrovna, sewed me into it, pins sticking out of her puckered mouth, a greasy apron wrapped around her enormous middle.

'Real velvet,' she muttered into the pins. 'Real velvet.' She stroked my back and looked as though she might actually cry. It was snowing from the heavy grey sky and the old men queuing up at the beer cellar in our courtyard wore the flaps of their shapkas down, raw red hands clutching their huge empty jars. There was one man with a swollen purple face, weeping red eyes and a running nose that dripped into his beard who always shuffled his way towards the front of the queue with a particular desolation—not chatting to the others, not even looking up.

1

'His mother loved him,' Dimitri used to say. I wasn't so sure.

Zinaida Petrovna tutted every time one of the men came over to our wall to urinate. The snow was banked up high, nearly reaching the window. My nineteenth-century double glazing had a foot's width between the interior and exterior panes and I was keeping a chicken, frozen, in the gap. I worried that Zinaida Petrovna might steal it while I was out.

She was charging me three-quarters of my monthly salary as rent for my one room and I paid her because I was living there illegally and Dimitri, my Russian husband, my cover, the person who was officially renting the place, had gone back to Ryazan after our last big row and showed no signs of coming back any time soon, thank God. But my documents hadn't come through and I still had none of a Soviet citizen's rights (surprisingly many, mostly concerning the procurement of food and housing).

Tonight, free and possibly even single, I was meeting Scott Weisman at Dom Literatov. It was Scott, in fact, who was indirectly responsible for my new status. Dimitri and I had had a row about him in the Savoy hotel. Well, I say row. It was more of a prolonged silence really.

The Savoy had opened three months earlier, the only half-civilised place in Moscow and with stricter entry procedures than the other hotels, so the prostitutes and seedy thugs who populated pretty much everywhere in those days couldn't get in. Unfortunately, though, neither could Dimitri. Not without a certain amount of effort at any rate. It was not a good start to the evening as far as the impending row was concerned.

We had pulled up in Dimitri's maroon Lada Samara, which had no heating (me in a big black fur and him in a thin, cheap imitation of a presidential great coat), and we skidded to a stop in the deep snow, just brushing against the brass barriers with red ropes that surrounded the entrance. Inside the barrier, under the hotel's glittering canopy, the actual pavement was carpeted. Doors guarded by policemen and hotel staff in top hats and old-fashioned frock coats revealed the warm wealthy glow of the foyer within—a chandelier, gleaming marble floors and pretty girls in smart uniforms with their names on their badges, all just graduated from Moscow State University's English faculty.

I had been having dreams. My nights were haunted by plummeting lifts, plunging planes, gangs with guns, buildings ablaze. I had woken up that night gasping for breath, with alcoholic dehydration and a pounding heart. I ran barefoot across the freezing, unpolished parquet to the kitchen where I stirred a spoonful of crystal-shining orange KoolAid into a glass of tap water. Tap water they said one shouldn't drink, but I didn't see any Russians dying. Actually, I did, but not from drinking the tap water. Dimitri, my husband, who slept with one hand flat against the wall (his little finger scarred from when he fell over running for the loo at school when he was six), woke up, like he always did, lit a cigarette and tried to comfort me. Sometimes he went easy on himself and we just went out for a drive. I would tell him about girls who got cars for their seventeenth birthdays, the keys presented in a box by their beaming parents, friends clapping round the blazing candles on the cake, the surprise gift parked neatly outside, a ribbon round the aerial. Or I described people who winter in the Caribbean or restaurants where they serve lobster and make crêpes Suzette at the table. I don't think he really believed me.

That night of the separation he took one sympathetic, though exhausted, look at me and said, 'You need to go to the Savoy.' And he was right. The dim greyness of Communist Moscow was too accurate a reflection of my mental state. He felt that only a Russian could really be expected to cope with this life. It amazes me now that he was then only twenty-seven. Judging by his eyes he could have been fifty.

I showed my passport to the policemen and the doormen and Dimitri walked manfully by my side, snowflakes melting on his shoulders, speaking to me in English. They usually fell for this at the Intourist but they weren't having any of it here. Dimitri lowered his voice to a whisper and one of the policemen leant down to hiss into his face. I lit a cigarette and waited, watched the fat snow fall. Dimitri stood on his tiptoes and whispered into the policeman's ear. That seemed to do it. One little threat and we were in.

The doors were opened and we went and sat down in the pink and gold bar. They served microwaved ready meals in here—that was how glamorous it was. Outside, where old ladies huddled in underpasses, their feet wrapped in rags, there were shortages so severe that even German food parcels were being accepted. People remembered the war and the Germans had not been forgiven. In the Leningrad blockade people ate rats.

'I wish you wouldn't threaten everyone,' I said, my hands clamped round a Campari and soda. I knew I shouldn't have said it. I knew he didn't want to be in the Savoy in any case. He did it for my sake. Taking me back to my world. A world in which he, of course, would always be uncomfortable.

Still, none of his generosity, in my view, justified an hour and a half's thin-lipped silence. Well, OK. Not total silence. He did say one thing. It was: 'I don't know why you don't just go out with Scott Weisman.'

He had met Scott. He did not like Scott. The easy American superiority, white teeth, blue passport, pocket full of dollars.

Good point, I thought as I rolled my eyes and sighed. When we got back to the dark, stinking doorway of our dingy flat, the symbol of our pathetic attempt at a relationship, he left me there, got into his car and drove away into the night.

I put my big iron key in the door and went inside. There was a dead rat in the bath. I had brought poison from London and it made them die of thirst. I sat on the bed in my fur coat, my knees pulled into my chest, and cried until I was empty. Not for Dimitri really. For myself, for my dad, who was killed in Belfast when I was nine, for all the other desolate people crying alone in the night. A lot of them, I thought, were probably in Moscow.

Then in the morning after the row (maybe even separation?), shaking with hangover, I phoned Scott and he invited me to the Dom Literatov party. He was a Russophile Californian doing an internship at the *New York Times*, intrepidly trawling round meetings of mothers of dead Soviet conscripts (there were a lot of them), attending memorial rallies for the gulag-dead outside the Lubyanka at which nobody got arrested (unthinkable even six months earlier) and hitting on damsels in distress (me). He was sharp and funny and looked like a Martian in Moscow with his cute glasses, short back and sides and pressed khakis. Maybe the GIs looked like this in sepia wartime Britain. He mistook my depressive sarcasm for searing intelligence and he loved me. He brought me jars of bacon bits from the salad bar at the American Embassy and he sat on my dirty floor with me drinking sweet champagne, singing Billy Joel songs and saying he didn't know any other girls like me.

Tonight was the night of our date. Zinaida Petrovna came round to the front of me for a look. 'Pryelyest!' she whimpered. I almost liked her. I put my stilettos in a carrier bag, pulled on black zip-up waterproof boots, my coat, hat and gloves, and trudged out into the gloom. I walked down the boulevard with my head bowed against the snow. There was an old woman sitting on a bench selling ice creams in squat cones out of a cardboard box for ten kopeks. An ancient orange and white tourist bus juddered outside the circus, choking everyone near it with thick black exhaust fumes.

At Dom Literatov people stood around in the slush smoking in groups and talking quietly.

'Hey, Zanetti,' Scott whispered into my ear, coming up behind me and putting his hands round my waist.

'Fuck off,' I said, and turned to kiss him on the cheek. 'I've left Zinaida Petrovna alone with my chicken,' I told him.

'That's the last you'll see of that,' he nodded, pulling his woolly hat off and treading the snow off his Timberlands, the stamp of his nationality.

The foyer was dimly lit and stuffed full of middle-aged men in appalling suits standing in front of clouded mirrors and combing the remains of their hair. I sat down on a stool and changed my shoes and Scott took all our stuff to the cloakroom and handed me my greenish plastic tag. Limonov (which translates as 'of the lemons'), or whoever it was, was already talking and most people were standing round the rostrum listening reverently. Scott took two shots of vodka off a trestle table and handed me one. I'd never drunk this stuff neat before. We clinked glasses and sank them in one. Hmmm. I could get a taste for this. We did it again and it is at this stage that my memory gets slightly blurry.

I remember throwing my arms round Limonov's neck and congratulating him. I remember throwing my arms round Scott's neck in a corridor we found behind a black padded door. I remember a KGB stooge telling us we were in an unauthorised area. I think I remember falling soon after that down a stone flight of stairs, though that may be a retrospective memory, constructed from my injuries. Something flickering at the back of my mind shows me a girl in stilettos slipping down the boulevard on the ice dangerously late at night.

And then it was morning. I was lying on my front and my mouth tasted of vomit. Someone was banging on the door and thin grey light was coming through the windows. My hand was right in front of my eyes and there was blood on it. I sat up and put my feet on the parquet. There were shoes on them. My knees were badly grazed and I was still in my dress. I touched my face and felt what could be a dramatic wound on my forehead. My jaw hurt. I looked round the room and saw that I had thrown my outdoor clothes on the floor. I must have left my boots at Dom Literatov. I ran through the memories I could dredge up. No big deal, humiliation-wise. So far I could cope with the damage. I took my shoes off and went to the bathroom to wash my face. When I had rinsed the blood off it was only a scrape really. Amazing how much blood can be produced from a scalp wound. I went to the kitchen where the old lady, whose name I never did find out, was boiling some cornflakes in a saucepan of water. She was houseridden and smelt of decay. A boy called Lyosha brought her useless food aid—dried goods with instructions in English, all of which told the recipient to add eggs or milk or some other unattainable thing.

'Good morning,' I said.

'Good morning,' she said.

'There's someone at the door,' I said.

'Yes,' she said.

I couldn't answer the door because of my illegal status. Apparently, my Russian sounded like an Estonian's but that wasn't good enough. Estonians would be told to produce documents too.

I took my KoolAid back to my room and it was only then that I saw Dimitri. He was asleep with one hand against the wall. Had he been there when I got home? Had he come in the night? My scream of surprise woke him up. He looked at me blearily.

'Your head,' he said.

'I know. There's someone at the door,' I told him.

He got up in his Y-fronts, lit a cigarette and heaved our enormous and ornate front door open. When I saw the policemen I ducked into the toilet. There is a Soviet joke which involves banging on friends' doors and shouting 'Police!' It is a very bleak Russian-style joke with reference to the 1930s purges. Anyway, the sight of actual police at the door was very chilling indeed. I assumed they had come for me. Dimitri and I once ran through the crimes I had committed against the Soviet state and estimated that I was fixing to spend about thirty years in a camp. Trading hard currency, smoking illegal drugs, travelling outside Moscow without a visa, living without a propiska and so on.

They stood in the hall and made Dimitri produce his passport (although it was called a passport it did not entitle the holder to travel anywhere. For that he or she would need an 'international passport' and there was pretty much no chance of getting one of these unless you were directly related to Gorbachev himself). Neither the policemen nor Dimitri reacted in the slightest way to the latter's near nudity. Dimitri smoked, the policemen checked his details.

'You're not registered here,' the more acned of the two stated.

'It's my mum's flat,' Dimitri said. I wondered if he had already told Zinaida Petrovna to confirm that or if he was planning to threaten her later.

Realising this wasn't about me, I came out of the bathroom, still in my velvet dress.

'This is my wife,' Dimitri said. 'She's mute.'

Hello? I raised my eyebrows at him in disbelief and nodded at the policemen, lips sealed.

'You are covered in blood,' the chatty one said.

I nodded in silent admission and then went and lay back down to die quietly of alcohol poisoning. I hoped Dimitri would not be staying.

The muttering in the hallway continued and Dimitri came into our room to put some trousers on.

''S going on?' I asked.

'Something next door. They want witnesses.'

The room between ours and the old lady's had been empty since we'd been living there, but last week, while Dimitri was away, a young couple had moved in. Though we theoretically shared a bathroom and kitchen, I had seen the girl only once, very late at night when I was running to the loo. She was coming in, drunk and heavily made up. The man I had seen three times, coming in and out, smart and slightly westernised. We had never spoken.

Now the policemen were opening the door to the room, their big leather boots noisy on the wooden floor, hammers and sickles on their steaming hats, an effect always achieved when coming in from the snow. You stand there steaming.

'Just in here,' they told Dimitri.

'Yes,' I heard him say. That was before he groaned loudly. 'Oh God,' he said, staggering back into our room followed by the boys in khaki.

I put my hand up to my forehead.

Dimitri signed a form to say he had witnessed the crime scene. I was next. I hauled myself up. Dimitri was white. They didn't speak to me and I, being mute, didn't speak to them. I peered round the edge of the door they had opened to look at the bodies of my neighbours. An axe lay on the floor. A woodcutter's axe. Fairy tale thing. The girl was lying on the single bed the couple must have shared. Her head, I think, had been completely severed. She was dressed in outdoor clothes. The naked man's injuries were, if possible, more horrific. I surmised, as I retched into my hands, that he had killed her and then killed himself by cutting off his leg above the knee and bleeding to death. There was blood everywhere. But I mean absolutely everywhere. The smell, overpowering, was of steak that has sat in the sun for a couple of days. Sweet and thick. At this point I threw up on to the floor in front of me.

That was sixteen years ago. I was nineteen years old. And that is what I remember. That and the fact that my chicken had been stolen in the night.

Chapter 1

THIS IS THE first proper posting I've had since my break-down. Moscow. It's not the first time I've been back since I left Dimitri for good, but I haven't lived here since I was a teenager and, since that night, I certainly haven't worn any velvet dresses.

I didn't want the job especially, but I thought I'd better show willing in case I got sacked. Might have seemed churlish to refuse. You don't want to come over all prima donna-ish when you are busy grappling with your sanity. I went mad in Qatar during the war with Iraq. Like, really mad. That's what falling in love can do to you. Anyway, I needed to rebuild a bit of trust on the paper.

Tamsin (who, amazingly, is still the foreign editor. It's not often people cling on to that job for more than a year or two. The senior people like that are the first to go when there's any kind of regime change. And there's always a regime change) and the op-ed (opinion and editorial) bloke took me out for lunch at that big seafood place in Butler's Wharf and we sat outside squinting at each other and cracking lobster claws with big metal tools that flashed in the sunlight.

'How's your Russian, Zanetti?' Tamsin asked, sucking butter off her fingers.

'Haven't seen him for years,' I muttered and she blinked at me questioningly. 'No, er... It's fine. It's good. It's fluent,' I said. 'Why? Where's Toby going?' Toby wears three-piece suits into the Moscow office (a shabby room in a big compound full of foreigners) and runs an illegal caviar business from which he scrapes off a profit.

'Miami,' Tamsin said, lighting a cigarette. The op-ed bloke coughed and dabbed at the corners of his mouth with a big white napkin. He is running for a Tory seat in the local elections next month. He will get it.

'Miami?! Miami?! What the fuck is he going to Miami for?' I laughed, feeling for my own cigarettes and then taking one of Tamsin's.

'We're opening a bureau,' she told me defiantly.

'Toby McFarquhar is going to be the *Chronicle*'s Caribbean correspondent? What's he going to do? Intrepid pieces about whether or not you really can have a relaxing time at a spa on Nevis?' I actually once read a piece about exactly this in the *Financial Times*. Somebody must have been very very pleased with his assignment that week.

'Zanetti. I am not about to start defending the paper's decisions to you. There are a lot of stories we are missing out on by covering them from New York and Washington.'

Uh-huh. He'll be writing picture captions for big splashes about which celebrities have been spotted on the beach that day with their tits out/in/bigger/smaller. And the odd murder, I suppose. All those mad Brits kill each other over affairs from time to time—nearly posh enough for a title but not quite, minds addled by the heat and the booze. I will definitely be lobbying for that job when I am in my dotage (not far off at this rate).

The only hope of Moscow's being remotely interesting is if Chechnya or somewhere explodes. It's not an attractive thing to admit, but if there isn't a war going on it's hard to get really enthusiastic about a job. Once you've been at the very edge of life it is hard to concentrate on the middle.

There is something about covering war (and, Lord knows, plenty of my colleagues have written books about it) that gives you an unshakeable, though perhaps warped, sense of perspective. When you have seen the absolute horrors of it, then nothing else seems to matter at all. The papers are full of articles that suddenly seem absurd in their banality. A Prime Minister lied about his motives for something? The public shouldn't eat fish?

Look, babies are having their legs blown off somewhere, men are torturing each other, women are being raped by soldiers, murdered in front of their families. Don't tell me about some dodgy paperwork and a health scare involving farmed salmon.

Well, that's the kind of attitude you pick up doing this job. And it feels like the truth. The trouble is that if you despise everyone who genuinely has an opinion (!) about fox hunting then you are going to end up pretty lonely. Most of us are pretty lonely. And it's not as though we are charging round the world putting an end to war and injustice either. We're just watching really (though my colleagues' books would mostly have you believe otherwise).

I suppose the big stumbling block to this 'I've seen the horrors' thing is that when a horror happens to you personally you are not quite sure what to do with it. You've spent so much time watching that you don't notice that you haven't learnt anything at all that you can apply to yourself. Look, I am already talking in the second person. Have you noticed that whenever anyone talks about something horrible hap-

I thought, not for the first time, that you don't need to punish people who have done unthinkable things. That just gives them something to rail against. They punish themselves if you leave them alone. They shrivel and twist themselves into a sleepless, peaceless, screaming ball of agony. I wanted to pity him. Then he told me about the things he had done personally in the villages and I sipped my beer and smiled blankly and thought that he deserved to live a very long life so that his torture was not unjustly curtailed by the longed-for sleep of death.

Death. Yes, that was the link. I was cleaning my teeth when I got the news. My room on the ranch was vast and bare with an enormous teak bed swathed in mosquito nets and with bamboo doors out on to the veranda. It came through as a text message to my mobile phone. 'Call me. Bad news. Eden.' Eden Jones. Colleague. Sometimes lover. He was staying at my flat in London while I was away, doing a stint on home news at his paper to see out his contract. He had just got an incredible new job writing for the *New Yorker*. Don't know how he pulled it off. Can hardly string a sentence together, but perhaps the fact checkers write it all for them.

I lay down on the bed under the nets and lit a cigarette. It was like a whole world under there. Ashtray, cold cup of coffee, newspapers, phone, laptop.

''S up?' I asked him when he picked the phone up.

'Faith, your mum's dead,' he said. I was grateful to him for not finding it difficult or embarrassing. For just telling me and not being desperate to get off the phone, cringing with the horror of his responsibility.

'Oh,' I said, wondering how I felt about this. 'What happened?'

She was sitting at her kitchen table with her friend Pauline eating Chinese takeaway. Pauline is Nigerian and is always trying to make Mum go on holiday to Lagos with her. I ask you. I mean, when I lived in Moscow all those years ago it was full of people from Lagos trying to catch a break. If they came to Moscow then, all I can say is that Lagos must be a real slime pit. That was my mind trying not to digest what Eden was saying.

So, they were eating chicken with cashew nuts, spinach in garlic sauce, Shang-hai dumplings and special fried rice. Mum told Pauline she had a headache and pinched the top of her nose. They were sharing a bottle of some crap by Ernest and Julio Gallo. Mum stood up. 'I feel a bit funny,' she said. Then she fell over on to the parquet of the kitchen floor. Dead. This, say medical people, is pretty much the best way to go. Painless, sudden, certain. An enormous brain haemorrhage. She was sixty-two. A decade ago I might have thought that was a reasonably respectable innings. Now it seems young.

I had been leaning up on one elbow to talk to Eden. Now I lay down on my back and watched the lazy brass ceiling fan slice through the thick air. There was a mosquito inside my net and I blew a stream of smoke at it. A song came into my head. By Mike and the Mechanics, I think. Anyway, it's all about death making everything too late. And now it is. Too late.

I stopped hoping she would come and find me years ago, of course. Though when I was first moved away to live with Dad and Evie I couldn't believe she'd let me go. I lay awake in bed waiting for the doorbell to ring. Believing she would come for me. If not tonight then tomorrow. I didn't know then that she would have been arrested if she'd tried. That is, she was arrested when she did try.

Then, not long ago, after I'd been doing a harrowing child abuse investigation in Jerusalem, I went to find her. Not that it was difficult. I knew where she was. I had her number. She'd always kept in touch with Evie, even before Dad was

killed. I took her an olivewood nativity scene from Bethlehem. She gave me some conditioner for my ridiculous blonde
Afro. She cried a lot. Then, after that, we were officially in
touch. But it turned out I was in touch for her sake, really. So
that she wouldn't be sad, wouldn't feel she had let me down,
wouldn't feel a failure. There was nothing in it for me. For I
suppose I had hoped what we all hope. All of us who go to find
someone, whether a parent or a lover—we hope they will take
us in and hug us and give us all the security and certainty and
love we have longed for all our lives. I don't imagine it ever
happens. I was looking after her again, like I'd done when she
was drinking. Like I'd always done. And now it was too late.
Too late for her to brush my hair again, for her to take me to
school sober, for her to make biscuits on my birthday or sing
me a lullaby. Of course it's too late. I am thirty-five.

The hearse broke down. We all stood on Streatham High
Road, about twenty of us, while a teenager in a black suit
phoned head office to get another one sent out. He put one of
those red triangles up in the road to warn other drivers and
he rolled his eyes at me, not imagining that I might be the
chief mourner. Nobody was crying.

I leant against the railings of a primary school that was
protected by high glinting fences with razor wire on top
of them and I smoked a cigarette. This flesh-slashing wire
apparently keeps out the fathers who might come to snatch
their children.

Another hearse pulled up and flashed its hazard lights
on while the pall bearers dragged Mum out of the back of one
hearse and put her in the other. I had bought one of those
flower arrangements that reads 'MUM' in big white chrysan-

themums and one of the blokes in black tails held it while the transfer was made. The flowers were supposed to be a joke, but actually they just looked depressing. Funereal humour—not funny.

'Right, we're off,' the driver said, and we all got back into our big black cars to follow him to the church. I understand that for a hearse to screech round corners at ninety miles an hour would be inappropriate, but the speed they do go at makes me breathless with anxiety.

'I don't think you're allowed to smoke in these things,' Pauline pointed out. I put my cigarettes back in the pocket of my leather jacket and drummed my fingers on the arm rest.

I had got in from Harare three hours earlier and I had not slept on the plane. I had drunk quite a lot on it though and now my lips felt dry and my thoughts were acid and tangled. I wished I'd eaten the British Airways slime-class muffin they'd brought me for breakfast.

Evie was waiting for me in the church. I sat next to her and held her hand. She smelt of violets and looked, today, like Coco Chanel. If anyone had been my mother it was Evie. She had her own children now, grown up and half gone, Mo to university and Shash to India to find herself on a mountain or whatever it is that people do. Evie's husband is based in Hong Kong and nobody ever sees much of him. A happier arrangement perhaps than the one she'd had with Dad—she looked after his daughter while he travelled around to wars and got killed.

Eden slouched in during 'The Lord's My Shepherd'. I thought if I could keep singing I might stop crying. 'In death's dark vale I fear no ill.' I felt that I spent a good deal too much time in death's dark vale. It seems to be part of the job. Eden had raked up a black suit from somewhere. He looked as though he'd slept in it but that's just how he always looks. His hair was wet from the shower and he had shaved seconds ago (very possibly in the taxi). He shuffled his way into my pew and put his arm round my shoulders. I looked down at his feet and saw that he had trainers on.

'Did you buy that, Zanetti?' he whispered, nodding towards the 'MUM' chrysanthemums.

'Mmm hmmm,' I said.

He shook his head and muttered, 'Christ.'

I looked at the altar and didn't really see it. It is hard to know what to do with grief. Perhaps if your spouse of thirty years dies you can bury yourself in the enormous reorganisation of your life that will be necessary. Maybe if a beloved parent dies you can talk to all their friends, paste photos of them in albums, tell your children about them. Tell your children…

But I didn't even know Mum very well. I was supposed to plough on as usual now. Even talking to Eden about it seemed a bit self-indulgent somehow, seeing as how I'd had so little to do with her. But there was a coil of pain in the pit of my stomach and it wouldn't go away. I told myself it didn't matter—that death is a part of life for everyone and that surely the death of most people's parents was a worse experience than this. I know Dad's seemed transparently cataclysmic. I shrugged to myself in my mind and thought of the Russian way of saying 'byvayet' (it happens). But here is my question: if, in evolutionary terms, this is just what happens, no big deal, comes to everyone, then what is the use of it hurting so much? Really. If it doesn't matter then why is it so fucking painful?

I think being English probably doesn't help. Or, that is, being English today. A hundred or so years ago everyone would have met death by about the age of five. I would by now probably have a few living and a few dead children. Death was then, and in some places is now, very much a part of life. Coffins were open, children were not protected from it. Nowadays we devote all our energy to pretending that we won't die and nor will anyone we love (if we fasten our seatbelts, have vaccinations, don't smoke, don't drink, eat broccoli, drink a litre and a half of water a day) so that when they do (and they do) we are left bewildered and confused. Not that those are two adjectives I would ever want to apply to myself.

And it was different from when Dad was killed. I was little then and I just longed for him to come back. I even prayed. I prayed that it might not be true, that he would turn up on the doorstep, dishevelled and apologetic. Of course, those kinds of prayers don't get granted. Which ones do, that's what I'd like to know? Asking for what you really want is always asking too much. So what is the right amount to ask? An exam result? A glance from a good-looking man?

We were out in the churchyard now. Eden seemed to have an arm round me still. Evie had slipped away. She was probably relieved to see the back of this woman who had come into her life unwanted and done so much to disturb it. But no, Evie was kinder than that. A supermodel from Pittsburgh, she never forgot where she came from and she always said that if she hadn't gotten this face on her, she'd have been living in a trailer park like her daddy, drowning herself in liquor. She laughed when she said it, but it was true.

'Ashes to ashes, dust to dust...'

I threw a handful of earth on to the coffin and felt dizzy and inexplicably angry. I have seen so many people all over the world weeping on top of coffins, their sons killed by some moronic militia or another. I've seen enough of this. Can't something nice happen for a change? I smiled at my own belligerence and turned away.

Pauline had wanted to make some limp sandwiches (well, I don't suppose she would have planned for them to be limp but that is how I thought of them) and tip some booze into everyone to numb the pain, but I couldn't face it. I just went home to Rosslyn Hill with Eden, who had irritatingly broken my coffee machine.

I lay down on the bed (a mattress on the floor piled with white duvets and pillows) and shut my eyes. Eden was fiddling around in the kitchen (a fridge, a cooker and a sink against the wall in the front room).

'I am an orphan,' I said.

'Me too,' he shouted back. 'Drink?'

'Yes.' I sighed. 'Might as well.'

Chapter 2

IT WAS STRANGE being on the Moscow flight. It is a scene. We were all sitting in the departure lounge and there were the usual packs of pierced teenagers with big blue labels on their rucksacks and smart blokes on the phone. A man in an ancient tweed suit, his brown briefcase actually falling apart in his hands, shuffled up to a woman wearing thick tights and stood over her until she looked up and noticed him.

'Archie!' she said. 'Are you speaking?'

'I'm replacing Greigs,' the man sighed, slumping down beside her.

At this news the woman closed her book in her lap. 'It was all such a shock,' she said.

Archie nodded. 'The shocking thing is how little I know about Fonvizin,' he said and they both laughed.

A couple of Russian glamour pusses pretended to be pleased to see each other and kissed enthusiastically.

'Shopping, shopping, shopping!' one of them said, holding up two armfuls of Bond Street bags. Her friend wiped the lipstick off her left cheek and held up her hand. It flashed

23

even in the fluorescent light of the Terminal Two departure lounge.

'Ooooh, sister! Who?' The first girl laughed, moving her sunglasses to the top of her head and leaning towards her friend's finger.

'Robin,' said the engaged one proudly.

'Fuck kind of name is that?' the other one laughed. 'Isn't it a bird?'

'Does it matter?' the ring wearer said, and she glanced backwards at an older woman pulling an expensive leather case with logos on it. 'Come on, Mama.'

Mama's hair was dyed and set, her sunglasses had been bought yesterday and she was dressed in the soft beiges and greys of enormous wealth. I smiled. Good for her. This woman, now in her sixties, must have grown up under Communism, queued for every last item of food in the 1980s, probably went out on the street with all her belongings—forks, tacky ornaments, lampshades—and laid them on a tea towel in the hope that some foreigner would buy something. She will have worked thirty years in a factory. She probably fed her kids and didn't eat herself. Her husband very likely died of drink years ago. And now she's on a shopping trip to London with her daughter. Good for her. But not good for my mama. Something Eden once said to me flashed into my mind. 'If it's not one thing, it's your mother.'

I glanced down at the book I was going to pretend to read on the plane. It was my pre-predecessor's 'Whither Russia?' book about the beginning of the Yeltsin era. I remember us all feeling that as Russia's democracy emerged from the darkness of totalitarianism just about anything could happen. Would the Communists take over again? Would they get a nationalist lunatic who would start randomly executing everyone vaguely swarthy? Or would freedom triumph and herald a new age of higher living standards, flourishing arts and sciences and chickens in every pot?

But what actually happened was what anyone at all far-sighted might have predicted. Democracy survived, but it did not fulfil anyone's expectations of it, did not deliver on its promises, and nobody felt much freer, just quite a lot poorer. And the system became as obscure and corrupt as that of any system in a country with the kinds of problems Russia got left with. Sort of Latin America but cold.

We crowded off towards the plane as instructed and I waited behind two men from Coca-Cola.

'We have one thousand participants,' one of them was saying.

'Do they already know the product?' the other asked.

'Nope. All virgins.'

'Great,' the first man nodded, fanning himself lightly with his boarding card.

Advertising in Russia is now as sophisticated as it is any-where in Europe. My favourite has this wise old peasant bloke who looks a bit like Tolstoy walking along the Moskva embankment with his totally westernised grandson who is wearing rollerblades and has a pierced ear. Tolstoy is bathed in this buttery yellow sunlight and is talking about the heart of Russia which turns out, I think, to be some sort of cranberry juice.

But it was back when I still had a Russian husband that advertising first arrived in Russia. It was hilarious. Nobody had been allowed in to do any market research and in any case they were dealing with a people who had not been adver-tised at in seventy years and had zero understanding of the concept. The first billboard that went up was in Pushkin Square. Until then there had been no graffiti, no litter, no signs, no competition, very little street lighting. Shops were called 'Bread' and 'Milk' and 'Meat' (which was a joke because at that time none of these places contained any of these goods and when you pointed out, exasperated, that the shop said meat on the door you would get the reply: 'So? It says "prick" on the woodshed.').

Anyway, this sign went up. It had a stick man on it and he was holding a can. The logo was a direct translation of the English and was, therefore, entirely senseless. It said: 'More a jar of water than a way of life. Sprite.' Nobody knew what Sprite meant (especially as it was transliterated so that it couldn't even mean pixie or elf or whatever it does mean). Nobody had ever seen a 'way of life' advert (presumably the Coke Is It ads were being lampooned) and why would anyone pay money for a jar of water? The English had been 'More a can of drink than a way of life'. Anyway, that was all a very long time ago now. Even Russians can't be convinced that McDonald's serves anything edible any more. In my day there was a three-hour queue in the snow to get in. I know because I queued. Well, there was toss all else to eat. Kids used to take orders from people in cars, duck under everyone's legs to queue jump and come back out with the food for a five-rouble commission. My friend Adrian always used to steal the napkins, straws, toilet light bulbs and loo roll. So did everyone in Moscow, so in the end they locked the light bulbs into immovable globes and stopped providing everything else.

I was staring out of the window of the plane now and the stewardess came to tell me to fasten my seat belt. I was sitting next to a cello. A girl with long blonde hair and a pierced eyebrow was on the other side of it.

'Can't put it in the hold,' she said. 'Too cold.'

'Right.' I nodded. Across the aisle a mail order bride who had just been to London to meet her husband was asking the woman on her right whether she thought £600 was a lot or a little for an engagement ring.

'Well, it can depend,' her English neighbour said, diplomatically.

'And is £350,000 a big mortgage and if he dies do I have to pay it off?' she wanted to know next.

'Is Walton-on-Thames a prestigious area?'

My favourite old colleague Don McCaughrean was supposed to be meeting me. He moved to Moscow with his wife (no, seriously) Ira. They met in Baghdad during the last war and it was love at first sight, never mind that he was a chronically obese and highly abusive alcoholic war photographer and she was a delicately lovely, clever, sober, straight and pragmatic student. She painted her toenails while our hotel was being shelled. She was far older and wiser at twenty-two than Don McCaughrean would ever be and he'd already had more than forty years of trying.

It's always strange to be back. There is something about even flying into Russian airspace that makes me relax. I'm not weird in Russia. It's one of the few places where I'm usually the least worldly person in the room, the most girlishly naïve.

When I got back to England after the murders I told a Russian friend who was miraculously in transit to Israel (one of the few ways out in those days) what had happened.

'They had been axed to death. Really horrific,' I said.

He shrugged. 'It happens,' he said. 'Byvayet.'

'Anyway, when the police came...' I began. His interest was aroused, somewhat wildly.

'The police came! Wow,' he said. 'That's incredible.' He wasn't being sarcastic. That really was, as far as he was concerned, the amazing bit of the story.

Out after the baggage carousels I couldn't see the bastard anywhere. I probably had a few too many vodkas on the plane. Well, OK, I did. I, and all the Russians, now lit a cigarette while we stood restless in the customs queue. There were hundreds of signs telling us not to, but we knew better.

British Airways normally lands at Domodedovo now, a place the Americans used to call 'the dome of death' when it was for internal flights only and renowned for the number of crashes that happened there. Now it's all revamped and ritzy, but we were going to Sheremetyevo. Almost, I thought, as though for nostalgia's sake. For at Sheremetyevo airport nothing has changed in twenty years.

The ceiling here is a design that centres round the non-stick cake tin. There are a million of them glued on up there, and there are even light bulbs in about forty of them. It is very bleak and gloomy and smoky and, well, basically, Russian.

Nobody I recognised had their face pressed to the misty glass when I came through customs. An old man pushed through the crowds with a bunch of carnations, running towards his wife. Huge blokes with gold teeth jostled to flog their taxi services and thin men in cheap suits held up signs with foreigners' names on them. The air was fetid—filled with clouds of cigarette smoke and the steam coming off a thousand unwashed and now very wet people. It must be raining outside. A little dog rushed towards its owner, dragging its lead behind it. She dropped her cases and picked it up, eyes full of tears.

A bloke in a leather jacket scanned the arriving crowds, his arm round a pretty young woman holding a baby. He pointed at me. She smiled. She looked just like Ira. Don? Don't be ridiculous. He lunged forward and hugged me, patting my back hard.

'Zanetti, you old slag. You look awful.'

'Don?' I said, gazing suspiciously into his face. 'What the fuck happened to you?'

He threw his arms out and beamed. Bashing a few people in the head as he did it, he turned a full circle, wiggling his arse when it faced me.

'Jesus,' I said.

'Not bad I think so?' Ira said, smiling as well and reaching over the baby's head to kiss me on the cheek. 'This is Donchik.'

I looked at the baby. 'Donchik?'

'After his daddy.' She blushed.

'What's left of his daddy.' I shook my head as Don picked my case up and started pushing his way out towards the gloom of the car park.

Don must have lost between six and ten stone. His face glowed with health. I swear he seemed to have fewer wrinkles and more hair. He was wearing a pair of jeans that fitted perfectly and he had no paunch whatsoever. A nice clean shirt tucked in, a new jacket. And he smelt. Not of sweat, booze, fags and war. He smelt of aftershave. I lit another cigarette.

Don hauled my bag into the back of a brand new Volvo estate, hunching away from the heavy rain as he ran round to open the passenger door for Ira. Me and Donchik were in the back, apparently. Don senior looked at me, started to speak and stopped again.

My hair was getting wet. 'What?' I asked him.

'Um... Listen... Faith. Can you put it out? No smoking in the car. The baby...'

'Oh. God. Sure. Of course,' I said, stamping the fag out under my cowboy boot. 'Sorry...I...' I sat down in the back seat and blew my last mouthful of smoke out in front of me. Don coughed. 'Shit. Sorry,' I said and opened my window. My left arm was getting wet.

'Oh, Faithy love, could you shut that? Don't want the baby to...' Don asked me, twisting round to reverse out of his space.

'Sure, no problem,' I whispered and zhuzhed the window shut.

'So! Here we are!' Don announced, paying the car park guy and accelerating out on to the motorway. An enormous arch told me in English and Russian that Rothmans cigarettes welcomed me to Moscow. Nice.

The baby looked at me. He had grave reservations. He was deeply unimpressed. He dribbled.

'Beautiful baby,' I said.

Ira leant round. 'Do you think it is so?'

'Absolutely. Looks just like his old man,' I said, lying. Looked just like a slug.

Ira was delighted. She laughed and nudged Don who smiled over at her. Bloody hell. This was going to be forty-five minutes of sheer, unadulterated nightmare.

Big Mercedes with blacked-out windows sped down the outside lane; little Ladas, grimly determined, skidded in and out of the other lanes, the faces of their drivers pressed against the cracked windscreens, peering out through the grey rain. I've driven this road a million times. It almost feels like home. Home without the heartwarming stuff. To me there is something that feels real about that. In the West you've got all your illusions of cosiness, comfort and longevity. Come back to Moscow and it will tell you the truth. You know the place but it's not going to welcome you or help you out. In fact, it usually confuses you. The billboards now are so overwhelming, vulgar, ludicrous. They disorientate you by obliterating the buildings beneath them and they are surreal in their attempt to flog sex, wealth and very thin cigarettes to a couple of old women staggering across an asphyxiating twelve-lane traffic jam.

Crawling into town on the airport road, we passed the fifty foot high sculpture of barbed wire that marks how near the Germans got to Moscow during the war. Pretty near. In fact the area called the Barricades is now part of Moscow, albeit a shitty not very central part.

When we passed Byelorusskiy Station there were people milling about outside. Time for some trains to leave. Fat women in headscarves pulling big dark bundles of who knows what along on pram wheels, their hands like hams, their feet wrapped up in lengths of material and stuffed into felt boots, army style. Years ago, when the stations were draped with red Communist flags and the signs along the platform read 'Glory to Marxism-Leninism', Dimitri used to drive me down here in the middle of the night, ours the only car on a twelve-lane road (Stalin wanted all roads to the Kremlin big enough to fit lots of tanks down—now they are clogged twenty-four hours a day with solid traffic), snow banked up at the pavements, the sky black and pierced with freezing stars. Women in furs sat round braziers, their roses in glass cases kept warm by candles. He would buy a whole bucket and I had to hold it on my lap all the way home. Amazing roses, all the way from Georgia. If you went to Byelorusskiy Station these days at two o'clock in the morning you'd probably get yourself shot.

'That guy who owns the strip clubs got shot here last night,' Don said, psychically.

'What? The Serb?' I asked, feeling for my cigarettes and remembering not to.

'Yeah. Wanker.'

'Even so...'

We all laughed. Don (going the wrong way if you asked me but I thought I'd just shut up) drove us down Tverskaya, the road that used to be Prospekt Marksa. Well, it was Tverskaya under the tsars, then Prospekt Marksa, now it's Tverskaya again.

The tsarist nostalgia makes me sad. Communism did have its downsides (gulags and what have you) but there was a lot that was wonderful about it and the tsars certainly did need getting rid of. The idea that a beautiful royal future for Russia was obliterated by the Communists is certainly a pile of crap. We trundled past Gucci, Louis Vuitton and all that stuff, the glittering shop fronts blurred by the rain. The shop where I once stood for four hours for cheese is now a Benetton. In those days there was white cheese and yellow cheese. I once asked what the cheese was, meaning what type of cheese, and the warty shop assistant scowled at me as if I was mad. 'It's cheese,' she said. They don't sell that cheese any more. It was nice. It had lots of tiny tiny little holes in it and it tasted of almost nothing, but was good with salt and black bread. Here's an old Soviet joke for you. It's about the shortages. It is not funny.

A teacher asks her class to name a word beginning with C. A little girl puts her hand up.

'Cheese, miss,' she says.

'Well done, Svyeta. Five points.'

Then she asks for a word beginning with G. Misha puts up his hand.

'God, miss,' he says.

The teacher is cross. 'There is no God,' she tells him.

'There's no cheese either but you gave Svyeta five points for saying it.'

Eventually Don put his window down to flash his press pass at the armed guard and he drove into the big foreigners' compound on Kutuzovsky Prospekt, home to the *Chronicle*'s office and flat. Now home to me. These are called Stalin buildings because they were built under Stalin and are big and solid.

There were more than five hundred cars crammed into the courtyard, completely asphyxiating the pathetic swings and sandpit in the middle.

'Listen, Faithy,' Don said, switching the engine off. 'We've got to get Donchik back home for his feed so I'm going to dump you here.' He got out and dragged my case out of the boot. He tossed me the keys to the flat that the housekeeper, Natasha, had given him the day before. 'Come over for dinner tomorrow when you're settled,' he said. 'I'll do my Cobb salad.'

I raised my eyebrows at him. Don cooking anything, consuming anything other than takeaway and beer, would have bowled me over, but Don making a salad? Well, the world had turned upside down.

'What have you done with my Don, you skinny bastard?' I asked, kissing him on the cheek. 'See you tomorrow. You still at Sadsam?'

'No! It's so polluted round there. No good for the baby. We've got a big dacha out at Peredelkino. I'll email you the address. See you tomorrow,' he said. Okey dokey.

Ira leant out of the window. 'Welcome to Moscow!' She grinned.

I waved and went into doorway number eleven.

The flat is on the ninth floor behind a big padded steel door. A fashion for these developed when crime got out of control in the early nineties. Having a steel door is unnerving as it is, but when it is padded with black leather it takes on a whole new dimension. There were four locks on it, two of them big fat metal fingers that wedged themselves into the frame at top and bottom and then two sort of crossbar things that jammed into the walls on all four sides. You would have to really really really want to get in here to attempt this door. On the other hand, I always think that having a door like this makes people really really really want to get in. Doesn't carrying a gun make you more likely to get shot? It's like having bodyguards. In any case, I was outside the fucking door for half an hour before I worked out how to do it. It was good to own it, though. Home! Home?

I love this flat. I've been to it before, to dinner with whoever the correspondent is whenever I'm in Moscow. It has bright pine floors, and huge windows overlooking the river, the Ukraine Hotel (one of Stalin's scary wedding cake buildings) and the gleaming marble White House. And the twelve-lane road. But it's high up and you hardly notice that. At the back the corridor kitchen looks across the whole city and along the river to the university up on Lenin Hills. (OK. Sparrow Hills. But I was used to the old names.) The bedroom has a depressing balcony over the car park but the windows are big and impenetrable-looking, the walls are white, the furniture is inoffensive and the lights of the city all around are comforting. I kicked my boots off and slumped on to the sofa, lighting a cigarette at last.

Not long ago, back in Baghdad, I had nearly let myself imagine a different life. I fell in love, did I mention? There seemed, briefly, to be a hope of sitting at a breakfast table with the papers, reading bits out, laughing, popping out for croissants. I almost believed we might lie on some pale beach, looking at the other people and imagining extravagant secret lives for them, speculating on what they'd say if we stole their towels. But it was not to be.

Someone had left a bottle of vodka on the coffee table and a shot glass. Good old Don. I smiled and poured myself a drink. A siren screamed in the street below and I must have fallen asleep. I dreamt about Mum. She was here in Moscow with me, brushing the tangled spirals of my hair and singing a song about a broken mirror. And as she sang she disintegrated slowly, until she was a little heap of rags on the floor and all I could hear was a sharp stinging bell.

I opened my puffy eyes and staggered towards the door. It was completely dark outside and the traffic on the road below had that lazy night-time feel about it, the red tail lights trailing all the way over the bridge to Kalininsky. God, that's called something else now too. Noviy Arbat. That's it. My socks slipped on the parquet and I lit a cigarette with my heavy silver lighter on the way to the insistent ringing.

'Who is it?' I shouted, struggling with the stupid fucking locks.

'Police,' a man shouted back. 'Open the door.'

I briefly considered that this might be some kind of joke, but I don't suppose anybody makes that joke any more.

There were two of them out there. One of them had his gun out of his holster. They wore the pale bluish-grey uniform of the Militisia and they looked very determined. I digested their presence slowly. If it was a joke it was getting very elaborate. I pushed my hair back out of my face and suddenly felt serious.

'Vera Sakhnova?' one of them shouted.

I put my non-smoking hand up to my ear. What? Who?

'Nyet,' I said, still sleepy. But hang on. Vera is Russian for Faith, it's what all my Russian friends call me. And Sakhnova is...well...Sakhnova is...it's my married name. I never did actually get divorced. Well, I never planned to marry again.

'Da.' I nodded. 'Eto ya.'

'You are being arrested in connection with...' the one with the gun paused, aiming his weapon at me, 'with the murder of Leonid and Yelyena Varanov.'

The other one took my arm.

'Hey! Fuck off. I don't know who these people are and I didn't murder them. I just fucking got here,' I shouted, pulling away.

'You are under suspicion of their murder in 1989,' the gun man said as his friend dragged me in my socks out of the *Chronicle* apartment and down nine flights of stairs to the squad car. On the way I began to have an inkling as to who Leonid and Yelyena Varanov probably were.

Chapter 3

I WAS VERY very pissed off by the time we got to the bottom of the stairs. I mean, do I look like a threat to society? I got my socks wet on the way from the doorway to the car and one of the bastards put a hand on top of my head, you know how they do, as he guided me into the back seat.

These cars have come on a lot since they used to stop to give you lifts in the middle of the night. For money, of course. For a long time after all the gangsters had got flashy new BMWs, the police were still driving around in rusting Ladas, looking like something in a 1950s cartoon. Everything is topsy-turvy in Russia. They have a huge body of literature to prove this—stories about people's noses having a life of their own, old ladies falling out of windows and things generally not being as they seem. In the west you feel fairly relaxed in an area where everyone has a brand new Mercedes. In Russia a brand new Mercedes is a sure sign of danger.

For a long time policemen were underpaid or not paid at all and they were constantly killing themselves and their wives with their standard issue Makarov 9mm guns. They were on the make at all times and would gladly take a bribe for pretty much anything.

Not only that, but police cars were for years the safest kind of taxi to get and you didn't feel quite as shabby taking the ride as you did when ambulances pulled over for you in the slush. This, though, was a state of the art car and I was not at all happy to be in it.

'Are we talking the communal apartment off Sretenka? Are you out of your minds? I remember seeing the bodies. I threw up. My husband was there. Have you hauled him in too?'

'Save it for the interview room, Mrs Sakhnova,' the bloke sitting next to me said.

'Fine. Great.' I scowled.

It was still raining. People associate Russia with snow but it's like North America really. Long hot summer, long rainy autumn and long snowy winter. It's most beautiful in the snow, but in Moscow the actual thick white blanket that you see in pictures doesn't last long. The cars, the heat of the houses and the pollution turn everything to slush pretty quickly, and for most of the winter people just slosh around in this filthy grey liquid, cars spattering the pavements and shop fronts with it, people employed full time to mop the stuff from shop floors and everyone's doorway piled high with wet boots and dry pairs of slippers.

Last time I was in the back of a police car in Moscow I was with my old mate Adrian, the bloke who used to steal the straws from Moscow's new McDonald's. I was job-sharing with Adrian. We were both supposed to be translating articles from Russian into English on a magazine that was breaking new ground by being the first to publish slightly anti-Soviet pieces. Nobody got imprisoned and people started to realise that Gorbachev was different. Things were changing.

I can't remember where we'd been that night of the police car but he was—well, he always was—very drunk, dribbling into his scraggy beard. Anyway, he stole the policeman's hat from the ledge by the back window. He suddenly said, 'Quick! Run!' and opened the door while the car was moving. The policeman swerved into the kerb and started swearing and I tossed him five roubles and ran after Adrian who had now dived into an underpass somewhere near the open air swimming pool. Russian open air swimming pools are amazing, though the best one was filled in to make way for the rebuilding of some ghastly cathedral. Stalin knocked it down for the swimming pool, but there really was no reason to be putting it back again. In the winter steam billows out of the heavily heated pools into the freezing air and it is like being on another planet swimming in the snow at night in an outdoor pool, the other swimmers invisible in the steam, flakes of snow melting on your head and into the water. To get to it you have to swim through a water-filled tunnel from the hot changing rooms.

'You fucking lunatic!' I screamed at him. He pulled the flaps on his fur hat down and grinned.

'You want it?' he asked, throwing the policeman's hat at me. I've still got it somewhere. It must be in one of the boxes I'll probably never unpack.

I was introduced to Adrian on my first day at work at *Novoe Vremya* (a friend of Dimitri's had got me the job, semi-legally). The building is now a bar just behind an enormous flashing casino.

'He has wonderful English,' the boss said. We were standing on a piece of greasy linoleum in the basement of a large pre-revolutionary building on Pushkin Square. This was the magazine's cafeteria. It was dark down here and lit by one very weak, bare light bulb. A fat woman in a white chef's hat and apron stood behind a counter next to a menu on which everything except 'kolbassa', salami, had been crossed off.

Adrian was sitting on an old plastic chair eating salami and drinking 'kakao', the evil-tasting coffee substitute the Soviets had had forced on them. It came as thin powder, and when you added hot water it still tasted like thin powder.

'Hey,' he said. He did not have wonderful English. He had not, in fact, spoken a word of English for three years. The boss,

Vasily Vasilyevich, thought he was Russian. Everyone thought he was Russian. I could hear that he was Texan. As his English came slowly back to him (and his Russian was always better than his English because everything he'd ever read he'd read in Russian) he told me that he had stowed away on a Russian fishing trawler from Seattle. On his family ranch in Texas he had always been the odd one out (short, ugly and clever). At high school he was the only one who didn't wear a Stetson and cowboy boots. He chose to study Russian as a rebellion—those were the days of President Reagan's Evil Empire speech. His classmates would drawl, 'All them foreign countries is a bunch o' shit.'

So he arrived in Moscow after a year at sea (seriously) during which he'd been found, of course, and put to work gutting fish. Then he'd changed his name to Kolya Kuznyetsov, got himself some counterfeit Russian documents in return for secret English lessons and finally found a job on the magazine.

I couldn't drink kakao and I had Evie send me real coffee from England which I had to go out of town to the international post office to pick up. Every morning Dimitri would drive through the snow with a cup of coffee on the dashboard and deliver it to me in the office.

'Can I have a sip?' Adrian would whine.

'No,' I said.

'Can I have a dollar?' he tried.

'No,' I said, but sometimes I gave him one. You could change it on the black market for three months' salary. Not that there was anything to buy with the roubles when you had them, except cans of kakao.

Adrian was very very frightened of Dimitri who, essentially, was the black market. 'If I tried to take his money he would kill me. I can see it in his eyes,' he said once, leaning forward over the typewriter we shared and picking his nose.

'Don't be stupid,' I told him.

Lying in bed that night, looking up at the ceiling high above my head, I asked him.

'If Adrian tried to take your money would you kill him?'

'Of course I would,' Dimitri said. 'I might kill him anyway now you mention it.' He laughed and rolled over to kiss me. 'You're beautiful,' he told me, holding a spiral of my hair. 'Especially in the moonlight.'

Lots of people were a bit scared of Dimitri, but he was sweet really. It was just a survival technique and you needed one back then. Probably still do. He stood out with his western clothes (trainers in the snow) and proud swagger. And he did despise Adrian but that was only because Adrian loved me. Sometimes he got drunk enough to declare himself to me. Usually just before he passed out and had to be put in the recovery position and left to fend for himself by the roadside.

I wonder where that policeman's hat is.

'Here we are,' someone in the front of the squad car said, and I saw that we had pulled up not outside some local station number 7 or whatever, but out at the procuratura, someone's lovely town house before 1917. It was by a tram line intersection and I stepped out into mud beneath a stucco porch, the whole building painted bright yellow and white, plaques on the wall telling you which departments were housed where.

'This is fucking ridiculous,' I said, as I was led, supported on both sides, into a brutally lit hallway where I made soggy footprints on the parquet. A big woman in red lipstick made a note of my arrival and nodded towards some swing doors. Even now nobody had painted over all the picture-sized marks on the walls where Lenin had hung for so long. He was gone, but his spirit remained.

I was left locked into a tiny interview room off a long yellow corridor. Two chairs, a vinyl-topped table, an ashtray (thank God) and a big metal machine that was presumably some kind of recording device. No two-way mirrors in here. I don't suppose they want anybody else looking while they beat the suspects half to death.

Personally, I wasn't frightened. My Russian is fluent so I know there will be no misunderstanding. Also, I didn't do it. But mainly, and who are we kidding, I was a westerner. It wouldn't look good to torture me or to imprison me on false grounds. If I'd been Russian things might have been different. Let alone, Lord knows, Chechen or something. I was very tired now.

I must have sat there cigaretteless for about twenty minutes before a woman came in with cigarettes, a lighter and a big folder which she plonked wearily down on the table. She was about my age, dyed ginger hair, big chest squashed into her uniform, long painted nails.

'Sergeant Molotova,' she said, smiling and offering me a cigarette. 'And you are...' She paused and flicked some switches on the machine, nodding at me to say who I was.

'Faith Zanetti,' I said. But I knew what she wanted and it was true. 'Vera Sakhnova. That is my married name, but I separated from my husband ten, no, twelve...um...fifteen years ago and I have not see him in that time.'

'Hardly surprising,' said Sergeant Molotova. 'He has been in Oryol psychiatric prison for most of it.'

I felt my heart start to pound now. Maybe I had a hangover. I had, obviously, never been to Oryol psychiatric prison, but it didn't sound very nice. I doubted that it was particularly nice. Also, I didn't quite believe her. There was nothing psychologically wrong with Dimitri and he wasn't violent or...or anything.

That the past was piling up on me now was surreal, since I had hardly thought about my brief Russian marriage since it had ended. My main, my abiding relationship in life had been with Eden, a man who in a different world might have been my husband, my 'life partner', the father of my children.

But my marriage. I had always thought of it as being a teenage romance, something that most people go through when they are trying to get their lives in order. Not something that was going to come back to get me. For fuck's sake, I had a job to do. Though I should think they'd be pleased with a little column tomorrow about arriving in apparently democratic Russia to be arrested practically straight off the plane.

'This is totally fucking absurd,' I said, drawing hard on my cigarette and leaning my elbows on the table. Dima hadn't been violent. Although... I thought of the time I had spent alone in our grotty room, waiting for two days for him to come back from what he described as 'a meeting'. I had just arrived from England; it was before the wedding even. He said I shouldn't go out without him and I hadn't dared disobey. Soviet Moscow was not a welcoming place. He came back wild-eyed and unshaven. I hugged him but he pushed me away and I noticed that his knuckles were frayed and bleeding.

'What happened to your hands?' I asked him, screwing my face up. I was wearing stripy pyjamas and a grey cashmere scarf. I don't know why I remember that.

'I shut them in the car door,' Dimitri said.

What? Both of them? I thought it but I didn't say it.

Did this mean he was violent, though? Russian men had to serve in the army for God's sake. They went through revolting peer group initiation rituals that the weaker ones didn't survive. People were starving in the streets back then (fainting in Leningrad apparently) and life was hard. So he'd been in a fight? It seemed silly and western to assume that fighting was a sign of actually having some sort of propensity to violence.

'Oryol?' I sighed. 'Why?'

'He turned himself in, Mrs Sakhnova. He came to us in 1992 confessing to the double murder that occurred in the communal apartment on Kolokolnikov Pereulok, Sretenka, in 1989. He said,' and at this point she rustled through her papers to get it right. 'He said: "I can no longer live with myself." Handed over his Communist Party membership card, passport, marriage certificate. Told us to take him in. I sat in on the interview. I was training. He was so calm, so strange, that we had him psychiatrically evaluated.'

I put my cigarette out in the white plastic ashtray and stared at Sergeant Molotova.

'Apparently, Mrs Sakhnova, he was protecting you.'

'Hello?' I said. I suppose I had known something a bit like this must be coming. I mean, they'd arrested me and all.

'He had always been our prime suspect but we couldn't track him down. The system was a mess back then. Everything changing.' That's for sure, I thought. 'Your landlady...' she looked at her notes again, 'Zinaida Petrovna, at the time confirmed hearing someone come into the apartment around four. The couple must have died nearer to midnight. When Sakhnov turned himself in you had returned to the United Kingdom with whom we did not have an extradition treaty...' She laughed. 'We did request permission to interview you but it was denied,' she said.

I raised my eyebrows. 'Why didn't I know about this? Why didn't you haul me in on the...at least five...visits I've made here in the meantime?'

Sergeant Molotova smiled. 'There was no reason for you to have been informed of a denied request for interview on the seven subsequent visits—it is seven, Mrs Sakhnova—you have made to this country while your husband was in custody for the crime.'

I lit another cigarette.

No part of me believed that Dimitri had killed those people. He had no reason to do it. Sure, he traded currency and had a not particularly legal vodka trading business in Vorkuta in the Arctic north, but that couple had only just moved in, did not seem especially dodgy and had nothing at all to do with us. My main suspicion was that he had been set up. He did have some not very nice friends. That was for sure. I mean, Misha for a kick-off.

I first met Misha in 1988. I had been moaning at Dimitri that he never introduced me to his friends (I have grown up a lot since then) and that we never went out anywhere. He would leave me in the flat and come back with a greasy roast chicken bought from a cook at a hotel cafeteria. I once asked what he'd been doing and he said (this is a direct translation from the Russian): I have been fucking dealing with fucking stuff, for fuck's sake. He once took the train to Vladivostok (this takes about a week) to pick up an Audi which he then drove back to Moscow and sold. I think they got stolen in western Europe and smuggled east on boats so that nobody had to drive them across any borders. Something like that.

Anyway, one evening he gave in. 'You want to meet my friends? OK, let's go and meet my friends.' So we did. This aggressive side to Dimitri was, I always thought, just a sort of public display. The way he felt he ought to be. What he liked was driving into the countryside and showing me where to pick mushrooms, walking arm in arm down the Arbat and buying me a coloured scarf, talking about getting a dacha one day and having an apple tree.

Misha, who lived in the hell that is the housing estates out at Yugo-Zapadnaya, had not one but two steel doors.

'People are always trying to rob me,' he explained, ushering us in with a fag between his lips and a sort of panther in his arms. Seriously, this cat was huge. Really big. It had bright green eyes and its fangs came over its bottom lip and glinted in the gloom of Misha's hall. Whatever it was it was not a normal domestic cat.

Misha was also large. You see a lot of Russian blokes like this, bulked up by the army, vodka and lots of bread, head shaven, face covered in small scars. He could have strangled me with one hand. He wore plastic slippers (like the ones people wear at swimming pools), shiny tracksuit bottoms over which his paunch hung, and a T-shirt with Madonna on the front of it (quite a prize in Moscow at that time). A pretty woman, well, girl really, no older than I was, brought in a plate with a doily on it and some chocolates. She had a black eye. I know that sounds weird and melodramatic but what can I tell you? She had a black eye. She seemed extremely scared of Misha. When she left the room again Misha said, 'My wife. Nastya.'

Nastya is the diminutive of Anastassiya, a country-sounding name then, though now I expect there are lots of baby Anastasias what with the Romanov nostalgia. He had probably picked her up in some Siberian backwater with promises of Moscow and then locked her in the flat and beat her up. She came back with vodka for the men and a bottle of cherry liqueur for me. Women are supposed to like sweet things.

I did not like it, but I drank a lot of it. I heard a baby crying from the other room, though Misha did not comment on this.

'I love Margaret Thatcher,' he said, when Dimitri and I had sat down on the velour sofa under a 1970s perspex chandelier. It was snowing outside and I remember wishing I was anywhere else. Anywhere at all.

'You do?' I smiled.

'I love her,' Misha confirmed. Then he lurched into English and said, 'How are you, old chum?'

He and Dimitri laughed so much that Misha went dark purple and looked as though something bad might happen to him. He stopped laughing suddenly, poured out the shots (I was apparently going to drink this cherry stuff in shots) and looked grave.

'To Andrei,' he said and put his hand on his heart.

'Andrei,' Dimitri said, and we drank.

This went on all evening.

'Who the fuck are all these people?' I hissed when Misha went to the loo.

'Friends who have been killed.' Dimitri nodded, very drunk now.

'Killed by what? Was there a plane crash? How come you know so many dead people?' I was not sober myself.

'Prison. Fights. You know the kind of shit,' Dimitri explained as Misha came in, tucking his T-shirt into his trousers. He was as broad as about four or five of me. I didn't really know the kind of shit, but I was beginning to get the picture. There was a culture in those days of revering anyone in prison, anyone who had ever been there. Partly, it was just so tough that if you survived there was respect due to you. But it also came from the Communist regime and the fact that there were so many political prisoners. Of course there was a lot of underground support for those imprisoned without trial, for those who had spoken out against Communism, who had written books or painted anti-Soviet pictures, all that kind of thing. This status ended up also being conferred on the violent thugs who would probably be imprisoned in any country. It struck me that the people to whom we were drinking were of the latter type.

The drunker Misha got the less safe I felt. He had shown me his tattoos (one of which was across his flobbly and hairy stomach)—a naked woman and a heart with 'Mama' written across it. He had sung two prison songs, very loudly, and when Nastya dropped something in the kitchen he grabbed a large assault rifle from behind his armchair and ran out towards the front door shouting, 'Come and get me, you cunting motherfuckers!' He staggered back, swinging his weapon terrifyingly and looking disappointed that there had been nobody there. He obviously quite fancied blowing somebody's head off.

'Wanna see the rest of my guns?' he asked me. Dimitri dug me in the ribs. There was a horrible nervous energy about Misha that seemed wholly destructive.

'OK.' I smiled. Nowadays I would probably recognise them all and maybe even know how to use a few of them, but then I was just appalled. How many did he need, for the Lord's sake? The one he'd been waving around seemed like it would probably do the trick all by itself.

When he had shown me his enormous sack of ganga weed from Afghanistan it was time to go home. The drunken back-slapping and tearful Russian goodbyes took ten minutes. Misha kissed my hand.

I got into the car silently and Dimitri pulled off, pissed out of his mind, into the snow. Nobody had snow tyres and at night the snow on the road turned to ice. There were a lot of crashes.

'That is why I don't take you to meet my friends,' Dimitri said softly, taking my hand. 'I am ashamed of this life.'

I leant out of the window and vomited neat cherry liqueur down the side of the car.

I was so shocked by the information that Sergeant Molotova was hurling at me that I forgot to construct a mental case in defence of Dimitri and, of course, of myself. At last the cogs in my brain started whirring a bit and the whole thing just seemed madder and madder and madder.

'Sergeant Molotova,' I said. 'This is completely crazed. I remember seeing these bodies. Neither I nor my husband was remotely involved in this.'

The more I thought about it, the weirder it all seemed. I think I even assumed that Sergeant Molotova knew it was stupid.

'You are lying,' she told me.

'Mmmm. I'm not, though, and I think someone of your experience must be perfectly capable of seeing that. I don't know who the fuck you've got in Oryol, but I don't see how it can be my ex-husband. My husband.' I was shouting now. 'It was the guy, surely. Killed her, killed himself. It was no mystery. Seriously.'

I could see from her face that this line of argument was worrying her. After all, she'd been present at the confession and had told me herself that it had seemed strange.

Someone banged hard on the door. 'Can't hold her much longer unless you've got something, Lyenochka!' he shouted.

'One moment,' she told me, and she stepped out of the room, not bothering to lock me in.

When she came back her manner was softer and she switched the tape recorder thing off.

'Mrs Sakhnova,' she began, not sitting down. 'Our detainee in Oryol is claiming that you, not he, are responsible for the double murder in question. Initially we dismissed his claims as the ravings of a lunatic. However, he had his hour with a lawyer and he retracted his confession. It's highly unusual, but he raised various issues we felt should be looked at, though we have not, as yet, reopened the case. I am not happy to detain you any further without another extensive interview with the detainee. You are free to go.'

I stood up. 'Oh, thanks a lot,' I said, sticking my muddy socks out at her.

She shrugged. 'As I say, you are free to go,' she repeated, and left the room.

Standing outside the procuratura at five o'clock in the morning in my socks, wet T-shirt and sodden jeans, I was not the most alluring prospect for the few passing taxis that there were. A couple of cars slowed down, took a look at me and screeched away. Nor, it had to be said, did I have the money on me to pay for one if it did stop. I walked along, dopey and wet, past the new Tryetyakov gallery where they've put all the icons and things, stepped round an unconscious drunk, his purple face pressed to the grimy pavement, his clothes sodden, and along crumbling alleyways of big grand European style apartment buildings, now mostly reconverted into enormous apartments with ballrooms and floor to ceiling stoves, having been chopped up into single roomed flats by the Soviets. As I stepped on to the bridge by the Kremlin it stopped raining and the sun was starting to come up over the river, the gold domes of all the churches inside the walls shining with newly restored religious fervour. I fished out my change and bought cigarettes from a sleeping teenager in a kiosk, banging on the window to wake him. He looked a bit scared of me with my wild hair, wet clothes and shoeless feet. I was home by six thirty, freezing cold, exhausted, my toes numb and soaking.

A fat lot of good it does having a steel door if you leave it open, I thought, going in, slamming it behind me and lying down on the bed. I knew what I was going to do tomorrow, though. I was going to Oryol sodding psychiatric prison. That was for sure.

Chapter 4

I TOOK A Valium and slept in my clothes, my suitcase still unopened by the double bed that the previous correspondent had shared with his wife. The children—there had been three of them—had slept in the other two rooms along the corridor. Their bunk beds were still in one room and a cot, dismantled by the movers but not taken, lurked accusingly against the wall in the one by the loo. I was not going to let this depress me. Hey, as if I needed more things to depress me when my mother had just died and then I got arrested for some ancient murder which had been quite depressing enough just to witness at the time, for Christ's sake.

I woke up completely dazed at about midday and staggered to the bathroom to run myself a burning hot bath, tipping in some hotel sachets of bath foam that I found in a little wicker bowl on the glass shelf over the sink. Moscow is, thank God, three hours ahead so I could just about get to the office and make a few calls before they got into work in London. Didn't want to start the job looking like a total arsehole.

While the bath ran I walked round the flat. It was a bright, fresh, buttery sunshiny day and all the trees in the courtyard and down by the river were golden, yellow and brown after the rain. I could see people walking their huge frightening dogs, wearing scarves and boots, their hair blowing about in the wind. I threw my wet clothes into a big box of a clothes basket and wandered, naked, into the kitchen. Natasha (where was she, anyway?) had left milk and coffee for me, some eggs, butter and bread. There was equipment here for a family of ten. A thing that looked as though it was for heating up babies' bottles, three different types of food blender, a six-slice toaster, enormous casserole dishes, a Moroccan tagine and a fruit juicer. Well, it was not going to get used, I thought. The most my fridge ever had in it was a bottle of vodka and one of those masks that you chill before you put them over your eyes to soothe them.

I lay in the bath and blew smoke rings up to the ceiling. I decided that I was probably the first person who had ever smoked in this bath. There was a memory trying to get in. I scrunched my eyes up in a feeble attempt not to let it. I remembered when I was little finding my mum in the bath, unconscious, her cigarette burnt out in her mouth, ash dropping into the water. 'If it's not one thing...'

I plunged my head under now and came up staring at a big sort of sticker of a cartoon dinosaur on one of the tiles and I briefly imagined bathtime here under my predecessor, a nanny with all three children splashing about, and I burst into tears.

I shouldn't have stopped taking the anti-depressants they put me on after Baghdad. A shrink and anti-depressants. I never thought it would come to that.

'Imagine if you had a thyroid problem—say, an underactive thyroid,' the doctor said to me.

'OK,' I said, totally unable to imagine this.

'You would take the medication and stay on it for the rest of your life without a second thought. Well, you have low serotonin levels in your brain and this is the medication you need to take to boost them,' he said, tapping at his computer to print out the prescription. 'You might also want to address your alcohol and tobacco consumption.'

Might I, indeed.

I took the pills and I saw the shrink and I got better so I stopped. But since I stopped I can't seem to stop crying all the fucking time. It's embarrassing, I thought to myself, and stood up to get out of the bath. There was a pile of clean, folded towels on a chair in front of me and I wound one on to the top of my head.

Eden was supposed to be arriving today. He was coming over to do his first big *New Yorker* thing—a piece about the crumbling Soviet prison system and how much had changed since the end of the Cold War. Not much was my guess, but that wouldn't be quite long enough for a *New Yorker* piece. They are usually about ten thousand words, I think. The only place in the world that lets you ramble on at that kind of length. Or, rather, the only publication brave enough to publish properly researched, exhaustive pieces of informative writing. He was planning to get some friend of his who managed the Metropole to provide him with receipts so that he could claim the expenses for a room and then actually stay with me thereby making a profit of about five thousand dollars.

I could probably get him to come to Oryol with me. Something on a psychiatric prison would surely be brilliant for his thing. I mean, psychiatric prison was where they sent most of the dissidents. They were big on drugs, and people would get daily injections of Christ knows what until they confirmed that they just absolutely loved Lenin. I sat down on the bed and called his mobile. He was just getting on the plane at Heathrow and would be here this evening, he said.

'Want to come to dinner with Don and Ira?' I asked. 'I said I'd go. They've got some dacha out at Peredelkino.'

'Am I supposed to know what any of those words mean?' Eden asked. I could hear a stewardess telling him to turn his phone off. I could almost hear him wink at her. At any rate, I heard her giggle. Was he really going to have time to actually seduce someone on the sodding plane? Probably.

'They've got a country thing out of town where the writers used to live,' I said. 'Don has promised to make a salad.'

'A what?'

'Exactly. Anyway, shall I tell him you're coming?'

'Sure,' Eden said.

'I got accused of a murder last night,' I told him, leaning off the bed for my cigarettes.

'Did you do it?' he asked, audibly hauling his bag into an overhead locker.

'Fuck off. Seriously. The police took me off for an interrogation in my socks,' I said, lighting the cigarette.

'Socks? Is that some Russian slang for something?'

'No. In my socks. I wasn't wearing any shoes.' I sighed.

'Why?' Eden asked, clunking his seatbelt on.

'Because…oh, fucking hell. I spent all night in a police cell…' I started to whine.

'Sir. The captain has started the engines and I must ask that you…' I heard the woman say and then the phone went dead.

I found that I kept forgetting to think about the dead couple. It was all a hundred years ago and I didn't know them or anything, but they were my first bodies and, at the time, it had affected me badly. I spent months wondering about them, about their relationship—clearly a bit on the rocky side. I wondered mostly about her, about her parents and what she'd been like when she was little. Somebody held a funeral. Somebody grieved and is probably still grieving. Somebody never got over the loss of her. My feelings about him were different. Back then, at any rate. I didn't have time to sympathise with murderers. But now. Now I don't know.

The 'office manager' was not in her seat when I arrived at the *Chronicle* bureau. I walked across the traffic-clogged courtyard and breathed in the smell of autumn in Moscow. There is something about this city, about the cheap petrol they use, the austerity of the buildings, the width of the roads, the determination of the people, the taste of the absolute vastness of the place, that somehow lands on your tongue even in the centre of the city. This country is huge, endless, wild and beautiful and you can almost smell the steppes, the Urals, the Arctic north, the deserts and the thousands of miles of forest even on the steps of the *Chronicle*'s office on Kutuzovsky Prospekt. Almost.

I pushed open the black padded door and wandered in. It's a nice little flat, light and parqueted like all the others, lower down with only a courtyard view at the front, but at the back you can see the playground of kindergarten number 83, lots of little bundles of child hurtling around on swings and a slide. I found Lyuda, now in her seventeenth year of working for the *Chronicle*, in the kitchen, smoking a cigarette and tapping her ash into a cone of lined paper that she had made into an ashtray. When she first got the job it was basically a spying brief with regular reports to the KGB on the foreigners' activities. Now it was more tea and phone calls. She was fiddling with the plug to the kettle and arguing with Arkady, the driver (fourteen years' service), who sat at the kitchen table, protecting his plate of salami with one arm while he ate it with the other.

'Hi,' I said.

They both lurched to attention as though I was the headmistress and had caught them rolling a joint or something.

'Good afternoon,' they both said.

'I'm Faith,' I told them and held out my hand. I had bought them a bottle of port each at the airport—an effort to bring something very English that they might actually like. I put them down on the table and Arkady turned his box round and round, thoughtfully.

'Is it cognac?' he asked, showing a gold tooth.

'It's called port. It's a bit like Georgian wine except nice,' I said.

'Portwine.' He nodded, obviously disappointed.

I should say that this was a name the Soviets gave to the most vile liquid ever produced. It was bottled in Georgia and maybe Uzbekistan and drunk by me during my early days in Moscow. I think a large percentage of it was petrol.

'Well, sort of,' I admitted. 'You'll really just have to drink it.'

I turned to Lyuda. 'Listen, can you do me a favour? Can you try and get me permission to visit the psychiatric prison in Oryol tomorrow? Me and my colleague, Eden Jones, who is working for the *New Yorker*.'

Lyuda ran her cigarette butt under the tap, put it in her cone and threw the cone into the plastic bin. She blew out her last stream of smoke and stared at me. She had a big friendly face with pink cheeks and a funny grin. She must have been about forty-five but had long hair pulled back by an Alice band.

'Tomorrow? You're not going to get official permission in that time, but I know the head of Russian Psychiatric Institutions from university, so I can ask her to give them a call for you if you want.'

'You studied psychiatry?' I asked her, wandering back into the main office. She followed me.

'No. It was her who studied cello. We were at the Conservatoire together but she broke her hand and moved to MGU to do psychiatry.'

'So what do you play?' I asked.

'Piano,' Lyuda said, throwing her hand out towards an old upright piano shoved into the corner of the room behind the filing cabinets and the Tass machine.

'Cool,' I said, and slumped down into a shabby brown armchair. My office was across the hall, helmet and flak jacket sitting welcomingly on the big desk. I hoped I would have to use them but was aware that this was something to feel vaguely ashamed of.

Arkady lumbered in, sniffing his now open bottle of port. He looked at the label, squinting in concentration. 'Twenty-five per cent.' He nodded, pleased.

'Listen, the police dragged me off last night asking me about some murder I witnessed the aftermath of in 1989. I'd only been off the plane about ten seconds and it seemed quite sort of funny and Soviet, so I'm going to do something about that, and unless you've seen anything in the papers or on the news that you think I should know about you can probably go home for now,' I told them.

'So, you were here in 1989?' Lyuda laughed. 'Wow. Why?'

'Boyfriend trouble. In a rat-infested communalka.' I nodded, and Arkady laughed too.

'Do you need the car?' he asked.

'Yes, I do actually. Why?'

'I'll go and fill it up then,' he said, saluted me and left.

I was already enjoying myself. Clean towels, no need to get my own petrol. What more could I want?

'I'll just call Marina,' Lyuda told me, and sat down behind her desk. She talked for about five minutes, rapping her fingers on a file in front of her and then she looked up at me. 'You've got to be there by ten. It's a long drive. I'll tell Arkady to meet you at the bottom of your staircase at 6 a.m.,' she said, and started collecting her things to go.

'Great,' I said, and got up to saunter across to my office. The shelves were full of the insightful books of every Moscow correspondent there has ever been, including the only one anyone has ever actually read—David Remnick's *Lenin's Tomb*.

It sounds so weird and morbid now referring to someone's grave all the time, especially someone who is actually in there. But under Communism it was just a landmark. 'Meet you at Lenin's tomb at six thirty.' Unless you had come all the way from Chukotka especially to visit the revered old corpse, it did not have any special resonance really. There was no thought of what was in there or what it signified. It was just like meeting someone at Big Ben or Marble Arch. Odd that abroad there was always a horrified fascination with the Soviets' having pickled their leader's body and put it on permanent display. You can still see him, incidentally. The soldiers standing guard still tell you off if you talk but they don't really mean it any more. In the old days it would have been like talking in the presence of Jesus or something.

I phoned Tamsin and knocked off five hundred words about last night, the angle being that in Putin's Russia foreigners still get hounded by the police immediately upon arrival, just like they used to when the Iron Curtain still hung firm between East and West, when the freedom of ordinary Russian people was still crushed by the hammer and lacerated by the sickle of Communism, when…etc. You get the picture. They love all that on the British papers. Not that you'd get a thank you from the desk or anything as extravagant as that.

Don had emailed me his address and directions. A little message popped up entitled 'see ya later!' and it was from 'DanI@ pipex.ru'. Arkady parked the car, a big red Volvo estate (another family thing I wouldn't be taking full advantage of), right out-side the office so that I just had to step into it like the queen. I was quite enjoying this. Eden had so far failed to show up so I texted him directions to give the cab driver at the airport.

I pulled out on to Kutuzovsky, leaning my arm out of the window into the autumn sunshine, and swerved to avoid a Jeep with blacked-out windows that seemed to want to run me off the road. I love driving around post-Communist Moscow. Every time I come back on a story it's the thing I get the biggest kick out of, traffic or no traffic. Years ago there were hardly any cars on the roads at all and now there's fairly permanent gridlock. But it's cool being able to drive here without having to faint in terror. They go fast and the road markings, such as they are, tend to be ignored. A lot of people don't have mirrors and the traffic police stop you as often as they can for a little bribe. They used to have the authority to shoot if you didn't stop.

Everything was cordoned off today round a big flashy bar opposite that appeared to have been firebombed (again). Don's directions were crap and I kept having to pull over to the side of the motorway and peer at my map before doing illegal U-turns across eight lanes. I wondered what the Rus-sian car death statistics were and thought they must be very high. Certainly I've seen a lot of corpses on the roads over the years, especially in winter.

Don was standing on the porch holding Donchik when I drove through his dark green picket gates that had a big 32 plaque attached to them. He waved and, with one arm, showed me where to park. As I got out of the car he took Donchik's hand and waggled it at me, grinning indulgently. 'He's saying hello,' he explained.

I put my cigarette out in the gravel at my feet and I noticed Don notice this but he managed not to say anything. I tried to scrape some stones over it with the heel of my boot.

'Hello, Donchik,' I said and touched the baby's cheek with my finger. It was surprisingly soft and I did it again.

'He's quite a charmer,' Don told me as I kissed his bristly cheek and slapped him on the back.

There was a hammock on the porch and a half-eaten plate of raw carrots and celery on the floorboards beside it. This was a real old Chekhovian dacha. 'Home sweet home,' Don said, marching in with Donchik who gurgled a lot. The whole thing, inside and out, was painted that rich Russian dark green and a bright glossy white. Ira (surely it must have been Ira?) had furnished the dark corridors with little paintings of the snowy steppes framed in thick gilt and with spiky lurking plants on high tables.

'Check out the stove,' Don said, leading me into the front room. I already had checked it out. It would have been hard not to. It was a huge, original Gzhel stove, blue and white painted ceramic from floor to ceiling, the size of a biggish car. All houses used to have these (though not always so ornate) and the heat from it would heat the whole place via pipes that went upstairs and out towards the kitchen and hallways. Hey, Russia could spare the wood for fuel.

'Wow. Does it work?' I asked.

'The bloke promised it would. It's real but the piping and stuff's new. He's coming to light it next week. Didn't trust us to do it the first time. What do you think?' Don was really proud of his stove.

'I think it's fantastic,' I said, and I did.

There was a chaise longue in olive velvet and a round cherry-wood table with a white lace cloth on it. Most amazing though was the painting on the wall. It was of Don McCaughrean and Ira. Ira sat on a chair, her hands folded demurely in her lap, but her head turned to look up at her husband who stood behind her, serious-faced but with the glint of a proud father in his eye.

I looked back at Ira and realised that it was clear from the painting that she was pregnant. She's very beautiful, Ira. Looks a bit like Anna Kournikova but without the tartiness. She's serious and precise, making jeans and a T-shirt look like a business suit.

'Don...' I started, but I didn't know what exactly I was going to say. I wanted to say: What the fuck's happened to you? Why don't you slap me on the back, pour me a vodka and tell me it's going to be as hot as a camel's arsehole in here with that stove going?

But I didn't want to say that really because...well, because he looked so fucking happy. This must be the real Don McCaughrean. The overweight, chain-smoking alcoholic slob that I had known and loved must have been a disguise he wore to hide his misery. This slim guy who ate sticks of celery, cuddled his baby and loved his wife...this was Don.

I wondered if his ex-wife and children knew about any of this, or would recognise him when he came to get them for the summer. I looked round again and saw some photos on top of the stove. One of them, I saw now, was of his kids. Here. Perhaps this summer. So, he was sorted. I sighed.

Ira came rushing in wearing an apron with the salient bits of the Venus di Milo covering her own salient bits. She kissed me, pressing a hot pink cheek into mine.

'Hello, darling,' she said. 'Look at me! Don's been doing the cooking really. I'm just doing some last minute marinading. Let me get you a drink,' she said and hurried out.

'I'll give her a hand,' Don told me. He looked suddenly flustered at the thought of his wife going to any extra trouble and him not being there to help. 'Could you?' he asked, handing me the baby.

'Oh. Sure,' I said, taking my leather jacket off and slinging it over the back of the chaise longue. I put my arms out and took Donchik round the middle, holding him uncertainly out in front of me. Don had already gone. Donchik screwed his face out and started to cry.

'Oh fuck. No, I mean, oh dear. Oh sorry,' I told him, and held him closer to me, bouncing up and down like parents do. I looked him in the face hard and he stopped crying, baffled. I stuck my tongue out and his eyes lit up. I stuck it out again and he reached for it with a fat hand. I did it again and he smiled, showing two pink gums.

'Hey! Don!' I shouted. 'He smiled at me! He smiled!' I ran towards the door and Donchik started crying again. I stopped and performed my trick again. It worked. I smiled back at him and we both laughed like a pair of idiots.

Don shouted from the kitchen. 'Zanetti, can you get that!'

'What?' I yelled back.

'The door!'

I walked out into the corridor with Donchik under one arm, still laughing, and pulled open the door.

'Fuck me!' said Eden Jones, staring at me and the baby. 'That was quick.'

'Yeah. Sod off. This is Donchik,' I told him as he leant down to kiss me. Eden Jones is very tall. I always think he looks as though he's come from an expedition into a desert (which reasonably often he has). Albeit the kind of expedition where you might wear a white shirt, jeans and trainers. But he's tanned with wrinkles round his eyes and he gives the impression of having sand in his hair.

'Don what?' he asked, dropping his suitcase on the floor but keeping hold of his Duty Free bags, presumably presents for the McCaughreans.

'Donchik,' I said. 'It means little Don.'

'Wow,' Eden breathed.

He looked older. Like an ex-husband you only see at Christmas. Something like that. Our relationship is never over. It just goes through different phases. And some of those phases involve seeing, living with other people. But all the time we belong to each other.

'I know,' I said.

There was some scuffling from the kitchen and Don came blustering out holding knives, forks and plates.

'Jones, you old bastard,' he said, sounding, for a second, more like his old self. 'Good to see you.'

'You too. What's left of you,' Eden said. 'You're emaciated.'

'Running.' Don beamed, delighted. 'Ten miles a day. Through the woods. Fantastic. Asthma's completely cleared up.' It was true. He wasn't wheezing. Then again, he wasn't smoking either.

He took us into the sitting room and Ira came in, apronless this time with a tray of glasses, cranberry juice and sparkling water. Don smiled at her and she put the tray down and took Donchik from me. I thought he looked mildly disappointed at this. At least, I hoped he did. Aunty Faith. Hmmm.

Eden handed Don a big orange box of champagne and Don looked briefly bemused. 'Yes, right,' he said, making a knowing face at Ira. 'She's forgotten we've got drinkers here,' he said, kindly, and set off back to get something to service the alcoholics.

I raised my eyebrows at Eden and he shook his head, laughing silently.

Don returned immediately with a glistening bottle from the freezer and two shot glasses. Eden waved his hand. 'I had enough on the plane,' he said, picking up a glass from the tray and pouring himself some water. So, just me then.

I took my shot glass and emptied it, relieved. But I had been made to feel like a drunk and was subdued by the special treatment I required. I lit a cigarette and sat down on the chaise longue. Ira and Don looked at each other.

'On the porch, Zanetti, you slag,' Don told me and I went to stand out on the porch by myself.

OK, I thought. You've made your point. You've got it all now. Health, love, child, peace. I wouldn't have been at all surprised if it turned out he'd converted to some religion. But I suppose he had really. I leant on the edge of the porch and looked across the garden. They were growing lavender and roses. It was sunset now, dusty and orange, and there were lots of people pottering around in their gardens in the houses nearby, long grass and sandy paths outside the fences, neat little bushes and herbs inside. In winter it would be almost impossible to get to some of these houses, staggering down the narrow dirt pathway in deep snow, the spikes of the fences just poking up from beneath it, smoke billowing out of all the chimneys and, surrounding everything, the thick dark forest. I would like to have shown this place to my mum, I thought. Probably more because I can't than for any other reason.

When I came back in Ira was explaining the origin of all their furniture. 'I go to auctions,' she said. 'People hid all their pre-revolutionary stuff. Under the bed, in the attic, in the cellar, in churches. Amazing how much survived, really. Now it appears at auction.'

It appears at Don's house. He hadn't, thank God, made salad. He lit a brick barbecue in a corner of the porch and did chicken and sardines and I sat there with my bottle of vodka, moving away from the baby into the garden when I needed to smoke. They had a white-slatted table out here and iron painted chairs.

Everyone was gripped by my story and Eden was predictably desperate to come to Oryol in the morning.

'Do you think he did it?' Don asked, sucking sardine juice off his fingers. Donchik was asleep in his pram under a mosquito net and Don checked on him at intervals of about four seconds.

'Of course he didn't do it. He was a black marketeer, not Don Corleone. It was two hundred years ago so I might be misremembering it, but it looked to me like the bloke, our neighbour in this shit-hole flat, killed his girlfriend and then chopped his own leg off or something. There's no way Dimitri had anything to do with it.'

'And you were actually married to this guy?' Don smirked, clearly not believing I was capable of such a soft-hearted action.

'Yes I was actually married to this guy. I was nineteen for fuck's sake. I wasn't always like this, you know,' I said, and Eden reached out to touch my hand. I snatched it away. No thank you very much.

'Right,' Don said, nodding in real understanding. He looked as though he was thinking about the transformations people make and feeling sad for me. Well, he could fuck off.

'Anyway,' I said. 'I'm going to this prison tomorrow to see what the deal is. It's a nice story for one thing: "My husband is in a Russian psychiatric prison." You know.'

'Fucking weird though,' Eden said, pushing his plate away from him and taking a cigarette out of my packet. For the first time that evening he was subjected to the McCaughrean marital glare, and he got up to join me in the garden, shouting his conversation over the edge of the porch. It was dark now and suddenly very cold, the Indian summer revealing itself to be a fraud in the chill of the autumn night. 'I mean, why would he confess?' Eden wondered. 'Who wants to be in Oryol Institute for the Insane half their life?'

I flicked my butt over the hedge and on to the pathway. 'He doesn't want to be there. I reckon someone set him up. If it's him in that prison at all, that is.'

'They can't have set him up,' Don pointed out. 'Then he wouldn't have confessed.'

'Yeah, but they could have said they'd kill him if he didn't. Or kill his mum or something,' I said.

'Is his mother still alive?' Ira asked.

'I've no idea. She was in 1989. She had him when she was about eighteen so there's no reason why not. A brother too, but later. Dad drank himself to death years ago, obviously,' I told them.

'Of course,' Don and Ira said in unison. 'Konyeshno.'

There was a pause and we could all hear the distant roar of the motorway into Moscow and the night insects chirping in the forest.

'You wanna come with us, Don?' Eden asked quietly.

'Why are *you* going?' Don wanted to know

'I'm doing a prisons thing for the *New Yorker*. You wanna come with us?'

Ira scowled. Don looked at her and sighed. 'Eden... Jonesy. I don't really do news any more. I...' He stopped, embarrassed.

'What the fuck do you do then?' Eden spluttered. Don had won a whole display case full of awards for his war photography.

Don sighed. 'I do a lot of commercial stuff. You know— hotel interiors for brochures, pharmaceutical products...that kind of thing.'

'You take photographs of aspirin?' I asked him.

Ira got up from the table and started carrying plates in. You could see that we were confirming her worst suspicions of what would happen if Don had his old friends round for dinner. He'd slip straight back. He'd put that weight back on. He'd smoke, he'd... It occurred to me that the extent of Don's drink problem could not have been cured by love alone. Presumably she'd given him an ultimatum. It's not something he could have done without counselling. Not the notoriously willpowerless Don McCaughrean.

'Where are the meetings?' I asked him, quietly.

'British Embassy,' he said. 'You should come.'

I was stunned. Of course there are a lot of sober people in the world. People who don't know what suffering is. People who can cope with their lives because their lives are copable with. We are not among them. I coughed, appalled.

'Me? You must be fucking joking. I'm not an alcoholic, Don. And what does it mean anyway? In California someone who drinks half a bottle of wine with dinner every night is an alcoholic. Here you have to drink more than three shots with breakfast even to be in the running. It's social convention, Don. I mean, if we're denied every tiny little fucking pleasure in life...' I stopped and poured myself a vodka. I hate all this. Sobriety—good. Inebriation—bad. Why? Who said? God?

There was a long pause during which Eden cleared his throat.

'Ah, a speech!' I said, and everyone laughed. But then nobody could think of anything to add.

'Yeah,' Don said, eventually.

'Yeah what?' Eden and I both said.

'I'll come.'

Eden walked back up the steps on to the porch and shook his hand in gratitude.

'Don't bring it up,' he whispered loudly to us. 'I'll tell her later.'

'Christ. It's not dangerous or anything, you know. They're not going to start shelling us. Just a hospital visit,' I said.

'Prison,' Eden corrected me.

'Whatever,' I said.

Well, it was true. It wasn't actually dangerous in itself, I suppose. Not directly. Though perhaps if I had known what would happen I might have left it alone. I might have thought better of it all.

When Don kissed me goodbye he said, 'Hey, Zanetti. I forgot to tell you. Scott Weisman's here. For the *Washington Post*. He says he knew you from years ago.'

Scott Weisman. God. So it wasn't just my marriage that was back to haunt me. 'Yes. I remember him. I'll look him up,' I said.

In the car on the way back Eden touched my hair. It was raining again and the lights of the city when we got there were blurred by the water streaming down the car windows. Eden brushed my hair once. He said, 'One day I'm going to brush your hair and buy you a pretty dress.' And he did. But the way he meant it I think he intended it as a kind of conclusion. He would do this and I would come out of my cocoon and become a beautiful butterfly, able to give and receive love. In fact, of course, he brushed my hair, I put the dress on, we had sex and the next morning it was business as usual. The sniping and bantering that I can live with. That, and his endless sexual adventures with any locals he can lay his hands on. He's going to like it here, I thought. The sexiest women in the world. Anyone will tell you that. In Soviet times the joke was about Russian women being fat as dumplings and wearing headscarves. Then westerners actually started coming here and the truth was out.

I put Eden in the kids' room. It was hard to think of it as anything else.

'Top bunk or bottom?' I offered him. The elusive Natasha, whom I still hadn't met, had made up both.

'Hmmm. Bottom, I think,' he decided, slinging his suitcase on to the top bunk.

I took my clothes off and got into bed naked, listening to Eden shower in the bathroom, hearing him unzip his washbag, the whirr of his electric shaver, the flick of the light switch. I thought about the baby we never had (I aborted—it seemed the only sensible thing to do when two war junkies are in danger of reproducing) and the baby that Don and Ira had had. I thought about my dad, dying on a Belfast pavement, his lungs filling up with blood. And about my mum, still probably unchanged by death in her box in the dark earth. And I thought about myself and what I am doing here. What am I doing here? War after war and country after country. Am I out to pasture in Moscow? Would nobody else do the job? I won stuff. I won a big silver plate after I got shot in El Salvador. I won a kind of vase thing after Bosnia (and fuck me that was hell—trapped in a cellar in Pristina for two weeks with Don lard-arse McCaughrean). Will I carry on? Will there be some flare-up in Abkhazia that I'll go to? I'll dodge some bullets, hide in a cave, sleep with an Atman, eat a goat, win some more hardware. And then what?

I touched my face and found it wet with tears.

I stood, lit perhaps by the moonlight, in the doorway of the kids' room. 'Is there room for me in there?' I asked.

'There's always room for Faith Zanetti,' Eden whispered, and I climbed in.

Chapter 5

WHEN I WOKE up Eden was in the bathroom again. It was strange to hear normal domestic noises. It was still dark outside. I put a T-shirt and pants on and padded into the kitchen, pushing my hair out of my face. I could smell coffee.

'Dobroye utro,' said Natasha, a small dark woman in a blue apron, pouring coffee from the stove into a big white mug. 'S molokom?'

'Morning. Yes, milk please. No sugar.' I held my hand out. 'I'm Faith...and I have a guest. Eden Jones. He is in the bathroom.'

Natasha nodded as though to explain that she was used to the ways of western promiscuity, having worked for the *Chronicle* for so many years now.

'He was in the kids' room...' I muttered. Hopeless. She wasn't asking for an explanation. She couldn't have cared less, presumably. But I felt shitty and I was using her as the accuser when really I was accuser and accused. That's what a shrink does for you. 'What time is it?'

'Five forty-five,' Natasha said, glancing at her bracelet watch. 'Arkady's already downstairs.' She blushed when she said Arkady. Very revealing, I thought, and smiled.

'Fuck. Better get a move on,' I said.

I banged on the bathroom door. 'Get out of there, Jones!' I shouted. He came out immediately, shaven and showered, a white towel round his waist.

'Hmmm, foxy,' I said, and pushed past him.

I brought my cup of coffee down to the car with me and was about to get into the front seat when I noticed that it was already occupied by Don McCaughrean.

'Hey! My car. My seat. Ladies first,' I said.

'Get in the back, Zanetti, you slag. When you behave like a lady I'll treat you like one,' he said. His hair was wet and I didn't dare ask if he'd already been for his run because I was pretty sure he had and didn't feel like listening to any sanctimonious crap before nine.

Eden and I got in the back and Arkady screeched out of the compound, spilling my coffee all over my white T-shirt.

Basically, it is a very long way to Oryol. But once you get out of the huge grey tower-blocked suburbs of Moscow it all gets quite Dead Souls. The roads, such as they are, really are lined with fairy-tale wooden houses, painted bright colours, with chimneys smoking and vegetable patches in the front yard. Chickens wander in front of the car and goats are tethered to fences. Your more enterprising pensioners sell lurid and sort of erotic beach towels from their washing lines (a very weird sight) and lots of people have set up stalls by the road selling apples, dried fish on strings (I have no idea who might want these or why) and, in an area just outside Oryol, big gingerbread biscuits in the shape of churches.

Every time Eden or I lit a cigarette Don opened his window and leant out. 'I'll tell you what though,' he said, just past Klin. 'There's nothing better for you than married life. You morons should try it.'

'Sure, Don,' I agreed and kicked Eden hard in the shin.

'Will you marry me, Faith?' Eden asked. Don looked round, almost excited.

'Fuck off,' I told him. Not for the first time.

'No, I mean it,' Don went on. 'I've never felt better in my life. It's amazing what love can do. And Donchik...' He smiled to himself.

'Don, mate.' I leant forward and put a hand on his shoulder. 'We're all really happy for you and everything and I'm sure we're probably a bit jealous. But, fuck me, it isn't half nauseating.'

Eden laughed.

'Oh, sorry,' Don said, crestfallen. 'I didn't realise.'

'Since when did you ever realise anything? You go around saying it's colder than a polar bear's cunt when you're out photographing a convent. I'm just saying...' I tried to explain.

When we were a hundred miles outside Moscow Arkady piped up as drivers always do.

'We're here!' he said, grinning. It was a joke. Under the Soviets no drunks or destitutes were allowed within one hundred miles of Moscow. Anyone found inebriated with no fixed abode was driven out of the city and dumped here. They were mostly ex-prisoners, released to find their families dead or gone or refusing to have them. The Soviets actually did quite a good job of housing everyone in some way or another, so the homeless were extreme cases. This meant, of course, that all towns exactly one hundred miles away from Moscow were total shit holes with loads of makeshift shelters and hostels for society's absolute lowest of the low.

I explained this to Eden who was competitively irritated to be the only one who didn't speak the language.

'Out you get then, Zanetti,' Don said. 'Seriously. You were really packing that vodka away last night. The bottle was nearly empty.'

'Thank you, Donald.' I nodded. I had to admit that I was feeling a bit queasy. I lit a cigarette and Don coughed. Ha!

After a couple of hours Eden was asleep and Don was talking to Arkady about the best way to prepare cabbage.

'I think a little grating of nutmeg makes all the difference,' Arkady said to Don who looked as though he might even note it down.

I gazed out at the countryside and thought about seeing Dimitri again.

The first time I ever saw him was in another lifetime. It's hard to describe now how the Soviet Union seemed then. It's not just another lifetime for me, but another lifetime for Russians, some of whom (the young ones) barely even remember pioneer camps, rations for matches and sugar, communal yard cleaning on a Saturday, the easy, lazy days of knowing your rent was paid and your gas and electricity would never be cut off.

There was a romance about it that I've never known in any other place. I imagine that sounds silly to any Russians who actually lived through it, but as someone brought up in Thatcher's Britain it did seem romantic. Nobody ever talked about money—there was no inflation and nothing to buy with money anyway. Nobody talked about possessions—everyone from Moscow to Vladivostok had the same tea sets, chests of drawers and sofa beds. Nobody talked about moving house— you couldn't. So you very quickly started extremely genuine, emotional conversations about life and death and literature. People seemed interested in each other. Crazy but true.

I must have been sixteen, on a school trip to Russia—the outing to the Bolshoi ballet. It was winter and Moscow was deep in frozen snow, gloomy and oppressive. As foreigners we were followed everywhere by scuttling men in fur hats and coats with the collars pulled up high around their faces. Nobody seemed to chat to anyone, either on the streets or on the beautiful ornate metro. There was almost total silence everywhere, bizarre given the enormity of the city and the volume of people. Giggling crowds of English schoolchildren attracted a lot of attention.

The tour bus was waiting for us at the entrance to the hotel—a place so huge that I got lost every single time I tried to find my room. We came down in cavernous dark lifts, nodding to the woman who guarded them, who took and gave back our key, who noted our movements. We drove through the dark city, past the Sputnik memorial, a vast silver rocket shooting up into the starry sky, past a statue of Lenin that stood in the middle of the road, his right arm raised, his face austere. We pulled up at the pink and white colonnaded entrance to the theatre and our tour guide protected us from the crowds of kids who wanted to buy our dollars and pounds, to sell us badges with Lenin on them and to practise their English. We were ushered into the foyer where people moved around in the layer of slush that covered the marble and through into the stalls of the auditorium.

Although the bright red stage curtains were covered with little hammers and sickles, there was something unsoviet about the colours and the opulence of the décor. The boxes were all shining gold, the backs of the wooden seats were sprayed gold and all the upholstery was a rich red velvet. I expected to see princes in full military dress and princesses in tiaras and pearls, not the shabby Soviet citizens in their 1940s clothes, steaming in the aggressive central heating.

Everybody hassled everybody else for not having checked their coat, cardigan or bag into the cloakroom, for fanning themselves intrusively with their programmes and for shuffling around in their seats too much. Then there was total silence. The curtains opened, the stage shivered with expectation and the first ballerina stepped graciously out of the wings on her points, her head bowed, her tutu shimmering. The crowd roared. A lot of the men stood up and called her name. Someone threw a rose on to the stage. The ballerina smiled. The crowd roared again. The ballerina leapt into the air and everyone went wild. It was like being at a football match. This was Soviet Russia and I was sixteen. Not that I've changed much. Sometimes I feel as if I was born world-weary, like Russians are (unless they're at the ballet). Or maybe not weary so much as cautious; wise.

In the interval the Russians all dashed for the mirrors. Men and women alike stood in full view of their peers and did their hair in the foyer, scratched bits of schmutz out of their eyes, smoothed their eyebrows, reapplied their lipstick. I went outside for a cigarette. The cold took my breath away and I wrapped my arms round myself, wondering how long it would take me to die. Not long, I thought. I had just put my cigarette out under my shoe when I felt a big warm coat slip round my shoulders.

'You're freezing,' Dimitri said, coming round to the front of me. He was holding a rose which he gave to me.

'What happened? Your date stand you up?' I asked him, but he didn't understand and assumed I was thanking him. He was not much taller than me, broad shoulders, sparkly black eyes and a mischievous smile.

'I can get arrested for talking to you,' he said.

I didn't understand.

'KGB,' he said, pointing to a bloke in a black coat at the bottom of the steps. The bloke raised his hand and smiled. Dimitri did the same.

'Right.' I nodded.

We established that I was staying at the Central House of Tourists and he said he'd see me outside it tomorrow morning. At least, I think that's what he said. At any rate he was outside it the next morning when we all crowded down to get on the bus. He stood back from us and I shrugged my shoulders at him through my ski jacket. How could I get away? Then, when I had one foot on the first step up to the bus and the tour guide had looked away to shoo some children with Lenin badges, he grabbed my arm and pulled me behind a car. We ducked down as though we were being shot at and I have never been so excited in my life before or since.

The sky was cloudless and blue and it was so cold that the exhaust at the backs of the cars billowed like white smoke. I could feel my eyebrows freezing. I wore pink woollen gloves with pearly beads sewn on to them and Dimitri looked down at them and laughed. Evie had bought them for me in her effort to properly feminise me. It was a losing battle, I thought, but so far I didn't have the money to buy my own clothes so I was pretty much forced to wear the skirts she got for me.

When the bus pulled away we stood up, laughing and I looked at his face. He seemed to be waiting for instructions from me. He had on the same thick black coat he'd been wearing the day before but no hat—some sort of rebellion, perhaps. He was older than me, maybe in his twenties, with lines round his eyes and a slightly tired look about his face. I offered him a cigarette and he took the packet out of my hands and scrutinised it.

'Silk Sut,' he read.

'Cut,' I said and started to light a match. He took the cigarette out of my mouth and put it in his with another. He lit them both and then blew on the lit ends of them before giving mine back to me. Drawing in his smoke he tried to savour the flavour, curling it round his tongue and blowing it out slowly in rings.

'I prefer Kosmos,' he declared, delighted. I assumed they were Russian. In fact I came to know them well and nobody in their right mind would prefer them to any other known brand (except perhaps Belamor Kanal papirosi). They go out all the time for one thing, which is perhaps why he blew on the ends of the Silk Cut that day. And perhaps not.

I looked around me and breathed in the icy air. We could go anywhere and do anything. This was freer than I'd ever been, behind the Iron Curtain, in Soviet Moscow. Everything we had done so far and would do today was illegal—fraternising with westerners was an imprisonable offence for Dimitri and I imagined our KGB minders would take a pretty dim view of my absconding.

We crunched through the snow hand in hand, down to the bottom of the hotel's pathway and I looked back at it, a twenty storey high grey concrete thing with a couple of black spindly trees in front of it and a motorway in front of that. Dimitri stood by the road and stuck his hand out. A little brown Lada pulled over immediately and we got into the back seat, Dimitri chatting to the old man who was driving. He put his arm round me and took another cigarette, also offering one to the driver. I gazed past the grime out of the window at this bright snowy day, unable to say anything comprehensible to anyone, trusting this bloke to take me back to the hotel later this evening, not even asking him where we were going.

I can hardly remember the feeling now. Not jaded or tired, not cynical or critical. I was open and excited and on the brink of life, all that business, seeing everything for the first time. I wound down the window and stuck my head out. 'Hello Moscow!' I screamed and Dimitri dragged me back in, terrified. I couldn't stop laughing.

We went to a café in the basement of GUM department store. Gosudarstvyenniy Universalniy Magazin. State Universal Shop. It was dark and we had to queue up to pick up a tray with a bowl of kasha on it (kasha is savoury porridge and is as vile as it sounds) and a glass of sweet milky coffee. We sat at a long table crowded with other people, sweating in their coats and hats, and we didn't speak. They knew I was foreign because of my bright yellow ski jacket but they didn't comment and I didn't comment. Dimitri and I grinned at each other across the table and he shushed me when I spat my kasha out, coughing in disgust.

We walked round Gorky Park and paid five kopeks for a ride on the ferris wheel, rusting even then, creaking up to its full height of about a hundred feet, agonisingly slow so that my whole face, hands and toes were numb and frozen before we were halfway to the top. We could see the gold of the Kremlin (no crosses on the churches then) and the frozen twist of the white-grey river making its way through town. We shared a cigarette and I clapped my gloved hands together to keep warm.

We hired skates and Dimitri knelt to lace mine up, frowning with concentration. Everybody stared at me, nudging their friends and giggling behind their scarves. Puffy yellow jacket, green woolly hat, pink gloves, short black skirt and white woolly tights were clearly not the look in Moscow that season. Dimitri held my hands and skated backwards in front of me, entirely effortlessly, as though backwards and forwards were the same to him. The ice was crowded and I fell over twice. It was getting dark when they played the

Soviet national anthem over a loudspeaker to announce the end of the session. There was an innocence about it. Or was it me there was an innocence about?

It was another life. But I remember the feeling. And it is in direct contrast to the feeling I was experiencing on the drive to Oryol. Oryol is not a nice place. It is not a wealthy place or a pretty place or a place that anyone would ever go to unless they were born there and couldn't afford to leave or were sent there as a result of being found to be criminally insane. Everything there is dirty. The slush is blacker than the slush in Moscow and the tramlines are defunct. Crowds of despairing people stand at bus queues and stray dogs roam around picking at the rubbish, of which there is no shortage whatsoever.

In a place like Oryol the prison is not really much of an eyesore. The rolls of barbed wire on top of the old red brick walls and the armed guards on the watchtowers, wrapped up against the cold, pretty much sum the whole town up.

'Fuck me,' said Don, glancing around with a shiver as we drove up to the third set of electric gates. 'This is depressing.'

'Yes, it is.' Eden nodded. He had woken up as we arrived in Oryol but he hadn't said anything until now. There was nothing to say.

The prison director, Avdotiya Yevgenievna, met us at this barrier. She had dyed orange hair in a big do that involved hairspray, backcombing and pins. She wore a very tight skirt and a big shiny blouse with a frill round the bosom and silver flecks round the cuffs and collar. She smiled enthusiastically.

'We are so glad to have you,' she said in English, leaning down to Arkady's window and switching back to Russian. 'If you just leave the car over there I'll take you in.'

'I hope it's OK—we've brought our photographer?' I said, peering up at her.

'Of course, of course.' She smiled, waving a hand to show us that as far as she was concerned, the more the merrier.

Arkady skidded into the space she'd indicated, pulled his fly-fishing magazine out of the glove box and pushed his seat back into my knees.

'OK, OK, I'm getting out, for Christ's sake,' I muttered.

Don and Eden, neither of whom had ever seen Soviet Russia, were silently appalled by the total bleakness of this place. It was, it's true, hard to completely pin down. Firstly the building hadn't been cleaned since it was built before the revolution and was therefore black with grime. Secondly the outside space, of which there was a lot, was just black, slushy dirt—no gardens, pathways, or exercise areas. Thirdly, there was a lot of barbed wire. And fourthly, the grim pallor of the few faces visible behind the hundreds of windows facing us was truly chilling—physically and emotionally.

Avdotiya Yevgenievna, though, sensed none of this. She had dressed up for the second group of foreigners ever to visit her prison and she was bloody well going to enjoy her day with the press.

'We had a delegation from Broadmoor here last year,' she said, eyes sparkling. 'Lovely people. A really exciting interchange of ideas. We all learnt such a lot. I'll show you the pictures later. Brian. Yes. Brian, the director's name was. Wonderful man.'

She picked her way through the mud to the steps of the main entrance. I swear I could hear moans and groans, the kind of noise they use in period dramas to denote entrance into depressing Victorian establishments.

Inside, the Soviets had put pale yellow lino flooring down everywhere about thirty years earlier and fluorescent strip lighting at very sparse intervals on the cathedrally high ceilings. A few of them still worked. Avdotiya Yevgenievna led us through some swing doors into a huge hall where fat women were using ladles to serve evil-smelling food to lots of extremely happy-sounding people. The pitch of conversation was fast and high and the diners, holding white trays, moved about as they settled themselves at tables with their friends, jostling and laughing and scraping the floor with the metal legs of their chairs. I raised my eyes at Eden.

'This was the staff refectory,' Avdotiya Yevgenievna explained. 'But I instituted a new system whereby the patients—I don't like to call them prisoners—now eat with us at lunch times. I think trust is a vital part of the patient/carer relationship.' `

She led us towards the counter and handed us all a tray. Oh, God, but we were going to have to eat some of this crap. I looked round the room and saw that men with guns were standing by all the doors, scanning the scene in front of them vigilantly. I glanced around for Dimitri but stopped myself, unable to imagine what I would say or do if I saw him.

'Surely some of them can't be trusted, though?' Don asked, obviously a bit worried.

'Of course.' Avdotiya Yevgenievna nodded sadly, holding her tray under one arm and gesturing with long red nails. 'But we don't give up on anyone!'

She was a better woman than I was, needless to say. I had already given up on every last one of them.

I held my tray out and a big lady, all of whose teeth were steel, ladled two golubtsi into one of the compartments. Ooh I remember these. They used to serve these at the canteen when I worked on Pushkin Square. When they were serving anything at all, that is. Minced meat wrapped in a cabbage leaf and baked in...semen? Something like that. At the next big aluminium vat I was given some slivers of potato in stinking grease and at the next a piece of bread. I picked up a glass of fizzy brown crap from a rack at the end of the service area and waited for Avdotiya Yevgenievna to show me where to sit down.

She did so. I was to sit next to the best-turned-out prisoner in the building. A clean-shaven, bright-eyed young man called David who wore blue overalls and a crazed smile. Eden sat on the other side of him and Don opposite. Avdotiya Yevgenievna watched us eagerly, sitting down as close as she could get to Eden and tucking into her food with enormous relish. 'Go on,' she said. 'You can talk to him about anything you like except his crime.' Don raised his eyebrows at me. Immediately, of course, all I could think about was his crime. Was it grisly? What constitutes a crime that might render you criminally insane? Or was it, like Dimitri's, just the way you talked about whatever you'd done. Avdotiya Yevgenievna leant over to me and put her hand up to her cheek for a pantomime whisper.

'Skinned his father alive,' she hissed.

I choked on a mouthful of cabbage, Don shouted 'Fuck me!' without meaning to and Eden's eyes widened in horror.

'So, how do you find it here?' he asked, holding a ball of unidentifiable meat up on his flimsy fork, the one kopek kind that bends if you try and get a so much as vaguely firm piece of food on to it. Avdotiya Yevgenievna translated.

'Great,' said David, pushing his clean tray away from him as though he had thoroughly enjoyed every bite of his meal. 'I have been almost completely rehabilitated and will soon be ready to rejoin society.'

Not my fucking society you won't, mate, I thought and coughed.

Eden kept looking at me expectantly, waiting for me to ask about Dimitri, but I was biding my time. I was tired and didn't want to face arguing my way in to see him, and if she agreed perfectly happily, I didn't want to face him. When Avdotiya Yevgenievna realised that we wouldn't be eating any more of the stuff on our trays she clapped her hands like a little girl in a 1950s film who is about to be taken to the circus.

'Andatry!' she exclaimed.

An andatr is basically a very big rat. But really big. The English word is coypu and nobody has ever seen one except on someone's head. The Russians make shapkas (the traditional men's fur hats) out of coypus. To Avdotiya Yevgenievna's apparent glee, they kept coypu on the premises for the prisoners to bond with or something. She took us back outside into the mud, swapping her stilettos for boots by the door and picking up a big blue scarf from a hat stand to wrap round her head and shoulders.

The coypu were out in a hut at the back of the prison and it was obvious which hut they were in because of the nauseating stench coming out of it and the rivers of coypu faeces that were merging with the mud around the door. Avdotiya Yevgenievna beamed madly as she showed us in. Eden had to duck through the door into the gloom. Don looked as though he might actually be sick and raised his hand to his face against the smell.

Once our eyes had adjusted we could see hundreds of wooden and wire mesh cages against the walls, the concrete floor just covered in coypu waste and the coypus themselves, horrifying in their hugeness. There were a couple of prisoners in there, one of them sweeping the floor and the other getting a beast out of its cage. The sweeper was a big bloke, the kind who might have worked in a shipyard and had tattoos before his mental instability caused him to butcher his girlfriend and her entire family, or whatever it was he'd done. He kept his eyes down. Avdotiya Yevgenievna came towards me in the gloom and leant into my ear.

'Cooked and ate a child,' she announced, and put her finger to her lips to ensure my silence on the subject. Hell, she had it.

The other one, a puny type with a droopy eye, brought the coypu over to meet us, stroking its greasy-looking fur with one hand. They are the size of a smallish badger and have protruding teeth and big claws. Coypus have long, fat tails and I can honestly say that I do not like them.

I felt I should ask a question. Don had gone back outside in a rush. 'So the prisoners care for them?' I asked.

'Patients. Yes. It's very therapeutic. Good for them to work with animals.' Avdotiya Yevgenievna nodded, indulgent.

'But why have you got so many of them?' Eden asked. It was a good point.

'We farm them,' she said, proudly. 'This is an andatr farm.'

It was dawning on me now. That was the smell. Not the living coypus. The dead ones.

'Fur,' I said out loud to myself.

'That's right!' She grinned.

'Who kills them?' Eden asked, stroking the disgusting animal held out to him.

'The patients,' Avdotiya Yevgenievna said, leading the way out now.

I made a face at Eden. So, the prisoners bond with the animals and then they kill them. Hmmm. Therapeutic. Yup. Well, I can see how.

'The government funding is not enough by itself for all the extra programmes we run. We have a number of small enterprises on site...' she added. I wasn't really listening, though. I was thinking about our friend in there snapping that coypu's neck the moment we left. It's probably a bit like letting prisoners box. An outlet for their violence and all that.

Don had thrown up in the mud. 'Sorry, I...' he apologised, shaking his head.

'Don't worry! Don't worry! I should have given you all a drink when you arrived. Hair of the dog!' Avdotiya Yevgenievna said. She assumed that Don just had a hangover.

Eden and I laughed. Once that would have been true. The old Don would have a can of beer in his jacket pocket for these emergencies. He turned back and took a picture of the shed, trying to retain a bit of dignity.

'Tossers,' he said to himself. It was not clear who he meant. The coypus, probably.

Avdotiya Yevgenievna was still enjoying herself immensely. A foreign delegation, photographer and all. 'So!' she declared. 'The slide show!'

Eden nudged me and it was obvious that this was the moment. I took a deep breath.

'Avdotiya Yevgenievna,' I began, and she turned to face me in the mud. Eden and Don kept walking towards the front steps. 'There is one pr—patient in whom I am particularly interested. I wonder if you could introduce me to Dimitri Sakhnov?'

She scowled, her brow wrinkling in concentration. She put one finger to the top of her nose and closed her eyes. Then, as a dark cloud engulfed the prison compound, she opened them again, smiling.

'Double murder! Chopped the boy's leg off!' she said.

'Um. Yes, that's right,' I said.

'Marvellous. This way,' she told me, actually taking me by the arm as though we were girlfriends taking a stroll in the park. We all went into the prison together and Avdotiya Yevgenievna shouted to a colleague. 'Marina Vasilyevna! Could you start the slide show for these gentlemen? I am just going to take Miss Zanetti for a private interview with a patient. Faith—may I call you Faith?—come this way.'

She picked up a set of keys from a hook and we must have walked about a mile up and down flickering yellow corridors, some with cells on them (locked doors with rusting grilles at eye level) and some with small dormitories, well lit with photos stuck on the walls and crucifixes and icons all over the place. I noticed that one bloke had a pin-up of the queen. Seriously. The queen of England. Lucky for us all that he's not at large.

The further we walked the more nervous I got. I could hardly breathe, let alone listen to the lecture I was getting about crime and modern society.

'Ninety-five per cent of my patients committed their crimes when drunk. I compare the problem to guns in America. The vodka manufacturers would claim that their product is recreational, but I believe it kills people. Teetotal communities have very low crime rates. Countries without guns have very low gun deaths,' she was saying. She slowed her pace and I felt sick. 'He's had a lot of attention lately. Suddenly started saying his confession was false, he's not guilty. Blaming his wife and whatnot. They took him seriously. He's been to Moscow twice for new interviews. Got back from his last one this morning. What's your interest, anyway?' she asked me, banging on the glass door of a dorm to announce our already extremely obvious presence. 'Sakhnov!' she shouted. 'Visitor!'

'I'm the wife,' I told her, walking into the room.

Chapter 6

THERE WERE SIX blokes in here. I glanced round at all of them. Four sat on their bunks, two squatted on the floor playing cards. All of them wore the prison boiler suit and all were youngish, in decent condition—rotting teeth, appalling odour and recent scarring notwithstanding. None of them was Dimitri.

I peered more closely into their faces.

'Hey! Sakhnov! Stand up!' Avdotiya Yevgenievna shouted, the first time I'd heard her sound remotely like a prison director, and one of the men playing cards got to his feet. He had a short beard, wild blue eyes and straggly dark hair. He looked at me, and said, 'Hey, Faithy. How's it going?'

It took me a few seconds to recognise him, so far was he from my mind.

'Holy shit,' I said, smiling. 'Adrian.'

'Can I have a dollar?' he asked, and I laughed and went forward to hug him, genuinely pleased to see him, however inappropriate it was to be pleased about anything in here. But I was pleased too that it wasn't Dimitri.

'Christ, you stink,' I told him. 'Really. You stink.'

He stood back and looked into my face. 'Faith, you've got to get me out of here,' he said.

The last time I'd seen him was just before I left. Dimitri was in one of his 'let's go round and taunt Adrian' moods. Sometimes he just wanted to go out and spend time with people he hated, just to compound his anger. We'd been to the market so decided to take some bread and sausage round to Adrian who sometimes didn't eat for days on end. There were only two markets in Moscow then. They were legal but somehow it was private enterprise, bizarrely sanctioned because the traders were all from the southern republics. Nobody, however, could afford anything there. You would see old ladies buying two potatoes and actually weeping when they handed over the money.

The market had everything. It was like paradise. It was indoors in a vast modern hall next to the circus and it smelt of eastern spices and pickles. Birds flew about in the rafters and rats scuttled beneath the tables. The whole place seemed to steam.

'Dyevushka! Dyevushka!' the traders called out at me as I passed. 'Girl! Girl!' They had gold teeth and funny accents and made Russian sound unpronounceable and clipped. They had black flashing eyes and brightly coloured skull caps; the women wore green and red headscarves and long skirts.

They sold bloodless halal-killed pigs, drained, white and whole on squares of muslin. They had oranges, lemons, grapes and watermelons, pumpkins, courgettes and yellow and red peppers. There were enormous white cheeses dripping on slabs, vats of dark honey, vats of pale honey, mounds of coloured spices. I loved the market. But even on my salary and Dimitri's vaguely ill-gotten gains it was a treat. Once every couple of months and you were grateful for it.

We felt like king and queen at the market. We were young and well dressed, rich and foreign. The Russians buying their pathetic potatoes stared at us and the dark people from the republics practically fell at our feet. As we paraded out that day with our bags of shopping, dropping kopeks into the hands of the children begging outside, Dimitri stopped and bought me a pink rose. A long-stemmed fat pink rose, sprayed down every ten minutes since dawn, its thorns picked off, its petals almost offensively luxurious in the snow and the appalling poverty. He brushed it against my cheek and smiled.

'Another planet,' he said, and shook his head. He always said I was like someone from another planet. So soft and impressionable, worrying about the hungry children and the old woman in our apartment, thinking about the future as though we'd be alive to see it.

When we got home Dimitri announced his desire to go and see Adrian. I knew where he was going with this. There was something both aggressive and self-destructive about it. At once a desire to inflict humiliation and a desire to experience it. My fingers were still cold and I didn't want to go out again, but Dimitri was determined. 'Come on!' he said. 'It'll be fun.' I knew it wouldn't be. Not because I didn't like Adrian or even because I disapproved of Dimitri's mocking him. I knew it wouldn't be fun because I had already decided to leave and go back to England. I didn't want to live like this forever and I didn't want to bring Dimitri back to a world he'd never understand. It happened like this.

We had gone up to Lenin Hills one night, late. It must have been two o'clock in the morning and I had a long sable coat over my nightdress, boots pulled on to bare feet. We looked out at the city beneath us in silence and I said, 'This isn't going to work, you know.'

He knew what I meant. He didn't dump responsibility on to me by saying 'What isn't?' or doing some babyish disingenuous thing of pretending he thought I was happy or some accusatory thing like asking me how I could do this to him. He just said, 'OK.'

He loved me and he wanted me to be happy, whether that involved him or not. But I wanted to explain.

'You don't know what the last line of *Casablanca* is,' I told him, desperate to clarify it for my own sake.

He said, 'What's Casablanca?'

I said, 'Exactly.'

And that was that. Except it wasn't. I didn't go immediately. I didn't even book my flight immediately. I just pretended I'd never said it and went to work every day, drank sweet Soviet champagne with Dimitri every night and waited for the feeling to go away. But it didn't. I wanted to go back to my planet and be with my people.

You see, Adrian was living alone off his salary from the magazine. This was a salary that already hadn't been paid for three months. At first they tried to pay us in food—tins of sardines and sprats (I don't even know what sprats are, but the Russian is 'shproty' and they come in aspic), cuts of salami and loaves of bread. But then that ran out too and people were fending for themselves.

Adrian lived miles out of town in the cheapest apartment he could find. 'If I want to do my ironing I have to have sex with the woman next door so she'll lend me her iron,' Adrian whined. He lived on about the three hundredth floor of the most depressing tower block in a vast complex of very depressing tower blocks. It was one of those places where taxis and cars of people's relatives just drive round and round shouting out of the window at pedestrians, 'Where's korpus seven?' and none of the pedestrians ever know, even when they are standing right outside korpus seven. I'm sure it wasn't true about the iron either. Adrian would never have had the remotest desire to iron anything, and anyway he only had one set of clothes. He probably used it as an excuse to get to sleep with the woman next door.

We trundled up in the small dark lift in silence. The buttons had been melted with a teenager's lighter and the bulb had been out for years. Hey, at least the lift itself was working. In most of these blocks old ladies have to allocate an hour or more to get up to their flats. Adrian wasn't surprised to see us. He was used to our mad weekend visits and I think he even understood what they were about. He knew Dimitri despised him and I think he may have grasped better than I did that Dimitri enjoyed watching Adrian's love for me and asserting his own possession of me. I should stress that my marriage was the last real relationship I ever had. I learnt my lesson. Male-female relationships are no great shakes.

He opened his door a fraction, all four chains on. 'Hey,' he said.

We went into the gloom. The light bulbs he stole were not for himself. At least, not for the giving of light. He sold them for vodka. There was not a single bulb in his flat and almost no furniture. A bed, a couple of metal chairs, a standard Soviet kitchen table, cooker and stuff. But no cupboards or wardrobes, no pictures or ornaments. Not even a television. Some amazing percentage of domestic deaths under Communism were caused by exploding televisions. Something like sixty per cent. No, I can't remember, but enough to be amusing. Clearly Adrian was taking no risks.

Somebody staggered out of the loo, bewildered at the sight of us, his bleary eyes squinting to get us into focus, his already very precarious balance thrown off with the effort of recognition. He fell against the wall but, still standing, continued to assess us.

'This is Pyotr,' Adrian said. 'He lives downstairs.'

Adrian was using the verb 'to live' in its loosest possible sense. I mean, he exists. But I'm not sure that living was what

Pyotr was doing downstairs or anywhere else. He was a classic Russian drunk. There is no way of describing in a realistic way how much these men (nearly always men) drink. One could say they drink vodka like water, but then even the most health conscious people only drink about two litres of water a day. Pyotr was in a state way past drunkenness. Drunkenness had been days or weeks ago. They start to binge. They spend an evening drinking a couple of bottles of vodka and they get very drunk, remember their army days, sing, hug each other, fight and pass out. Then they come round and carry on drinking. For days. Eventually, though the motor functions are still working, they are pretty much comatose. I mean, actually comatose. Like in a coma. With huge parts of their brain completely shut down. You see them out on the streets, staggering along the pavement in urine-soaked trousers, lying on the ground bleeding from head wounds they got in a fight, defecating under trees in Moscow's (and everywhere else's) parks.

Pyotr stared at us, uncomprehending. He moved, lumbering towards the kitchen, and sat down at the Formica table, his hand clasping a thick, greasy vodka glass.

Adrian followed Pyotr and we followed Adrian, pulling off coats and scarves, kicking off shoes on the way. Dimitri couldn't help lining his shoes up neatly by the door like his mum had taught him. Incidentally, here is a tip for visiting in Russia. Make sure your socks or tights have no holes in them and do not smell. And that they match. They are on show more than you might like.

Adrian kept reaching up to touch his beard and moustache and then to adjust his filthy glasses. He snorted rather than spoke.

'Sit down, guys,' he said. He smirked because he used the American slang ironically. He despised everything American including the language, though when he got really drunk he would admit to missing Taco Bell and something called Chuck E Cheez. I don't know what it is. Vile killer food of some kind or another.

Anyway, we sat down. Dimitri noted all American slang for use when he moved to Florida as nature intended. He muttered 'sit down guys' to himself, quietly enough to be audible only to the very sober. He got a salami and a loaf of black bread out of a carrier bag we'd brought and put them on the table.

'Crazy,' Adrian said and went to the fridge to get a jar of gherkins. He brought a bottle of Czech beer for me. A treat.

When Dimitri had cut up the bread and sausage with his penknife (cutting the bread into half slices) and Adrian had knifed the metal seal off the top of another bottle of vodka we all, even Pyotr, looked briefly out of the window as if to check that the weather really was bleak enough to be doing this. It was. Just miles and miles of grey sky, tower blocks and falling snow. Adrian stood up.

'When I first came here the Iron Curtain was firmly in place. When I first came here this was the Evil Empire. When I first came here I expected a nuclear war to break out any day. But what did I find? I found a country with full employment. I found a country with a great education system free for all. I found a country with a health service that did not discriminate between rich and poor. I found friendly people and a place I can call home. But what do we see now?'

He got a bit louder for that last line and we all looked up at him.

'What do we see now?' he repeated.

We weren't sure whether or not we were supposed to answer. The kettle on the hob started to whistle and the small kitchen filled with steam.

'What do we see now?' he asked again. 'We see a place standing at the crossroads of civilisation. We see a nation united in uncertainty. We see—'

Pyotr banged his fist hard on the table and shouted. 'Nu, ladno. Nye pizdi. Nalivai.' This translates as: 'Well, OK. Don't cunt on. Pour it out.'

Dimitri laughed. Adrian was silenced. He poured the vodka and the three blokes drank, winced, smelt a slice of bread each, popped a gherkin into their mouths and looked at the bottle again.

I poked my big toe through the hole in my tights and felt it freeze on the lino.

As I say, I have grown up a lot since then. I looked at Adrian now, even shorter than he was before, dwarfed by hardship, definitely a whole lot older, thinner, more defeated. Well, I imagine twelve or so years in a psychiatric hospital could do that to you.

'Faithy, Faithy. For old times' sake,' he grinned. 'Get me out of here.'

I had to smile. I put a hand on his shoulder. 'Shit, Adrian. Why the fuck have you done this? I spent the whole sodding night at the procuratura because of you. And *how* could I possibly get you out? I couldn't even get you transferred to hard labour. You're not even you. Who are you anyway?'

Adrian spat on the floor.

Avdotiya Yevgenievna shouted into the room. She had not gone far. 'Sakhnov! Respect for your visitor!'

This made both of us laugh. There is a piece of Russian drinking slang that allows drinkers to say to anyone not drinking, 'Don't you respect me?' Apparently, not getting completely arseholed is hugely disrespectful to the assembled drunks.

'You don't respect me,' I told Adrian.

'I will if you get me the fuck out of here,' he whined.

I felt heavy with responsibility and, God knows, it hadn't even started yet.

'You know I'm not him, right? You know I'm me. Tell them. Tell the American embassy.'

However sympathetic I feel I am very good at absenting myself. In fact, it usually takes me at least twenty-four hours to experience the feelings associated with any particular event. So I can be in bed with someone, having sex with them, and it's only the next day that I have any idea whether I loved it or hated it, fell into their arms with defenceless abandon or wanted to throw up. And the way I avoid feelings is to concentrate on the detail. The detail here was how repulsive Adrian seemed with his beard and his prison smell and his pleas.

I sighed and sat down on a metal chair. The blokes playing cards had exactly zero interest in what was going on. It is people like these who provide westerners with a duty, an actual moral duty, to enjoy themselves. Do you think that these prisoners, living in revolting conditions with no hope of anything better even if they do get out, would feel guilt or anxiety about sipping cocktails on a beach or eating sushi in a forty-fifth floor revolving restaurant? They wouldn't, and on behalf of them we must make sure we take pleasure in what we've got and not ruin it all with doubt. Easier said than done, of course…

'Why haven't you told them? Why now? Why are you in here? Adrian,' I moaned, exasperated. 'Help me at least a tiny bit.'

He pulled at his beard. He looked frantic. I wondered what drugs they had them all on. Opiates, probably.

'The Americans have no record that I was ever even in Russia. All my old documents are Soviet fakes. Good ones as well. I'm Nikolai. Kolya Kuznyetsov. I've been officially Russian for years. You know that, Faith. And now…well, now I don't even have that stuff. Now I'm Dimitri Sakhnov. All the papers he gave me, passport, everything, are in his name with my picture on them. Hey, nobody believed I was American fifteen years ago. Now…it's hopeless.'

'God, Adrian,' I whispered, and took my cigarettes out of my jacket pocket. 'Can I smoke?'

'Give the boss five bucks and you can have sex with us all,' Adrian told me.

'Tempting,' I said and lit my cigarette. I looked at him and flinched at the realisation that even Adrian, changed, crazed by incarceration, would perhaps rape me if it weren't for the guards.

'So, you're saying that Dimitri set you up for this, are you?' I asked him, wanting to cry, fighting something down.

'That's what I'm saying,' Adrian told me, staring me right in the face.

'I don't believe you,' I said, almost hopefully.

'Fine. I know you're going to go and find out, though. You won't be able to help it, Faith Zanetti. The first thing you'll find is that Dimitri is dead. Thank Christ. That's why I'm doing this now. If I'd tried before he'd have killed my kids. He would as well.'

I tried not to flicker. There was a lot wrong with all this and I didn't want to start grieving for a Dimitri who might be alive and well and living in Palm Beach. It was hard to help it, though. That first smile he gave me outside the Bolshoi a hundred lifetimes ago came into my mind and my stomach tightened with sadness.

'What kids?' I asked.

'I was teaching English in the country. Married the physics professor. They were babies when Dimitri came to see me,' he said, quietly now, tugging at his beard, eyes glazing over.

'Told me I had to "give myself up".' He moved his fingers into speech marks, a gesture I hate but that looked particularly urban and incongruous here.

'What makes you think he's dead?'

'You hear things in here. I heard something.'

At this point Avdotiya Yevgenievna barged back into the room. 'Time's up, Sakhnov,' she barked, earrings dangling, her neck flushing. I hauled myself out of my chair and turned on Adrian. I had had enough.

'So, Adrian. It's been great to catch up,' I said, putting my cigarette out in a ceramic mug that held an inch of cold tea. I sighed. The weight of my involvement in this thing was now becoming oppressive. But I would think about that tomorrow. For now, I was trying to stay as blank as possible.

'Faith! Faithy! Are you going to help me?'

'Sure,' I said, and I fished a dollar out of my jeans and gave it to him. He stared at it, bewildered and looked back to my face. We both laughed. 'I'll try, Adrian. I promise I'll try. I don't know what to do yet. You've really landed me in a lot of shit.'

Adrian slumped down on to the edge of his bunk bed. One of his cellmates swore. 'I didn't think you'd come unless you had to,' he said.

'No,' I answered. 'Perhaps you're right.'

Avdotiya Yevgenievna grabbed my arm and hissed into my ear, 'Raped his girlfriend and hacked her to death with an axe. Chopped her husband's legs off.' Her morbid excitement had been funny at first. Now it was wearing a bit thin. I thought of the line in *As Good As It Gets* when Jack Nicholson says, 'Sell crazy some place else. We're all stocked up here.'

'Neighbour,' I corrected her. 'I know.' Clearly she had thought I was joking when I had told her I was his wife. Or maybe her mind only processed information about hideous crimes.

I raised my hand to Adrian as we left. I was almost tearful with fondness and sadness. If only I had known I wasn't going to see him again I would have hugged him so tightly that my heart would have broken.

Before we left, Avdotiya Yevgenievna gave us each, me, Don and Eden, a hat made of coypu fur.

Chapter 7

DON WAS PARTICULARLY pleased with his hat. He said he thought it lent him the gravitas he had hitherto been lacking.

'McCaughrean,' Eden pointed out, 'a rat fur hat is about the amount of gravitas you deserve.'

'Thanks, Jonesy.' Don smiled, delighted.

We had been trundling along the dismal road out of Oryol for about ten minutes before anyone even bothered to ask me how my meeting with my mass murdering husband had gone.

'Hey, Zanetti,' Eden eventually enquired, blowing a plume of smoke out of his window. 'How was your mass murdering ex-husband?'

I took my hat off and put it on my lap. It was annoyingly impossible not to stroke it like a cat. 'It wasn't him,' I said, lighting my own cigarette. 'It was this friend of mine. Went native years ago and left no record of being American. Says Dimitri set him up.'

'Dimitri's the ex-husband?' Eden wanted to clarify, not wildly interested. 'But not the convict?'

Don put on what I suppose he thought was an American gangster godfatherish voice. 'I was framed, boss,' he complained. Then he changed it to the voice he must have imagined that Lee Harvey Oswald had had. 'I was just a patsy.'

Eden and I thought it best to ignore him.

'Well, not actually ex, but yes.'

This information perked Eden up a bit. 'What? You're married? You're fucking married? You never got a divorce! No way!'

I laughed and took a long drag on my cigarette, crossing one cowboy booted leg over my knee. 'Sure. You may address me as Mrs Sakhnova from now on.'

Don was beginning to catch on now. 'What? Zanetti's married? That's huge!'

'Right. So if you wouldn't mind showing a bit of respect that would be great.'

'Do you have kids?' Don wondered, leaning round from the front seat which he had bafflingly been allowed to occupy. Again.

Eden, who was sitting next to me in the back, shook his head. 'Wow,' he said.

My marital status did not seem to me the most exciting part of my current dilemma and I pointed this out to the idiots in the car.

'Fair enough,' Eden conceded.

'Married!' sighed Don.

'Oh, for fuck's sake,' I said. 'This bloke, Adrian, has been in prison for about a million years for something that he absolutely definitely didn't do. I don't believe Dimitri did it either but one thing is totally for sure and that's that Adrian didn't do it. He wouldn't be able to pick a fucking axe up off the floor, let alone swing it at a part of someone's anatomy.'

I opened my window a fraction and flicked my cigarette butt out. Arkady was humming an old Rosenbaum song called 'Boston Waltz'. It's so melancholy that it could probably make a person cry for their lost loves, lost youth, opportunities not taken, smiles not returned, if they were on a podium collecting their fourth Oscar. But here, out on the road from Oryol to Moscow, it sounded like the end of the world. It's about leaves dancing in a crumbling Moscow courtyard and it's about loss.

'Shut up, could you?' I said, and he did.

Don craned round to look at me. 'Feeling a bit edgy, Mrs Sakhnova?' He smirked.

I stared at him, uncomprehending. 'Yeah. Yeah, Don, I am feeling a trifle edgy this evening. The thing is, right, the Russians think I murdered two people when I was nineteen because someone they think is my husband told them he was just protecting me when he confessed. *But,* and get this, not only does the patsy think Dimitri did kill them but he also says he framed him for the murders *and* he is now dead. Did you somehow miss some of this? Were you distracted by a rare butterfly?'

Don looked slightly abashed.

Eden raised his hand like a confused schoolboy who had been away with chicken pox when long division was happening. 'I've got to tell you, Faithy, I actually missed the "and now he's dead" bit myself,' he said, pushing his shirt sleeves up above his elbows. Arkady swerved to avoid a flock of geese that was waddling across the road. I slid into Eden's lap and my lighter fell out of my jacket pocket on to the floor.

'Oh. Well, now I've told you. Adrian said he'd "heard" Dimitri was dead. That's why he's making his psychotic bid for freedom now. By telling everyone he can lay his hands on that it was me what done it. He didn't think at this stage it would be worth trying to claim he's an American citizen. Probably a good call.'

Don hadn't said anything for a couple of minutes and when he turned to face me again I thought he might be about to make some terrible joke, but in fact he said the first helpful thing that anybody had said to me since the beginning of this whole nightmare the day before yesterday.

'It seems to me,' he said, scratching at his nose, 'that you should try and find out about this couple and why someone wanted to kill them, or why he killed her himself or whatever. If we have no clue who they were then of course the idea that Dimitri or Adrian or you killed them is absurd. But if they were like, I don't know, child traffickers or something, then it might fall into place a bit. It might not kill you to get in touch with Dimitri's family while you're at it. Say he's not dead? You know, you might call him up and he'll say, "Hey, Faithy, long time no see. Incidentally, about those people who got killed next door fifteen years ago…" Hmmm?'

I smiled and leant back in my seat. 'Yeah. Thanks, Don,' I said.

'Any time,' he agreed, holding up his hand for me to slap. He paused a second before shaking his head and saying, 'Faith Zanetti. Married.'

I flicked the back of his neck. 'Fuck off, McCaughrean. OK?'

It was after midnight by the time we got back to Moscow but there was a message from the desk that they wanted to run a last minute spoiler about a journalist who is claiming that Putin's FSB (KGB basically. It's had its name changed loads of times since Ivan the Terrible set it up but that's the only thing about it that ever really changes) keeps drugging her and putting her on planes to weird places and stealing her tapes and notes. It's probably true and if it isn't it easily could be and I'm sure they're doing it to someone else. The point is that the *Sunday Chronicle*, which you might think was essentially the same thing as the *Chronicle*, had got an exclusive interview and the *Chronicle* had found out and wanted to make it look rubbish and old hat-like by running the story first. For, although the papers are both owned by the same sleazy magnate, they are highly competitive in a bitter and pathetic way. So I sat in the office writing this thing from cuts and rumours (I did put in a call to the woman but she obviously wouldn't speak to me as she'd been paid for the exclusivity by the *Sunday*) and watching Eden turn off the lights in my flat one by one high up across the way.

I fell asleep at the desk and dreamed about Dimitri so vividly that when I opened my eyes in the grey dawn light of the office I could have believed he was there. We had been to the Ukraine to stay with his aunt and uncle in a tiny village where the roads and pavements were just dirt tracks and everyone was vaguely related to each other. But even here there was a House of Culture where propagandistic films were screened and orchestras came all the way from Kiev to play. It was a grand colonnaded building with a statue of Lenin in the forecourt and a disco every Friday where Uncle Sasha put on his black shiny shirt and played his synthesiser.

We really did go there once. It took a night and a day on the train and we took champagne with us and went first class. The snow seemed deeper and thicker in the Ukraine, the glasses of tea that the wagon lady brought us in Hammer and Sickle iron holders seemed hotter and sweeter. The station where we got off had no platform and no signalman's hut. Nothing. Just a sign, buried in the snow. Uncle Sasha had come to meet us and he helped us down into the waist-deep powder. He wore a huge fur hat, felt valenki (peasanty over-boots) and an ancient fox fur coat. In his enormous chapped hands he held a bunch of carnations for me.

'Welcome, Muscovites!' he said. For although he did know I was English, Moscow was about as far away and as otherworldly, as glamorous, a concept as he could manage.

Sasha had built himself a very grand house with money that Dimitri had sent him from the not spectacularly legal vodka business in the far north. The house was hideous. Made entirely of concrete with small double glazed windows, a large asphalt drive and two wild dogs on chains to guard it (the last being a common feature of the modern Russian home in those days—the chains were thick, long and noisy, the dogs never released from them). It was set a couple of hundred yards away from the two parallel rows of old, decorative wooden houses that constituted the village. These had been there for about three hundred years, rotting fairy-tale cottages with smoking chimneys and carved roofs and window frames. Gogol's short stories were set somewhere like this with their mud rivers of spring roads, crazed inhabitants and phantasmagorical happenings.

Inside, Sasha and his wife had both a television and a sound system which they demonstrated proudly to me. If Russians didn't count as foreigners by virtue of being fellow Soviets, then I was the first foreigner any of them had ever met. When we got drunk under the plastic New Year tree with flashing Santa Claus lights I sang them 'Let It Be' and recited Shakespeare sonnets (well, the only two I know— 'Shall I Compare Thee to a Summer's Day' and 'When to the Sessions of Sweet Silent Thought'). I felt I ought at least to show my credentials.

The next day we went out on to the river for an ice picnic. The men cut down trees to make a fire on the ice and the women (me, Aunty Zina and Aunty Pavla) unpacked the marinaded meat and threaded it on to skewers while the children skidded around madly. The location wasn't doing my sanity any favours. The sky was so low and so white, the snow falling so thickly, the ice on the river so deep, that I couldn't tell where the snow ended and the sky began. Only the spindly black trees on the opposite bank helped to ground me. That and the sweet cognac that vast Aunty Zina eventually produced.

This was where the dream took place. Dimitri was bringing wood over to the fire and the ice began to crack. He fell through and, though everyone rushed to save him, the current was strong and he was quickly carried under. We followed him as he floated visibly under the ice, his face up, his eyes wide open. He was shouting, 'I am not dead, Faith. I am not dead.'

I woke up, my face lined with marks from my jacket sleeve. I walked round the office to make sure he wasn't there, aware of how mad this was, but unable to stop myself. I took one of Arkady's beers out of the fridge (beer does not count as alcohol in Russia and is a perfectly acceptable morning time beverage) and bit the top off. I am good at that. I sat in the ageing brown velour sofa and put my feet up on a metal desk. I made the call I have made so many times in my life. Not, however, for the past fifteen years or so. I still hadn't forgotten the number.

Dimitri's mother does not have a phone. There was a time under the Soviets when quite a lot of people didn't have a phone. If you wanted to call another city or even another country (inadvisable from a getting-hounded-by-the-KGB point of view), then you had to do it from the local post office where you would queue, sometimes for hours, to book your call and then again for a booth to become available. When one of these old wooden booths flashed free, you would go in, pick up the heavy black Bakelite receiver and quote your call number to the operator who was on the end of the line and also physically about two yards away. She, always she, would then connect you and, always, listen in just in case. It didn't really seem like a hassle because everyone had to do it. People also sent a lot of telegrams. You would pick up a form and fill it in with one of the nibs they left on the counters, dipping it in the wooden pot of congealed ink. Then you took your message to the counter and paid by the word. I once sent a message to Evie with the word 'fuck' in it. Though I had written it in English the post office woman recognised the word and made me delete it. Out in the provinces things are still like this now.

Anyway, when I used to call Dimitri from Evie's house in Putney all those years ago I had to dial the upstairs neighbour—owner of the building's only phone. Very possibly Ryazan's only phone. She kept chickens on her balcony, apparently. Not some romantic Babylonian garden balcony, but the notoriously dangerous concrete slab kind outside one of the windows on the twentieth floor of a big grey 1970s Brezhnev apartment block. Hey, if you want eggs…

I had learnt how to say: I am calling Dimitri Sakhnov. The woman, whose name I never knew, would say: Call back. I would wait five minutes for her to go down and get Dimitri and then I would call back and he would pick up. We had arranged times but he often missed them and I would be desolate. Again, I have changed a lot since then. I think it was probably some father-related problem. When the main man in your life drops dead early on it must surely do things to your view of men in general. See—I told you they made me see a shrink after Baghdad.

'I am calling Dimitri Sakhnov,' I said now, recognising the croak of the woman who had been picking this phone up since the mid-1980s. I lit a cigarette. The woman hung up. I redialled.

'Da?' she said this time. Usually she said a word that translates as 'I am listening'.

'Hello,' I said. 'I am Dimitri Sakhnov's wife and I am trying to get in touch with anyone who knows where he is.'

The woman coughed the kind of cough that I will be producing in about thirty years if I carry on smoking at my present rate and live that long. 'Galina still lives downstairs but she doesn't talk to anyone. Not since he went to prison. Don't phone me again. I've got problems of my own.' Given that this lady was elderly and Russian this was doubtless true. I, however, was on my way to Ryazan to see Dimitri's mum.

I left a note on Lyuda's desk to ask her to look up some information on the murder victims and any living relatives they might have, went upstairs to the flat for a shower (Eden was fast asleep on the bottom bunk) and was on my way back out of Moscow by six thirty a.m. I had brought Elvis with me to keep me company. All western music seems incongruous in Russia. It makes you feel like you're in a film, driving out on to the ring road against the rush hour traffic listening to the velvety molasses of the King singing 'I Just Can't Help Believing'. The rain had let up and I could taste the chill that meant the snow would start soon.

Last time I did this drive I was holding a big metal bucket of roses between my knees and Dimitri was driving. He loved being able to buy the whole bucket and not just a single rose like the other Joes. Or Ivans. It was snowing and I was amazed he could see the road at all, his cigarette clamped between his lips, black eyes blazing forwards into the night, collar turned up against the cold. The car had no heating and my legs were freezing against the metal.

When the gaishniki (traffic police) waved us over with a glowing baton Dimitri swore hard and skidded into the lay-by.

'Pizdyets,' he said. Cunt. He said it a lot. Weirdly, and, as it turned out, stupidly, I was comforted by the golden light of their little hut on this remote forest road. It was nice to know that there were people out here, smoking and drinking vodka, playing cards, working out their shift.

'Zhaba,' he said. 'Whatever you do, don't talk to them. They are not people. Not really. Not like you have in the West. They are wolves.'

Zhaba was my nickname. It means toad and people were always shocked when he called me that. It was a stupid joke. When a woman tried to cross the road in front of his car, Dimitri would hit the horn and shout, 'Zhaba, blyad!' Fucking toad! I once complained that he didn't consider me properly female since he called all women toad except me. So I became Zhaba.

Dimitri couldn't frighten me about the traffic police. He was always saying melodramatic things like that which I dismissed as hysteria. He took his documentation from behind the sun visor, left me in the car and went to join one of the gaishniki in what looked like a lovely and well-heated hut. I smoked three cigarettes. I picked all the petals off one of the roses. I noticed that the headlights were on and I worried that the battery would run down. I fiddled around trying to turn them off but I couldn't find the right lever. Terrified by the thought of spending a freezing night in the car, I beckoned the remaining gaishnik (who was pacing up and down with his baton and occasionally giving me flirtatious looks) over to help. Without speaking I pointed at the headlights and pointed at the controls. Helpfully, and bringing with him a gust of freezing air and sour breath, he leant in and switched the lights off.

Now I thought I had been reasonably (a) cunning and (b) obedient in not speaking to the bloke. Obviously, however, by not speaking I had revealed beyond doubt that my Russian wasn't up to much.

'Innostranka?' he asked, squatting in the ice by the side of the car now and leaning his elbows on my open window. 'Foreign?'

I suppose I wanted to talk to someone. I suppose I was scared and getting lonely. I think I was worried about Dimitri in there for so long. Usually they took the bribe in seconds and sent us on our way (apart from that time they chased us down a motorway and fired a shot because we were late for a dinner and Dimitri hadn't wanted to stop). Perhaps I arrogantly imagined that my foreignness would free us.

I smiled and said, 'Yes. English.'

'English, eh?' he said. And then he arrested me for being out of Moscow without an out-of-Moscow visa.

It was four hours later that Dimitri had managed to bring the bribe into proportion with my crime. They impounded the car and sent us walking back to the city. Dimitri wasn't speaking to me. We trudged through the snow, me stumbling and slipping, Dimitri ploughing steadfastly forward, before a car stopped for us and took us all the way back into town. We had left the roses to die in the car which Dimitri came to bail out a week later. The next morning we took the train to Ryazan and this time I didn't speak all the way there.

There was lots of building going on along the road now. Big grey blocks of flats shooting up all over the place, the Turkish builders already on site, yellow hard hats bobbing about in the early morning gloom. I drove past rows and rows of neon-lit kiosks selling alcohol of all kinds, cigarettes, flowers, teddy bears, pairs of tights and various kinds of erotica. Most of the people on the pavements were the street cleaners and last night's casualties, staggering homewards, bleeding, lost, disorientated. The few upstanding citizens already setting off for the metro ignored them.

I had gone out past the hypermarkets and furniture warehouses (all of which had, of course, gone up since last time I did the journey) when Don called me on the mobile. I swerved over into one of the lorry parks where emissions are checked. Mayor Luzhkov decided, quite rightly, that Moscow stank of petrol and decided to ban the use of the old Soviet crap within Moscow's borders. It has made a very big difference. True, the city still stinks of exhaust and there are more than a hundred times more cars on the road than there were under Communism, but the stench of that old stuff really was asphyxiating. Or not, as the case may be. There was no asthma until the Iron Curtain came down. Weird. Anyway, here were all those old khaki lorries that look as if they have driven all the way from Samarkand (and they mostly have) having their emissions checked by skinny drug addicts.

'Hey,' I said. 'Up early.'

'Donchik is usually up at about five thirty and I like to let Irochka get her sleep,' he explained. I kept feeling I had missed something in all my years of knowing Don. You know, like what a lovely bloke he is. What an angel. All I ever saw was a big fat drunk with a foul mouth and, yes, a heart of gold, but not one that would ever translate into genuine acts of kindness to those closest to him. Was I blind or had he really changed that much? I knew what the answer was, though. I was blind. He had found someone who believed in him and that was all he ever needed. Even thinking this made my eyes water slightly. Maybe it was the petrol fumes.

'Give her my love when she wakes up,' I said. 'What is it? I'm taking your advice. On the way out to Ryazan to see Dimitri's mum. Still alive, apparently.'

'Oh, great,' Don said and I could hear the baby gurgle. 'Listen,' he went on. 'I have weird news. I got Ira to run the names of your murder victims past a mate at the FSB and he pulled the report up and read it over to her. Mostly just routine stuff, description of the crime scene. Injuries and stuff. He's faxing it to me so you can have it when you get back. One interesting thing was that the guy died from a blow to the head with a blunt object, not the axe wounds. It wasn't the butt of the axe—fuck knows how they know that—and the murder weapon wasn't recovered.'

This reminded me of a documentary I'd seen called 'Death on the Staircase'. It covered the case of this bloke who claimed to have gone out to check the pool lights and come back in to find his wife in a bloodbath at the bottom of the stairs. All the prosecution had to do to get their conviction was to show the crime scene photos. The woman didn't have injuries to her brain or the kind of fractures that go with being beaten to death and there was basically no motive. But normally when you get pissed and fall downstairs you hurt your foot slightly. You don't die in a sea of your own blood. Anyway, the point is that head wounds are apparently very complicated.

'Don. I'll see it when I get back, OK? I can't concentrate now,' I told him, lighting a cigarette. I was getting weird looks from the lorry park people. Some of the drivers seemed to be considering an approach though surely the women who service these men didn't pull up in their own cars. As far as I knew they were mostly children, orphaned girls and boys who had run away from their institutions.

'No, no. Sorry. Listen. That's not the thing. I don't know what this means or whether it means anything, but it doesn't fit with your description of what went on,' he said. My phone battery was dying and it peeped at me to communicate this.

'Don. What?'

'Well, Yelyena and Leonid were brother and sister. Not lovers or husband and wife or anything. Brother and sister. Yelyena had a daughter whose date of birth was about a year before they were killed.'

As he said this my battery breathed its last and I put the phone down on the passenger seat and screeched off towards Ryazan.

I didn't know what to do with this new information. It had never occurred to me for a moment, even on the few occasions I'd seen them before they died, that they were anything other than lovers. But I realised now that I'd never had any reason to make that assumption. Something about it, though, and I'm no forensic psychologist, did seem to make it less likely that Leonid had lost it and killed Yelyena and himself. Maybe, to any kind of criminal investigator, it wasn't less likely at all. Maybe some enormous percentage of crimes are based in sibling rivalry. Maybe Leonid was mentally ill and Yelyena had tried to restrain him. But it didn't ring true. I was going to have to face the possibility now of a third party. Dimitri or someone else.

And the daughter. I wondered where she was and how easy she would be to find. Her existence though was less of a surprise than Leonid and Yelyena's relationship (incestuous maybe?). It is a very Russian thing for women to leave their children with Granny up to a certain age. I have met hundreds of people who seem to be living a single life with boyfriends and a career and you suddenly find out that they had a child at nineteen with their first husband and it lives in fuck knows where with the grandparents. Even so, Yelyena and Leonid's life was taking shape now in my mind and I found it disconcerting. So disconcerting, indeed, that just as I had arrived at the welcome to Ryazan signs I had to pull over at the side of the road and throw up. Perhaps it was the liquid breakfast. I tried to think of the last time I'd eaten and realised it was lunch at the prison in Oryol. I'd hardly wolfed that crap down either.

Feeling really ropy, I leant against the car and rested my arms on the roof, my head slumping down on to them. I could smell meat and when I looked up I saw one of those roadside barbecue things where some thug cooks bits of pig on skewers and gives them to you in newspaper with ketchup and a piece of bread. I quite like it actually, though under Communism the source of the meat was very dubious indeed and I'm sure I ate some cats and rats and stuff. I bought a kebab off this guy in a shell suit and found that I was starving. I put it on the passenger seat and dipped the lumps of meat in the ketchup, dribbling the sauce down my T-shirt, until I had stuffed the lot into myself. Wiping my mouth on the back of my hand, I saw that I had arrived at the Sakhnov estate.

Not like Tolstoy's rolling estate at Yasnaya Polyana. This was an estate as in a hell-hole maze of grey skyscrapers each indistinguishable from the next, some left half finished in the 1970s, all surrounded by rivers of mud. I went for the policy of not thinking about which one Galina lived in and trusting the back of my mind to know. If you start thinking about where you're going in these places you immediately get lost. It's like trying to describe to someone how to drive. Suddenly I have no idea which is the brake and which the accelerator. You just have to trust yourself to know. I hope pilots and surgeons do not employ this method. Anyway, in this case it worked.

I parked in the sludge and looked up. It had made me so sad the first time I'd come. I was a fuck of a lot tougher now.

We had gone up in the lift and Dimitri had been so excited to introduce me to his mum. There was no real word for girl-friend then and one was always described as 'nyevyesta', fian-cée, like they do still in Italy, even when the likelihood of a wedding is on the slim side. Galina Alekseyevna had hugged me when I walked in the door out of the gloom and stench of the communal corridor by the lift. She was much younger than I'd expected. She'd had Dimitri when she was a teen-ager. I see now that she had probably dressed up and had her hair done for our visit. She had lipstick on and dyed blonde hair, silver high heels and a big fluffy jumper dress with a dog or cat or something on it. There was something about the bravery of dressing up like this in such an utter shit-hole, a provincial Soviet town (once beautiful and anciently impor-tant but horrifically industrialised by Stalin), a place in the unimaginable vastness of Russia where nothing would ever happen, where the grinding drudgery of life had continued unabated for hundreds of years, something about all that that broke my heart.

Dimitri had walked forwards into the hallway of his childhood home, the brown and gold swirly carpet surely an original feature. He sat on a low stool and took his trainers off, placing them neatly with the other outdoor shoes and putting his slippers on. There were photos of the boys at various ages on the walls in plastic mock gilt frames and a smell of some-thing frying in Soviet oil making the air thick and sweet.

Today, though, so many years later, Galina Alekseyevna was not dressed up. Nor did she look surprisingly young. She looked like a Russian woman from the provinces who has lived through the end of Communism and to whom life has never been kind.

Chapter 8

WHEN SHE OPENED the door her face registered pretty much nothing. She nodded and said, 'Vika said you'd phoned from a Moscow number.'

In all official buildings in Russia, like the procuratura, there are big square patches in the paintwork where portraits of Lenin used to hang. In Galina Alekseyevna's flat the patches showed where the photos of her elder son had been. I sat on the low stool and pulled my boots off. Galina pushed a pair of grey felt slippers towards me. They might easily have been the ones Dimitri had worn all those years ago.

Now she shuffled off towards the kitchen where a tin kettle was boiling on the hob. Nothing in here had changed but it all looked older and sadder and emptier. Galina picked a packet of cigarettes up off the Formica table and lit one, inhaling deeply and shaking her match out as she did so. Her face was ravaged by cigarettes and misery and I actually reached up and touched my own face, knowing that the same fate was in store for it. Does it matter? Life is so short in any case. What if we followed the advice of glossy magazines and

drank lots of water, ran miles every day, injected our faces
with anti-wrinkle freezing agents? Would it make any difference? Surely these concerns are the result of not having any
real concerns. The people of Angola don't spend much time
worrying about how many glasses of water it would take to
really make their skin glow.

I sat down at the table and rested my face in my hands.
'I'm sorry about what happened,' I said. 'You must have been
very disappointed in me.'

She had been so excited when we got married. She wore
a lilac hat that she bought in Leningrad. She had walked up
and down the corridors of the Ryazan House of Weddings as
though she was parading around Versailles. She thought it
would mean escape and who could blame her. Dimitri would
move to London and she would follow. She would walk in
Regent's Park, see the Beefeaters at the Tower of London and
shop at Harrods. But it didn't happen, because I ran away.

'We can't control our destinies,' she said, turning to
switch the stove off, wiping one hand on her filthy flowery
apron. She moved as though she were in pain.

'How is your mother?' she asked me.

I looked out of the window at the other tower blocks, the
tiny people moving around in the mud below and the grey
sky that looked as though it must stretch all the way to the
Urals without letting the sun through and I burst into tears.
Well, not actually burst. But my eyes stung with tears and I
felt an empty pit of sorrow in my stomach.

'She...she died. Actually she died,' I said, shaking my
head with the senselessness of it all. It was only when I had
dried my eyes and blown my nose on the tissue Galina passed
me that I realised she probably meant Evie. Evie, who had not
made it to the wedding, had come over once when Dimitri
and I lived in the communalka in Moscow and Galina had

come up on the train to meet her. We took sandwiches to Gorky Park and Galina couldn't stop saying how beautiful Evie was. Well, she was. Still is. A beautiful stepmother like in a fairy tale. It occurred to me now that we never told Dimitri's mum that Evie wasn't really my mum. It didn't seem worth the complication somehow.

Galina sat down and put two cups of tea on the table. She stirred sugar into both of them and sighed deeply.

'You look older,' she told me. 'How are you? Did you remarry? Children?'

I smiled weakly. It was like being in one of those films about single women who are always being hassled about whether or not they've got a boyfriend. Except not like that, because in those films the woman is young and attractive, not shattered and worn like me. And those films, of course, notoriously have happy endings.

'No, Galina Alekseyevna. I never divorced Dimitri. I've never... No. No children. I...er...I had a...I have a career. A job.'

Even as I said it I realised how meaningless this was going to sound. I mean, maybe if I'd been a doctor or a human rights activist or something then it might have been worth it. No family but look at the families I've helped. That kind of thing. But here I was, raddled and war-weary with nobody to love and nobody to love me. A bit of a boring old cliché but none the less true for that. And I didn't need Galina Alekseyevna to make me realise that these are the only things that matter in life. Nobody lies there on their morphine drip breathing their last and feeling really pleased that they wrote that feature on America's obesity problem. I felt empty and weary.

'Oh yes?' Galina asked without interest.

'Yes. I'm a journalist. Mostly a war correspondent. I covered Iraq...' I couldn't be bothered to continue and Galina wasn't listening. 'Do you...do you ever hear from Dimitri?' I asked. Well, this was what I was here for.

Galina sighed again and lit another cigarette although her last one was still burning out in the ashtray. I sipped my tea and it made me feel sick again. Perhaps I was going down with something. Nauseated with life. That kind of ailment. Very common in these parts.

'Faith. Faith. Faith,' she began and then paused, glancing out of the window and closing her eyes briefly. Though run down and shattered, she had bothered to smear a bit of creamy blue eyeshadow over her eyelids. 'After you left he wasn't well. He was thin and anxious, always up in Vorkuta doing his deals, but he never seemed to have time for his family any more. He stopped bringing things—Tampax, coffee, washing powder. I thought he was dying of grief. And then... Then he didn't come home for months. His brother hadn't seen him either. Igor is a good boy. Married now, you know. Two children. Sweet girl, his wife. Loyal. Reliable.'

Yup. OK, OK. I get it.

'And then... Well, then a woman came from Moscow in a uniform. It was evening. I was putting Tina to bed. I went to the door and she looked at me with...with pity, Faith. She told me that Dimitri had confessed to a murder that happened in your building just before...well, before you left him. He had confessed and the sentencing would be in private but she said she should warn me...that's what she said: "I want to warn you". She said she should warn me that though it was unlikely he would receive the death penalty since he was having a psychiatric assessment, it would be no less than twenty years.'

I was wondering whether or not I was going to throw my kebab up. It is always at these moments, these huge emotional moments, that I choose to think about something completely prosaic. The message being, I suppose, that life goes on. The fact that you are in the midst of horror or upheaval doesn't mean that your digestive system is not going to contact you. Perhaps quite the opposite.

Oh, I wanted to hate her. I wanted to dismiss her. I wanted to shout that relationships are complicated. That I didn't just run off and break his heart. That we had problems and culture gaps are so unbridgeable and... I don't know. But really I just felt sorry. I wanted to hug her and tell her I would make it all better again. I wouldn't, though. Indeed, I was almost certainly going to make it a fuck of a lot worse. Well, no, he's not in prison. But he is dead though. I hear. And it had been so long since I'd been here. If someone had asked me exactly what it was like in Dimitri's mum's flat I might have had trouble remembering. Now it was as though I had never been away. There is a Russian song that goes: 'Eto bylo davno. Eto bylo nye davno.' 'It was a long time ago. It was not long ago at all.' That's what it was like here. Things can feel so distant, as though they happened in another life to other people, and yet you can remember where the forks go and what they feel like and how the bedroom will smell.

'Have you...er...have you been to see him at all?' I asked, assuming that I already knew the answer. I mean, the fact that they've got this dwarfy American bloke in there instead of Dimitri is a bit of a giveaway.

'What's the point?' she said. 'I don't want to know him. He confessed. He killed Yelyena, Lena, with an axe. And the boy. I have spent ten years wondering if it is my fault. Did I do something to him? Was he on drugs? Sounds so silly now but we were naïve in those days. We didn't know about drugs. We thought only in America. Only the capitalists. It was an innocent time before the end. The children weren't as they are now. Things weren't like this.'

That is actually true. Communism was a religion to the Soviet people. If you obeyed its rules and believed, there was a lot of comfort to be had from it. The crime rates really were very low. It was an incredibly safe place where young people didn't take drugs or watch violent or pornographic films. They weren't allowed to, it's true. But those are freedoms that a lot of people are happy to do without. It is a well-known fact here that around the age of thirteen or fourteen children started to question the Communist ideal. Many lost their faith at this time and many had their faith strengthened. At any rate, when the thing came tumbling down on top of them, so many Russians felt that their whole belief system had been ripped away from them and they were alone in a meaningless and chaotic world.

There was something about the fact that she named the victim that made me prick up my ears. I was thinking about this and the fact that Dimitri had clearly not been here, not been in contact with his mother for as long as Adrian had been in Oryol, when I heard a key in the door.

'Hello, love,' Galina said, looking suddenly a bit happier, brighter. Her body sprang into a kind of maternal action and her eyes opened a fraction wider. She stood up to do things, I imagined, like provide slippers, take a coat and administer a kiss.

'Ciao,' said a female voice.

Just as Galina was saying 'I have a guest', the Italian speaker burst into the kitchen.

'Who the fuck are you?' she asked, grinning. She had hair that was dyed bright lurid red. It was shortish and twisted and matted into little spikes that were sprayed solid and looked like some sort of volcanic eruption on her head. Her left eyebrow was pierced with a sharp spike and she had a gold ring in her nose. She wore thick mascara and shiny lipstick to match her hair. She was a fat girl in huge baggy jeans that fell low enough around her blanc-mangey hips to show a red thong at the back. Her black jumper was slashed as though with a knife but it was presumably retailed in that state. She opened the fridge and took a can of beer out.

'Want one?' she asked. I loved her newness—how she couldn't have existed a few years ago, before all the change. She was a product of post-Soviet Russia and a good one.

'That would be great actually.' I nodded, smiling. 'I'm Faith. I was married to Galina's son, Dimitri. Well, I still am married to him but I haven't seen him for years.'

She raised her eyebrows and froze for a fraction of a second. It looked like an expression learnt from a soap opera, so popular here now, so unthinkable before. ('Ranshe', meaning before, is a word you hear a lot. People drone on endlessly about how much better things were 'ranshe' even when actually they weren't. There is a joke that mocks the old ladies who look back fondly at the Stalin years. Q: What was there before—a chicken or an egg? A: Before there was everything. Chickens, eggs, salami!)

'I'm Tina. Valentina.' Tina beamed and sat down. Galina came back into the kitchen without her apron on and with a lash of colour across her lips. 'So, you ditched Dimitri, poor Dima, huh?' Tina smiled, clearly not giving the slightest toss. 'Do you think that's why he went and hacked those people up? Went insane with grief and found his catharsis in a murderous rage?' She laughed and lit one of my cigarettes. 'Hmm. Benson and Hedges?' she read with a good English accent. 'Cool.'

'I don't believe for a second that he did it,' I said. 'I was there. He was as shocked as I was. I don't know what's going on, though. Anyway, you say they came to tell you he confessed. Well, he didn't. I went to Oryol psychiatric prison yesterday to see him and it isn't him. It's someone else using his name and I guess all his documents. Dimitri isn't and never was in prison for that crime.'

Tina smiled as though this was the funniest and most exciting thing she had ever heard. 'Holy fuck,' she said. 'Hear that, Galya? Not him. So where is he then?' She said the last bit in a mysterious ghostly voice. She was not taking any of this seriously.

Galina Alekseyevna, however, was staring at me open-mouthed, all the colour drained from her face. When I looked back at her she put her hand up to her face and began to sob. Tina got up and walked round the table to put her arms round Galina. She gave her a big lipsticky kiss on the cheek and rocked her slightly, comforting the thin old woman with her luscious enormity.

When Galina had put her hand up to indicate that she was sufficiently recovered to carry on with this nightmare meeting, Tina sat back down, as happy and bouncy as she'd been when she came in a couple of minutes ago.

'Anyway, why the fuck do you care? Buggered off back to London then, bugger off there now, that's my advice. Only joking.' She giggled. She was now beginning to seem slightly mad.

'I care because the guy they think is Dimitri retracted his confession the other day and said I'd done it. He's a friend—was a friend—of mine. I got hauled into the procuratura in the middle of the night and hassled shitless. They know they can't get me on anything, but for some unfathomable reason they are taking the retracted confession seriously even though they have no idea it isn't Dimitri they've got in there.'

'How did you get into Oryol? I thought visitors weren't allowed?' Tina said. Perhaps not mad then. She was on the ball, at any rate.

'I'm a journalist. I'm the bureau chief of the London *Chronicle*. Just got here the other day.'

'Whoa,' said Tina. 'Cool.' Then she started rolling a joint. Galina pretended not to notice. She simply didn't look at what Tina was doing.

When she lit it she closed her eyes in pleasure and inhaled. 'Want some?' she asked me. 'It's good Afghan.'

I had one drag and then ran for the loo. When you need to remember where something is you remember it. That's my experience. Nothing had changed. Pink plastic was the theme of this and a billion other Soviet bathrooms from Europe to Asia.

I vomited every last drop of moisture in my stomach. I could hear Tina laughing in the kitchen. I splashed my face with water and tried to wipe some of the ketchup out of my T-shirt with a flannel.

When I got back to the kitchen Galina had spread the table with pictures of her elder son. Some were the ones she'd taken off the walls, others she'd pulled out of albums. She'd kept them in a Duty Free carrier bag from Heathrow that, I could see, was something I'd once brought with me in another life. Here was Dimitri in the army, muscular and smiling in a picture that was almost sepia and could have been taken in the 1920s, though in fact he'd gone into the army in the mid-1980s, after I'd met him. He'd been arrested for dealing in hard currency and basically agreed to stop trying to evade conscription in return for not getting a prison sentence. Something like that.

He had tried twice to avoid conscription. On one occasion he slashed his wrists here in Ryazan while his mum was away. It had to look convincing and he'd nearly died. It was an insanity plea and it worked. The next time he'd got a friend to break his leg with a crowbar. Success again. But only temporary. They always hounded them down in the end if they didn't have the money for the bribes. Of course, of all the boys who got sent to the war in Afghanistan, none of them was related to any member of the Soviet nomenclatura.

There were school photos and university photos, nearly all of them in black and white. Dimitri clutching his books and folders, smiling into the camera with a gang of friends all of whom looked as though they had since perished in some awful tragedy, though they probably hadn't. It's just that atmosphere that old photos have. There he was on holiday at the Black Sea in what looked to be knitted swimming trunks. And there was me. Sitting on the lawn at Evie's house in a blue dress I'd bought at Camden market. It had white daisies on it and was a fifties thing tightly belted at the waist. I had my wild hair tied back in a ponytail and I remember posing for it. I asked a friend to take the photo so that I could send it to Dimitri and I was smiling at him with all my heart. I picked the photograph up and almost wept for that girl who looked so hopeful. By that point I was pretty much braced for the wedding pictures.

It had been so hard to get permission. The papers seemed to take a hundred years and it feels as though I spent a decade queuing up at the Soviet embassy in Kensington, filling in forms about who I wanted to marry and why and where we would live and did I want to bring him out of the Soviet Union. When I told them I was going to go and live there it was treated almost as a defection and someone from *Izvestia* came to Evie's to take my picture but I don't think the piece ever ran. And I can't even remember now if I really wanted to get married or not. I can't remember if I loved him. I know I loved the idea of him and I wanted to do something my friends weren't doing. I didn't want to go to university and I didn't want to work in a shop. I wanted to live.

I let my hair loose and the people in the House of Weddings stared at me. I stuck a pink rose in it and wore a long white satin nightie and a string of pearls. This was not the usual attire. The other couples queuing up to do the deed were more conformist. The girls were all in vast net things with hooped skirts that made it hard for them to sit down.

They wore frosted lipstick and white plastic hairbands with white plastic flowers in them. The boys, hungover to a man, wore cheap shiny suits and clip-on bow ties. Not many people had their families with them, but we had Galina Alekseyevna and Dimitri's little brother Igor who was then about fifteen. Afterwards we went and had our photo taken at the tomb of the unknown soldier in Ryazan's war cemetery and then we had supper…here. In this flat. And there were photos to prove it. I made pizzas which seemed exotic then and Evie had sent a case of wine over with me so we drank it but nobody understood why we didn't have vodka instead. In bed that night Dimitri said he would make me happy. He kissed my eyelids and called me princess. Galina had given up her double bed for us and gone upstairs to her friend's for the night.

'Do you have any idea where he might be? Where he might have gone?' I asked the women now.

Galina shook her head and smiled at me through her tears. 'Thank you, Verochka,' she said, using my Russian name, the affectionate form at that. 'You took him away but now you have brought him back.'

I didn't have the heart to break the rest of my news. Especially as it was only a prison rumour, and who could rely on that?

'What about Vorkuta, Gran? Couldn't he have gone there?' Tina wondered, putting her joint out at last. The smell was doing nothing for my stomach issues.

Gran? God, last time I saw Igor he was basically a child himself. Everyone had grown up, even people's children had grown up. And me? Both parents dead now, a couple of awards for voyeurism, an on-off relationship with the man of lots of people's dreams. But not mine. And Igor was such a tiny little bloke. This girl was huge.

'Here's Igor. He's an oboe player.' That's what Dimitri had said. But look what he had produced.

Galina shook her head. 'No. We'd have heard,' she said. She turned to me. 'My brother lives up there. He worked for Dimitri in the vodka business before…before you.'

We all sat there, three women at a table of photographs, all with our own private thoughts. I would like to have cried. It's so unfashionable to admit that things matter. You break up with someone and the television tells you that you have to move on, that he wasn't worth it, that you deserve better. Somebody dies and it tells you to remember the best of them, to take the lessons they taught you out into life with you. But really? Well, really, the wounds we get from these things stay with us forever and change us. Not always for the better. Sometimes loss really does leave a hole that will never be mended. Sometimes the pull of the past is stronger than the lure of the future.

'Hey! Is that your Volvo out there? Can I have a lift back to Moscow?' Tina asked, her perkiness in no way affected by the past half-hour's conversation.

'Um, sure,' I told her.

'Great,' she said. 'Let's go.'

Chapter 9

I DROPPED TINA off outside the Cherry Casino.

The conversation all the way back to Moscow had gone like this: Tina, drawing on her cigarette and sighing or shaking her head, 'It's been so hard on Gran, writing Dimitri out of her life, you know. Fucking hard. Couldn't live with the shame, I reckon.'

I thought about the Kray brothers' mum and how she had maintained that they were lovely boys long after it was public knowledge that they nailed people to the floor and stuff. It almost seemed disloyal of Galina to cast him off so quickly, but perhaps she just couldn't face all those years of missing him and of wishing things were different. Presumably she's had all that anyway, though.

Tina smoked so many cigarettes that I was very nearly tempted to mention it. She said she had a boyfriend in Moscow but her granny disapproved of him because he's black.

'He's a guitarist,' she told me. 'In a blues band. His dad came over from Cameroon to do a degree at MGU. Went straight back there again afterwards too.'

I nodded. Funny the countries that had these understandings with the Soviets. You used to get a lot of Iraqis here too, at the universities and taking honorary posts in various government departments.

'Gran pretends she doesn't like Job because he's a guitarist. Really it's because he's black. I took him to Ryazan once and he stayed at the flat. They bumped into each other on the way to the loo in the night and Gran was totally terrified.'

I laughed.

The journey had gone quickly with Tina in the car. I liked her and felt sort of proud of Russia for letting her come into existence. There aren't actually many places in the world where women can be whoever they want to be, and you wouldn't immediately think of a former eastern bloc country as being one of them. She was cool.

She hopped out of the Volvo on to the pavement as though she owned the whole city. She hauled her red rubber rucksack on to her back and ruffled her hair. I waved and she grinned at me. 'If I hear anything about Dad I'll let you know!' she shouted as I pulled off.

I slammed the brakes on and tried to back up to where I'd been. Tina was walking away into the early evening crowd on Noviy Arbat. The shops were closing and the bars were opening. Everyone was on the move.

'Tina! Tina! Come back here!' I screamed at her out of the car window but she didn't turn round. I was about to get out and chase her when a Range Rover slammed into the back of me. There was a loud crunch followed by the sound of shattered glass falling on to tarmac.

'Fuck!' I muttered to myself and I banged my fist on the steering wheel.

Arkady was none too pleased to be called out to deal with this. It meant standing around for all eternity filling out forms and arguing with the police who refused to move either vehicle until the procedure was complete. I walked back over the bridge to the compound, staring up at the Ukraine Hotel, already a relic of another era. When I first saw those buildings (there are seven of these Stalinesque Gothic wedding cake buildings in Moscow) they sent a shiver down my spine. I think it was the one at Vosstanie. So black and evil-looking, so imposing and vast. Designed to make a person feel like a minuscule little piece of nothing in the face of this huge and malign power. The fact that people actually lived in them meant nothing to me. The fact that one of them is the university, a place presumably humming with youth and vibrancy, was irrelevant to the sinister doom of these spiky dark buildings.

The Ukraine Hotel is the same inside as it is out. It is no less terrifying trying to find your way down the long narrow corridors, carpeted by a thin strip of worn maroon fabric down the middle of the parquet, than it is standing outside pondering your insignificance. They are like the corridors in *The Shining* but much more frightening. The place can hold so many guests that it is never more than a quarter full (it has twenty-eight floors all with hundreds of rooms) so that, huddling in your big sparsely furnished room as I have done twice now, you feel that you are alone in the place with only the demons for company.

There is a cinema and theatre down by the river near the Kremlin called the Estrada. In this building Stalin housed his henchmen and it was here that his purges hit hardest—the inner circle. They say that many families jumped together out of the windows of the Estrada when they heard the midnight knock on the door.

I don't know how much of that happened in the wedding cake buildings but it is definitely what they seem made for.

Dimitri and I used to come to the Ukraine Hotel to steal tyres sometimes. There were shortages of everything including windscreen wipers, rear-view mirrors, tyres and petrol caps. There was nowhere you could buy them so you had to steal them. Dimitri said that the Mercedes tyres were the best. Often Mercedes, brought in by German diplomats, were parked outside the Ukraine. Perhaps there were pretty prostitutes who worked there. Anyway, Dimitri would bring his own jack, put our shabby old tyre on the Mercedes and put the nicely grooved German one on our Lada Samara. This can't, I now think, have been a good idea. Just in terms of our own safety.

Dimitri and I also used to come and drink at the Ukraine Hotel sometimes too. It was such a slime pit that they didn't bother trying to keep Russians out and we would sit at the bar slurping sweet champagne and vodka with fizzy blackcurrant stuff which I paid for in hard currency. Sometimes we ran into Scott Weisman and Dimitri would challenge him to drink vodka or ask him about the American army in an effort to make him feel like a wuss. It didn't take much, frankly. Scott brought Russian girls he met on the metro. (This was not seedy in those days. In fact lots of couples claimed to have met on the metro, the buses or the trams. To approach a pretty girl on public transport was entirely normal and highly acceptable behaviour. They would say something that is only two words, 'Mozhno poznakomitsya?', but it means, 'Can we get to know each other?') He needed to impress them without daunting them. I think that was the policy. Frankly, just a flash of his passport would have more than done the trick.

I looked at the Ukraine now with the sun setting behind it and it just looked shabby and bleak. Something that had once been powerful but had now been revealed as too big and lumbering to be viable. A dinosaur. Just a bit further down the river was the new silver shopping mall bridge, rubbing the Ukraine's nose in it as if it needed it.

❀ ❀ ❀

I found Eden at his laptop, ruffling his hair with his hands, shoulders hunched, ashtray full, two cups of cold coffee by his side.

'Hey,' he said, looking up sleepily and smiling. 'Where've you been?'

'I've been to London to see the queen,' I murmured. 'No. I went to Ryazan to see Dimitri's mum. She totally believed he'd confessed and was guilty. Tried to disown him. Took all the pictures of him off the walls and stuff. Now she's kind of elated that he's free and in hiding or whatever. I didn't dare tell her Adrian said he was dead. She didn't seem that interested in the detail or anything, but guess what?' I said, throwing myself on to the sofa and leaning up on one elbow.

'What?' Eden asked, lighting a cigarette and tossing the packet over to me.

'He's got a teenage daughter.'

'Who has?'

'Dimitri has.'

'God. It's like EastEnders, your life. And you never knew this?' Eden wondered, pushing his sleeves up and facing me, leaning back in the swivelly chair. Before I could answer he was off again. 'Seriously. Or some Shakespearean comedy where they don't recognise their own children because one of them's got a hat on. Mum! Dad! Son!' He was losing control.

'Shut up, will you. I never knew this. In fact, I didn't know it until about half an hour ago. Crashed the sodding car in shock. Basically there was this girl at Dimitri's mum's house, all pierced and trendy and calling Galina Alekseyevna "Granny". I just assumed she was the brother's daughter, Igor's daughter, though now I think about it of course she couldn't be. This girl must have been about sixteen or so which means she was born before Dimitri and I got married. Igor was only about fifteen himself when we got married. Anyway, somehow I'm not registering any of this until she leaps out of the car ...'

Eden interrupted me. 'What was she doing in the car?'

'I gave her a lift to Moscow. She's got some boyfriend here that Granny doesn't approve of. Anyway, she jumps out of the car and promises to let me know if she hears anything about where her dad is. She was totally cool about it. Almost laughing at me, actually. I mean, presumably she's thought he was in prison her whole life and now she finds out he's not and just isn't that interested. Hates him for it or something. Fuck knows. It's weird. Maybe she's in denial.'

'Or maybe she knows exactly where he is and always has done?' Eden suggested.

At this point Natasha walked into the room with a pot of tea on a tray.

'Oh, lovely. Thanks, Natasha,' I said, thinking about anything but her and the tea. An absent thanks, necessary and unnecessary. Now I know it seems weird but I even started to wonder whether or not I *had* known about Dimitri's daughter before. Had he maybe told me and it had been irrelevant to me so I'd forgotten or somehow put it to the back of my mind? No, of course not. Of course I would know something like this if he'd told me. So had he not told me because he thought I might not want to get involved with him if he did? Or was it some other kind of secret? And why didn't she seem to care very much? I was still in a daze of thought when Natasha dropped the tray on the floor in sudden reaction to a loud boom that shook the whole city and actually made me hold on to the edge of the sofa.

'Holy fuck,' I said. Eden leapt up and ran to the window in a motion at once fast and slow. The actions were those of speed, of rushing, of urgency, and yet the pace was agonisingly slow, almost like a dance about someone in a hurry, but to very ponderous music. Natasha whimpered and started picking the smashed crockery up off the floor, glancing around nervously and shaking as she cleared, perhaps hoping to bring the event into the realm of the mundane with her concentration on the domestic chore.

'Jesus, look!' Eden shouted, pointing out towards the Kremlin. There was a plume of black rising into the sky.

I was already on the phone asking Arkady to bring the car round. He sighed, annoyed, I suppose, since he'd only just got back from my crash and needed to take it to the garage and get the lights fixed. I told him he could drop us off on the way, and put the phone down. If we were going to get close to this we certainly wouldn't be able to park and I didn't want to be dealing with that at the same time as looking at whatever this was going to turn out to be.

I stood up and picked my jacket up off the floor. The phone rang. It was Tamsin.

'Reuters are reporting a huge explosion in the shopping arcade on Red Square,' she said.

'Yeah. We heard it. I'll file something in an hour or two. OK?'

'Soon as poss, Zanetti, please. Nice spoiler on the journalist.'

'Thanks,' I said. 'Talk to you later.' And Eden and I ran down the stairs to the car, not bothering to wait for the lift. 'Why are you coming?' I asked him.

'I love all this stuff,' he said, and I laughed. He was never going to survive as a serious writer.

'Fucking swarthy fucking bastards,' Arkady said, as we pulled up on a side street near GUM. Russians are not world-wide renowned for their racial tolerance. You often find yourself talking to completely normal-seeming intelligent, funny and urbane people when they suddenly say something like: 'Of course, she's very full of herself. Jewish, you know.' It is a type of anti-Semitism that a lot of people seem to find acceptable. So, rather than just a plain 'I really hate Jews', someone uses the word 'Jew' (in the case of anti-Semites you will notice that they mention it unusually often) in a wholly negative description of someone else, using it as part of the reason why, as should be clear to the listener, this person is awful. Like: 'We had a row. You know, he was one of those North London Jewish boys.' Or: 'Well, having facelifts is such a Jewish princess thing to do.' Almost subtle. Yet as vile, of course, as a more obvious slur.

For swarthy Arkady used the word 'smoogliy'. A brilliant word and so much more evocative than swarthy.

'Hello?' I said to him.

'Fucking Chechen scum,' he explained.

'Ah. Yes,' I said and Eden and I leapt out. 'Arkady thinks it's Chechens,' I shouted over to Eden.

'Not unlikely, is it?' he asked as we ran towards the shop.

'Not really,' I yelled, weaving my way through the screaming crowds of people who were running away.

It looked as though the whole place was on fire and sirens wailed from all around, police cars, ambulances and fire engines screeching up on to the pavements and spewing out their shouting teams of uniformed experts. There were people bloodied and covered in plaster dust, but not many of them. It was after hours and there can only have been cleaners in there at this time. I had lost Eden now and by the time I got to the Red Square entrance to the shop by the new church the police were slapping taped cordons up and shouting at people not to cross them.

'Was it a bomb?' I asked a boy with acne and a police uniform.

'Yes,' he snapped, and that was about all he'd be sharing with me this evening. I started walking round the outside of the building. I love this place. It is staggeringly beautiful, even now that it's full of Clinique and Galeries Lafayette and Armani. It runs along one whole side of Red Square, with St Basil's at one end, the reconstructed red brick gates and the history museum at the other and Lenin's tomb and the Kremlin wall opposite. St Basil's is the one you see in every television news stand-up ever done from Moscow. It has five onion domes decorated like a gingerbread house and it was built under Ivan the Terrible who, rumour has it, gouged the architect's eyes out when he had finished so that he would never build anything so beautiful again. Outside the church is the big wooden execution block where people were beheaded. Then there is the purple marble mausoleum where Lenin lies, still guarded by stony-faced boys bearing bayonets. The Kremlin wall behind the tomb is bright red and above it you can see the white churches with their gold domes, now with their gold crosses restored to them, though the Kremlin tower still has a beautiful red neon star on the top of it. I'm glad they didn't take that down.

The GUM department store is a vast pre-revolutionary thing, built in that St Petersburgy mock Venetian style with long colonnaded aisles in pastel colours, ornate ironwork bridges and a pretty fountain. Each aisle houses about two hundred shops and there is a pink aisle, a blue aisle and a green aisle. Under the tsars people came here to buy their most lavish clothes, silverware and gilded crockery. When I first came in here, with Dimitri on that school trip to Russia, the staggering opulence of the building was overpowered partly by the militant heating that just blew you away with its searing force, and by the pathos of the shabby little shops tucked away in pre-revolutionary grandeur and selling three cotton pillowcases for three kopeks or tins of sardines, plastic hair combs and matrioshka dolls for tourists, kept behind glass on account of their relative preciousness. Now it's flashy again, or it was before the explosion, but its romance is gone. You can go and buy Armani jeans anywhere in the world and the thing that was so special about GUM has, like so much in Russia, been consigned to the past.

Most of the windows on the ground floor had been blown out, so the explosion must have been downstairs. I was about to go back to the office and wait for the presidential address before I filed when something occurred to me. The guards at Lenin's tomb. They had been standing there the whole time, after all.

I ran across the cobbles towards the pair of soldiers and shouted, 'I'll give you a hundred dollars if you tell me what you saw!' I stood still and waited but neither of them flinched.

I shrugged my shoulders and lit a cigarette but just as I did the Kremlin clock struck ten and the parade of goose-stepping replacements in their gleaming jackboots came towards us swinging their arms with each high kick. The changing of the guards. This is something I first saw one winter's midnight in 1987 and I was awed by the power of the Soviet Union and all that it entailed. Well, it was the desired effect, let's face it, and they were good at it.

As the boots clicked and the hardware clanked I could swear I heard someone hiss, 'Unknown soldier, ten minutes.' I smiled and checked my jacket pocket for the cash. I looked over at GUM and saw that fire engines had now surrounded it and the hoses were out. Crews of paramedics dashed into the building and the police were going completely crazy, cordoning off more and more of the surrounding area and moving their cars about the place to secure the area. A police car drove right down the middle of Red Square. A militsionier leant out of the window to shout at me.

'Madam. Please leave the area. Immediately.' I nodded and shuffled what I hoped was deferentially towards the gardens where the tomb is.

Two cigarettes and a call to the desk later and my boy was there, still in uniform and looking absolutely terrified in spite of the dark and the obvious distraction of a huge blaze over at GUM.

'So?' I asked him, unable to meet his jittery gaze.

'The money,' he said quietly with some kind of accent. Maybe that southern country thing that Gorbachev was always lampooned for.

I handed him two fifty dollar bills and he leant down to stuff them into the tops of his jackboots.

'We're supposed to look at each other for the whole hour but I never can. Two women in the black Muslim clothes went in with a big box. I noticed because it was after closing and not many people were around apart from the street sweepers. Then, and this was the freaky bit, they ran away. Like really running, like you never see women doing, just before the bang. I sort of knew it was coming. Fucking Chechen scum,' he added for good measure.

'Thanks,' I said. 'What's your name?'

'You're fucking joking,' he hissed. Well, it was worth a try. He'd have to be 'an eyewitness' then. I'm not saying it would have been difficult to find out his name from the Kremlin press office, and actually I probably would do that so that I could mention the nearby guards at Lenin's tomb who remained unflinchingly at their posts though their lives were in jeopardy—you know the type of thing—but if he was off the record he was off the record.

I called Arkady to tell him I was coming. He said Eden had already found him and I should meet them over the road outside where the Intourist Hotel used to be. They pulled the Intourist Hotel down. Now I'm not saying it wasn't by far the most hideous thing ever constructed by humankind, but I spent so much of my time there as a married teenager, watching the prostitutes (all of whom Dimitri knew and some of whom he had been out with) in their fishnets and wigs smoking those tiny thin cigarettes with a flower on them and listening to the Arab students arguing in hissing secretive whispers. Gone! Flattened. Well, it did keep getting firebombed. It had too many offices in it for its own good and everyone in business got firebombed at some stage or another.

I noticed that my hair was full of white dust and felt sad for all that pretty stucco that had been obliterated tonight. I walked towards the empty space where the Intourist in all its smoked glass, aluminium plate and concrete glory had been, past where Moskva Hotel had been. It was beautiful. Even though Stalin commissioned it. It was grand and grey and ever so slightly asymmetrical. When the architect took the designs to Stalin, the dictator accidentally approved both of them and, too afraid to disobey or to question the decision, the architect built half and half. I love this story. Mayor Luzhkov was apparently less amused.

I was just waiting for the lights to change so that I could cross the road when someone came up behind me and put his arm hard round my waist, locking my hands to my sides. The other hand, a leather glove on it, covered my face and I felt my throat close up in terror. I was expecting to be bundled into a car and thrown down on to the back seat to be sat on and choked.

'Guess who?' said a voice. Lilting American accent.

I elbowed Scott Weisman hard in the stomach at the same time as breaking free, spinning round and shouting, 'Scott Weisman!'

'Oof,' he said, doubling up. 'Long time no see.' A really long time. In fact, maybe not since I was nineteen and he was a newspaper intern. Not since the days of Dom Literatov and nearly splitting up with my husband in the Savoy.

When he was standing again I threw my arms round his neck and kissed his cheek. I found that my eyes were damp. Annoying, this new propensity of mine. He was broad-shouldered and dressed like an off-duty president. Despite the casual slacks, T-shirt and jumper, his wealth and health were unmissable. He wore heftier black-rimmed glasses now and his thick short back and sides was flecked with grey.

'Shit! So long!' I said, beaming. 'You look just the same.'

He ruffled his black hair and smiled. 'You too,' he said. 'You too.'

We paused, taking each other in.

'Hey,' he said. 'You know that bastard husband you had back then? Fucking robbed my flat at gunpoint after you left. Kicked the shit out of me.'

My face fell and I scrabbled for my cigarettes. I tried to make a joke out of it. 'We are still very happily married, thank you, Scott,' I said, putting one in my mouth and lighting it with my Zippo.

'Uh-uh. Don't think so, sugar pie. He told me you'd done a runner because of some gross thing you were involved in. Some murder you'd gotten into the middle of in a drunken stupor. Obvious bullshit. Said he was going to try and clear your name. This he was telling me whilst actually kicking my head as I lay on the floor in my hallway, tied up by some dickhead henchman. Then when I called the police he'd apparently disappeared. Couple of years later someone from the procuratura called me in San Francisco, can you imagine, to tell me they'd got him.'

I sighed and we started walking together. I pointed to my car and he nodded in understanding.

'He always was very jealous of you, Scott,' I said, smiling at the issues from centuries ago even in the face of all these new horrors.

'Oh, well that's hunky-dory then.' He laughed.

We crossed the bottom of Tverskaya by the Danone shop in silence and soon reached the car.

'I'm beginning to realise that he wasn't what he seemed. A lot of stuff has come up, Scott. I don't suppose he mentioned his daughter while he was trying to beat you to death, did he?'

'Really? What, some provincial teenaged marriage? Shit.'

'That kind of thing. Want to come over for dinner tomorrow?'

'Sure. You're in the old *Chronicle* flat, right?'

'Yes. About eight?'

'Great. Eight sharp. I'll be there with bells on,' he said, and he patted the top of the car as I got in. When we pulled away I saw him get his phone out of his big cashmere coat to phone his desk in New York. But I had the eyewitness scoop.

'Who was that?' Eden asked, flicking through his notebook.

'Scott Weisman. *Washington Post*. He's a friend of thingy at AP. I actually know him from ages ago. He just told me Dimitri robbed him after I left. I must have some kind of social fucking autism that I can't recognise a violent maniac when I'm sleeping with him. I was married to this bloke. He was nice. I'm finding this stuff really hard to believe.'

'Zanetti. You've never been the sharpest tool in the shed. You know. Always a couple of republics short of a union. Sandwich short of a pic—'

I hit him. 'Shut up, Jones. You are annoying me. When are you moving out?'

'Actually, I'm rather settling in. Was that a dinner party you were arranging for tomorrow? Shall I do my cassoulet?'

I sighed. 'That would be great,' I said. 'I fancy cassoulet.'

Tamsin loved my piece about the explosion and they ran it with a sort of side piece about how a burka could disguise anyone, with photos of all the paper's famous columnists dressed up in burkas and rendered (obviously) unrecognisable. I had put the soldier's suspicion that actually the bombers had been men into the piece. I'd also got a terrorism expert to speculate on the record that the bombers might well not be Islamic at all as they would have been far more likely to martyr themselves than to run away. It was beginning, and a senior FSB told me this on the record, to look like some mafia-type commercial crime related to the astronomical GUM ground rent.

I was so tired that somehow, after everything, it seemed natural to fall into Eden's bunk bed with him again.

Chapter 10

IN THE MORNING Natasha woke us up with coffee. Any pretence that I might have made that we were not a couple had now been pretty much given up on. I reached down to take a sip of coffee and slopped some over the parquet so I got up.

'You can sleep in my room if you want,' I told him, crawling under the bunks to try and find my pants. 'Seriously. This is silly.'

Eden laughed and grabbed my hand, pulling me back down to lie with him. 'Faithy,' he said, and kissed my cheek. 'What about Don? Don't you think I could do it? Give it all up for a quiet life?'

'Eden. It's the crack of dawn,' I pointed out.

I stared at the wire mesh of the bunk above me and thought about it, though. I pulled myself out of his attempted embrace and lay still but alone.

'It's not that I don't think you could do it, Jonesy. It's that I couldn't,' I said. 'It terrifies the shit out of me. House, husband, no travel, no calls in the night, no cigarettes!'

Eden had to climb over me to get up out of bed. He was pissed off.

'You say all this bollocks, Faith, but what are you going to do? Carry on like this? For how long? You don't see many sixty-year-old foreign correspondents. You want to end up on the desk sending people out to great places while you sit by yourself in the Groucho Club, pitied by the girls lining up to go to…Bosnia or whatever? Do you?'

It wasn't a long speech but it was enough to make me really hate him. 'Don't come into my flat and talk to me like this. If you don't like me the way I am, sweetheart, then find someone else to hang out with.' Why can't we just wake up, comment on the weather (vile) and drink coffee like normal people? I turned over in bed to face the wall. 'And don't even think about trying to pretend to me that you could effect some sort of butterflyesque metamorphosis like Don. He was probably like that underneath already. You're just a squirming nest of vipers under your expensive shirts. If China ever came up you'd be in Beijing like a shot, leaving me changing nappies in Harlesden.'

Now he bothered to laugh. 'Why do we have to live in Harlesden?'

'Because we do,' I told him. Smiling myself now.

This was true, though. Eden had been dying to go to Beijing for fifteen years but nobody would ever send him. They always thought of him more as a fireman, someone to send out to a conflict. China was in large part an economic story too, so he just didn't cut it in the minds of his editors. This drove him crazy. Nonetheless, I was annoyed with myself for saying it. If I was challenging him it must mean that on some level at least I was taking his offer seriously. Ugh. I should never have let them send me to a shrink. I was fine beforehand. Apart from the lunacy and the breakdown, of course.

'Look. I don't know why you have to go into attack mode every time I try to suggest that we spend more than three nights in a row together,' Eden said, calmer now and putting his trousers on.

'Because I do,' I muttered mostly to myself. 'Because I do.'

'Hmm. Sharp as a tack with the answers this morning, Zanetti,' he huffled.

Natasha made us scrambled eggs on toast and outside the window a few tentative flakes of snow were starting to fall. Six months of winter were about to kick off. We ate in virtual silence and I lit a cigarette after only three mouthfuls. Why are relationships like this? Why is enjoying each other's company not enough? Suddenly you are being picked apart and hassled and told what's wrong with the way you live your life.

I went off to get dressed and to watch the news while I was doing it. Satisfyingly, they'd hauled some small time mafiosi in for the GUM explosion. Not, obviously, that this meant they'd got their men. If anyone knew about miscarriages of justice it was beginning to be me. When I came back Eden was sitting at the living room table making a list.

''Chup to today?' I asked him.

'Making cassoulet. Will I be able to get goose fat at Stockmanns?' he wondered, craning round to face me, ludicrous in his crumpled T-shirt and broken glasses. He was wearing them more and more. Were we getting old?

'Yes,' I told him. 'I should have thought so. No prisons?'

'I don't have to deliver until the end of November.' He beamed, delighted with himself and quite rightly. What a job.

'Right.' I laughed. 'OK. I'm going to the American embassy to see if I can persuade them that Adrian exists.'

First I popped over to the office where Lyuda was on the phone to the FSB press office trying to get them to release the reports on what I was beginning to think of as My Crime. I put my finger on the button to cut her off.

'Got them. A friend of mine did it through a contact. Thanks, though,' I said.

Lyuda, who was wearing an outfit made entirely of crochet today, was briefly crestfallen. But she had news.

'I've been trying to find out about the Varanovs and it seems that they were in fact brother and sister,' she said, riffling through some papers on her desk to find the relevant sheet.

'Yes, I know,' I told her, quite pleased with myself though entirely baselessly so since it was Don and Ira who had done all the research.

'Twins in fact,' Lyuda said.

Whoa. OK. That was new and somehow, though I don't know why, more interesting than mere brother and sister.

'Shit. Really?' I said, getting my cigarettes out.

'The parents are still alive and they live up north somewhere,' she said, at last getting the scrap of exercise book where she'd made her notes. 'Yes, here we go. Vorkuta.'

Right. Vorkuta. The first time I ever heard the word it had made me shiver with fear. Another of Stalin's feats of shittiness. Displace the Komi reindeer hunters (basically Eskimos) and build loads and loads of mines in a place where snow falls in July and it is light for only about four months a year. Ever. That is, in the daytime. Then move loads of people there to work down the mines. But maybe that wasn't the source of my horror. Maybe, even back then, I knew that Vorkuta would be a place of doom for me.

Vorkuta. Where Dimitri did his vodka trade. Where his uncle, according to Galina Alekseyevna, still lives. Also the place where Yelyena and Leonid Varanov apparently grew up.

'If you could get me a number for the parents by the end of today that would be great,' I said, and I leapt out of my seat to go and hassle someone at the American Embassy. This was all getting very weird and interesting now, like some investigation you start getting really into. But this time it was personal. I smiled to myself and imagined myself the gritty heroine of a violent film shot in grainy colour.

Arkady drove me and, on the way, I called Don and asked him and Ira to come over for some of this cassoulet. 'Don't forget the report,' I told him. I felt sure, like someone with instincts (all of which are always a pile of crap—do not ever trust them), that there would be some answers hidden in it somewhere.

The American Embassy is cool. Well, less so now, perhaps. But years ago it was a place of mystery and wonder. It had a video rental shop and a salad bar with real genuine imitation bacon bits. There was a gym. There were fences and guns and if you were Russian and could get in the Soviets couldn't drag you out again. Now it was an area of an unforgiving world that was forever mall-like. All the men had a short back and sides and nobody had gone more than two hours without a shower. A comforting black woman with long purple nails told me to wait there, so I sat in a new sofa shipped in all the way from Kansas and read *Time* magazine. I smelt aftershave, coffee and bleach. I asked where the nearest ladies' room was. I went into it and was sick.

I drank water from the cooler so cold that my teeth hurt and then a press officer came out jangling with all the identification tags round her neck. 'Faith Zanetti. Candace Hershowitz,' she said.

I shook her hand and we went down lots of corridors, through a metal detector that wailed at me to take my belt off, and into a conference room that had a view over the river. The windows were slightly smoked and I could see leaves blowing about and people adjusting their scarves as they crossed the bridge. It all felt like another world that couldn't touch me while I was in here.

'Here's my problem, Candace,' I told her. 'In 1989 I was living in Moscow with my then husband, well, current husband, estranged husband. Whatever. A Russian. Dimitri Sakhnov. Here I was and our next door neighbours got murdered in the night. A couple of days later I left my husband and moved back to England. A couple of years later my husband turned himself in for the crime. The murder of the people next door.'

Candace was taking notes and occasionally looking up at me in total bafflement. She wore a Star of David with diamonds in it.

'Anyway, I arrived in the country the other day to take up my new post…can I smoke? No, didn't think so. So, I arrive in the country and am arrested on suspicion of this murder a billion years ago. My husband, who has been in Oryol psychiatric prison for over a decade, is retracting his confession and accusing me. Obviously, they released me fairly quickly what with the total lack of new evidence and stuff. I then went to Oryol to visit my husband. But it wasn't my husband. It was an American citizen and old friend of mine called Adrian Smith who says he was somehow framed by Dimitri.'

Candace put down her pen, took off her glasses and let them dangle on their bobbly silver chain. 'Ms Zanetti,' she said. 'What is the nature of your request?'

I took my cigarettes out and put them on the table just for comfort. Candace eyed them with loathing.

'I'm getting to it,' I said. 'Adrian is in prison. He entered the country illegally in the mid-1980s and assumed a Soviet identity. He's been here ever since, living as a Russian. Mostly, as it turns out, in prison. I want you to acknowledge him as a US citizen and get him out of Oryol either as a free man or, at least for starters, extradited to America. What do you think?'

Candace, who had resumed her notes briefly, coughed. I could see she didn't give a shit but was, much against her will, obliged to ask certain questions for formality's sake.

'This is extremely unusual, as I am sure you can imagine, Ms Zanetti. I will make some preliminary inquiries' (which she pronounced innqurrriz) 'and get back to you as soon as possible.'

She stood up, shook my hand and showed me out as quickly as she could. Frankly I did not hold out much hope. I called Arkady and told him not to wait for me.

I put my belt back on, got out of the compound and walked the few hundred yards over towards the Arbat. It's pedestrianised and pretty, a wide street with black iron street lamps topped with glass globes all the way along it, pastel-coloured buildings with ornate balconies, old men playing the accordion and tourists buying antiques. Couples stroll along here just like me and Dimitri used to. He stopped in the snow one gloomy Sunday and bought me a big black peasant scarf with pink and red flowers on it. I've still got it somewhere. The Arbat seemed so melancholy then, with hardly any shops and hardly any shoppers, but beautiful anyway in a crumbling faded grandeur kind of way. Now it was bustling with life, restaurants from all the southern republics pouring out the smell of spices and the pitch of arguments. I sat down on a bench to smoke. A green wooden Moscow boulevard bench, surrounded by a blanket of yellow leaves. I lit a cigarette and watched the people go by.

I remembered I'd come down here once with Adrian on a lunch break. A lifetime before he ended up in Oryol, back when we were young and life was simple, if only we'd known it. We'd heard a rumour that someone was selling beef jerky out of a cardboard box. Barely credible, and anyway I had no idea what the fuck beef jerky was, but we strode off into the slush to investigate the truth of the tip-off. Adrian pulled the flaps down on his greasy andatr hat and wrapped his scarf three times round his neck. Arm in arm we approached a man just outside the hunting and fishing shop who fitted the description we'd been given. He sat at a table in the snow with his arms folded on top of his box.

'What have you got in there?' Adrian asked him.

'An American delicacy, comrade,' the old man replied.

'I'll give you a dollar for the lot,' Adrian told him, holding out the green bill that I'd given him a couple of weeks earlier.

'Done,' the bloke told him, standing up, handing him the box and folding away his table. A day's work more than satisfactorily completed.

Adrian took his prize, triumphant. Though you normally had to queue for hours for anything so much as vaguely western, there had been no demand for this stuff, presumably stolen out of some maniac's suitcase at the airport. This was a huge business and, when an American friend of mine did have her case stolen, I knew where to go to try and buy her stuff back. We got all the clothes and most of the items in her washbag off a stall on the outskirts of Izmailovo market.

Adrian refused even to open his box until I had bought bread from the shop on my corner called 'Bread' and butter from the invalids' shop. These were places that nearly always had actual goods on sale. You were only allowed to buy from them if you had a pass proving that you had fought for the Soviet Union in a war or were a certified invalid. Or, of course, if you had dollars you could slip the shop assistant. Five bucks would get you an enormous slab of butter cut from an even more enormous slab and wrapped in greaseproof paper, ten eggs just handed to you over the counter (you were supposed to bring your own receptacle), milk poured from the urn into a jar (again provided by you) and four whole salamis. Once changed into roubles, five bucks could get the shop assistant a fur coat.

We went back to my flat and sat on pillows on the floor tearing the elaborate wrappers off the beef jerky. I got some half-sweet Soviet champagne out from under the bed and we began our feast.

'God, I love this stuff,' Adrian said, salivating over his scraggy beard and tearing a strip off the cured beef with stained teeth. 'Yes,' he said, closing his eyes in not very appealing ecstasy.

I nibbled a bit off the end of mine. Beef jerky is disgusting. Absolutely vile evil stuff that speaks to me of Satan. It is a bit like Bombay duck which in Russia is called 'vobla'. This is odd since vobla is dried fish, usually sold by ancient crones who stand in the freezing dark outside metro stations waving them at you as you pass in the hope that you will be lured by the delicious smell. You won't. Arkady, and many other professional drivers whether military or civilian, keep a dried fish behind the sun visor to chew when the need arises. It is most commonly eaten straight off a sheet of newspaper and accompanied by a jar of beer purchased, more often than not, in my old courtyard. Perhaps it was the champagne that was so badly marring the taste of the beef jerky (how do they make it taste like rotten fish?). And perhaps not.

After polishing off about ten of these ghastly things, and, hell, we must have had five hundred, Adrian went out to buy beer. I gave him three vast preserving jars from under the sink that must have belonged to the old woman down the hall, and I waved to him as he queued, occasionally jostled by the old timers.

'Geez,' he said, when he came back. 'That took, like, *ages.*'

It did not, however, take him ages to get so completely arseholed that he passed out on my floor, snoring loudly. He sipped straight from the jar and sang sad Russian songs about people dying alone out on the steppe. Then he moved on to bawdy army songs with swear words in them that he'd learnt on the fishing trawler. One of them is about a thousand verses long and takes in a different profession (tractor driver, sportsman, astronaut) with each verse, hinging upon the phrase 'fuck your mother'. Just before he actually toppled over, spilling the last drops in the jar that he clutched like Pooh bear with a pot of honey, he said, 'God, but I love you.'

When Dimitri got in I was asleep in bed and Adrian was on the floor where he'd fallen, though I had slung a blanket over him. There is no shortage of blankets in Russia. They don't, or didn't, have duvets, just very thick woollen blankets which they put in sort of duvet covers with big diamond-shaped holes in the middle. It must have been two o'clock in the morning and Dimitri tripped over Adrian, smashing a jar and causing the American to moan loudly. I switched the light on.

'Hi,' I said. 'Where were you?'

Dimitri came and sat on the edge of the bed and stroked my hair. 'As far away from your world as I could have been.' He smiled, kissing me on the forehead. 'Let's get this bastard home,' he sighed.

I thought that sounded like a hassle and objected but Dimitri refused to sleep in a room with this pissed heap of rags snoring on the floor. It wasn't an entirely unfair point.

I had to go with them to give directions because this was before any of our joint visits to Adrian's. There were no other cars on the road and we were silent all the way, Dimitri smoking angrily. When we pulled up outside Adrian's depressing block, where a couple were drunkenly having sex in the bushes by the entranceway, Dimitri said, 'Did you sleep with him?'

I laughed. 'What is wrong with you?' I asked him.

Dimitri hauled the still comatose Adrian off the back seat, carrying him effortlessly over to the door which he kicked open, leaving him in the filth by the lift. 'Jesus fucking Christ,' he said, when he came and sat back down in the car, his face twisted with revulsion.

'What?' I asked.

'He pissed himself,' Dimitri said.

At work the next day Adrian and I broke the typewriter on purpose with the magic button so that Adrian could take his hangover home.

I thought about him now in prison and wondered if there might not be an extent to which he was enjoying himself. I lit another cigarette and started walking back to the office. He was proud of the appalling hell of his year on the trawler, below deck in windowless stinking cells, standing knee deep in fish entrails, slicing and gutting. He enjoyed the staggering scuzziness of what he thought of as his Soviet life. Normal Soviets, of course, led perfectly ordinary lives, looking after themselves and their belongings as well as possible, taking pride in their careers and their families. Adrian's life was more like that of a Soviet drunk, someone who had already been in prison and never managed to pull it together afterwards. In any case, he was pleased with it on some level. But I supposed that must have changed. He had a wife, after all, and children. I thought I would go and see them and was surprised he hadn't asked me to take them anything, to do anything for them, when I'd been in Oryol.

I got back to the office and made Lyuda get Avdotiya Yevgenievna on the line. While she was doing it she pointed with her cigarette at a pile of the Russian papers that she'd been through with a highlighter pen. There was something about a teenaged lesbian pop duo that I thought the paper might like. I'd run it past Tamsin later.

Lyuda waved when she'd got the prison director for me and I took the call in my office, kicking my feet up on to the desk and fishing my cigarettes out of my pocket.

'Hello. Avdotiya Yevgenievna? Thank you so much for yesterday and I'm sorry to bother you again so soon. I was wondering if there is any way I could get a message to Adrian...Dimitri Sakhnov? Or even to speak to him if you could allow it?'

Avdotiya Yevgenievna paused. Then Avdotiya Yevgenievna coughed. I lit a cigarette and waited.

'Avdotiya Yevgenievna?' I eventually said.

'Miss Zanetti,' she replied, her voice trembling as though I had just told her we could only ever be friends. 'Miss Zanetti, I am sorry to tell you that patient Sakhnov was found dead in his shower cubicle this morning. He blew his head off with a sawn-off shotgun. The cleaners are still in there...'

Now it was my turn to be silent. Had I known something like this might happen? That night they dragged me off to the procuratura. It was all too sinister to end up being a misunderstanding.

'He blew his own head off?' I whispered, putting my feet on the floor, sitting up straight and hunching over the receiver. There was something about this reeling sensation of initial shock, those first few minutes when you hear the news you could never have expected or had long dreaded: something almost familiar about the feeling. A closure of the throat, a sinking of the stomach, a pounding of the heart and one's face unable to stop itself scrumpling up, hands instinctively covering it in an attempt to deflect the blow, your brain not yet registering that the blow isn't physical. But none the easier for that.

'Definitely. Suicide. Nobody else involved. Well, except Seriozha who smuggled the gun in and gave it to him in return for a...well, a...a sexual favour. He's been arrested.'

'Seriozha?'

'Yes. The priest,' she said, matter of fact. Or was she almost pleased?

'Right,' I said and hung up.

I could sort of feel the sugar draining out of my bloodstream and suddenly knew why people in shock get given sweet tea.

'Lyuda!' I croaked. 'Lyuda. Sorry. I've had some bad news. Could you make me a tea. With a lot of sugar.'

I put my elbows on the desk. I knew Adrian had not killed himself. So far I only had one suspect and he was rumoured to be dead. But that was assuming that Adrian had told me the truth. If someone else had set him up...

And, perhaps so as not to face the present head-on, I thought about the past. A trip Adrian and I had made one snowy hungover day, the sky bright, the earth frozen, out into the countryside, I can't even remember where. Or why. We took an elektrichka (an electric train) out to a stop where nobody was waiting and got off, wading through knee-deep snow, laughing at each other. We walked through a little park with a defunct monastery in it—gold domes, crumbling white walls, the doors banked shut by the drifts—and we sat on a bench. Adrian had brought a bottle of Georgian wine, some vobla and a few slices of bread wrapped up in foil. It felt like a feast. I wish I could remember what we were doing there.

I picked up the phone and dialled Galina's neighbour in Ryazan, thinking, as I always did, about the chickens on the balcony and almost imagining that the KGB were still bothering to listen in.

'Hello. It is Faith. Dimitri's wife. I was wondering if you could ask Galina to call me back. I want to go and see her brother in Vorkuta.'

The cough on the other end sounded worse than ever. I even put the cigarette I was fingering down on my metal desk when I heard it. She recovered and cleared her congested throat.

'Moved out last night. Don't know where she's gone. Left me a tea set and some napkins,' she said.

I had my hand over my mouth and mumbled my goodbye. I only just made it to the loo, kneeling over the bowl and emptying my insides again. I wiped my mouth, still on my knees, and thought that I slightly preferred this new physical reaction to things getting harrowing. The mental one was harder core.

I stood up and looked at my drawn face in the mirror, pushing my hair back to get a better view. So, Dimitri is definitely still alive, I thought, pleased in a way to have still more confirmation. Definitely still alive.

Chapter 11

EDEN'S CASSOULET WAS in its pot. I pushed open the padded door and it felt like walking into someone's home. Not mine, surely? The radio was on a jazz station and the whole flat smelt of cooking.

'Hi, honey, what's cooking?' I shouted, and Eden came out of the kitchen actually wearing an apron.

'Hey,' he said. 'You look shit.' He kissed me on the cheek and handed me his glass of red wine to sip.

'Nice,' I said.

'The French place delivered it.'

'I'm going to have a shower and guess what? Adrian shot himself and Dimitri's mum moved out of the flat she has lived in for thirty years. There was no sign that she was about to move yesterday. Now she's gone,' I told him, throwing my arms out for emphasis.

Eden wiped his hands on his apron and went into the kitchen to turn the music down. 'Adrian shot himself? The bloke in prison? I thought he wanted you to get him out?' he said, lighting one of my cigarettes. Part of me wanted to think about Adrian and be sad. Well, more than sad. Whatever would be appropriate for a wasted life and a violent death. But I was so mystified by it all, and now just about beginning to feel a bit scared. I would have to leave my emotional reaction for later.

'Yup. He did want me to get him out. And of course he didn't shoot himself.' I sighed. 'Shower,' I said, pointing towards the bathroom. Eden followed me as I found a towel, took my clothes off, and stomped away from him. He asked question after question, almost more upset than I was, until I finally told him to fuck off.

'OK, but hurry up. They'll be here in a second. Don phoned to say they're bringing the baby but he'll sleep in his car seat.' Eden raised his eyebrows in acknowledgement of Don's bizarrely changed status. Only a year ago if we'd known Don was coming round we'd have filled the fridge with beer and made sure there was a clean duvet to chuck over him when he passed out on the sofa. Now I was worried someone should make a salad in case he found the cassoulet too stodgy. Well, I wasn't actually, but I could have been.

I was just leaving the room when Eden gave me some more news. 'A woman from the procurator's office called. Her name's by the phone. They want you to come in next Wednesday at two and don't leave the country in the meantime.'

Great. Superb. Had Adrian left a note? Evidence against me? Well, it was Thursday now. I was determined to prove myself innocent by next Wednesday. Quite apart from the fact that I now had to know what happened that night. And why.

While I stood there under the burning water I considered trawling Moscow's jazz and blues clubs for a half-Cameroonian guitarist who might lead me to Tina. It would once have been easy. There were only two places. A cellar out at Sokol that was really a kind of heavy metal dive though they'd take anyone who'd play. The band was confined to a protective cage and it was so dark down there it was hard to make out the performers in the gloom, let alone the other customers. There were always two or three tables reserved for the heavy metal freaks who tended to be comatose, face down in the ashtray, waiting for tomorrow. Then there was a disused theatre behind the Arbat somewhere. It was a beautiful Art Nouveau building with swirly wooden decoration on the boxes and above the stage. It was abandoned in the fifties some time and someone suddenly had the idea of ripping out the seats and staging gigs. The noise and the people somehow made the building seem more rather than less desolate and sad.

Now, of course, there were thousands and thousands of jazz and blues clubs here. I could see at least two out of the window of the flat. All the old buildings have huge cellars that used to be used for storage, if for anything. They are a whole extra floor of building and, once money started to matter, it became clear that they could be used. Some of them just got squatted by the desperate street children and their pimps and dealers. I knew I was going to have to do some long features about these creatures and was trying to put it out of my mind. The child-related stories that Russia throws up are too grim to stand. And that is not even including the unspeakable horror of Beslan.

But these same cellars also make perfect seedy dives and romantic restaurants. There's a place called the White Cockroach where trendy-looking people crouch at tiny round tables smoking in the flickering candlelight and some famous guitarist sits on his stool and strums. It would be a nightmare trying to find Job and I knew it.

I heard the doorbell ring and got out of the shower, the whole bathroom steamed up. For the first time since I'd got here I felt really clean. I bent over and rubbed my hair dry, cleaned my teeth with Eden's plastic pot of powdered toothpaste and put on some deodorant. That's the routine as far as beautification goes. I did though go into the bedroom to find clean pants, socks, jeans and a T-shirt. All of these items had been ironed by Natasha. God, she must have done nothing but iron when there was a whole household of people to deal with. I intended to sleep in this, the flat's double bed, tonight, with or without Eden Jones. At least then it might start to feel like home. I liked the gleaming wooden floors and the bright white paintwork, the black and white tiled bathroom and the high windows with their dramatic views. Maybe I should put pictures up or something. I thought it would have been nice to tell Mum about it, but now I couldn't decide whether this was a fantasy dragged up by her death, or whether, had she still been alive, it really would have been nice to talk to her. Death skews everything. But we all know that. I mean, look at Princess Diana. Drop dead and your memory is sanctified, whatever you may or may not actually have done in life.

I could hear a baby crying.

'Hey, Faithy,' Don said, lunging towards me with a big smile and a bear hug. 'You look great.' He pointed to a bottle of champagne on the table to indicate that he had brought it with him. I acknowledged it, smiling.

'Really? Jones just told me I looked shit.' I laughed and went to kiss Ira who was holding the aggrieved little Donchik. She handed him to me while she shrugged her coat off and I showed him his reflection in the hall mirror. This he seemed to find hilarious and he grinned, baring a tooth I didn't think he'd had before.

'A tooth!' I said, taking him back to his mum, who had settled on the sofa. Mummy and Daddy glowed with pride, at least some of it reserved for me, perhaps the first person who had noticed this development independently.

'You've got the knack.' Don nudged me significantly before sitting down with his wife.

'Yeah. Right.' I smiled and went off to get them drinks.

Eden was stirring. 'Fuck me, this is going to be great,' he said, tasting some of his cassoulet from a wooden spoon. It was dark outside now and I could see the red star still on top of the university in the distance up on the hill. I took a bottle of fizzy water out of the fridge and, climbing up on to the work surface to get to the back of one of the billions of cupboards, I found champagne boats.

'Wow. Look!' I said to Eden.

'I am,' he told me and he slapped my arse. I climbed down.

'Fuck off,' I said. I was just on my way back into the other room when I thought I'd best tip him off. 'Mention the baby's tooth. They'll make you a godparent,' I said.

Eden grimaced in bafflement.

Don paced round the flat looking out of all the windows as though planning a series of photographs for *National Geographic* about Moscow views. 'Brilliant,' he concluded, sipping his mineral water carefully.

Ira was cooing to Donchik in an attempt to get him to sleep. The television was on silent, the news, Putin standing on a podium looking rat-like and dictatorial, both of which he is. That presenter with the moustache was occasionally offering comment.

'Hey, did you bring the thing?' I asked Don.

'Fuck. Yes,' he said and went to get his jacket off the peg. He had elected not to change his shoes for slippers but to stay in his socks. I wondered if this was not partly to show off that the big toe of each sock had actually been darned. This was the life Don now had. His ex-wife must really hate Ira. Or was that just my cantankerousness? Maybe she was happy for him. Maybe she knew him well enough to love him and want the best for him. And, hell, this was definitely the best he was ever going to get.

He handed me a big manila envelope and I sat down to drag the documents out and examine them. While I was doing this, Don tried to help Ira get the baby to sleep by making grotesque faces. This looked seriously counterproductive to me, but I was hardly in a position to comment.

I glanced at the description of the crime scene, which was basically how I remembered it, though it was strange to see it laid out like this in neat columns and signed statements with times meticulously recorded and even the most mundane things carefully described. Then I flicked through the rest of the stuff, the signatures of the officers who had been called out, Dimitri's signature as a witness and my own signature. Somehow sad to see our handwriting side by side like on our wedding certificate. Above my own writing was a description of me offered by the police officer on the scene. The word 'mute' had been underlined. I wondered why that hadn't been raised at my interview and decided that perhaps when Adrian had confessed he had been told to say that he'd threatened me to stay silent or something. Which had been almost true except that it wasn't Adrian and it had been to protect me from arrest for being an illegal resident in a private home rather than for suspected murder. 'The witness was dressed in a black evening gown. Her face, hands and clothing were severely blood-spattered and she was in a state of inebriation,' the policeman had written. I bit my lip. I tried to consider for a billionth of a second whether it maybe had looked bad for me that morning. Whether there was a time during the investigation when I really might have been a suspect. After all, I did leave the country almost immediately. But surely nobody could have imagined that a nineteen-year-old English girl...

'Shit,' I said.

Don and Ira looked up at me, both of them putting a finger to their lips.

'Oh. Sorry,' I whispered.

Ira crept away with the baby.

'Put him in that middle bedroom,' I suggested.

Ira nodded, padding on her slippered tiptoes towards the door.

'Shit,' I said again at normal volume.

'What?' Don wondered. 'Something interesting? It all looked a bit dry apart from the brother and sister thing.'

'Twins, apparently,' I said.

'No? Fuck me,' Don replied.

'But did you see the stuff about me?' I asked him, thinking that the description didn't seem at all dry. In fact totally fucking blood-soaked.

'To be honest with you, I'm not that brilliant at reading Russian. Better at the spoken,' he admitted, sipping his water again. I wondered how his AA meetings were going and I tipped my glass of champagne down in one.

'It's just... I don't know. Shit. It's weird. I heard Adrian apparently killed himself today. You know, the guy who's supposed to be Dimitri but isn't. I went to the American Embassy this morning to try and do something about him. He was probably already dead. But... Shit.'

'What? Faith? What?' Don came and sat next to me on my sofa now and put a hand on my arm. OK, clean living was one thing but touchy feely was quite another. I shook him off.

'I don't know. Something's weird. If you read this report it really looks as though... Don, when the police came round I was covered in blood. I think I fell down some stairs or something, but Dimitri told them I was mute so they wouldn't know I was foreign and I was... Bollocks. I think it really might have looked like I had something to do with it. And then I left the country straight away...'

Don laughed and I was grateful. Relieved. 'Zanetti? Honestly,' he chortled and I was safe again. Or at least, I thought I was.

I flicked back to the scene of crime stuff on the first page and, now that I was smiling again, there was something else that caught my eye and made me laugh even louder. Every item in the room had been recorded in writing and then positioned on a kind of map. You know, 'leg of male victim' kind of thing. Sitting on the sideboard all by itself, as innocent as anything, was a 'small uncooked chicken'. *My* small uncooked chicken! They had nicked my sodding chicken and then mutilated each other!

'They stole my fucking chicken!' I exclaimed, waving my evidence about and leaping up. I ran into the kitchen. Eden had taken his apron off and was holding the enormous casserole dish, about to make a ceremonial entrance.

'The dead twins stole my chicken!' I said, shaking the piece of paper in front of his eyes.

'Sounds like a tabloid splash,' he said, and the doorbell rang.

Scott Weisman swept into the flat in a slightly presidential manner which I love. He unlaced his boots, talking non-stop, cheeks pink from the cold.

'Sorry I'm late. Had a deadline and then I thought to myself, Hey, I'll take the metro for old times' sake. Remember the first time we hung out together and we met at the top of the escalators at Ploshchad Revolutsii and went to that Georgian place where that guy got killed that time?'

'Yes,' I confirmed. 'You had a red ski jacket on and I thought we might get murdered for it.'

'Right.' He nodded. 'You know what? I gave that jacket to this kid in an underpass.'

'Gave?' I asked him, cocking my head to one side. The gypsy children play British bulldog in underpasses, knocking the wealthy to the floor and relieving them of their possessions.

'Kinda.' He smirked. 'Well, who needed it more? Them or me?'

'Um, you,' I guessed.

'Right,' he agreed, pulling some Afghan woolly sock slippers on over his white sports socks and standing up to kiss me hello. 'I brought you an avocado,' he said, hanging his jacket up and pulling the fruit out of a deep pocket.

'Thanks,' I said, taking it. 'You've met Don, and this is his wife Ira.'

They shook hands, Ira giving hers weakly to him as though he might kiss it. Instead he pumped it up and down like she'd just beaten him at tennis.

'Ochen priyatno,' he said. 'Good to meet you.'

I like this about expat life. There is a congenial atmosphere and an expectation that everyone's going to be friends, that we're all of a similar type. We get the deal and we've immediately got that in common. Whether or not it happens to be true it does provide instant friends in any city in the world. 'Hi, I'm here doing a story for the *Chronicle*. Fancy a drink?' A huge international family, and a fond one at that.

Eden was fiddling around at the table, lighting candles he'd dug out of a drawer and stuck on to saucers and generally doing loud things with cutlery.

'That's Eden Jones. He's the cook for this evening and a new staff writer at the *New Yorker*,' I said.

Scott dashed over to Eden and slapped him on the back. 'Didn't I see you in Afghanistan, dude?' he asked him.

'Don't think so. Baghdad?' Eden suggested.

'Definitely Afghanistan.'

'You must be thinking of someone else.'

'You Brits all look the same,' Scott laughed. 'Weren't you once going to go to China for us, though?'

Eden nodded, almost meekly.

'Touchy subject,' I shouted across the room.

'Sorry. I hear it's a shit-pit,' Scott said and Eden laughed.

A couple of sloshes of champagne and shuffling of seats later Eden said loudly in French, 'A table!'

Now I normally will not tolerate anyone speaking any language other than their own first language or the first language of their interlocutor. Occasionally, when finding oneself in a country where one's own first language is not the official language, it is allowable to use certain words of that country's language to describe things that perhaps do not have a name in one's own first language. On this occasion, though, still shaken from the crime scene thing, I let it pass.

We all sat down and Eden started ladling sausages and huge pieces of goose into bowls and passing them round. I looked over at Scott and was amazed at how little he had changed. I always expect the world to move on so much, but here we were, back in Moscow, the years not difficult to fill in. He went back to the States, did a few years of domestic reporting, headed up the Los Angeles bureau, did Rwanda and then got posted here. A few disastrous relationships, a few tragic passions. I made this up, of course, but felt pretty sure that my guesses were right. Especially Rwanda, because I'd seen his byline. But, self-centred and generally rude as it was, I only had one thing on my mind this evening. My murder.

'So, you remember that night we went to the Limonov thing at Dom Literatov?' I said.

'Ugh. Faith. Are we going to trawl through this all evening?' Eden sighed, ladling out the final portion. Don and Ira met each other's glance. They would probably be on a macrobiotic diet for the next six weeks to get all the red meat out of their system.

'I'm not trawling, for fuck's sake. A friend of mine died today and it's my...well, you know, it could be my fault. Or at least, it's not unrelated to me, pretty obviously.'

'Fair point,' Eden muttered, and sat down. It was only later that I realised why he hadn't wanted to hear about the evening in question. He suspected, clearly, that there might be things about it he would find unpalatable. And there were.

'Sure,' Scott said. 'You were hilarious. Never drunk neat vodka before, she says. So I give her a shot and she does about fifteen in a row. Hey, when you have a talent for something you have a talent for something, right? Then she's trying to make out with everyone in the room, staggering round on these incredibly high heels...'

Don and Ira were laughing, Eden was pretending not to listen, fiddling around with some CDs in the candlelight, and I had my head in my hands. Encouraged by the laughter, Scott ploughed on.

'By midnight she had dragged me out into this back room and we were...well, it seemed rude to turn her down, right?' Ira was almost weeping with laughter, but I had stopped eating.

'Hello?' I asked, stunned. Eden turned Billie Holliday up. A lot.

'Sure...' Scott said, and then he realised I was serious. 'Faith? Not really? You actually don't remember this?'

I took a bite of a sausage. 'Of course I don't remember. I had fifteen shots of vodka for Christ's sake.' I laughed. 'I could do with one now, actually.'

Eden took this as a cue not to have to be involved in this conversation and got up to get the vodka out of the freezer. 'At your service,' he mumbled as he got up, and I realised he'd been getting arseholed all afternoon while he was cooking.

So, I had sex with Scott Weisman.

'Anyway, this KGBeshnik comes in and yells at us and we're running out pulling our clothes back on when Faith goes flying down these stairs and smashes her whole face up. Do you remember that bit?' he asked, Ira still choking with laughter.

'I thought only Russian girls did this kind of thing!' she squealed, and Don started to look a bit nervous.

'I'll just check on…' he whispered, and lumbered out of the room. Eden put a vodka down in front of me and I drank it, whether Don McCaughrean liked it or not.

'Actually, that does ring a bit of a bell,' I admitted, trying to run a finger through the still wet tangles of my hair.

'I tried to take you home but you wanted to go clean up in the ladies' room. I waited for, like, hours and then I got caught up in Limonov leaving and by the time I sent a waitress in to see if you'd passed out in there or something, you'd gone. It took me forever to get my coat back because you had the tags in your purse and I ended up handing twenty bucks to some warty-faced bitch. But the freaky thing was, when I got outside I was still looking around to try and find you—I assumed you'd got in a cab. But I did see Dimitri, your Dimitri, parked right outside the building, leaning out of his car window smoking a cigarette. I tried to wave to him and I know he saw me but he pulled off. Remember I'd met him before at that thing you had?'

Ira wasn't laughing any more and we were all waiting to see what he would say next. Ira shuffled in her seat. Eden coughed. But Scott didn't say anything else. He just carried on with his food, and the table was silent. I was digesting the implications of what he'd said. Basically, if he was right, and I supposed that he was, then Dimitri could not have been asleep long by the time I got home. Unless I'd passed out on the boulevard and slept. Or gone somewhere else on the way back. I couldn't get a meaning out of it. I took a sip of wine. Eden had started to gaze around the room, settling, eventually, on the view. He broke the silence.

'Look. Snow,' he said, so we looked. The whole night sky was thick with fat, lazy flakes.

Even in the middle of this unsavoury story it was magical and everyone round the table was six years old again, gazing out at the first real snow of winter. Something about Russia seems to put life into perspective. Something here makes you stop looking in and makes you look out. Maybe it really is just the snow.

'Cool,' I sighed. 'Beautiful.'

When the miracle of nature pause was over and we'd all collected our adult selves I got back to business.

'So,' I said, 'you just let me stagger home by myself covered in blood and you never even called?'

'What are you, crazy? I called about every ten minutes the next day. Your phone must have been cut off or the exchange down or whatever. Then you'd left and the asshole came to rob me with this quarterback of a guy with a head like a soccer ball and hands like some kind of...you know? Prison tattoos? This huge ogre with a piece of metal piping...'

Now Ira was completely grim-faced, her little gold earrings bobbing in disapproval. Normal Russians were embarrassed by these thugs whom all westerners seemed somehow to encounter. I took the bottle and poured myself another vodka, drinking it without a speech or a fanfare yet again. I tried to cut some bread, a baguette that Eden had put out on a rustic board, but instead managed to lodge the knife in my finger.

'Fuck,' I said. 'Sorry, everyone.' And I rushed off to the bathroom.

I knew who Scott was talking about, though. It was Misha.

I shoved open the bathroom door, clutching my finger as the blood dripped on to the tiles in big dark drops. Don was in there, sucking at a vodka miniature he'd obviously brought with him. I could hear others jangling in his jacket pocket. When he saw me he slumped down on to the side of the bath.

'First drink for a year, honest, Faithy. I've been as fucking sober as a judge's anus, I swear.' He almost sobbed. 'It was that little tooth. I took one look at that little bloke's first tooth and I lost it…I just…I lost it.'

I sat down next to him and leant my head on his shoulder, blood seeping through on to my jeans now. 'It's OK, Don,' I said. 'It's OK.'

'After the divorce and everything…all the booze… I assumed I was impotent, Faithy. I just assumed…and now he's got this little tooth…and I dunno…'

I rinsed my finger and wrapped some loo roll round it. Then I made Don eat some toothpaste and we went back to face the music, a bit of solidarity at last, I thought. What a bitch that I liked him more when he failed.

'Thanks, Zanetti,' he said, nudging me quietly as we sat down at the noisy table (Eden had started on about the West Bank).

'Any time, McCaughrean,' I told him. 'Any time.'

Chapter 12

I DIDN'T HAVE to do any kind of big investigation into where Misha lived. I knew exactly where he lived. In a pathetic attempt at marital bonding I had copied the names of all Dimitri's friends, their phone numbers and addresses, into my vast black Filofax (I was the first person I knew to have one—a present from Evie—and it's still my address book today despite all technological revolutions rendering them obsolete). I decided that since we were a couple all our friends should be in common. All I can say in my defence is—I was nineteen.

I know what a wifey thing to do this is because I've seen other people do it. The wife leaves a 'we are not here right now' message on the answering machine and makes social arrangements to see other couples. The wife's friends, therefore, call the house and pass on regards to the spouse. These days the husband's friends call him on his mobile and never show the remotest interest in his girlfriend or wife, finding the whole emotional attachment issue embarrassing and distasteful. As I say, I was nineteen.

Did I think he would still live there? I suppose I almost did, and at any rate it seemed like a good place to start. I left Eden asleep in the double bed we'd shared and thought how handsome he was as I crept to the bathroom with a sheet round me. All sandy-haired and tanned, his face gently lined by the effort of this life, his broad shoulders hunched to wrap themselves round a pillow. Any normal woman would be pleased to have him. I smiled to myself and heard Natasha come in the door.

'Dobroye utro!' I shouted, closing the bedroom door behind me. 'Good morning.'

'Cold out there,' Natasha said, and I could feel the cold come in with her on her cheeks and coat. It was unusual for her to have acknowledged the temperature. Russians usually only admit to feeling the faintest chill when it is below minus forty. Anything under that and they say, 'Call this cold? When I was a boy out in the steppe we thought of this as warm...' She hung up her beret and silk scarf carefully on a hook, took her apron down and plunged her feet into her slippers. 'Coffee coming right up,' she said, smiling brightly.

I envied her. Patronising? Probably. But wasn't it easy? You come in, you do your job, you go home. Just for a second I wanted that life. Was it possible just to run away and start again? I would like to have left myself behind and got on a plane to...anywhere. I could be a waitress in San Francisco, I could work in a sandwich shop in Paris... Or I could drink my coffee and go and see Misha.

I popped into the office and there was a message for me from Candace at the American Embassy. I called her back immediately while Lyuda played a Chopin nocturne on the office upright piano. It was disconcerting but not unpleasant. Arkady put his Walkman on and buried himself in *Moskovs-*

kiy Komsomolets, the Russian equivalent of the *Sun* and, interestingly, the paper from which the *Chronicle* most often lifts stories.

'Hi? Candace? It's Faith Zanetti at the London *Chronicle* returning your call,' I said.

'Ms Zanetti, thank you for getting back to me. I made some calls regarding your alleged American citizen, Adrian Smith. Firstly,' she said, and I heard her rustling her paperwork, 'I did speak to the psychiatric prison in Oryol and they informed me that the patient you claim was using the name Dimitri Sakhnov but was, you said, in reality Adrian Smith had committed suicide. I am sorry to have to give you this news.'

I lit a cigarette and put my feet up on my desk. 'That's OK. I heard yesterday afternoon. Thank you,' I told her, glancing around for an ashtray.

'They had no idea of his being anyone other than the person he was registered as being, however, and stated that it was extremely unlikely that this man was an American citizen since his spoken Russian was entirely unaccented. The body of the deceased patient was retrieved from Oryol by a Russian woman claiming to be a relative. I am sorry not to have been more help,' she said.

'Thank you for your efforts,' I said, putting the phone down, defeated. Not that I expected any huge revelations, but it seemed sad that Adrian's whole existence had been obliterated, even from a bureaucratic point of view.

I interrupted Lyuda's playing. She had a green silk number on today. 'Could you get me the details of the woman who collected Dimitri Sakhnov's body from the prison in Oryol? Tell them I want to go to the funeral or something,' I asked her. I felt reasonably certain that at any rate I had pretty much found Adrian's wife.

Arkady drove me out to Misha's block, on a big estate near Prazhskaya. I didn't want to call him to say I was coming in case he suddenly moved house. These days a lot of Moscow looks quite beautiful, if a bit inhospitable and imposing. Mayor Luzhkov cleaned it up for a big anniversary, but he didn't clean up any of the bits that foreign dignitaries weren't going to see. These are the bits where everyone lives. Huge, endless tower block estates surrounding the city, all a bus and a tram and a metro ride away from the centre.

Time, luckily, was on my side today as far as the paper was concerned. The Americans were having an election and foreign news was swamped with profiles of the men in the running, the people who would or wouldn't vote for them and other long pieces of Americana, like features on the regeneration of the NYPD, abortion clinics in Arizona and gunshops in Georgia.

Here, nothing much had changed but me. Sometimes I wish things would change more, just to keep pace with me. Going back to a place like this makes me feel like a time traveller, as though I ought to have got younger on the way. How can this place still exist when the me that first came here doesn't? I stood in pitch darkness in the lift that rattled up to the tenth floor, the orange glow of my cigarette the only proof of life. I was starting to feel sick again and I clamped my teeth together and tightened my stomach. The corridor up here smelt bad in an indefinable way. Just old and grotty, rubbish left lying around, animals' and probably people's urine dried on the floor and lower walls. The sour smell of neglect and decay. I rang on the bell.

After a few seconds I heard heavy movement on the other side of the faded yellow metal door. Someone looked through the peephole. I was standing, as exposed as I could make myself, right in front of it.

'Who is it?' Misha barked. I could tell it was him.

'It's Faith. Vera. Dimitri's English wife from years ago. We met...' I was shouting when I heard him start to unlock the door. This took a few minutes. When he finally opened it he gestured me in with a semi-automatic machine gun that he had brought to the door with him.

'You never know,' he said, glancing down at it and then back at me in explanation.

'No,' I agreed. 'You never do.'

Misha didn't look the same. Well, not unrecognisable, but not the same. He looked thirty rather than fifteen years older. He had grown his hair back and it was thin and grey. He had a thick beard that was grey too, perhaps grown to cover scars. He was fat now rather than just hugely bulky and muscular, and his breath was short and wheezy. He was missing a front tooth.

'You haven't changed a bit,' I said.

'You neither,' he coughed. This worried me. I was lying. Was he?

The flat was overheated, which explained his T-shirt (though not the fact that Christina Aguilera was on it) and shorts. He also, as ever, wore flip-flops though this was not as odd in Russia as it might have seemed in other areas of the world. They are an acceptable slipper here and are also obligatory wear at swimming pools and hospitals and places like that.

The corridor was dark and narrow and carpeted in cheap turquoise stuff that bounced underfoot. He showed me into a room where a boy—well, maybe a teenager—was sitting on the floor in front of the television playing a game with mythological animals in it, a grey brick maze and a character, presumably the boy, with a sword and a whip. Could this be the baby who had been crying in the background years ago?

'Borka!' Misha bellowed. 'Get up and say hello to the lady.' He had put the gun down on a heavily laminated fake wood table, but not in such a way as to suggest that he wouldn't be picking it up again. It was big. A bit like the things the police carry at airports, cocked for the extra fear factor. A stuffed panther stood near the window, patches of its fur coming away in clumps. He looked familiar.

'Ciao,' Borka mumbled without looking up. Was this Italian slang some new fashion?

'Little cunt,' Misha said, half to the boy and half to me. 'No fucking manners.' He shrugged his apology and I put a hand up to make clear that nobody should stand on ceremony on my account.

There were two sets of net curtains on the windows. One simple kind just to render the windows blind and then, on top of them, some frilly ones for decorative purposes. The windows themselves were modern, double glazed and dirty. I assumed. The carpet in here, as in so many places, was deep brown with yellow swirls and there was a black leather three piece suite (ghastly phrase) which completely dwarfed the room as if the enormous television didn't do it all by itself. Against the walls were the ubiquitous display cabinets in dark wood, containing glasses and cups, plates and the odd crystal animal, the kind of thing you collect from the back of the Sunday magazines. Though I'm not sure where you get them in Russia.

There were a few photos of Borka on the walls. At least, I assumed it was Borka. A small, frightened-looking child, gazing into the camera from the swings, the school stage and a swimming pool. Now Borka had gel in his hair, baggy jeans with pockets in them and, I noticed, a silver toe ring on one of his bare feet.

'Sit down,' Misha said. I sat down. 'Anastassiya! Nastya!' he shouted. A woman called back. 'Bring tea. We've got a guest.'

Misha sat down in one of the armchairs and filled it to capacity. Quite a feat, actually. He placed his arms on the arms and spread his legs. 'Nice to see you after so long,' he said. 'You shouldn't have broken Dimitri's heart, you know. It shouldn't have been done.'

This sounded like a threat of some kind and I was about to make my case. You know—life is very complicated and things are never as cut and dried as one party might like to make out. Whilst of course one cannot do anything about being left, being heartbroken is a matter of choice. We can't affect what happens to us always, but we can choose how to react.

Thankfully, this was not required. Misha suddenly began to laugh loudly and rather unnervingly. He had, apparently, made a joke.

'Well, Misha, I'm glad you mention him actually. You know we are still married? I was hoping to meet up and maybe, well, maybe do something about it. I dare say he might want to get married again by now and he wouldn't have been able to locate me, so I was just...really... I'm working here now. Just came over as the correspondent for the London *Chronicle*... it's quite a prestigious broadsheet. Well, it was until about 20 years ago, but it's got a big circulation and...'

Nastya came in with some tea. This was definitely the same girl as had come in fifteen or so years ago. She was maybe even carrying the same tray. She smiled at me and laid a big doily down on the table. She put a vast teapot in the middle of it, all inlaid with silver and gold and blue patterns.

'Ochen priyatno,' she nodded to me, still bowing to arrange the stuff on the smoked glass coffee table. 'Nice to meet you.'

She didn't have a black eye this time, but she did have the look of a lifetime of abuse. Though obviously very beautiful, and I imagined about my age, she was thin and worn, her faint wrinkles not, like mine, laugh lines, but worry lines. She was in a pink velour tracksuit. Hideous and vile but, I happened to know, expensive and actually fashionable. She was dangling a lot of expensive rapperish gold.

'Coke, mum,' Borka said.

'Coke what, Boris?' she whispered.

'Coke, please,' he hissed and she scuttled out of the room. Misha burped and threw his hand out to show me that I could pour the tea if I wanted.

'Lovely lady, my wife,' he said.

'Yes,' I nodded. He was looking me up and down as though wondering where my pink tracksuit and gold chains were.

I could hardly lift the sodding teapot but I poured us out some tea and was just finishing when Nastya came back in with the Coke in a big crystal glass, ice and lemon, for her son. They probably had one of those vast brown fridges that makes ice in little crescent shapes.

'Oh, sorry. Let me,' she said, coming back over to serve us. Borka swore at his screen.

'Boris!' Nastya reprimanded.

'Little cunt,' Misha commented.

I unwrapped and ate a chocolate from a chunky glass dish on a stalk. I sipped my tea and then stirred some sugar into it. Nastya went back to the kitchen. I could smell something frying in grease and thought I might be sick. It was becoming my new thing.

I cleared my throat. 'So, I was wondering…'

Misha stopped me with his hand. 'Bad news,' he said. 'Dimitri's dead. Car crash up north. Vorkuta. Tragic. Couple of weeks ago.'

Well, it was succinct at any rate. Though not, I was now sure, true. Whether or not Misha knew it wasn't true was another matter, however. After all, this may well have been the source of the 'rumour' Adrian said he'd heard.

I tried to look stricken. I mean, I was a bit stricken, but not specifically by this news.

'Oh my God!' I said. 'I half expected you to tell me he'd been put in prison or something. But I never thought...'

I looked up at him to see if the concept of Dimitri's being in prison had elicited any kind of reaction. It was difficult to see with the hair and the scar tissue. His eyes were so swollen and watery with booze and pain that it was hard to see anything in them at all.

'Sakhnov? Prison? You must be joking!' he barked. 'They could never pin anything on him. They were after him once for that thing you were mixed up in at the flat...but there was no chance. Once he knew you were safe he was out of here, off the map...'

He tailed off. Mixed up? Mixed up! I wasn't fucking mixed up in anything. I had nothing to do with this shit! That was the kind of thing I wanted to scream. But screaming around Misha didn't seem like a good idea. It did occur to me that it might have been Misha who helped frame Adrian. Who did the threatening.

'Poor old Sakhnov. You shouldn't have messed him around like that. He was a jealous guy. We went round and saw to the American dickhead you were fucking. That was a laugh,' Misha explained, smiling to himself in wistful fondness at the memory. Ah, what larks. He tapped his fingers gently on the arm of his chair.

I decided to ignore his comments. I would have been outraged had it not been for the fact that I had only last night discovered that actually I had been fucking that American guy.

'Was there a funeral?' I wondered.

This was the first thing I had said that Misha really reacted to. His eyes opened slightly wider and his body took on more of a shape, a rigidity that it had lacked before.

'Funeral? Yes. Yes, there was. Yes. Just me and a couple of mates,' he said, quickly, lying so obviously that even his son looked up from his game.

'Right. Where?' I asked, nearly enjoying myself.

'Novodyevichy,' Misha said quickly. 'Yes. Novodyevichy.'

'OK. Well. Thanks,' I said, getting up. 'I'm so sad to hear the news. I'll write to his mum, perhaps.'

Misha hauled himself up too. Not without difficulty. He followed me out of the room, picking up his gun on the way. You need a gun if you're near a door. That seemed to be his view.

'I wouldn't do that,' he said. 'She died years ago.'

I liked the idea of Dimitri being buried in Novodyevichy though. Well, I liked it now that I was certain he was not dead. Novodyevichy is where Dostoevsky is buried, Chekhov, Gagarin…Kim Philby. It may also be the loveliest place in the world. Dimitri and I crunched round there in the snow one day looking at the graves. The Soviet ones are fabulous because there was no God, so no crosses or sombre-faced angels. There is a grave with a statue of its occupant on the phone, while another bloke has a busty nude on his; the space-men are all carved in their space suits, the writers hunched over their typewriters, fag in mouth; the obstetrician is chis-elled in bronze, scrubbed up and holding a newborn baby in the palm of his giant hand. Khrushchev is in there too. He was unfortunate enough to die in the 1970s and has a really grotesque black and white symmetrical thing surrounding his bust.

The hilariousness of the senior Soviets revered enough to be buried in Novodyevichy only makes the monastery itself more moving. There are a lot of gold onion domes in Moscow—enough that you can even get used to them and stop seeing their heartbreaking beauty. It is possible to wander down the straggly little paths up to the gate, stamping your feet against the cold, and not expect to be stricken by wonder and awe. Novodyevichy was allowed to work as a monastery, in a very small way, even under the Communists but by the time Dimitri and I climbed the steps to the church things were almost in full swing again. Not that anybody had publicly announced it, but people had started to sense that they were no longer going to get arrested for going to church and that nobody was going to question reopening the chapel next door to the main building. Gorbachev never quite went as far as going to church, unlike Yeltsin, but changes were afoot.

It must have been minus twenty that day. My eyebrows and the inside of my nose were frozen and the tips of my gloved fingers had gone numb. I was paying a lot of attention to these phenomena and hardly noticed that we had gone through some wooden swing doors into heaven, or the stage just before it. It was so dark in here that all I could immediately see were thousands and thousands of flickering candles and walls of gold. The air was full of intoxicating incense and Dimitri fell to his knees. I would almost have liked to cross myself but I didn't know how. A choir was chanting Orthodox mysteries somewhere in the gloom and a bearded priest in black robes swung a censer at them, muttering divine truths.

'Dyevushka!' an old lady hissed, bundling towards me in rag slippers and a headscarf. She tore the hat off my head and shoved it into my arms. Then she pointed to my gloves. She couldn't do it, though. She couldn't spoil it, hard though she tried. It was the first and probably the last time that I nearly believed in God. And He lived here. Here where Dimitri Sakhnov could never dream of being buried even if he were dead. Which he isn't.

So, I'm standing at Misha's front door about to say goodbye. But just before he opened the door for me we both heard noises outside. The lift doors opening and shutting, voices in the corridor and then, at last, a ring on the doorbell. Misha lifted the gun to a firing position and stood with his back to the wall. God knows what had happened to him in a doorway one time, but it must have been bad.

'Da?' he grunted.

'Ya. Ya. Dyadya, eto ya,' said a laughing girl whose voice sounded weirdly familiar. 'It's me, Uncle,' she was saying.

Misha beamed all over his face and opened the door to let in Tina, wild Valentina from Ryazan, and Job, her half-Cameroonian boyfriend. Tina hugged Misha and kissed his grisly beard. Job shook hands with him warmly and said, 'Zdorov, bratan,' which is a very hard slangy way of saying 'All right, mate' and has all sorts of criminal and prison-related implications.

They were taking their coats off by the time they saw me. Job, shortish and wearing Timberlands and a hooded snow-boarding jacket that made him look like an American tourist, looked blankly at me, speechless, waiting for an introduction.

Tina grinned and rushed forward to kiss me. 'Hey! Faith! That's sooooo weird! What are you doing here? How do you know Uncle Misha? Well, he's not really my uncle but he's been a friend of the family for, like, forever,' she said, swinging back round to stroke Misha's face as she babbled. 'Thanks for that lift, sister. Don't know what I'd have done,' she said, pulling a woolly bobble hat off. Since I saw her last she had dyed her hair electric blue. 'This is Job. You know, I told you about him,' she said, sitting on the floor to take her boots off. Job leant over to shake my hand.

'How you doing,' he said in English, spotting my un-Russianness immediately as people always do if you don't wear make-up or jewellery.

I nodded at him. 'Good,' I said. 'A trifle bewildered, but otherwise basically good.'

Misha looked seriously uncomfortable and followed Tina into the living room. Job and I went with them.

Tina kicked the oblivious Borka in the back with her stockinged foot. 'Hey,' she said. Boris didn't look up.

'Hey,' he said back.

Tina was comfortable and clearly came here a lot. Nastya rushed in and kissed her.

'Nastya! Nastyusha!' Tina beamed, throwing her arms round her. 'Hope you haven't been letting Mr Big here push you around!'

'Foo! It's like having two teenagers in the house,' she said, gesturing towards the hideous Misha, still holding a semi-automatic machine gun, as though he were simply a problem child.

'Oooh. Before I forget,' Tina said, running back to her coat. She carried on speaking from the hall. 'Dad said I should give you these. It's parked up on Gogolyevskiy Bulvar, just by the metro.'

Misha put his gun on the table and sat down in his armchair, not meeting my eye. Tina chucked some car keys at him which he caught and held on to. 'Thanks,' he mumbled.

It was time for me to pipe up. 'Tina, how is your dad?' I said.

'Tragic. Tragic,' Misha said under his breath, trying to catch Tina's attention. She failed to hear or see him. She was unwrapping a sweet and Job was trying to seem nonchalant, glancing through the CD collection. She popped the caramel into her mouth and spun round to look at me, smiling.

'Good. He's good,' she said, eyes glittering.

'Not dead?'

'Not half an hour ago...' She laughed, and then she realised and laughed even louder. 'Oh, Mishochka! You haven't been talking shit, have you? He's such a shit talker,' she said to me. 'Papa's always in, like, semi-hiding. He thinks he's such a big shot. Gran's so convinced he did that murder she won't even acknowledge him.'

'What murder?' Misha perked up. 'At the communalka?'

'I don't know. Like two hundred years ago. Really gory thing with an axe. He went to ground for a bit because someone was trying to fit him up and then he phoned her up and she said if he ever tried to contact her again she'd spit in his face. I just sort of pretend he's dead when I see her. As far as she's concerned he's gone. It's weird how little it comes up actually. Unless *you're* around!' she said. She was hugely amused and completely unruffled by the whole thing. Little did I know then that she too had been spun a web of lies and half-truths. I, on the other hand, was shaking with proximity to my prize. She took a ball of cling film out of her pocket and started unpacking her grass, kneeling down at the edge of the coffee table to join me on the floor. 'It was crazy. I think you saying he didn't do it really set her off.'

'God, Tina. I've been trying to track him down! You could have told me. Can you give me his number?' I said, sitting down cross-legged on the carpet and attempting to seem casual.

She threw her head back and howled with laugher. Then she faced me, serious, and tapped the side of her nose. 'Sorry. State secret,' she said. 'Anyone got a fag?'

I passed her a cigarette and she rolled it between her fingers to empty the tobacco out. She mixed the grass up with it and carefully poked the mixture back into the cigarette. She lit it and inhaled deeply.

'Crazy,' she said.

'Tina, I called your gran and the woman upstairs told me she's moved out.' I was getting confused myself now, but there was something comforting about Tina's nonchalance. Maybe, after all, this could all turn out to be a horrible misunderstanding.

Tina blew her smoke out in a stream and handed the joint to Boris, who had stuck out his hand without looking away from his game. Nastya, who had come back in with a bottle of cherry brandy on a tray, clucked disapprovingly. She put the brandy down, went over to her son and took the joint off him, slumping into the sofa and taking an enormous drag herself. Okey dokey then.

'Whoa. Moved out?' Tina smiled, rolling her big eyes. She wore a lot of mascara. It was strange that such brutal piercings could look feminine on her. She was such a blancmange of a girl that perhaps anything would look sexy. Her combat trousers certainly did. 'She's been hassling the shit out of me on my mobile. She worked out I knew where Dad was, man. She made me tell him she wanted to see him "immediately".' As she said immediately she saluted as if in answer to a military command.

Nastya patted the sofa in invitation to Job who plonked himself down next to her and took his share of the joint. The smell was making me feel sick now. I wanted to get out of there. I could feel my face getting hot with the smoke and the overheating and the general and total weirdness. I stood up and thought I might fall.

'OK,' I said. 'Could you do the same for me? Tell your dad I want to see him immediately.'

I took a biro out of the pocket of my leather jacket and wrote my mobile number on the back of the *Chronicle* visiting card.

She looked at it. 'Cool,' she breathed. 'No problem.'

And I left. That is, Misha showed me to the door with his big gun and everyone gave me a stoned wave as I walked out. I could hear them laughing like crazy before the front door was completely shut, but they may not have been laughing at me.

Chapter 13

THE DOOR TO the flat was open when I got back. I assumed Natasha was taking out the rubbish or something and I walked in talking to Eden, whose shape I could see in the armchair.

'Well, I'll tell you one thing,' I said, kicking off my cowboy boots. 'Dimitri Sakhnov is alive and well and in touch with his big huge teenaged daughter.' I padded into the front room carrying my jacket. 'Jones?' I shouted, wanting a response.

Don McCaughrean turned to look at me. 'He's gone to look at Butyrskaya Prison,' he said.

'Oh,' I said, and sat down, lighting a cigarette.

Don looked terrible. Somehow he seemed to have put on weight even in the last twenty-four hours. Mostly on his face which was puffy and aged again, his eyes watery, his skin blotchy. His hands were visibly shaking.

'Need a drink?' I asked him.

'Thanks, Faithy. Yeah. Yeah. I need a fucking drink like a pimp needs a whore...' he started.

189

'Yup. Yup. OK, Don. I'll get you a beer,' I said. 'Steady your nerves.'

Natasha was in the kitchen making coffee. 'Your friend looks…' she said, getting the milk out of the fridge.

'Yes. He is,' I agreed and leant past her to grab a bottle of beer.

I bit the cap off and took it into the sitting room for Don. It had started to snow again, I noticed. The whole room took on a pale grey glow.

Don swigged from the bottle and seemed to relax a bit. 'Shit,' he said. 'Don't know what to do, Zanetti. I missed my meeting. You're not allowed to go pissed. Irochka's gonna kill me. She'll kill me. She'll chop my plums off and fry them up with some cabbage. She'll poke chillis up my arsehole. She'll—'

'Don, calm down. She loves you. She'll understand. You'll sober up, you'll apologise and promise not to be such a tosser in future and it'll be fine,' I told him.

'You think?'

I got up and put my hand on his shoulder. 'Of course,' I said. 'Here, have a fag.'

He pulled it out of the packet as though it were the very elixir of life itself. Which perhaps it is.

'I can't go home like this, Faithy. She'll grate my scrotum on to a dish of wild mushrooms. She'll—'

'Don. Shut the fuck up. No, you can't go home like that. Where have you been anyway?' I put my hand up. 'No. Don't tell me. Listen, let me make a couple of calls and you can stay with me until you're better. OK?'

'God, Zanetti. I've always loved you, you know…'

'Don't start.'

I called over to the office, sipping the coffee that Natasha had brought me and starting to feel, frankly, worse. I tried not to worry that I was going mad again. But Lyuda had news.

'I found her,' she said, audibly exhaling cigarette smoke. 'She even signed the body out as Valera Kuznyetsova. Wrote her real name, address and phone number. The funeral's today at...hang on a sec...at four o'clock at the monastery of St Vladimir out near...Vladimir. Yup. Not far from Vladimir. Arkady says he knows it. Are you going to go?'

'No, I'm going to stay here and cut my toenails. Of course I'm going to go,' I said. 'Did the desk call?'

'Yes. They say tell Faith they are really sorry but they're all America'd out today and there might be a slot tomorrow.' I could hear the other phone ringing in the background.

'OK. Why don't you get that? Tell Arkady to meet me downstairs in ten minutes.'

I was just walking back into the sitting room to deal with Don when the phone rang.

'Yes?'

'One other thing,' Lyuda said. 'I found a number for the twins' parents in Vorkuta. I called them—really bad line— and there was a friend there who said they'd be in after eight. Do you want to take the number down?'

'God,' I said, writing down the number. 'Lyuda, you're amazing.'

'Yes, I am,' she agreed and hung up.

Don had finished his beer and looked much less green.

'OK, baby. Funeral in Vladimir here we come!' I yelled, punching the air.

'Oh baby!' Don laughed. 'You do know how to treat a lady. Hey, you know what, I might take a few of these along for the ride.'

I picked up my jacket and cigarettes and Don went into the kitchen for the beers. 'I'm giving up tomorrow, Faithy, I swear,' he said, coming out and loading them into the pockets of his silly photographer's coat with all the little compartments for your films and lenses and beers and stuff.

'Hey. Don't look at me. I'm not your wife, honey, and I never will be,' I said, smiling. 'Let's go.'

Don toddled after me, grateful, hopeless. 'Not ever?'

'Not ever.'

Vladimir, unlike Oryol, is not grim at all. Well, that's a lie. Of course it's grim. It's in Russia. So, it's lonely and bleak and sad and beautiful and sits quaking in the unimaginable vastness of the landscape, knowing that nothing can make it safe. But apart from that it's quite nice. It's a tourist town with a big monastery and millions of beautiful churches. Not a tourist town as one might understand that in the West. It hasn't got nice hotels, expensive shops or pretty cafés. But there are stalls that sell guidebooks and, under Communism, it was one of the places, a stop on the 'Golden Ring' tour, that foreigners came to so it was kept relatively clean and didn't get too built up or polluted (only a little bit). A lot of the old houses survived and there are original market rows which now have shops in them again. The tram lines are still working and most people don't look as if they are actually dying of hunger.

It's not far from Moscow at all but it felt a fucking long way with Don McCaughrean in the car, let me tell you. He burst into tears about every ten minutes, droning on about letting Donchik down at the same time as swigging bottles of beer.

'You haven't let anybody down, you stupid bastard,' I explained to him. 'This is who you are. You fuck up a lot. Then you say sorry. You weren't a skinny teetotaller when she met you and she loved you then. Donchik couldn't give a fuck if you have the odd beer. Stop going on about it.'

'It was that little tooth...' he droned from the back seat. 'That tiny little tooth.'

'Yes. You said.' I sighed.

Part of me was pleased to have the old Don back, but a large part of me felt sorry for Ira. So she had another child to look after just like Misha's wife did. Don would say sorry and he would be so remorseful that there would be no room for her own anger at him for not holding it together and being a support for the family. She would end up comforting him for the fact that he'd behaved like an arsehole. Nothing in it for her at all—it was all about Don. I suppose his ex-wife would recognise this narcissism very well. And Ira would look after the baby and Ira would look after Don and Ira would get old with the weight of responsibility firmly on her shoulders forever. Fuck me, if Eden Jones thinks I'm giving it all up to live in a cottage with roses round the door he can fuck off.

'What's that, Faithy?' Don wondered. I think I must have unwittingly said 'fuck off' out loud.

'Nothing, love. Nothing for you to worry your pretty head about,' I told him, craning round to see if he'd got ugly again. He had.

'We're not really dressed for a funeral, Zanetti,' he pointed out.

'Bollocks,' I said. He was right. I was so excited about how close I was to finding out what was going on with all this crap that I'd sort of forgotten that this was going to be an actual funeral with a coffin and people crying. Adrian wasn't going to turn out to be miraculously still alive and dealing cars or whatever. Adrian really was dead. Killed, I could swear, by Misha. This thing was about Misha and I could almost taste it. Dimitri had always been scared of him. Why did Misha come round to our place and murder those twins? Fuck knows. But he did, and then he made it Dimitri's job to tidy up for him.

'Never mind,' I said. 'We both look pretty depressed. That'll have to do.'

Arkady, who had been unusually silent all the way, suddenly spoke. 'I once fell in love in Vladimir,' he said. 'The most beautiful girl I've ever seen. She wore a blue dress the day I made love to her down in those fields over there.'

I looked across at him and saw that he had tears in his eyes. Don and I both looked over at the fields, a muddy wasteland with a light covering of grey snow. Perhaps it had been different back then.

'Her dad was Jewish. Worked at the university. When he got sent to Siberia she and her mum moved out there to be near the camp. We lost touch,' he said, and went quiet again. God, this country.

By the time we got to the place on the other side of town we were all funereally subdued. The church was behind high red monastery walls that would once probably have been painted white. There were three black Mercedes almost blocking the forty foot high arched wooden gates, and Arkady pulled up behind them and got his magazine out. Don and I had to walk sideways to get past the cars into the monastery enclosure itself. There were a few spindly trees poking up among the gravestones and some of those enormous grey and black crows lurched around pecking at the ground. The service had started, and when we walked through the double doors to get into the church, nobody turned to look at us. It was immediately clear that this place had only just been turned back into a church. It was more like a town hall or maybe a local museum. There were a few empty display cabinets and marks on the walls where things had been taken down. At the altar a few icons had been put up but they were brassy and new and lacked the majesty they needed to truly impart the presence of God. The priest waved his censer bravely, but it couldn't muffle the smell of bleach. The mourners stood round the coffin which was, I saw when I got close and stood on my tiptoes behind a woman wearing a lot of perfume, open.

They do normally do this as a matter of course, but you would have thought that when the deceased was actually missing vital pieces of his head, someone might have made an exception to the rule. Nope. There he was, lying in front of the ten people who loved him best (or so I briefly imagined), half his face and most of his head covered by a black cloth. There was no hiding what lay beneath it, though. The rest of his face and head had collapsed with the lack of bone to support it and was an almost two dimensional thing, lying flat and too spread out on top of an ordinary looking, if very short, body in a black suit. I put my hand over my mouth but Don, good old Don, started taking pictures. The woman standing nearest Adrian's head and chanting the prayers along with the priest looked up at the first click, but seemed not to fully understand what was happening, or at least not to care. She was wearing a short arctic fox jacket, tight black trousers, an Hermès silk scarf, very very high heels with gold chains across the ankle and expensive sunglasses on her head. She was heavily, but well, made up. And not crying. From her position and the way she was leading the ceremony I decided that this must be his wife. The blokes I assumed must be Adrian's children stood next to her, old enough not to be little boys but young enough not to be teenagers. Maybe ten and twelve or eleven and thirteen. They both wore black cashmere jumpers and black jeans and both had a pierced ear with a gold stud through it. Their heads were fashionably shaved and they fidgeted and sniggered. Neither showed the remotest interest in the coffin. Both of them had a look, a familiar turn to their mouths. But I couldn't say that either of them really looked like Adrian. Then there were a few old people and a couple of shabby blokes, presumably from the local village. But no tears. No wailing. At the absolute most a mild interest. I suppose the burial of ex-cons is no big affair.

I cried though. I did. It was just a couple of weeks since Mum's funeral, after all. For God's sake. Not that that had much in common with this. And I was so mixed up somehow in what Dimitri had done to Adrian. And I cried too for how long ago we had known each other and how young we were and how happy. Well, everything's relative.

When the mourners, such as they were, started moving away from the coffin I stayed behind a second. I supposed the burial would be later. Perhaps tomorrow. The idea was that people could come and pay their respects. I thought it more likely that the suit might get nicked. Don followed the crowd out, clicking and shuffling and running in front of them. God knows what he was trying to get. Just something for his private collection, I suppose.

I stood by the coffin and fished around in the pocket of my jeans. I pulled a dollar bill out from the roll I had scrumpled in there and I tucked it into the side of the box, by his hand.

'There you go, Adrian,' I said. 'Have a dollar.'

I wished I'd brought some beef jerky too. I understand those ancient burial rites that involve giving the dead lots of nice things to eat. It seems so awful to just leave them there like that, no food or water, no company, nothing comforting to take with them on their way. I wished I had put something in Mum's coffin. The nativity set I'd bought her in Bethlehem maybe. Or some photos. I know it's silly, but seeing Adrian there like that I wanted to put a blanket over him and hold his hand for the journey. But I suppose he'd already started on it.

Don was outside sharing a beer with one of the shabbier-looking members of the funeral party. Adrian's wife, who

really did not look like a physics professor, was smoking a cigarette very elegantly indeed. I went and introduced myself.

'Hi. I'm Faith. I was a friend of Adrian's, of Kolya's, years
ago. We worked on the same magazine in the eighties,' I said,
stamping up and down a bit. It was getting cold and the huge
birds were circling the trees. The trees didn't look as if they
could possibly take the weight of these things.

She looked me up and down, disbelieving. 'Hi,' she said,
barely parting her extremely glossy lips, at once invitingly
and dismissively. I thought she must confuse a lot of men.
She was very obviously blanking life out, perhaps for the sake
of her children. There is a certain type of Russian woman,
pragmatic to the point of cruelty. There are places here that
westerners would hardly believe exist—their inhospitable
brutality something that we generally don't have to contend
with. And they were born beautiful and saw a way out so they
took it. Don't ask them any questions and don't expect them
to explain themselves. I wondered what she was like as a little
girl in her closed nuclear town or wherever it might have been,
picking mushrooms with her granny, having her hair pulled
into tight ribboned bunches.

'Um. I went to see him in prison the other day, actually. I
went to see him because he was there under the name of my
ex-husband, my husband, Dimitri.'

Valera Kuznyetsova's face remained almost completely
expressionless. None of this, presumably, can have been
a surprise to her. She did just perceptibly raise an eyebrow,
though, in a mockery of surprise, but it was a gesture of total
lack of concern. What was, however, surprising to me was
how amazingly rich she obviously was. And how clearly well
travelled. You don't develop the blow-dried lipsticky look of
the wealthy Lebanese by hanging around the outskirts of
Vladimir.

'Do you, er, do you still live in the area then?' I wondered.

'Still got the house. The boys come with my mother a bit,' she said, softly. 'We're mostly based in Berlin.' Russian grannies usually do the childcare. Going to Granny's can mean going to the Urals or to Tashkent or to Samara for six months or more. Russians in England usually get Granny over a couple of months even before the birth.

The Russo-German boys in question were standing behind a tomb smoking a cigarette. Their attempt to hide this was pitiful. Or perhaps that was the point.

'Did you see Adrian at all, while he was inside?' I asked, lighting my own cigarette. It was very nearly dark now, and all the grimmer in this provincial Russian churchyard for that.

'Nyet.' She shook her head. 'A guy came and told me to keep quiet, to leave it alone. So I kept quiet, left it alone. I thought this would happen sooner.'

'Someone told you not to contact your own husband ever again and he would soon be dead and you obeyed them?' I was raising my voice slightly now.

Valera shrugged. She had met my eye only once, and during this whole conversation she had looked as though she was glancing around for someone. Also, she was over six foot tall and had to look down to meet my eye in any case. Languorous to the point of near death, she clearly could not be bothered to move her head to that extent. Or, at least, wanted to come across that way. Just Adrian's type, though. Everybody's type really. That's why these women export so well. Super models, trophy wives.

'He gave me money. A lot of money.' Her lips turned up slightly at the memory of how much. And I didn't blame her. Not really. There are decisions to be made in life and she'd taken one. For herself. For her sons. 'And passports for

me and the boys. German ones. So...' she concluded. So. I
did what anyone sensible would do. That was the implica-
tion. And after all, she left hanging in the air, I only married Adrian because he told me he was American. Had she
felt duped when he revealed he only had a Soviet passport
himself? Was she already pregnant with the first boy when
she found out?

'What did the...er...what did the guy look like?' I asked.

'What guy?' She stared at me now as if I was mad.

'With the money,' I said, breathing out smoke into the
cold air like a dragon.

'Oh, him,' she said, looking away again. 'Big guy. Prison
tattoos. Shaved head. He brought this huge cat with him...'

She remembered everything about the day her life
changed. She could probably have talked about it for hours.
But she didn't have to. Misha.

At last a smile spread across her face and she waved madly,
walking quickly towards one of the black Mercedes.

'Hans!' she cried, as a man in a long camel coat held up
some car keys and smiled back at her. 'Boys!' she commanded
as she broke into a run. The boys followed, arguing child-
ishly. And in German. Hans had disappeared into one of the
cars and mother and children ducked down to get in too. The
headlights on all three cars came on simultaneously, blinding
the rest of us in their glare, and they swept off into the night
like a prime ministerial motorcade.

I trod my cigarette end into the mud. 'OK, let's go,' I
said to Don, turning round to face him. No Don. I went back
inside the church. No Don. I wandered around outside near
the Volvo in which Arkady had fallen asleep. No Don. I saw a
neon sign across the potholed and unlit road that said *Café*. I
pushed the door open and went into the steamy, fluorescent-
lit room. A fat woman in a greyish-white apron and hat was

behind a counter ladling things out of big metal trays on to chipped white plates. Don was sharing a bottle of vodka with a bloke from the funeral.

'Fucking hell, McCaughrean. Come on! We've got to go!' I shouted from the doorway.

All the other men in there, all dining alone, hunched over their pelmeni (dumpling things), a mug of vodka by their plates—they all looked up at me, blank and swollen-faced. And they all looked down again.

'Come and have a shot, Faithy,' Don implored. 'For old times' sake.'

'What old times, you idiot?' I said and stood by their plastic table as Don poured me a drink into his glass. I knocked it back and wiped my mouth. Don's new friend held out a piece of salami and I took it. Russians take the advice that one shouldn't drink without eating very literally. Surely it means that if you have a good meal you can drink another couple of glasses of wine and no harm done. Just because you eat a gherkin or some salami after every shot of vodka it doesn't mean it isn't eating your insides away. It does take the wincing aftertaste off though.

'Come on, boozy. Let's be off,' I said.

Don and his mate hugged and kissed each other three times on the cheek as if they'd just been remembering their old army days.

We crossed the road arm in arm, Don and I, and got barked at by a stray dog. Arkady woke up and started the engine in one motion when I knocked on the window.

'What a fucking great bloke he was,' Don said. 'Teaches phonetics at the school where Adrian and Valera used to work. Said there was no way Adrian was American. He picked Valera up on her first day at work after leaving university. Just started humming "Oh say can you see" and she melted, apparently.'

I laughed.

'Hey, Zanetti. You don't think Ira...?'

I laughed again. 'No, Don, I don't. If Ira wanted to go and live in London she would get a job with a big bank and move to London. It's not like that any more. Not for women like Ira, anyway. She actually likes you, I think,' I said, staring out at the dark road. The snow was coming thick and steady now. There would be a covering in the morning.

'I love that woman, Faith. She is a wonderful, wonderful woman,' he said, and burst into tears. I was beginning to think there might be something in this teetotal business.

We got back to the flat to find Eden at his computer drinking a bottle of red wine. It was odd to keep coming home to someone. I've never done it before. 'Hi, honey,' I sneered. I'm not good at these things.

'Hey,' he said, looking up slightly sleepily, not noticing my ironic tone. He ruffled his hair and shut the lid of his computer. 'You're late.'

'Went to Adrian's funeral in Vladimir. It was fucking weird,' I said, coming into the room, followed by Don. The vodka had hit him hard and he could barely stand.

'Wotcha, Jones,' he said.

Eden raised his eyebrows to question me.

'He fell off the wagon last night. Something to do with the baby's tooth,' I explained. 'He's going to have to stay until he's cleaned up.'

'Right.' Eden nodded, smiling. He was as pleased as I was, I think. 'Ira called looking for you, McCaughrean,' he said, and Don blanched.

'Shit,' he said. 'What do I do?'

I sat down at the table and took a sip of Eden's wine. 'Show her some fucking respect, McCaughrean,' I said. 'She's not your mother. Tell her you've been drinking and you don't want her to see you like this. You'll be up and running again in the morning.'

Don nodded. 'Right. Right. Yeah,' he said, opening and shutting, unzipping and zipping all his pockets to look for his phone. When he found it he hobbled towards the bathroom to make his private call.

'So,' Eden said. 'A funeral?'

I sighed. 'God, it was weird. It turns out Adrian's wife lives in Berlin with some new bloke and they use the Vladimir house as a dacha or whatever. She's seriously rich and apparently Misha, who I'll tell you about in a minute, anyway, he's a bloke Dimitri used to work for, really evil guy, came round and paid her off. Not like she even cared by the sounds of it that her husband was going to be incarcerated until the end of time under a false name… Come to think of it, how did she even know he was dead? Must be our Misha again…ugh.'

Eden poured more wine out. 'Get your own glass,' he said. I pushed my chair back and went into the kitchen. 'So who's Misha?' he shouted.

'He's this… He's a thug. The one who went to beat Scott up. Some kind of mafioso friend of Dimitri's. Dimitri's daughter was round there, at Misha's.'

Eden humphed. It began to dawn on me that he was really disgusted by the Scott thing. 'Scott Weisman. What does that make it? Forty-seven?'

'Oh, for fuck's sake. It was fifteen years ago,' I said, nudging him hard. He had the radio on a pop channel and switched it off.

'Yeah, I know,' he said, smiling. 'I know. He phoned,' he added. 'Weisman. His flat got completely trashed while he was here last night. He's spooked and says he's sleeping at the office and to call him.'

I was chilled by this news. The closer I got to the centre of this thing the less clear it was becoming. I felt sick again and got up to go to the loo.

'You went to *see* this Misha character?' Eden asked me as I went.

'Yeah. I told you. And Tina was there, talking about having seen her dad ten minutes ago, totally relaxed about the whole deal as though nothing's going on. *I don't get it*,' I said, throwing out my arms and running now to the toilet. I made it just in time. Was vodka suddenly not agreeing with me?

On my way back past the bedrooms, I saw Don, passed out in his clothes on the lower bunk. That's the Don McCaughrean I know and love, I thought.

Chapter 14

'Fuck ALL THESE funerals,' Eden said. 'Let's go out.'

So we left Don to his own devices, such as they were, and, when I'd more or less recovered, we went out for dinner at Skandinavia. It's a restaurant on Pushkin Square, near where I used to work with Adrian, though it's all unrecognisable now. The monstrous old concrete cinema is a casino and nightclub, lit up like Piccadilly Circus, and the little hut where we used to queue for something they called pizza but wasn't is now the entrance to a French restaurant with white linen cloths and a real sommelier from Paris. The rich Russians like to feel that they are getting it right.

In summer Skandinavia puts tables out in the courtyard under big yellow awnings and they put a bar and kitchen outside where they do burgers and seared salmon and stuff. If you sit here for long enough you will eventually meet every ex-pat in Moscow. But in winter the outside path doesn't look like anywhere you could ever put anything. They don't clear the snow, giving it a fairy tale look, and the building is cutesy and wooden with an arched doorway and potted pines outside. Mostly they serve herring, which is, apparently, what they eat in Scandinavia. Oh, and crispbreads.

We ordered a bottle of Sancerre and sat in a smoky alcove (well, it was smoky after we got there) laughing about Don. The bloke from the *Independent* was there with his wife and he called over.

'They running your stuff, Zanetti?' he asked. 'I can't get a spider's arse in with the fucking elections.'

'Nothing,' I said, trying to look disappointed. Seriously, though, if there was some big terror attack, like if the explosion at GUM had been a hostage taking thing or something, I probably wouldn't even know Adrian was dead yet. I certainly wouldn't be able to be schlepping out to Vladimir for the funeral of every Tom, Dick and Harry that my ex had managed to get sentenced to life imprisonment. God, poor Adrian.

The explosion had been 100 per cent confirmed as a mafia thing. One of the shops hadn't been paying its protection money and was blown out of the building. But people are tense in Russia at the moment. Nobody has got over the Beslan tragedy (tragedy, obviously, being too small a word for what happened, all words being too small) and President Putin is milking the terrorism issue as enthusiastically as Bush. So the explosion really rattled people. There is an atmosphere of anything being thinkable now.

'Bummer,' the *Indy* bloke said, and his wife, who was wearing denim dungarees, rolled her eyes and lit a baby cigar.

'He can't stand to have to spend time with the family,' she said. Someone told me they had four or maybe five children. I mean, who would want to go home to that? Neither of them, obviously. The Russian nanny must be in control.

We walked home through the first slush of the year and Eden tried his pitch again. Though first he warmed me up with a few prison stories. There is a prisoner in Butyrka who thinks he's Jesus. Not only this but a lot of the other prisoners and even a fair percentage of the guards believe him. He's been healing them and stuff.

'He's in for armed robbery.' Eden laughed. 'Must say, my headache went away when he touched my forehead, though.'

We were walking down Tverskaya towards the Kremlin and people were pouring out of the Chekhov theatre where they were showing *Uncle Vanya*. Eden touched his forehead to demonstrate and then looked a bit serious as though he was beginning to wonder if maybe…

Butyrskaya prison is an ancient castle in the middle of Moscow and a truly ghastly place to be incarcerated. Prisoners here dream of living only four to a two-man cell, eating proper meals, ever watching television or reading a newspaper, being allowed out for exercise. They are usually around twenty to a two-man cell and they take turns sitting and lying down on the bunks. The suicide and murder rates are phenomenal and they leave the cell for about an hour a week. The stench from the slop buckets is enough to make the least queasy person in the world vomit immediately. Like the Crosses prison in St Petersburg where the poet Anna Akhmatova queued for days for news of her son in the 1930s, prisoners wave their pale hands pathetically out of the slats in the windows in the hope that a loved one will be there to see them. Then they spit notes over the walls through straws made of paper. Man's inhumanity to man, as practised by the incarcerated at Butyrka, would make Stalin himself weep.

'So, basically, since Jesus moved in, they're all washing each other's feet and sharing food and not torturing each other or anything,' Eden told me.

'That's brilliant. Can I steal your story?' I said, linking arms with him as we turned to pass the National Hotel and the

Tsar's old stables, a big exhibition hall until it burnt down last year. Now it's just a shell. Considering that they've knocked the Moskva Hotel down and the Intourist just up the road, it's surprising anyone has any idea where they are at all.

'I don't see why not really. It's only going to be a couple of lines in a wider piece so I can't do it justice myself. Have it,' he said.

'No. You're being stupid. It's so brilliant. Keep it.'

'Have it.'

'Keep it.

'Have it.'

'OK.'

Tamsin was going to love this. 'Is This Man Jesus?'

'D'you think we can get Don in to do a picture?' I asked.

'Don't see why not. The governor's really nice. Professional clarinet player,' Eden said, turning up towards the New Arbat and the old army surplus shop. This is a four-floor building taking up a whole block of road, probably about the size of Selfridges. Since everyone male used to serve in the army and a huge percentage of them stayed on and made a career out of it, this shop was once seething with people, bombarded with calls. 'Have you got a size forty-two sergeant major's greatcoat without the belt?' Now it's empty. Or have Nike already bought it?

'I'll tell you what, Faith Zanetti,' he said. 'I'll move my stuff out here from London. We'll both promise not to do any wars. You haven't done one since Iraq anyway. And we'll see how it goes.'

The war was still going on in Iraq, of course, but there wasn't the same blanket coverage that there had been at the start of the invasion. I laughed. 'I'll tell you what, Eden Jones. You finish your prisons thing. You go back to London or wherever the hell you like. And we'll see how it goes.'

We were quiet for the rest of our walk, which was another half an hour at least, and we soon dropped the linked arms thing to light our cigarettes. I told myself that I didn't want to hurt him. But I knew it was the other way round. I didn't want him to hurt me.

You can be a physical risk taker but that certainly doesn't mean you are an emotional risk taker. In fact, I expect that people who plunge into relationships, who are always in and out of love, risking their heart every time they see a beautiful creature in a white shirt with chocolatey eyes, don't need to go around ducking bullets and diving away from explosions. We all get our kicks in our own way. And the adrenalin rush is the same.

When we got 'home' (Don's home now too, for God's sake) Eden went straight into the shower and I went straight for the phone. I dialled six times and then gave up and booked a call through the inter-town operator. If you're dialling Vorkuta you can expect trouble. They say that the only good thing to be said about the place is that it has a direct rail link with Moscow. It takes two days but at least it's there. I imagine the teenagers hanging out at the station, gazing at it out of their windows with a mad longing, dreaming that one day they will board the train towards the light. I am serious, incidentally, that it only ever gets light at all for a couple of months in the summer. It is a part of the world that was not meant to be inhabited. But Stalin was good at that.

'Connecting you now,' the operator said.

'Thanks. Mrs Varanova?' I asked, hearing a woman's voice at the end of the line.

'Yes. I am Varvara Varanova,' she said.

The name Varvara always reminds me of a rhyme Dimitri once told me to try and curb my curiosity about his life. 'Lyubopytnaya Varvara, na bazarye, nos otorvali.' Curious Barbara had her nose ripped off at the bazaar.

'Hello. My name is Faith Zanetti. I am so sorry to bring this up after so long,' I said, slightly nervous. I so didn't want her to hang up on me.

'Is this about the twins?' she asked. 'When we get a call from Moscow it is usually about the twins.'

She sounded composed. Almost eager. Maybe she didn't get to talk about them as much as she would have liked. I think this often happens to bereaved people. Everyone always dances round the subject in order to avoid offence, but I have found in life that people are absolutely dying to talk about their deceased. So to speak.

'Yes. It is I'm afraid. But I don't have new information or any information at all really,' I said, and I could hear a disappointed exhalation. Eden came out of the shower wrapped in a towel and I gestured wildly to him to supply me urgently with a cigarette and a vodka. These mimes are more difficult to perform than you might imagine when you are having a very delicate telephone conversation, the other end of which is the end of the earth. 'I was their next door neighbour in Moscow and I was there the night of the murder, though I was asleep or out when it actually happened, I think. It was a long time ago and I was young...'

'Yes, dear,' the woman said, reassuringly. She could hear my awkwardness and felt for me. I really really didn't want to tell her that I was one of the suspects.

'Anyway, I was wondering really whether you thought there was anything that the investigation missed. Anything you wanted to... You see, a friend of mine was in prison and died there. And he didn't do it. And I'm trying to find out who did do it.'

There was a long pause and I really thought she'd hang up. I drank the shot of vodka Eden put in front of me and rapped my fingers on the top of the bureau.

'Well, Faith...it is Faith, isn't it? I think they did get the right man. My little Yelyena, Lena, should never have married him and I told her so at the time. He was a nice enough boy but she knew he had problems with jealousy even before he proposed. He had already threatened one of her other beaux with a knife and she should never have married him. But she was pregnant and it was so difficult for young people in those days. They needed an apartment and they would never have got one if they hadn't married. Lenochka refused to have an abortion.'

She was babbling now, telling me the whole story, but my attention didn't wander. Everything was starting to fall into place and my stomach was dropping away from my body. Then she stopped.

I waited for her to speak again but I could tell that she was crying, so I was as still as I could be. Frozen to the spot. And as the world was changing, Eden was in the next room, tapping at his computer, as though the snail was in his shell. I couldn't believe he wasn't here, holding my hand, looking as stricken as I felt. I wanted to call out to him but I thought I might lose Varvara Varanova.

She pulled herself together and I looked out at the snow falling thick and fast again now, blurring the headlights of the cars so far below, and settling on all the window ledges of the Ukraine Hotel, making a meringue out of a Gothic horror.

'If only he hadn't come and taken the baby. If only he hadn't taken the baby,' she said, weeping again, sobbing for her own lost babies and the only grandchild she might ever have had.

'Mrs Varanova,' I said, trying to stay a bit calm, trying to keep the tremor out of my voice. 'I know where the baby is. She is OK. In fact, she is very well indeed. I know where she is.' As I said it, it suddenly occurred to me that perhaps I wouldn't be able to find her again. I clenched my eyes shut with the agony of the situation. I knew Varvara Varanova wouldn't dare believe me.

'Valentina. You know where our little Valentina is. Vladimir! Volodya!' she called, screaming into the childless emptiness of her flat. 'Volodya! She is found!'

I could hear a man rush to the phone. I heard them hug. Varvara began to laugh and cry with joy and Vladimir Varanov took the receiver just as I was saying, 'She calls herself Tina. In the western manner.'

Chapter 15

I WAS WOKEN up in the morning by Ira McCaughrean banging on my front door, Donchik grizzling in her arms. It was an hour before Natasha was due to arrive and the persistent bell-ringing and knocking had failed to rouse any of the resident blokes. I was bleary and staggering, half thinking it might still be the middle of the night.

'Hi, Ira,' I said, opening the door wide in my T-shirt and pants to let her in.

I had not slept well. I dreamt I lived in an American sort of 1970s concrete house deep in a forest, with lots of plastic furniture and big metal-framed windows. I was walking around it and it was my house. I had lived there for ages. But every door I opened showed me an unfamiliar room and I couldn't find the light switches. I went into five or six rooms before I woke up in breathless terror.

For hours I lay and thought about Tina and her grandparents, and Dimitri. I had promised them I would get her to call them, though it was not within my authority to do this by any stretch of the imagination. Had Dimitri already been married to Yelyena, to Tina's mother, when he married me? If so, maybe I was not technically married to him at all?

'Where is he?' Ira asked me, throwing her coat into a heap underneath the coat rack and laying Donchik on the floor in the front room to tug at his snow suit.

'In the spare room. Passed out in his clothes. He should be OK today,' I said. 'He was out by about seven yesterday. He's very ashamed of himself.' I don't know why I was defending him. They were both adults and what they did was their business. I suppose I just didn't want her to take his relapse too seriously, especially as I imagined he'd be doing it relatively often.

'Ashamed of himself? Ashamed of himself. Not worried that Ira might not be able to cope with Donchik by herself? Not concerned that Ira might be afraid for him? Just ashamed of himself,' she said. I appreciated her point.

'Coffee?' I offered.

'Yes. Please,' she smiled, sighing and following me into the kitchen with the baby on her hip.

Irochka is incredibly well turned out. Even today, in her relationship trauma, her nails were unchipped and her skin was pale and flawless. Her hair was a neat bob these days and she wore tight jeans and high-heeled boots, a lilac cashmere cardigan and diamond studs in her ears. I mention this because I was in a greying T-shirt and a pair of M&S white cotton pants with my hair a huge, tangled Afro and my eyes puffy with exhaustion and hangover. To make matters worse I lit a cigarette.

'I don't want him to come back, Faith,' she said, resting Donchik on a counter and making him gurgle by touching his nose and smiling.

'Ira,' I said, spooning coffee out of the packet into the cafetiere and lighting the stove with the gas clicker. 'It's really none of my business. You'll have to tell Don all this.'

Ira was undeterred. 'I know that. And I'm going to. I just want to chat to a woman about it first. You know, get it clear in my head. And you are the only woman I know who knows Donald.'

I was flattered. I'm not normally considered to be another woman. I'm often an honorary man (especially in the Middle East where if they considered me to be fully female it would be hard for me to do my job) or one of the lads though, obviously, in sexual situations I am a woman. And I have female friends in the press pack, sure. But they don't come to talk to me specifically because of my gender as Ira was doing here. Perhaps it's a Russian thing.

'Oh,' I said. 'Sure.'

'He seemed so manly in Baghdad. So in control. And I didn't mind him drinking. For a Russian woman to rule out a man who drinks would be suicidal. But he was protective.'

'Yes,' I said, putting the pot on the stove, my cigarette clamped between my lips.

'I'm not saying I need any protection. Of course I can protect myself. But I was moved that he offered it. I felt I could rely on him. But the night the baby was born, Don was so frightened he had to leave the room. I was in there on my own with the midwife and he couldn't even hold my hand because he was so frightened.'

'I see,' I said, thinking that I'd much rather have a baby without Don McCaughrean in the room, given the choice.

'It's not that I needed him there. I wasn't scared. I'm Russian. But he stopped offering his protection that night. And he's still sweet and gentle. Naturally he is. But he's so obsessed with the idea that his new happiness means he has to kick all his addictions—cigarettes, alcohol, danger—that it's become more important to him than I am.'

'So, you didn't ask him to...?'

'Of course not!' She laughed. 'I liked that he felt able to live without his props now that he had me, but then I started feeling…I don't know. I started feeling like it wasn't because he was liberated that he didn't need his props any more. It was because he had me as one big prop to replace the others. He was leaning on me so hard that the other stuff became superfluous.'

I nodded. God, she had it all worked out. 'I'm just going to put my jeans on. Will you watch the coffee? Turn it off when it's finished bubbling.'

'When it bubbles,' she confirmed, imitating the way I said 'bubbles' in Russian with my English accent.

'No.' I waved my finger. 'When it goes quiet after it has… you know…bubbled.'

We both laughed and I went to get a bit more dressed.

It was muggy in the bedroom and the light was golden because of the dark yellow curtains. There was an ashtray by the side of the bed and a glass with red wine dregs in it. Eden emerged from the tangle of duvet.

''S up?' he asked.

'Ira's here,' I told him.

'Oh God,' Eden groaned, and turned over with the duvet pulled up over his head.

Ira had poured the coffee out and got milk out of the fridge by the time I got back. Donchik was sitting on the floor playing with a set of keys and Ira was at the table smoking one of my cigarettes.

'Sorry, I stole one…' she said.

'Please.' I smiled.

'Anyway, what I'm saying is that I thought…well, I thought he would ease the burden of life. That when we were a couple I could relax and let him take half the load. But it didn't work like that. I ended up with my load and then his as well. And with a baby…well. With a baby that's not possible.'

I sat down with her and sighed, taking a sip of my coffee. 'No. But it's what most women do, isn't it?' I said.

'I am not most women,' Ira pointed out, quite correctly.

'No. You are not. And nor am I,' I laughed. 'Sorry. I was just being cynical. I think you were perhaps a bit romantic about it if you really thought... Well, it's just that most married women I see are simply carrying the whole thing off for everyone. Alone. It's what I've always wanted to avoid.'

Ira put her cigarette out, half smoked. She had wanted to experiment with the use of a prop, but it hadn't worked. 'Yes. Most women do end up looking after themselves and everyone else. Do you imagine I didn't know that? I have parents, you know. But I believe...I believe in love. I think it's much less common than people think. I think you are lucky if you capture the smallest glimpse of it. Like a little flicker of an angel's wing, just to prove they exist. And then—gone! But if you can catch it... Well, it's what operas are about, Faith. It's what literature and poetry are about. It's our glimpse of God on earth and you have to be looking or you will never find it. If you have decided not to look then you don't stand a chance.'

At this point Donchik toppled over forwards and banged his head on the side of the cupboard. Ira ran to scoop him up into her arms and he buried his face, red and crumpled in shock and misery, in her breast.

I had not been expecting a lecture in spirituality. Her speech had left me watery-eyed. Having once been someone who hadn't shed a tear for years, my breakdown in Qatar had left me almost permanently weeping, Prozac or no Prozac. I felt pathetic in a way, but in another way it was a bit of relief. Surprisingly, it does actually make you feel a bit better afterwards. This was news to me at the time.

'Yes. You are right. Of course, you are right. But love doesn't mean... Well, it doesn't mean that you're going to make it,' I said, finishing my coffee and lighting another cigarette.

'No. No, it doesn't at all. But I think that's such a waste, don't you? We could have made it. But he is so tied up in himself that he doesn't have room for me. You know?'

'Yes. I do know. I think I might be a bit like that. Eden's always... You know, Eden always wants me to...and I can't. I've got enough problems.' She was working my own interview technique on me. Be confessional yourself and everyone starts confessing like crazy.

'But maybe he could help you with your problems? Maybe he could take half the load? Everyone can see you two are made for each other,' she smiled, as though I was a mad blind woman, the only one who couldn't see that the emperor was naked. 'I just wish Don had tried. I wish he could have seen me there with my arms open to him, instead of looking around him everywhere and finding a mirror,' she said, getting up with Donchik now fast asleep in her arms. 'Would you mind telling Don that I booked him a room at the National and his stuff's in the lobby? I'd tell him myself but I don't want to wake him. And I don't want to hear his pleas. More responsibility at my door. No thanks. I've had enough. Vsyo,' she said. 'Vsyo.'

I followed her to the front door in a bit of a panic. I wished she hadn't left me with the message for Don but I thought she was absolutely right about what he would do and what that would mean for her. He loved her, but he was an introspective selfish bastard too. I was almost pleased that he hadn't changed too much. It had been disconcerting.

Ira kissed me three times and then came back for a hug. 'Thanks, Faith,' she said. 'Thank you for talking.'

OK then. Didn't really think I'd said much of use. She had been the picture of sagacity. Not me.

I shut the door and leant against it, thinking about what she'd said. At least I would have done if Don hadn't staggered out of the bedroom at this moment, his clothes crumpled, his face bloated, greasy strands of hair falling across his forehead, sweat patches in his shirt and a bottle of beer already in his hand.

'Hey, Zanetti. What's up? It's as hot as an A-rab's fucking armpit in here. Can't you turn the heating down?'

'No,' I said. 'It's controlled for the whole compound. Open the window.'

He was right and it is one of Russia's main problems. Well, I suppose there's Chechnya and unemployment and AIDS and everything. But apart from that, there is the heating. It comes on too late, after you have already been very very cold for a month. Then it comes on at such a blast that you sit around sweating until April. Getting ready to go out is appalling. It takes at least five minutes to get all your stuff on, by which point you are bathed in sweat. Then you step out of the front door and the sweat freezes to your skin. Shops and the metro are the worst. Weirdly, they are heated for the people who work there, all of whom wear short-sleeved thin cotton shirts. The public, who outnumber the staff by thousands to one, are in their outdoor clothes, sweltering in the dry and blistering heat in their fur hats, coats, jumpers, scarves and gloves. Then, in April, whether there is still snow on the ground or not, the heating goes off. In August there is no hot water throughout the city for three weeks while they do pipe repairs. You have to go the bath house and have a sauna. Which is nice, if not especially handy.

Don looked down at the beer in his hand and then he looked back up at me. 'I might give it another day before I go home, Faithy,' he said.

'Yeah,' I said. 'I should.' Perhaps I would tell him tomorrow. 'Listen. Make yourself at home, McCaughrean. I need to pop into the office. Eden found Jesus in Butyrka yesterday. I'm going to try and get us in. You'll do the art, won't you?'

'Totally. I've always wanted to meet Jesus,' Don said, swaying slightly. In my view, the meeting wouldn't do him any harm at all.

I put my boots on, picked up my jacket and took the lift downstairs. It had stopped snowing and the courtyard was slushy and, as ever, choked with the running engines of all the cars waiting for their occupants to appear from the doorways. There must have been hundreds of cars parked out here and another fifty trying to drive round the lot. That may be why I didn't at first notice the black Zil limousine juddering outside the office door. It was only when one of the blacked-out windows was rolled down and Tina leant out that my attention was really captured.

'Hey! Faith!' she yelled, smiling brightly, her piercings glinting in the dim light. 'Get in!'

She pushed open the door and jumped out, her vast bottom wobbling in a pair of khaki combat trousers. She had red Dr Martens on and a lime green puffa jacket. She was holding a cup of coffee from the Coffee Republic up near the Chaikovsky Conservatoire. She clicked her heels like a butler (or is it only Nazis who do this?) and bowed ironically to allow me to step into the vehicle.

'Er… OK,' I said, and tumbled in. Tina leapt in after me and plonked herself next to me in the black leather seat. It was very dark inside and the windows were actually curtained in frilly purple stuff like a Victorian hearse or something. It was only when my eyes adjusted to the light that I could see that Tina and I were facing Misha. And Dimitri.

Chapter 16

DIMITRI SMILED AT me. The same slightly boyish, slightly knowing smile he had given me outside the Bolshoi that night a hundred years ago, suggestive of sex and excitement and yet innocent and wondering at the same time. If I hadn't clamped it into place over the past couple of decades my heart might even have lurched. He looked older but it suited him. His thick black hair was now salt and peppery, completely grey over the temples. His oil-black eyes still glinted with energy, but also now with, well, maybe wisdom. He was better dressed than he used to be. Not tall, but broad-shouldered, he now wore a well-cut suit that showed that off. A white shirt, open at the collar, and black brogues that I was pretty sure had been bought in, or at least via, London.

'Hello, Faith,' he said.

All this time I had been so confused, so desperate to know what was going on, what had happened that night and why, so eager to find Dimitri and ask him, but now that he was sitting in front of me the calm that I had always associated with him swept over me. This was what Ira had just been talking about. I sat back in the seat of this sinister Zil limo, not sure whether or not I might actually be being kidnapped (after all, I hadn't tried to escape yet), and I relaxed for the first time in years. Dimitri had the situation under control, not me, and it seemed possible, just looking at him and how unruffled he was, that there was some perfectly reasonable explanation for everything. I smiled back at him.

'Hi, Dimitri.'

Misha didn't look at me. He behaved as though he was in some kind of trance, gazing into the middle distance, his huge hands clasped in his lap. I could see the bulges of his guns under his leather jacket. Dimitri appeared to be unarmed. Unusual.

Tina was grinning all over her face, triumphant. Maybe her dad had taken some persuading to see me, or maybe she was just stoned.

'How are you, Faith?' Dimitri asked me, a tender look in his eyes as though he had been longing for this meeting since he last saw me. I wondered what he must think of me now, my hair wild, my clothes shabby, my boots scuffed, my leather jacket smelling of smoke and wear. Could he see the girl from the Bolshoi in here somewhere? I felt that I had lost her. It seemed to me to be a very Russian thing to grieve for the loss of yourself as if for someone dead. This country was really beginning to get to me. And I was grieving.

I was weepy again, for God's sake. I was thinking of that Eric Clapton song that goes: 'Would you know my name, if I saw you in heaven?' That song always makes me think about my dad. He was killed when I was nine. Would he recognise me now, a thirty-five-year-old woman, her face lined with the more subtle scars of battle, her eyes aged by sorrow and all the long years? Would he know my name?

Dimitri looked at me as though he recognised me, as though he would have known me if I had been reincarnated as an elephant.

'I was sad when you left, Verochka,' Dimitri said quietly, not for a moment looking away from my eyes. Staring into them to catch my every thought. And he had always known, I remembered now, he had always seen what I was thinking about. Who I was thinking about. Sometimes it had been a little frightening, but his attention didn't leave me for a second.

'I'm sorry,' I said.

He waved a hand as if to put it all in the past, to show that he completely understood now, as he had done then. 'This is going to be the beginning of a beautiful friendship,' he declared in English, smiling.

'What?'

'It's the last line of *Casablanca*. I know it now. Not that any of this,' and here he went into English again, 'amounts to a whole hill of beans in this crazy world.'

I laughed and leant forward to touch his hand. 'Oh, Dimitri. Dima,' I said. 'I was nineteen.' God, what a stupid sodding way to dump someone that was. Pretentious. Affected. Ludicrous. Come to think of it, I don't think I had the faintest idea at the time what the line was. But I couldn't really have used *Top Gun* for a reference. Hardly the same romantic impact.

'I know,' he nodded, putting his hand on top of mine. It was only now that I registered that the car had been moving for some time. Tina was smoking a cigarette, Misha still staring ahead, the driver behind another piece of purple curtain, invisible in the front.

The past fifteen years, my whole adult life, seemed to have slipped away from me. We were discussing the end of our relationship as though I'd got on that plane the day before yesterday. I was embarrassed, felt self-conscious not to look so bright and so beautiful as I had done back then. It felt wrong that Dimitri was speaking so softly to this raddled old tart.

'Don't be ashamed,' Dimitri said, touching my hair with a smile. 'You are still beautiful, Verochka. You are as beautiful as you were that night at the theatre, out on the steps, holding the rose I gave you. Maybe more beautiful now that you are a woman.'

'I'm not ashamed, for fuck's sake,' I said in English, but quietly and to myself. I knew my defensive crap wouldn't wash with Dimitri. I had always known that. I felt naked and ridiculous. A gawky girl with braces being told she is a vision of loveliness. Tina caught my gaze and rolled her eyes as if to say, Dad's spouting his crap again.

When the car eventually stopped Dimitri got out and held the door for the rest of us. It was only at this point that Misha said, 'Zdorov.' Well, it was better than no greeting at all. And I remembered Adrian again and how we used to joke about people like Misha when we saw them in the street in our lunch break.

'Go and ask him what he thinks he's staring at,' I'd say, and Adrian would set off to do it and then change his mind and come back.

'He's really big though,' he'd say, whining, and we'd laugh.

We seemed to be down one of those streets that led to Tsvyetnoi Bulvar where the circus is and that old market that Dimitri and I used to go to. 'Isn't this where...' I began.

'Yes. Do you remember the market? They treated us like the tsar and tsarina there,' he said, smiling at me again.

Tina stamped her fag into the slush and stood, shifting her weight from one foot to the other, by the front door waiting for someone to come and open it. We were outside a huge grey apartment building which had probably once held communalki like ours, flats requisitioned by the Communists and made into communal hell-holes with a family per room, often as many as thirty people sharing a toilet. Now, though, the entrance had been surrounded by tall iron railings and an electric gate with a code that we must have come through in the car. Everything was clean, even the steps and the newly painted door itself, as black and shiny as 10 Downing Street. The whole place smelt of money.

'Dad! Come on! Fuck. I'm freezing,' Tina complained.

But it was Misha who finally put a key in the door and led us into a plush front hall with grey marble stairs carpeted in deep red and followed up towards an old wooden lift with gates by shiny brass banisters.

'Good morning, Mr Sakhnov,' an old lady with glistening grey hair smiled as we came in. She was sitting at a walnut desk, drinking tea from a chrome flask. 'Miss Tina,' she added. 'Sir, madam.'

We all said hello and Misha opened the lift gates so that we could get in. He pressed a button for the second floor. A button that may well have been made of ivory. Certainly of bone.

'Doing well,' I nudged Dimitri.

'Can't complain,' he laughed, somehow charmed as though I had made a hilarious joke that only he and I could possibly understand in all its many nuances.

We stepped out at the second floor and there were four doors here, all towering and vast, those twenty foot high double doors you get in Parisian apartment blocks. But here, three of the doors had been sealed. The locks had been removed and painted over, the gaps made solid. I understood that Dimitri's flat, assuming it was his flat, had once been four separate communal apartments, amounting probably to twenty rooms.

It took five minutes to access this lavish home, what with codes and keys and bars and things that beeped and flashed.

And then, at last, we walked into what can only be described as, though I doubt it was ever used as, a ballroom. Two hundred people could have danced here without bashing into each other and I could feel, just stepping inside, that the floor was, in fact, sprung, for Christ's sake. Sprung and made up of parquet hexagons, pieces of cherry, walnut, pine and something else, laid symmetrically and varnished so that the whole room sparkled. In the centre of the ceiling was a crystal chandelier big enough for a ballroom in the Winter Palace, and against one wall was the original floor to ceiling stove tiled in a kind of British racing green. It actually had a fire burning in it.

Dimitri coughed in both deference and command and a smiling, round-faced South American woman came rushing out of a side door to greet us. She was wearing a traditional black and white maid's uniform with a frilly apron and what looked like black tap shoes. Her Russian was heavily accented.

'Here you are. Here you are. Give me your coat, madam. Valentina, take your shoes off, dear.' She fussed around us, taking outdoor clothes, advising on choice of slippers from the pile and offering tea, coffee, hot chocolate. Well, the last fifteen years had been good to Dimitri. This was a long way from our grotty room in that communalka on Kolokolnikov Pereulok, where he ate sprats straight from the tin, smoked papirosi and went out with a gun shoved in his belt.

Misha shook hands with Dimitri and went back out of the front door. I heard the shuffle of his footsteps recede and tried to read Dimitri's glance—one of slight relief, perhaps.

'Holy shit,' I said, skidding into the middle of the room on my slippers. I spun round with my arms out. 'This is amazing.'

'It's yours,' Dimitri said, smiling at me indulgently, as though he'd put it all together especially for me.

'Hey, fuck off. What about me?' complained Tina, laughing, and putting her iPod headphones into her ears. She had the look of someone about to skulk off to her bedroom.

'What about you?' Dimitri shouted after her. 'I bought you a lovely flat.'

'I prefer it here,' she said. 'I miss Juanita.' Juanita smiled and kissed Tina's fat cheek which, incidentally, seemed to have a lot of blue glitter on it. Tina took a left and disappeared out of sight. Dimitri shook his head in parental despair.

'No. It's not mine, Dima. It's yours,' I pointed out.

'We are still married,' he said, nodding at Juanita's fifteenth offer of tea. 'So, if you want it...'

He held an arm out to show me into another room, a sort of study. He swaggered in with a walk that, though perhaps a bit too cowboyishly masculine, was safe and sexy. I saw a programme once, presented by the ghastly orange-haired Pip Deakin from the BBC (who hates me because I grassed him up once when he faked being sniped at and then I wouldn't sleep with him), about the body language of power. There was a shot of Clinton and Bush striding down a cloister somewhere. Pip said, 'Look at them trying to out-strut each other. This is not how normal people walk.' And nor was this.

There was a very ornate dark wooden fireplace in here that looked like the kind of thing you get in an English stately home. Again, a fire burned in the grate. In fact, the fire, though blazing happily, was rather dwarfed by the grate. I sat down in a large cream sofa that completely engulfed me and I looked around. There was a big photograph of Humphrey Bogart smoking a cigarette, incongruously positioned above the fireplace. A seventeenth-century portrait of an admiral might have been better suited to the spot. Dimitri stood next to it and looked up, pleased.

'It's an original. Karsh,' he said.

'Wow,' I nodded.

On another wall was another original—a movie poster for *Casablanca*, tastefully preserved behind glass. Next to it was a life size photograph of Ingrid Bergman, cut out around her curves. Perhaps it had stood up at the door to a cinema in Hollywood once. But now it was laminated and fixed to Dimitri's wall. I was beginning to get it.

The coffee table in front of me held a white vase of pink roses. It was the flower I wore in my hair at our wedding and he assumed it was my favourite, though actually I don't think I have ever had any flower-related preferences. I knew in a flash that when Juanita came in with the tea it would be Earl Grey. Would there be digestive biscuits too? All the things I had teased him about not being able to provide.

'Oh God, Dima...' I started to say, but I didn't know how I might continue. I had no answer to all this. I felt that he really could have spent fifteen years creating my dream home in the hope of one day luring me to it. I had forgotten this too. He had loved me. But too much. Much too much.

'Don't say anything now,' he smiled. 'Just stay. Faith. Please. Just stay a day or two and then make up your mind. You have to give me another chance.' He was kneeling down by me now and, oh God, he was actually holding a small egg-shell blue box with a bow around it. He looked up at me in what might have been supplication, but there was a twinkle of real power in his eye, of knowing I would melt, of knowing he could make me do anything. It was a kind of madness.

I needed a bath, I needed some sleep, I needed a drink. I needed to get the fuck out of here. A knot in my stomach warned me that this might be harder than I might like.

It was a Tiffany box and I, a war correspondent for God's sake, a shabby, alcoholic, chain-smoking woman old enough to have a family of seven, opened it. I pulled at the ribbon and took off the lid and removed the tissue paper, just like a pretty heroine in the film's final scene. It was huge. A huge, huge diamond on a gold band. I would hardly be able to lift my hand up with this on. But I tried it, and it fitted and it was... well, it was kind of fucking incredible.

'I'm sorry,' he said, standing up again now and lighting two cigarettes, one for each of us. 'I couldn't afford it last time.'

'Dima,' I said, shaking my head and staring at the rock. 'I can't.'

'Of course you can. Don't do this English crap. Take it. You don't like it? Sell it. Don't give me any—ooh, no, I couldn't possibly...'

I laughed. He did good impressions of English people, albeit in a heavy thuggish Russian accent.

'It is a present. I will be offended if you don't take it. Do what you like with it afterwards.'

'OK. You're right,' I said. 'Sorry.'

And anyway, I did like it.

I hadn't noticed the tea and biscuits arriving. I took a bite out of one of the digestives, trying out moving with the ring on.

'Just a couple of days,' Dimitri said.

'Dima, I don't have a couple of days. I need to talk to you about the Varanovy. I'm being accused of this murder. I came to see you in prison and I found Adrian. Now he's dead. He said you forced him to confess to those murders as you. And Scott Weisman told me you beat him up. And Adrian's wife said Misha paid her off and... Dimitri, you have to tell me what's going on!'

I suddenly remembered Scott's message. I hadn't called him back but I just couldn't believe that his new robbery could be related. I mean, it was all a thousand years ago for the Lord's sake. Wasn't it?

I took a sip of tea and started to feel calm again. There was an edge of madness to Dimitri that I could see now, in the flat, in the obsession with *Casablanca*, in the biscuits and the tea.

'I know. It's time,' he nodded, squatting in front of the fire with his cigarette, his eyes grave. 'We've got to protect you. I'm worried Adrian might have told them something.' He looked at me, guarded, checking my reaction, preparing his own.

'Hello?' I said in English.

'Something to incriminate you. There was a rumour… you have to understand that with these businesses…you know I bought the mines in Vorkuta? Big businesses, you know— there's always trouble. I've been using other names for years. But I worried it would reach Adrian somehow. I put out a rumour I'd been killed in a car crash. Had a guy turn my car over up there, put a body in it, set it on fire… Partly a tax question. Tina officially owns the business now.'

It flickered through my mind to ask where they got the body, but it seemed like a mere detail just at the moment.

'It turns out Adrian did hear the rumour and he always said, when he offered to go down for you, he always said that when I died he'd tell the truth and get himself out of there. He'd say he was Adrian Smith and I was Dimitri Sakhnov and it would all be over. I think we both thought… I was taking drugs then and you were safely back in London… I don't think either of us believed it would be more than a year or two before the vint killed me. And I didn't care. As long as you were safe …'

I realised I was holding my biscuit in mid-air, the ring catching the firelight and sending dramatic glares around the room. 'When he offered…' I began, and realised that my voice hadn't come out right. I coughed and started again, lowering the biscuit to the plate. 'When he offered to go down for me?' I shouted now, shrill and weird.

Dimitri laughed at me. 'Absolutely. You don't think he loved you too? I tried to persuade him not to do it. He was adamant. Almost keen. You remember how mad he was? They started talking about extradition, you see. I hid all the evidence...and I had a good contact inside...but in the end ...'

'What the fuck is vint?' I asked him, but something in the back of my mind knew. I'd read a piece about it somewhere. That woman from the LA *Times* did something on it. They gave it to pilots to keep them awake in the war.

'Oh, God. Verochka, it was a dark time. My heart was broken,' he said, and he punched the wall. Quite hard. 'You don't know what it was like. You never knew. You were from another planet. I grew up here. One of my uncles died in the mines in Vorkuta; my father drank himself to death after they took his Party card away. My school friends—drunks, suicides, prison. This place was forgotten by God. This was not somewhere for human beings. And you...standing there at the theatre, your little face so happy and gentle. From another world. You were the only light in my life. You were my hope, my escape... My Faith.'

I took another sip of my tea and it was only this second sip that tipped me off. There was a bitter taste that wasn't to do with the slice of lemon. There was medication in here and my limbs were already feeling too heavy to move.

'You bastard,' I said, tipping the rest of the tea on to the floor. 'It's fucking drugged.'

Dimitri smiled and walked over to me, calming me with his assurance. 'Faith. I asked Juanita to put a couple of drops of valerian in there. I knew we'd be having a difficult talk. It's herbal. There's nothing that can harm you in there. You know I would never harm you.'

God, was this true? I tried again to move and this time it didn't seem so hard. Was I overreacting?

'I've got some in mine too, you know,' he said, and laughed, sitting down next to me and taking my jewelled hand in his.

There was a pause during which I concentrated hard on not throwing up. It seemed like a bad moment to vomit.

'The vint was terrible. I was injecting. I heard voices, I didn't sleep. I never slept. I didn't go and see Tina for a long time. She was living with Mum in Ryazan and my brother would sneak her out, tell Mum he was taking her to the playground, and I would see her, but not then. Not with the vint. And one day I had a vision. A hallucination. Of this. Of sitting here with you. In a room like this, giving you everything you have ever wanted. And I knew what I had to do,' he said, his voice dropping.

'Dimitri, listen to me,' I said, trying to break through his madness to his calm. I felt I could get through if he'd let me. 'Who killed Yelyena and Leonid? Did you kill them? Why didn't you tell me you were married to her? Why did they move in there?'

Dimitri's face became very serious now. He ate a biscuit. He took another sip of tea, my cup lying on the floor still, the tea just reaching the edges of what looked like a Bukhara rug. Deep red and black.

'Verochka. Can it be true that you don't remember? Do you honestly not know?'

He was frightening me now. I didn't know what I knew. I couldn't remember anything. He got up and left the room.

'Wait here,' he told me, so I did. I smoked a whole cigarette before he got back holding a cardboard box which he handed to me on the sofa. It was open and very old, falling apart almost. Inside there was something in a carrier bag. I pulled it slightly nervously out of the plastic. Some material. I shook it out and it felt so familiar. Squinting my uncertainty, I held it up and shook it out. My throat tightened. It was my black velvet dress. From that night. Had I never noticed it was gone? No. It had got mixed up in that horrible night and my flight away from Dimitri, back to London. I had never thought about it again.

'Faith. It was soaked in their blood. You were covered in their blood.'

OK, I was going to be sick now. I put my hand over my mouth and stood up, begging with my eyes to be shown to the loo. Instead Dimitri grabbed a waste paper bin, a big red leather thing which thankfully had an ordinary metal bin inside. I leant over it and Dimitri held back my hair while I was sick.

I wiped my mouth with the back of my hand. 'Thanks,' I said, uncertain, somehow humiliated.

'OK?' he asked me, shrugging his jacket off and throwing it over the back of a Louis XV chair. I smelt the once familiar smell of him as he did this and nearly gagged again. He put the bin outside the door from where I assumed it would miraculously disappear. I wanted to run out into the street, back to the office, back to Eden, back to somewhere where I was Faith Zanetti. But I sat down again, next to the dress.

'It's not their blood. It's mine. I fell downstairs at Dom Literatov,' I said.

'Are you sure?' Dimitri asked me.

I didn't reply because we both knew the answer. No. I wasn't sure. I wasn't sure about anything any more.

'I loved you, Faith. I loved you more than life. But there was a long time when I never believed you would come and marry me. There were other girls... Can you forgive me?'

I stood up again now. 'For fuck's sake, Sakhnov, what are you talking about?' I screamed. I tried to use the language Faith Zanetti might use, but I kept hearing a teenaged girl.

'I'm talking about Yelyena. About Lena,' he said. 'She got pregnant. I didn't know what to do. I never lied to her. I told her about you and she was realistic about it. She wanted what she wanted. She wanted to get married so that the baby was legitimate and she wanted to move to Moscow,' Dimitri paused, as if tasting a bitter memory. 'You know, she never did tell me about her brother. He wasn't completely…right, I heard. In the head. But she did tell me, after the wedding, that there would always be another boy she loved best too. I didn't realise… I just thought it was some other jerk from Vorkuta… I met her in Vorkuta, right? Visiting the family. Faith, it was that marriage that never meant anything to me. Faith? Not ours. Never ours…'

I drew my breath in and walked over to the window. You could see the whole Kremlin from here. It would have been illegal for normal citizens to live here once, because of that. You weren't allowed to fly over it either. Even in this grim, grey weather, the gold domes sparkled with joy and majesty. I could not say the same for myself. Speaking of sparkling…

'Dimitri,' I said, taking the ring off and putting it on the table. 'We are not married.'

I thought he might do something mad, something violent. But he just nodded and looked into my face. 'In my heart we are,' he said. 'In my heart.'

I looked right back at him and felt myself returning to life. Dealing with the shock of seeing him, with the barrage of information he was throwing at me. 'I didn't kill those people,' I said. 'I didn't kill them.' I got up and flicked my cigarette into the grate. I leant back against the fireplace and felt myself warm up.

Dimitri positioned himself in the middle of the sofa, where I had just been, and told me the story of the night the Varanovs died.

'Faith. I was asleep in bed when you got in from the party. I'd been in Ryazan since that row we had about something stupid. Something childish. Lena, and, it turned out, Leonid, had moved in while I was away. I was going to tell you all about it as soon as I got back. I thought you'd understand. She left Tina with her mum back in Vorkuta. She was trying to get work in Moscow. She trained as a dentist. Anyway, I heard you come in. You had little shoes on, no boots, you were blue and shivering, your stockings were torn. You were drunk. So drunk that you weren't looking straight. You went into the bedroom, fell over on the way, and you looked in the windows for a chicken you'd left there. You kept saying, "My chicken. My chicken's gone." You thought Zinaida Petrovna had taken it. You were shouting, up and down the hall, "Who took my chicken?" I got out of bed and tried to get you to come and lie down, sleep it off, but you'd started banging on the old woman's door, then on Lena's door. You went into her room and switched the light on. I was following you, trying to stop you. The chicken was there, it was in their window and you opened it and took the chicken out. Leonid was in bed, asleep, and he woke up slowly and saw you taking this frozen thing. He had nothing on and he came towards you. You screamed and swung the chicken at his head. You killed him.'

'I killed Leonid Varanov with a frozen chicken?' I smiled. It seemed so mad, so weird. Just like the tabloid splash Eden had been on about. Like the brilliant 'Freddie Starr ate my hamster'. But Dimitri wasn't laughing.

'Yes. You did.'

I stopped smiling. 'Who cut his leg off then?' I was defiant, but my confidence was shattered.

Dimitri shook his head, seeming baffled by my stupidity. He carried on as though he was submitting evidence or something. 'This is when Lena came back. She heard all this screaming from outside and picked up the caretaker's axe for protection. She thought someone, maybe Leonid, was being robbed. She rushed in with this weapon and saw me and you in her room, Leonid on the floor, and she started swinging the axe at both of us. She was shouting that she loved me and how could I have gone with someone else and what did I think I was doing to her. I got the axe off her and I'd put it down on the floor, I think. And that's when you went crazy. Maybe with jealousy. I hope…' and he actually smiled slightly, 'I hope it was jealousy.'

I was completely incredulous. 'You *hope* that I went mad and murdered a woman with an axe and chopped the leg off a dead naked man out of jealousy? This is something that you *hope*?'

I stood up to carry on protesting my innocence. This was the maddest story I had ever heard. And yet, out of the dimmest, darkest recess of my mind I saw a terrifying, blurry naked man looming at me and felt the chill and weight of a frozen chicken in my hand.

And I lost consciousness.

Chapter 17

WHEN I WOKE up it was just getting dark outside. Juanita was putting my folded clothes in a pile on the end of a chaise longue. I lay in a dark four-poster bed and appeared to be wearing a white bathrobe, monogrammed in Cyrillic for DVS, Dimitri's initials. I hoped it had been Juanita who'd undressed me.

'God, what happened?' I asked, sitting up. There was a dressing table in here with a big ashtray and a silver brush and mirror set on it, the chaise longue, big windows with the dark velvet curtains pulled to and a door to what looked like a very nice bathroom.

'Ah, you're awake,' Juanita said, smiling at me. 'I think you fainted. When did you last eat? I've made you some soup. I'll go and get it.'

I wanted to blame Dimitri and his drugged tea but actually I believed him about the valerian. I have been feeling more than usually ropy lately, I haven't eaten properly for ages and...well...

Something had come back to me before I passed out and it felt like the truth. Isn't this what happens? Don't you delete the very worst stuff from your memory as best you can? The things you just can't cope with. I mean, I hadn't entirely lost my mind. I still didn't believe half of what Dimitri had said about the axe. I conjured up the image of an axe, for chopping wood. A heavy thing with a big rusting blade. I was sure I just wasn't strong enough, let alone homicidal enough, to have been swinging one of those around like a medieval knight. And I tried to see myself, mad and drunk, spinning round and round with both hands on the wooden handle, a splinter sinking into my palm. Might I have done that? Yet surely, I mean, *surely*, they would have arrested me immediately if there had been a trail of blood leading from their room to ours? I pictured this too, sinking into the unvarnished wood, staining it, and as I saw it in my imagination it seemed real, as though it could actually have been there. But wouldn't my prints have been all over the axe? They never even took my fingerprints. Had Dimitri cleaned up all night? I could see him, hunched at the bathroom sink, rinsing and scrubbing, taking a brush and some soap to the floor. Had he bribed the police at the time? This too was perfectly possible. There he was, slipping a hundred bucks into his passport for them to find accidentally on purpose. Something he did a great deal of. A lot of his story, I thought, my head still spinning slightly from having sat up too fast, was implausible to say the least. Or it had seemed that way when he told it.

But I think…I do think that I may have hit a man over the head with a frozen chicken. A terrifying naked man who was shouting at me. No wonder they never found the murder weapon. It had thawed by the time they got there. That's Russian heating for you.

I massaged my temples with my fingers and glanced around for my cigarettes. On the bedside table was a silver cigarette case. I leant across the clouds of pillows and duvets

to get it. I clicked it open and found it full of Silk Cut cigarettes. Next to it was a heavy onyx lighter which I didn't even
try to lift, but poked my face up close to light my cigarette
and inhaled deeply. This made me feel even dizzier and I was
beginning to really want to go home. Juanita came in with
soup and iced water on a tray and she was followed by Tina,
who bounced along behind her with a towel on her head.

'Hi, sick lady,' she beamed. 'Hey, if I had to talk to Dad for
that long I'd pass out too.'

I smiled. 'I don't think it was that,' I said. 'Just too much
to drink, too much news and too little food.'

Tina jumped up on to the bed and crossed her legs. 'Ooh,
news! I love news,' she said, and took a cigarette out of the
cigarette case. I held mine out to her so that she didn't have
to reach for the lighter and she put it to the end of hers and
sucked. 'Here's my news. I'm dying my hair green,' she said,
blowing her smoke out with a laugh.

'Yeah. I wish that was my news,' I sighed. 'Won't it stain
the towel?'

'We've got a lot of towels. We can easily make it your
news?' Tina suggested. I felt old talking to a rebellious teenager. They make rebellion, irreverence, look so ridiculous
that you can't help being sage by comparison.

'Hmmm. No thanks.' I shook my head. I don't think
they'd let me into the Kremlin press conferences with green
hair. It was bad enough already what with the scruffy thing.

'So?'

'What?'

'What is your news?'

Juanita put the tray in front of me, across my legs like in a
hospital. There was a single pink rose in a vase on it, as well as
food. I drank (or is it ate?) a spoonful of soup. Now ordinarily
I hate soup. Why would anyone want their food puréed into

a mush unless they a) didn't have any teeth yet or b) had lost all their teeth. Soup is a thing that they feed to you through a tube when you can no longer manage the effort of moving your jaws. However, on this occasion I thought I'd better eat something before I passed out or threw up again. It was a weird sickness. It seemed to be to do with not eating rather than eating. I was starting to think a doctor's visit might be in order. Not that this was something I was clamouring to do in Moscow. There was the British Embassy doctor who was basically there to run AA and distribute Prozac. There was the American Medical Center which costs a fortune and demands your credit card on entry and then, if it's serious, transfers you either to Finland or to the Kremlin hospital where you might as well start out in the first place. The rules in Russia are: do not, in any circumstances, get old or ill or incarcerated.

Chicken soup, though. Hmmm. Perhaps an exception was about to be made.

Tina seemed to notice my surprise. 'Juanita makes the best chicken soup in the known universe,' she said. 'Used to work for a Jewish family in New York before she came to us. Crazy, huh?' She used the word 'klyova' a lot.

'So you speak English? This soup is fantastic!' I called after Juanita as she slid out of the room. She came back in blushing and tugging at the sides of her apron. She really had the servile thing down. Still, I imagine she was well compensated for it and I knew what the alternatives were in downtown San Salvador. Or wherever.

'Thank you, madam,' she said, in English, and disappeared again.

'Lots of bad news, Tina. A lot of bad news,' I said, reverting to our previous conversation. 'When I was married to your dad there were some bad things that happened. Bad things that never got sorted out,' I said, climbing out of bed and opening the curtains with a thick tassled cord. The view on this side was of the front courtyard and the street, a few cars straggling along, their headlights dim in the light snow.

'Yeah,' she said, uncrossing her legs and stretching out. 'I know.'

I sat down on the chaise longue and put my hand on top of my pile of clothes. My plan was as follows: one, put on clothes; two, leave.

'I'm sorry,' I sighed, letting my head slump into my hands, singularly failing to execute my, frankly, brilliant plan. I'd like to say I wondered whether or not to tell her. Whether or not to plough on. But I actually couldn't help it. You know how people break under interrogation and suddenly, having denied things for years, just confess everything, including things they were never accused of? I felt a bit like that. Something about being in Russia makes lying, makes pretending anything, seem silly. The truth, the enormous bleak truth of life is staring you in the face and you're going to lie about something to someone? It just doesn't work. 'I only found out...only realised...I didn't know they were your...I didn't know them at all. It's only in the last few days that I sort of uncovered any connection between me and them. Dimitri never told me his ex-wife was coming to live there. I didn't even know he had a child before now, and after they were dead...well, it was gruesome and I sometimes dreamt about it, but I didn't think it had anything to do with me, let alone you, who I couldn't even imagine...and your grandparents... in Vorkuta. Tina—your grandparents want to see you. I know you probably don't want any contact and...'

I had been talking to my knees this whole time. Why I had been talking at all I can't imagine. I no longer had the excuse of being nineteen. 'I'm thirty-five' really isn't an excuse for anything except perhaps not sleeping with someone who is twenty-four, or whatever. My defence? I don't know. Just that it was all new to me and she seemed to be the only person in any of it who was remotely shocked or confused. I just thought she knew. But she didn't. She looked blank-faced at me for a bit with her mouth hanging open, her cigarette hanging off her bottom lip. I looked blank-faced back at her and watched the information get processed, cogs turning in her mind. Then a switch clicked.

'My *mother*? My mother died in a car crash! She did! Didn't she? My mother… The woman who had her head axed off was my *mother*! And who exactly was the guy? My real fucking father or something? Is that it? I got adopted by some psychopath at the scene? Well, *is it*???'

I was staring at her now with my hand over my mouth. Like an idiot. I stood up to move towards her, though God knows what I thought I was going to do. She leapt up to standing on the bed, looking as though she might jump at me. The towel had fallen off as she got up and green dye was trickling down her face.

'I mean it, you total fucking cunt. WHO WAS HE?' she screamed. I could hear Dimitri and Juanita rushing across parquet floors from afar. I took my hand away from my mouth.

'He was your uncle, Tina. They were twins,' I said. Nothing to stop me now, but I did pause. A little pause before the next unthinkable thing I was going to say. I was quiet now, almost relaxed, almost so tense I might have had a heart attack. It was hard to decide which. 'I think I might have killed him. But it was an accident and I swear I didn't do anything else.'

'I never fucking thought you did. Dad always said it was a robbery but that it looked bad for you and needed covering up. It seemed like a big joke...' She leapt off the bed, stumbled and stood in front of me. She drew back her hand with a grimace and whacked me so hard round the face that I fell over. She was a big girl.

Dimitri and Juanita appeared in the doorway as I fell and Tina went running towards them. She tried to push past but Dimitri held her wrists as she screamed and sobbed. Eden was right. My life was turning into an episode of EastEnders. It wouldn't become Shakespearean until later. And then not a comedy.

'You bastard. You evil fucking evil bastard,' she wailed, and punched him in the face. As he staggered backwards with the force of her blow, she ran past him into the hall. Juanita chased her.

'It's OK, dove. Tinochka!' she implored, but a few seconds later I heard the front door slam.

I climbed up to lean against the dresser and Dimitri came towards me, arms outstretched, his face already deep red where his daughter had hit him.

'Faith, my love. Are you OK? What did she do to you? Don't worry—she'll come round. She's always been jealous of your memory a bit...she'll come round,' he said, cooing as if to an injured, but still dangerous, animal. I exhaled hard, putting my cigarette out in a big crystal ashtray.

'Dima. It's nothing to do with me, with us. I thought she knew. I just imagined you'd convinced her that... I thought she knew ...' I murmured, genuinely sorry now. I had done something terrible to that young woman. Something she would never recover from. 'I swear I just thought she knew. I've been so tired and confused...'

Dimitri's eyes widened as he began to realise what I had done. 'Oh God,' he said, his whole body somehow seeming to loosen in defeat. 'I should have warned you.'

He stood silent for a moment and then, panicked for perhaps the first time ever, he said, 'Tina.'

I started pulling my clothes on fast now. 'I'll help you find her,' I said. 'I'll make it better, I promise.' Suddenly I felt less dizzy and sick. Soup or just resolve? I don't know, but I was dynamism itself. I had been fucking up in every area I could think of and I wasn't going to do it any more. For the first time since I arrived in Moscow I was clear-headed. The memory of a naked Leonid and the stupid frozen fucking chicken was almost a relief. Now I knew. And I almost knew I had had nothing to do with the axe business. Had it been Yelyena who had lost her mind? Had Leonid in reality attacked her and himself as I'd always suspected? Was Dimitri telling me I had done the other stuff so that I would be grateful for his protection? I didn't know any of this, but I did know I hadn't done the rest.

Far from being the Mr Big behind the scenes, it was clear that Misha was, and perhaps always had been, Dimitri's henchman, his bodyguard. He hadn't left when he walked out of the door. He was still standing there now, brandishing one of his guns. Was he supposed to stop me leaving or did Dimitri need a permanent guard when he was at home? I didn't bother to ask, but he was coming with us, apparently.

'Tinochka seemed upset,' he said to Dimitri, concerned.

'Yes. Faith just told her that Yelyena Varanova was her mother.'

'Fuck,' Misha nodded, opening the lift gate for us.

'Yes,' Dimitri said.

'I thought she knew,' I mumbled, getting in.

It was good to be outside in the cold air. I had at least some bloody sense of perspective now and it seemed feasible that we would find Tina and calm her down somehow, that I would go back to Eden and tell the whole story like a joke, and that, armed with another version of the night of the murder, I could explain myself to the procurator on Wednesday.

'Shit,' Dimitri spat, 'she's taken the fucking car.' He took his mobile out of his jacket pocket and turned his back on us to make a call to the driver. 'Asshole,' he hissed, finding the driver's phone to be off, presumably on instructions from Tina.

We beeped our way out of the security gates and looked up and down the street for a taxi.

'She'll have gone to Job,' I said. 'Do you know where he lives? Where he plays?'

Misha and Dimitri both shrugged.

'I had his number but his phone got stolen,' Dimitri explained, as if to excuse his paternal sloppiness.

A car skidded over and we got in, both men looking to me for direction.

'Umm. BB Kings. Do you know it?' I asked the driver, a young Armenian man with gold teeth, prayer beads on his rear view mirror, and a photograph of his daughter with huge Quentin Blake ribbons in her hair on his dashboard. He nodded and swerved out on to the main road.

'It's a blues club... He's a blues guitarist, isn't he?'

'Is he?' Dimitri said, lighting a cigarette and sitting back in his seat, shoulders back, head up, trying to regain some composure. Misha was doing his absent thing up front, amazingly effective for someone so enormously huge. Though generally very chivalrous, Russian men do not automatically let women sit in the front seat. Perhaps because it is more dangerous. Women and children in the back sort of thing. So Misha, who we must silently have agreed was the most expendable of our party, took the seat unquestioningly.

In the old days, when taking taxis was dangerous because there weren't any and you had to just get into whatever car stopped with whoever was driving it, there was a decision to be made. Sit in the front and make friends in the hope that once he knew you he wouldn't kill you? Or sit in the back, your hand on your nerve gas spray, hoping to be so unobtrusive that he'd forget to kill you? I always did the chatting thing and I seem to have survived. Things are safer now.

It must have been early evening because the streets were busy, small steaming crowds of people bustling around the glowing entrances to the metro and the traffic horrendous. You can sit completely motionless on the boulevards for twenty minutes at a time, edging forwards through the slush, pitying the filthy begging children and their bedraggled mothers.

Dimitri reached over and touched my arm, again the look in his eyes difficult to gauge. Not apologetic certainly, but wanting something, asking for something or, perhaps, demanding it.

'I just wanted to say... I need to apologise for something bad,' he said.

Oh, great. Excellent. Because I was running a bit low on bad things to think about.

'You were right about your friend. Your American friend Scott. I was very... I think I got a bit obsessed about you and him. After you left, Misha and I...well, we went to his house, and... It was a bad thing to do. I was already taking vint and... I don't know why I did that. I have wanted to apologise to him, to ask his forgiveness, for so many years now. It is something that has plagued me...'

I turned to look at him. So proud and defiant. He wouldn't want to be pitied by me or by anyone, so I tried not to think about how sorry I felt for him. He was so eaten up by guilt, by his feelings for me (which I thought pretty obviously had more to do with him than with me) and by all that had happened so long ago.

'Oh, don't worry about it,' I said. 'He's probably already forgotten.' This couldn't have been a more brazen lie, especially since he'd been burgled within moments of seeing me again this week. But Dimitri seemed happier immediately. It wasn't until now, crawling up past Kropotkinskaya Station, that I remembered what Scott had said. My whole fucking brain was giving up on me. Too much booze.

'He saw you! Dimitri, he saw you outside Dom Literatov! How could you have been asleep in bed when I got back if you'd only just been outside Dom Literatov?' I was shaking slightly with the slow and shivering realisation that everything Dimitri had told me was a lie.

He laughed. 'Such a little investigator, Zhaba! I got home, you were out, I went up to ask Zinaida Petrovna where you might be and she told me. Said she'd sewn you into your dress. The one that—'

'Yes, yes,' I said, understanding that he was going to wrap this up too.

'So, I drove out to get you. It was late; I thought you'd appreciate the lift. Anyway, you weren't there. I did see Scott but I didn't feel like talking to him so I drove home and went to sleep. I don't know where you were. Maybe staggering down the boulevard. How do I know? I suppose I must have beaten you home,' he explained.

Oh, God, but it sounded completely reasonable. Was it me who had no grip on this? All Dimitri's explanations were so calm and smiling. There was only one thing that really surprised me. How did he remember all this from more than fifteen years ago? What time he got home, who he spoke to, the things I said?

'Oh. Right,' I sighed, patting my cigarettes in my jacket pocket and ruffling my hair.

'Verochka. You are so suspicious of me!' Dimitri said, twinkling his eyes.

'Hmmm. That's because you beat my friends up,' I said, half wanting to tell him that I'd had sex with Scott that night. Just to shock him. Just to show him that I knew at least a few things he didn't know. Though he seemed to have lost that anxiety he'd once had. So totally in control now. So strange.

We pulled up outside BB Kings and asked the taxi and Misha to wait. Dimitri and I ran down the side of a shabby 1950s brick building on a main road to find the cellar door. A neon sign pointed to it and we pushed it open and hurtled down the stairs. A waitress was wiping the tables down in a long narrow room. It was dark and the grille was down over the bar. It smelt of stale smoke and spilt drinks. A set of drums stood at one end of the room. The walls were covered with pictures of jazz and blues legends.

The waitress looked a bit nervous to see us.

'Hi. Do you know a guitarist called Job? He's black?' I asked her. She shook her head and wiped another table. We turned to leave but she called us back.

'I do know a black guitarist. Plays here sometimes. Kuku. I've got his number in my phone. Do you want to call him?' she asked.

We waited while she fetched her coat and scrolled through the numbers in her phone. Dimitri punched Kuku's straight into his.

'Kuku?' he asked. 'Hi. I'm looking for a guitarist. His name is Job. Do you know him?'

I couldn't hear what Kuku was saying on the other end but it must surely have been something like; 'You think we all know each other because we're black?' But actually, he did know Job, and he told us he played at the Blue Note round the back of McDonald's on Pushkin Square. I realised how stupid I had been on Thursday to imagine that I wouldn't be able to find Job by trawling the clubs. It was a pretty straightforward procedure to find a black Russian man in Moscow.

Dimitri snapped his phone shut and thanked the waitress, pushing a thousand roubles into her hand.

'Thanks,' she said, looking up, bewildered, still holding her coat.

Back into town through the ugly clot of traffic and we were at the Blue Note within about an hour.

The club had opened by now and we had to pay to get in, again skulking through a weird little side door on the other side of a very grand theatre, handing our money over to a bloke with a Mohican who put our money in a metal tin and gave us raffle tickets from a book in return. The coat check girl hadn't arrived yet so we went behind the desk and hung our own coats up, taking the tags from the top of the hangers. Someone was playing scales on a clarinet. We had left Misha in the car again.

The club was almost empty, fifty or so little round tables with candles on them set round a low stage. A barman cleaned glasses and the clarinet player sat on a barstool, a glass of white wine sitting near her.

'Anyone know if Job is playing tonight?' Dimitri asked the only two people in the room. The clarinettist stopped playing and the barman stopped wiping.

'Da. Igrayet,' they said in unison. 'Yes, he's playing.'

'His girlfriend was here a second ago. She drank about ten tequilas,' the musician said, tossing her hair over her shoulder.

'Ten,' the barman confirmed, looking from the half-empty tequila bottle to the empty shot glass on the zinc in front of him.

'Not sure where she went,' the woman said, and started playing again.

Dimitri looked anxiously around the room as though Tina might somehow be hiding under a table. It was at this point that she emerged from behind a curtain opposite us. She saw us, but was obviously having trouble focusing.

'Fuck off,' she said. 'Get the fuck out of my life.'

But her heart wasn't in it and she was lurching our way. She fell heavily before she reached us, knocking over a table and four chairs. Dimitri and I rushed to help her up but she was unconscious.

'I'll get Misha,' I said, and Dimitri nodded.

At the flat (Dimitri's, not mine), Misha carried Tina to her room in a fireman's lift. It was tasks like this that Misha was built for. Her bed was another four-poster, but this one was designed like a hamburger, round, with the base and frame making up the sesame-seeded bun, the mattress the meat and the sheets, pillows and duvets in red, green and yellow to be gherkins, ketchup and, perhaps, onions. It was disgusting. But sort of funny. 'Lisa-Marie Presley had one,' Dimitri smiled, proud of himself.

There was a vast sound system in here and a plasma screen television mounted on the wall next to a big picture of Angelina Jolie in Tomb Raider. Misha put Tina down and Juanita came rushing in to deal with her. Her second cata-tonic patient in one day.

Tina came round with the first cold compress. She opened her eyes, looked at us, raised a finger in a fuck off and shut them again. Her hair was dry now but the green that had streaked her face had dried there, making her look ready for Hallowe'en.

Dimitri sat down on the bed next to her. 'Come on, Ratty,' he said. 'Don't be cross with us. Do you think I didn't tell you to hurt you? You always knew your mum was dead; it's not as though anybody lied. I wanted to spare you this. Faith and I had nothing to do with it. We tried to help but there was nothing we could do.' Another little lie that sounded basically believable.

Tina kept her eyes shut. 'Faith said she killed the man. My uncle. She *told* me she killed him.'

Dimitri laughed. 'Tinochka. Faith doesn't remember anything about it. She's blaming herself for no reason. I was there. I was sober. Faith and I tried to stop him. He was never right in the head,' he explained. So was this the truth?

Tina sighed and dragged her eyelids up over her eyeballs. 'I want to see my grandparents,' she said. 'We are going to Vorkuta and you are coming with us.'

I looked behind me like someone in a sitcom. Misha had left the room and there was nobody she could have meant but me.

'OK,' I said. It seemed the least I could do.

'Now,' Tina demanded, sitting up in her giant hamburger. 'Now!'

I looked at Dimitri and he shrugged.

'I've got to go home to change,' I said.

'Misha will take you,' Dimitri told me, spinning into action now. 'We can get the midnight train.'

Chapter 18

EDEN AND DON were sitting at the living room table. There were three empty wine bottles between them but their glasses were still full. There was only one lamp on in here and with the snow outside there was something romantic about the sight of them. So this was what they'd been doing all day, while I was receiving rings and blows to the head and whatnot.

Eden looked up and smiled at me.

'Uno!' Don shouted.

'Bollocks.' Eden sighed.

These hard-drinking, hard-living hacks who had seen the horrors of the world and lived to survive them were playing the children's card game, Uno.

'Hi,' I said. 'I got kidnapped on my way to the office this morning.'

'Oh,' Eden replied. 'Lyuda said you hadn't gone in. You escaped then, did you?'

'Oh, fuck off,' I said, coming over and sitting down with them. 'I haven't actually tried to escape yet so I'm not completely sure whether or not I've been kidnapped, but one of my captors is downstairs waiting for me.'

'Have a glass of wine,' Don said, holding the bottle upside down over his own glass. 'Oh. Bugger's empty,' he said, disappointed. I had a sip out of his glass.

'Been with Dimitri all day,' I announced, determined to get a rise out of these bastards. 'Apparently I did kill that bloke back then. He says I killed the girl too but I didn't. And guess what? The girl was the mother of his child—Tina, who lives with him now and has a four-poster bed in the shape of a giant hamburger.'

'A giant hamburger!' Don exclaimed, excited.

'Like Lisa-Marie Presley had?' Eden asked.

'How the fuck would you know that?' I wondered. 'Anyway, we're going to Vorkuta now to see her grandparents. You know, the parents of the dead twins—*one of whom I killed!*'

'Oh, don't be ridiculous. Of course you didn't,' Eden said, getting up. 'They're not going to be that pleased to see Dimitri, are they?'

'I don't imagine he's going in. Aren't either of you remotely surprised by any of this?' I asked them, standing up now and lighting a cigarette.

'A hamburger,' Don mumbled, shaking his head in wonder.

'Oh, for God's sake,' I shouted, and left the room to go and get ready.

Eden ran after me. 'We're coming too! Aren't we, McCaughrean?' he shouted to Don.

'What? Where? No way,' Don said, getting up and putting his cigarettes in his pocket ready for the journey. 'I'll bring some vodka, shall I?' he asked, loudly.

'Good idea,' I yelled from the bedroom where I was putting socks, pants, another pair of jeans and a couple of

T-shirts into my old brown leather suitcase. 'Jones! Have you got a jumper I can borrow?' I asked.

'Yup,' he said, coming in. 'I'll pack a couple for both of us.'

'Are you really coming?'

'I'm seriously not letting you go to the Arctic north with this guy by yourself,' he said, his cigarette between his lips as he spoke. 'Are you insane?'

'I think I might be, actually,' I said. It was getting to that point.

'Did you ask him about Adrian and stuff? What's the story?' Eden asked.

'I don't know. He's all really reasonable about it. He is *very* rich. He says Adrian volunteered for me, that I did do it, that he, Dimitri, was on drugs and Adrian was only going in until Dimitri died which he was apparently about to do.'

Eden stopped packing. 'It doesn't sound *that* reasonable,' he suggested.

'Well, it does when he says it,' I said, impatient.

'In fact I'd call it a trifle implausible. I'd call it a load of bollocks, Faith. I'd call it a pile of shit. I'd call it an absolute...'

'Yeah. All right. All right. I know. He's very persuasive. He stops me knowing what the fuck I think. We'll sort it out in Vorkuta, OK?'

'OK,' Eden said, dubiously, raising his eyebrows.

Eden and I had overnight bags, Don had four bottles of vodka in his pockets and his camera bag and we were ready to go.

Misha got out to open the doors to the Zil and saw Don and Eden tumbling along behind me. 'Fuck are these cunts?' he said, feeling for some hardware.

Don went up to him, pressing his body against Misha's and staring up into his face. 'Call me a cunt again, mate, and I'll fucking slice your head off,' he said.

Misha moved to slice Don's head off but I stopped him. 'They're friends of mine. Coincidentally they are also planning a trip to Vorkuta tonight,' I said, pushing Don into the car.

Misha did not comment but went to sit up front behind the frilly purple stuff with the driver. I was surprised the driver hadn't been sacked or executed after turning his phone off for Tina, but I suppose people had other stuff on their minds.

'What the holy fuck is wrong with you, McCaughrean?' I asked him. 'I mean this is a really serious relapse. You are almost as much of a fat arsehole as you used to be and you've only been boozing for about twenty-four hours. That guy could kill you with a flick on the forehead from his index finger.'

'I'd like to see the arse-wipe try,' Don said, still blearily defiant.

'I can't believe he's coming,' I said to Eden.

'He'll be OK in the morning,' Eden said.

'That's what we thought yesterday,' I pointed out.

'True,' Eden conceded.

'Where is this shit-pit we're going to anyway?' Don asked.

'Arctic circle,' I told him, and he fell asleep with his face spread greasily out against the window.

We drove on a bit in silence, the Moscow night glittering on around us.

'So, what does he say about beating Weisman to a pulp?' Eden asked. 'Something really really reasonable, does he?'

'He says he's sorry,' I mumbled, a bit abashed. Suddenly all the stuff Dimitri had been saying didn't sound quite as good as it had when he said it.

'Oh, well that's OK then,' Eden nodded, pushing the curtain out of the way, winding the window down and leaning his elbow out. 'Nice choice of husband, Zanetti,' he said. I had been thinking that too, I had to admit. It's just that somehow my personality didn't work when Dimitri was around.

We must have made a peculiar sight, worming our way through the crowds at Yaroslavsky Station that night. Eden and I, scruffy but handsome westerners, followed by two brutes: the completely arseholed Don McCaughrean and his camera bag, and Misha, grim-faced and built like a tank. I would soon be seeing a tank and so be able to verify my information.

Dimitri and Tina were waiting for us by the ticket office, surrounded by women in headscarves pulling bundles along on pram parts. Swarthy southern people sat on top of their huge piles of luggage, almost all of which was wrapped in material and tied with rope or string. Suitcases were obviously too expensive or simply unnecessary.

The lighting in these stations is horrible. Very pale yellow, just enough for basic visibility. The dregs of society were here in the warm. Men with their faces eaten away by drink and disease, their beards caked in food and vomit. Children addicted to glue and probably prostituting themselves huddled together in little groups to sleep, for warmth and for protection. There are actually people, to use the word people in the loosest possible sense of the word, who come to the stations to kill these children. As if it wasn't the lowest, most depressing and repulsive thing to want to have sex with them. Nope, they came up with something even worse.

'Hey!' Tina shouted out, pleased to see us, though lacking a bit of her bounce, I thought. 'Hey, handsome,' she said to Eden, holding out her hand for a kiss which, slightly to my surprise, she got.

Dimitri had his arm round her and had obviously been working his magic. I introduced everyone properly and

Dimitri shook hands with Don and Eden forcefully, with, I thought, an edge of threat. But he smiled and nodded, keeping his thoughts, as ever, to himself.

He had been insulted, I remembered, that I couldn't read his thoughts as well as he could read mine. We'd been in bed once and it had been raining heavily outside, maybe a big Moscow thunderstorm, lighting up the bright yellow crumbling buildings and lonely courtyard birch trees.

'I'm imagining that we're out at a dacha now. A big wooden dacha with a wild garden leading down to a lake. There is a birch forest near us and we can hear the rain in the trees and the birds taking shelter. There is a bowl of apples, Faith. Can you see them?'

I shut my eyes and I thought I could. I smiled, thinking about the romance of this. In my imagination it was another time, before Communism. There would be horses walking up and down the lane outside, children shouting to their French governesses. 'Yes,' I said.

'What colour are they?'

I opened my eyes. 'What colour are what?' I asked.

'The apples.'

'Oh!' I laughed and shut my eyes again, pulling the sheet up around me. 'Green,' I said. 'Bright green.'

Dimitri pushed me away and got out of bed, dragging his trousers on. 'They are red!' he shouted, and slammed the door on his way to the bathroom.

He had taken this as a sign that my love was not sufficiently deep.

He went back to the ticket office now and returned to us with a handful of first class tickets. Me and him, Tina and Misha, Don and Eden.

'Dima, I'm not... I'll go with Tina,' I said, firmly, swinging my bag on to my shoulder.

'Khorosho,' he said. 'Good.' He wasn't going to let go of his magnanimous patriarch image in a hurry.

He fished in his suit pocket and pulled out the Tiffany box. 'This is yours, Zhaba,' he said. 'Take it.'

I didn't feel like a row either, so I put the box in my leather jacket, smiled at Dimitri and nodded in thanks.

'Did that bastard just call you a toad, Zanetti? Want me to sort him out for you?' Don asked.

'Shut up, McCaughrean, would you?' I said. 'He just gave me about a hundred grand's worth of ring.'

'Oh,' said Don. 'Right.'

We got on the train with ten minutes to spare, shuffling down the corridor to find our compartments while the carriage woman shouted instructions at us. Most people had already settled in, sitting at the tiny tables in their flip-flops and tracksuit bottoms, unwrapping chicken legs and boiled eggs from foil, drinking sweet champagne from plastic cups.

A whistle blew just as Tina and I had crowded into our compartment, the bunks with their starched cotton sheets and pillow cases not yet made up. The train creaked and groaned into life, dragging its enormous load out into the vastness of Russia, away from the deceptive light and bustle of Moscow and into the real country, a wild country where wolves and bears howl in the forests and people's precarious little lives perch on the edges of the wilderness like grains of sand, ready to be blown away by nature's brutality. Stalin got legions of prisoners to build this train line and the ones who survived then had to build their own labour camp at the other end. He wanted to open up the Arctic where it never gets light. Obviously, it didn't work, though there are still people up there.

The trains from Vorkuta that carry on into the Polar-Urals are always disappearing, stuck in snow drifts, derailed and buried. Delays of forty-eight hours are common.

Actually, I say it never gets light and that's not quite true. In the summer it does get light but it never gets dark. But it's not real light, like natural proper sunlight. It's a kind of dusky half-light that stops you sleeping but doesn't really keep you awake. The surreal horror of these places is not to be believed. I have been up this way before, but this would be my first trip to Vorkuta.

Tina sat down and pulled an old-fashioned American lunch box with a picture of Elvis on it out of her oversized rucksack. 'Korol,' she said. 'The King.'

I had already sat down but I got up again now and pulled my jeans down on one side to reveal my pelvic bone and my tattoo of Elvis's signature.

'Hey! That's cool!' Tina said, genuinely impressed.

'I know,' I said, genuinely pleased.

Tina opened the lunch box and got out two cylindrical things in foil. 'Here,' she said, handing me one.

I sat back down and unwrapped my tortilla. It was filled with sour cream, guacamole and spicy meat.

'Wow,' I said in English. It didn't need translating.

'Juanita is fantastic,' Tina nodded, her mouth stuffed full of food. 'Crazy.'

I ate some of mine and we looked at each other. I liked Tina. She wasn't far off the age I'd been when…well, back then. I wished I'd been more like her.

Don leaned in from the corridor. 'Vodkas, anyone?' he asked, waving a bottle and some plastic cups.

'Yeah,' I said, holding out my hand. He balanced himself carefully with his legs spread far apart and poured a huge cup of vodka out for me.

'There you are, Miss Zanetti,' he said, and he looked questioningly at Tina.

'None for her,' I told him and he doddered away. She raised one eyebrow at me, the one pierced with a spike. 'Sorry. I'm thirty-five,' I told her in explanation. Well, someone was going to have to look after her. I wondered if Mum having died had put me next in line in a way I hadn't yet completely understood. A couple of weeks ago wouldn't I have been sneaking Tina shots, one of the girls, fuck the rights and wrongs of it? Yes, I thought I probably would. On the other hand, I had done this girl plenty of harm already today.

I drank the vodka down in one. *That* was what I'd needed all day. Never mind tea and sympathy. I felt the enormous shot warm every part of my body. I felt my muscles relax into the seat and my lips turn up in a smile. Everything was going to be OK, I thought.

I flicked my phone on (fuck—very low battery and I hadn't brought the charger) and called Tamsin in London to tell her I was going to Vorkuta.

'That's brilliant, Zanetti,' she said absently. 'Six hundred words by tomorrow. But we can't run it until next week.'

Six hundred words about what she hadn't said and I hadn't offered. I was hoping something would come to me while I was talking to her. Also, we wouldn't be there tomorrow. Did she have no idea where Vorkuta was? Of course she didn't. The day after tomorrow was when we'd be arriving. And also the day I'd be leaving.

'God, that's better,' I told Tina, wiping my mouth with the back of my hand and tucking into my tortilla. Tina nodded at me in understanding.

I looked up at her in horror. I could feel it coming. I wasn't sure if I was going to make it. 'I'm going to be sick,' I said, and ran outside, darting up the corridor to the loo which was, thank God, vacant. I leant over and threw up down the hole on to the tracks, a faceful of snow coming back at me as I did. The first time one ever sits on one of these loos in the snow it is a big shock. I shivered, more with fear than with cold. I didn't like this being sick. Not from the physical point of view but because it made me feel out of control, like when I lost my mind. And I couldn't bear to lose it again.

We were well out of Moscow by now, though even here it must be quite a rare winter where it's this snowy by November.

'You OK, Faith?' Eden asked me as I went back past his compartment. I stuck my tongue out in a sick face and Don laughed.

'Zanetti's been barfing!' he shouted, very pleased with himself. I stuck a finger up at him.

'Get some sleep,' Eden suggested.

'Yeah, thanks,' I said, and went back to join Tina, shutting the door behind me, locking it and lodging the block of wood the uniformed carriage woman had given me into the door handle as an extra anti-intruder precaution. Our beds had been brought down while I was gone, and Tina had leapt into hers, leaving her boots on the floor. She had the blanket up to her chin and looked sweet and babyish with her green hair, her stained face and her silly metal bits. She grinned at me.

'OK?' she asked.

'Nichevo,' I said. 'It's nothing.'

Tina laughed. 'Da? Nothing much!' she said. 'When did *you* last have a period?'

I had been getting something out of my case and I froze. I was staring into my washbag. My period, actually, wasn't due yet. Or was it due about now? In any case I ate so little and drank so much that it couldn't be relied on. But I'd been pregnant before. And aborted. That's why this throwing up hadn't alarmed me as much as it should have. The feeling was *familiar*, for God's sake. She was right.

I sat down on my bed and stared at Tina who was still giggling. 'It's OK,' she said. 'You're in and out in two hours. I did it last year.'

'Yes. Yes, I know what they do.' I nodded. 'Oh, shit.'

I pulled off my cowboy boots and lay back on top of the covers with my clothes on. I looked over at Tina again and she had fallen asleep, her eyelids swollen with the nightmare of her day. She was snoring with her mouth open and she made me smile.

I stared at the ceiling, white plastic and decorated with a repeated sketch of the Moscow Kremlin in red pencil, hammers and sickles and Communist stars still on top of all the buildings.

I reached down for my jacket and took my ring out of its box. I put it on and stared into it like a crystal ball. It lit up even this little compartment. Eden Jones was less than five feet away, not knowing my secret. His secret too. I heard Don out in the corridor, shouting drunkenly.

'Fuck me! I just got an arsehole full of snow, Jonesy! Seriously. I was taking a dump and this fucking blizzard flew up my jacksie!' I could feel his weight lumbering from side to side as he tried to get back to his place. I put my hand over my stomach.

'Hi,' I whispered.

Chapter 19

Dimitri shut himself in his compartment all the way to Vorkuta. Tina went in to ask him for some money for the restaurant car in the morning after the first night and he gave her enough for a meal at the Tsar's Hunting Lodge (a very nice restaurant just outside Moscow) so she didn't need to go in again. Misha stood guard outside all the way. I wondered if Dimitri wasn't perhaps praying or meditating or something in there.

Then Tina and I hobbled through the train, carriage after carriage, almost losing our footing every time we had to leap across the gaps from one carriage to the next. Don and Eden were already there. Don was having four cans of beer for breakfast and he was in tears. Eden was reading a fat and depressing-looking book called *Gulag* in preparation for all the research he was planning to do for his piece in Vorkuta. He was drinking coffee at the dirty little table, covered with an already stained paper napkin. The view from the window was almost lunar in its lack of...well, anything.

There were pieces of fish on drying bread displayed on glass cake stands on the buffet counter and I ordered a few of them with a glass of tea. Tina had a beer and a big bowl of kasha (that savoury porridge with butter and salt on it). Her bounce was back, she'd wiped the green off her face and she was excited.

'I grew up always knowing my mum was dead,' she said. 'I've even seen a picture of the car she was supposed to have been driving. Everyone trying to protect me from the truth, I guess. Pah! So, having new grandparents is kind of a plus? And they'll have pictures of her and shit. Do I look like her?' She posed.

I shook my head. 'I don't know, Tina. I can't remember.' I had aged about a hundred years in the past twelve hours.

After breakfast, during which Don cried continually about missing Donchik and letting Ira down (I still hadn't dared tell him), I bought five bottles of Borjomi mineral water and went back to the compartment to lie down. I must have lain there pretty much all the way to Vorkuta. I felt I needed the rest.

At some stage the forests gave way to little gingerbready villages and huge lakes starting to freeze, and then, at some later stage, every other effort at landscape or habitation sur-rendered to the tundra—hundreds of thousands of miles of icy snow. Though the train was, if anything, overheated, the chill of the inhospitable scenery somehow crept in and, when we woke up on our second morning in transit, pulling into the bleak grey attempt at civilisation that is Vorkuta, every-one was chastened.

I had my secret and the others had their own private thoughts. Except Misha, who I honestly don't think had ever had a thought.

We got down off the train into the near dark (it was ten o'clock in the morning), the carriage lady passing us our bags with a grim smile, as if we really were gulag prisoners arriving at our final, our very final, destination. There have not been enough civilian visitors to Vorkuta, there probably never will be, to make up for the number of prisoners transported here to work down the mines, transported here to work and eventually to die. Some of them petty criminals—light bulb stealers. Some of them violent criminals—brother and sister murderers. Some of them dissidents—middle class types who wore glasses and dreamed of Paris. None of them deserved to come here. Nobody deserves to come here.

When Stalin settled it there were a few Komi people, reindeer herders who lived out on the ice. No buildings, no electricity, no running water. He plunged brutal black mines into the ground, the shafts visible above the surface of the bleak flat landscape from everywhere. Electricity cables hang from pylons, strewn across the nothingness to the grey tower blocks in which the inhabitants of Vorkuta drink. Cars skid around in the slush on the road, some of them western and flashy, owned by people probably employed by Dimitri, to run the mines and sell the vodka to the needy. Or, mostly, to put it on the train to Moscow.

There are tramlines but the trams don't run any more. There are a couple of schools but only a few rooms of them are used now. Everyone who could leave has left. Children are sent to relatives somewhere, anywhere, else, even if their parents can't afford to get out themselves. The Komi who are left, recognisable by their broad faces and slanting eyes, are the town's homeless drunks. Their livelihood was taken away when reindeer hunting was banned and they were forced to go down the mines. And in return for the obliteration of a way of life that had continued unmolested for thousands of years they got vodka. And they used it.

'Oh, shit,' Don said, standing on the station platform and looking round him as his eyelashes and nostrils froze.

'Jesus,' Eden breathed.

Tina, the most colourful thing that had ever come here, glanced about in horror. She had put her bobble hat over her green hair. She shivered dramatically. Only Dimitri jumped off the train revived. He wore a floor-length sable coat and a black shapka. Misha was in bright American winter wear. Don, Eden and I alone looked a bit nippy. Stupid twats of westerners half undressed in the snow. The Russians had seen it all before.

Two big black Mercedes purred by the track, and two big furry drivers stood by them, opening the passenger doors as soon as they saw us. Dimitri walked briskly over to one of the cars and brought out a white fox fur coat which he handed to me. 'Put it on,' he said. 'You'll freeze.'

I had already frozen and anyway I had my secret to protect. The coat was long and soft and had a big hood which I pulled up. Eden looked at me and said, 'Wow.' I noticed that Dimitri noticed.

And I also noticed that Dimitri was the king of Vorkuta. You could see it in his eyes and in his stance. Not that I would ever have thought of him as anything less than regal in Moscow, even in the old days, but here it was clearly an acknowledged fact. This was his territory.

'OK,' he said. 'You guys go about your business. You can take that car and driver.' He held out his hand to offer Don and Eden a brand new Mercedes all to themselves. 'The driver is Ivan. He knows everything about the area and can get you in anywhere you need to get in. At one o'clock he will bring you to meet us on the edge of town and we'll go out to the tundra. It's not to be missed,' he said.

There was no question of anybody not following the man's suggestions. 'We will take this car and see you later,' he said, showing me, in my amazing new coat, Tina and Misha into the other one. There was a fear in the pit of my stomach that would only be explained by what happened later. But for now I put it down to the view.

Buildings loomed out of the darkness, a few, but somehow not enough, of their windows illuminated by a pale yellow light. And the darkness itself was not quite right. Not quite dark but nothing like daylight. There was the occasional row of shops—'Milk', 'Meat,' 'Bread'—but they were all shut and boarded up. The few people who were out on the streets looked drunk or mad or both, wrapped in rags and bits of animal fur, two or three of them actually clutching their bottles. I saw one mother, fur hat and coat, holding hands with two toddlers, bundled up tightly in snow suits, battling the weather, presumably to get them to nursery. I felt tears roll down my cheeks. Now, at least, I knew why I was crying so much. It would never have occurred to me before, before Mum died, before Tina had pointed the obvious out to me. But that woman, struggling down the pavement in Vorkuta, hoping that one day her children would get out of here—she was my sister. I was overwhelmed with such solidarity that I wanted to stop the car, to give them a lift, to take them to Moscow. But I just wiped my tears and let the car cruise on to the Varanovs' flat.

Dimitri and Misha waited downstairs in the car. I was under instructions to take Tina up.

'They know you're coming,' he said. 'It's better they don't know I'm down here. Understood?'

Tina kissed her dad on the cheek as he stood in the entranceway of what was, hands down, no contest, absolutely the most disheartening block of flats on the planet. And it barely even is on the planet. Normally the heating kicks in as soon as you come through the metal and glass double doors in Russia. Even the area by the letter boxes, all of them here hanging open on their hinges, a hundred blue metal flags, motionless in the cold air, is usually unbearably hot. But not here. Putin's government was not about to waste state money heating this shit-hole. And you could almost see their point.

'Yob tvoyu mat', said Tina. 'Fucking hell.'

The aluminium lift doors were open but there was no lift in the shaft. Icy wind blew down it into our faces when we leant in together to check it out. They lived on the fourth floor and Tina leapt up easily. Towards the end I held, breathless, on to the cold steel banister and pulled myself up. I was so stupid. Weak, breathless, sick. And it had taken a sixteen-year-old to offer a diagnosis.

The Varanovy must have been watching and waiting for our car. Hell, they had probably watched the Moscow train arrive in the distance from their grey double-glazed windows. They were standing, beaming, outside their front door, in the unlit corridor, so happy that, when they saw us, they weren't immediately sure which one to hug. But after half a second's pause they threw themselves on Tina, pulling her hat off, kissing and pinching her cheeks, tearing her puffa jacket away to take a proper look at her, to squeeze the tops of her arms and then fall on her, tearful, to kiss her again. They dragged her into the flat and I followed, very nervous indeed. But I needn't have worried. So I was the murdering bastard's second wife, not that they need know this (and they had no idea of my involvement in the murders, thank God)? So what? I had brought Valentina home and that was all they cared about.

Mrs Varanova had dressed up for the occasion. She wore a tweed skirt that had fitted her properly twenty years earlier, a silver blouse with a big bow at the front and thick blue tights. She had a grey cardigan round her shoulders and her hair was dyed gingery orange and set in a sort of Margaret Thatcheresque style. She wore orange lipstick and a gold chain. Mr Varanov was one of those Russian bulls of men. He was barrel-shaped and red-faced with a brown nylon suit on and a cream nylon shirt. They wore matching black felt slippers and offered us the same, all the while weeping and laughing and touching Tina.

'Oh, my darling,' Mrs Varanova said. 'I thought we'd never see you again. So beautiful! You've grown up so beautiful.'

I was slightly surprised that they were able to ignore the hardware in her face, the colour of her hair and the butchness of her clothes, but it was true, she was beautiful.

They fussed us both into the living room and sat us on a shabby velour sofa near the source of heat, an antique paraffin heater, and in front of the display cases. Display cases that were full of baby photos of Tina and two portraits of the twins.

I looked at them, aged maybe ten or eleven, smiling from beyond the grave, and I couldn't see anything that I recognised. I wanted it to be important, to show me who they had been and what they had been like. I wanted it to jog my memory so that no doubts remained. But they just looked like happy twins in brightly coloured sweaters. I stood up to look more closely and it was then that I saw the shot that made my stomach lurch. It was Yelyena, hardly more than a child herself, holding Tina in her arms, a tiny newborn baby. And somebody had been very inexpertly cut out of the picture. Dimitri.

'Look,' said Mr Varanov, whose name was Vladimir, after Lenin, he told me, proudly. Under Communism everyone called Ilya named their sons Vladimir so they could be Vladimir Ilyich like Lenin himself. It always makes me laugh when people introduce themselves, but Russians seem used to it. He showed Tina a photograph of herself crawling across the floor. This floor.

'I've been here before?' Tina smiled at them, overwhelmed and a bit subdued for her. She lit a cigarette and Mrs Varanova, Varvara, who would obviously liked to have said something, instead went to get an ashtray. You could see, you really could see, that Tina looked a bit like Varvara. And I think Varvara knew it too.

'Of course, love. You were with us until you were just over one and a half. Lena, your mum, went to live in Moscow and then...well, then you were with us until your...until he came for you,' Vladimir said.

Tina stood up and walked over to the window, moving the net curtain so that she could see the post-apocalyptic landscape beyond it. 'So, I'm home,' she sighed and Varvara burst into tears again.

There were chocolates and tea and Varvara wanted us to stay while she cooked a duck she must have spent months' worth of pension on (or more likely just ambushed it on the tundra), but Misha was soon ringing on the bell. Tina had hardly spoken while she looked through photographs of herself in knitted babywear, her mother holding her in various locations around town, her mum and uncle on holiday in Tashkent where they had visited a cousin one summer, her mum and uncle, so strangely alike, in a million different poses, staring into a million different cameras. Dimitri didn't get a mention and nor did the extraordinary violence of the twins' death. It was enough after all the suffering that Tina was here and was alive. When it was time to go she hugged the old people tightly, one under each arm of her bright jacket.

'You will come and live in Moscow. I will look after you now. I have a flat, bigger than this. I never use it. I want you to sell your stuff, give it away, I don't care. Here,' she said, fishing out the money Dimitri had given her on the train. 'For your tickets.'

The Varanovy looked at her sadly, unable to accept it as she held it out. Tina put it down on the stool near the coat stand and neither of them forced it back on her. They would come, I understood, and I think all of us were tearful. Certainly it seemed to be my thing.

Downstairs, Misha was waiting. 'All right?' he asked Tina when we got outside. He was being kind.

'Yes,' she nodded, smiling and she kissed his scarred, bearded cheek.

When we got back in the car I took a sip of my water. I had now not had an alcoholic beverage for more than twenty-four hours. My body was not enjoying it.

If anything, now that it was after midday, it looked almost darker than it had before. Dimitri glanced at my hand and saw that I was wearing my ring. I, personally, had forgotten, the huge weight of it notwithstanding. He grinned at me and winked.

'I knew you'd come round,' he said, and he breathed out in what looked like relief or, even, elation. He put his arm round me and squeezed my shoulders. 'Verochka. My Zhaba,' he said, and he was smiling all over his face.

'It's not…' I started to say, but I just didn't have the will any more.

'Right,' Dimitri declared. 'Ladno. Let's go goose hunting!'

Chapter 20

THE DRIVERS HAD both been instructed to drop us on the edge of town, in a spot about two hundred yards away from a disused housing estate where all the miners and their families had once lived. Now Dimitri was using about a quarter of the workforce to do four times the work. They lived, he claimed, in a nice modern thing at the other end of town. I can't honestly imagine 'nice' being a word one could ever apply to anything in Vorkuta. Actually, to be fair, the word he used was 'normalniy', normal, but that, honestly, seemed a bit of a stretch too.

If you'd seen us here from above, standing alone in this white desert, we would have been moving specks of black in the endless landscape of snow, just near the slightly bigger speck of black that would be Vorkuta, and at the end of the snaking line of the railway stretching away towards Moscow.

It was impossible to tell where the horizon was in the sea of endless grey. Don and Eden were leaning against their car, smoking with the driver.

'You look like the snow queen,' Eden said when I got out of our car with Dimitri, Tina and Misha. I did, too.

In front of the big shiny beetles of cars was a tank. It was old and camouflaged and had its number and regiment sprayed on the side in white. It was, in fact, a 1937 T-35. The guns had been ripped off and it was missing a few panels, but it was recognisable. I couldn't believe it was still capable of movement. I also wondered where it had been and what it had been doing until now. The western front?

'OK, guys,' said Dimitri, delighted. 'In you climb.'

'What did he say?' Eden asked.

'He said "Get in",' I told him.

'Oh,' Eden said, dubiously. Misha was already going for the small door in the side. He looked nearly as excited as Dimitri.

'How was your thing about the gulags?' I asked.

'We went to the main prison headquarters,' Eden said. 'It was fucking grim, frankly.'

'Yeah,' Don agreed. 'Grim.'

There is a barrier that often stands between westerners and Russians and it was standing here now, an almost visible thing, like an iron curtain. It's a 'life is tough' thing. I once sat on a plane with some generals from Krasnoyarsk. Their heads were swollen with alcoholism, their lips purple, their shoulders as broad and stooping as the back of a Tupolev. They were trying to chat the stewardess up, but they might as well have been Martians. She didn't have a human or even a mammalian reaction to them (not even revulsion) because they were from a place, from a life, she was never going to understand. 'Grim, eh? What a shocker,' I laughed, and started to get into the tank.

'Dad's always been promising to do this with me!' Tina said, and got in after Misha. I followed her and the others clambered after me.

Inside was pretty much the same as outside. That is, metal. There were no windows and only the gunner, who stood up with a lookout in the turret, could see the real world, such as it was. Misha was going to drive, peering out above the anti-quated controls through a scratched and nearly opaque panel in front of him. Dimitri, it seemed, was the gunless gunner. The floor was covered in grease and slush and we were clearly going to be sitting on it. Which, when wearing a white fox fur, seems a bit of a shame. Now I know there are people in England who don't like the idea of wearing fur. But all I have to say to this is—it's cold in Russia and people have got other things to worry about. Like not dying and stuff. Societies have to get pretty affluent and problem-free before animal rights start being an issue. I mean, cruelty to animals is one thing, but having an objection to killing them for meat or clothing is a long way off in Russia.

There were two boxes of vodka, in all twenty-six bottles, and a paper bag full of radishes in here. There were also six VEPR hunting rifles, stacked up against the front wall. They are like AK-47s but for hunting. These ones were brand new, black shiny barrels and unsullied, sleek slings. Misha, who could barely fit his arse in the small swivelling metal seat in front of the pedals and levers, took his place. Dimitri threw a couple of tarpaulins over the floor and invited the rest of us to sit down. It wasn't agonisingly uncomfortable until Misha started the engine and we were moving. Then the shuddering shook all our bones until I thought they might break.

'You might get a free one,' Tina whispered to me and it took me a couple of seconds to realise what she was talking about. Ugh. A miscarriage in a tank would be...well, messy for one thing. Though she was right about the lack of choice it would involve. Choice. We are all brought up to want it. In America and Britain it has been presented as a kind of human right. I've never really understood its lure, though. People think they want it but are always secretly glad to be relieved of it. As I would have been in this instance, I suppose. God, what a fucking thing to have happened.

Dimitri pulled the little door shut, stood up with his head in the turret, and the whole machine filled with petrol fumes, the engine pumping blistering heat out into the cavity of the thing where we were all sitting. Feeling sick and overheated I backed away down to the other end, but here it was as cold as outside and my bum soon went numb. I was thinking of telling this to Don to cheer him up but I didn't quite have the enthusiasm. Dimitri came down, energetic and edgy, and bit the top off four bottles of vodka (I remembered where my talent for biting the tops off beer bottles was, in fact, learnt). Supporting himself on the sides of the tank, he staggered along to pass one to Misha. We weren't bothering with the formality of shots or toasts or even pouring it out. He gave one each to Don and Eden and kept another one for himself. Out of his coat pockets he brought a big green glass bottle of champagne and handed it to me.

'Ladies,' he nodded, gallantly, smiling a bit and twinkling his eyes. And I like the Russian gallantry. It takes English men in Russia years to learn. They get there still pouring themselves wine at a table full of women, letting the door close on girls they are actually taking on a date and…no, but seriously…allowing women to get half the bill. Meet these blokes a few years later and they are practically laying their coats down in the slush for you. In Russia no woman will talk to you otherwise. And I know it hardly suits me, but I like it.

Dimitri was happy. I was wearing his ring (I still hadn't quite dared take it off, though I'd never meant to put it on) and he had taken this as a sign. And I think now that he genuinely believed that when we got back from this trip I would move into that flat he had done up for me. Well, for me apart from Tina's room, that is…

I had tried not to drink for the day while I decided what I was going to do about my problem. But I still hadn't decided. In fact, I had no idea, and I really did need a drink. I twisted the cork out of the champagne and took a swig. Better already. I passed it to Tina and got my cigarettes out of my jacket, which I was still wearing under the fur. The petrol fumes were asphyxiating anyway, so smoking didn't seem to make much difference. I was terrified that Tina might suddenly tell me I shouldn't be drinking or smoking, but then it occurred to me that she just assumed I'd be aborting, thinking nothing of it. That's a sixteen-year-old for you. At thirty-five it is a different proposition. Now or never and everything. And I had always thought that never was my preference. But that was a positive decision in a way. Now it would involve negative action. And the last thing I was about to do before I knew exactly what I thought about it was tell Eden Jones and hear his views on the subject. Thanks.

It's like a war zone, Russia. Even when there isn't a war going on (which, let's face it, there usually is). It's a country that makes you feel ashamed of your own little worries and concerns. Am I getting fat? Well, not that I've ever had to wonder that, but you know the kind of thing. It pulls life into perspective and lets you escape from the mundane details of your life all at the same time. Escapist but somehow confrontational. Well, it has always had a reputation as confusing (there is a forever quoted Churchill line on this with which I'm not going to bore you). Anyway, my point is that I found it amazing that I could be out here, in this appalling wilderness, worrying about problems as small as a child, a relationship, one little life.

Suddenly the tank lurched to a halt, sending Don, who was sipping his bottle of vodka with his eyes closed, sprawling flat on to the floor, his vodka slopping out all over the tarpaulin.

'Oi, get off, you poof!' he shouted, dozy, assuming some-one had pushed him over. Misha was shouting down to Dimi-tri to open the door.

'It's Sasha,' he yelled.

Dimitri smiled and opened the door, leaping down into the snow. We all shrugged and made 'no idea' faces at each other and Dimitri came back in, took a couple of bottles of vodka and hopped back out again shouting something to whoever was outside.

'Who the *fuck* is wandering around out there?' I said, just as Dimitri was coming back in and shutting the cold air out again. It was bitter outside. Your spit would definitely freeze before it hit the ground. Don was too pissed to notice, but Eden was beginning to look a bit blue. He had two jumpers and a jacket on but you really need polar exploration stuff here.

'Sasha's been roaming for ten years. There are a few of them. Escaped from prison and stole a tank. You can't get across the snow in anything else. They can't go back but there's nowhere to go either. Some of them have got their families with them. They live like this,' Dimitri explained.

This seemed just too bleak to be imaginable. Even for Vorkuta.

'I've seen the prison. This is preferable,' Eden nodded when I'd translated for him.

'What do they eat?'

'We've got people who take stuff to them. Sasha thought we were doing a delivery. That's why he stopped us,' Dimitri said.

'He stopped us in a tank?' I asked.

Dimitri nodded and leapt back to his gunner station. Tina had drunk most of the champagne now and was gig-gling to herself about nothing.

'Got to bring Job up here,' she said. 'He'd be so freaked out.'

'Unlike us?' I asked, taking the champagne off her.

Tina laughed at me. 'You seemed like one of us until we got you here, man,' she said.

It's true. Russians have always told me 'Ty nash chelovyek'. You're one of us. But you have to have Russian blood coursing through your veins for Vorkuta not to put the fear of God into you. And, after all, it turns out, I am English.

Eden had taken Don's lead and had sunk half a bottle of vodka before shutting his eyes. People often have this reaction to Russia. If you drink enough it'll go away. It won't, though. It actually gets closer.

The tank juddered to a halt again and Dimitri leapt down, excited. 'OK. There's a rifle for everyone, but don't start shooting until your eyes have adjusted,' he said. 'If you do you'll get snowsick.'

He jumped down with all the rifles in his arms and handed one to each of us as we passed him, crunching our boots into the snow. My feet were frozen before I'd taken a step and I pulled a tarpaulin out after me to stand on. The snow was only as deep as the last fall. It quickly turned to ice and was, in all, probably forty feet deep at least. That was why it took a tank to drive across it. Anything else would start to sink.

'Whoa. Fuck me,' Don said, stumbling out, falling into the snow, standing up again.

He spat some snow out of his mouth, looked around and started to sway. You had to concentrate if you wanted to stay upright. It was so difficult to see the horizon, to understand the difference between land and sky that it was like being underwater doing somersaults and forgetting which way is up. That is snowsickness. Weirdly, perhaps because there was no artificial light with which to compare the eerie glow of the natural light, it seemed brighter here than it had in Vorkuta. It must now have been about three in the afternoon. The men were all holding their bottles, but me and Tina had left ours, empty in any case, inside.

'Goose!' Tina shouted, looking up and starting to aim her gun.

'No!' Dimitri snapped at her. 'Not yet. Get adjusted first.'

She was right, though. There was a V of geese flying over us, on their way to wherever they go. Somewhere nicer, I hoped.

It was Misha who started shooting first. He looked around him as though he might be about to pass out, gaze unfocused, feet exaggeratedly steady, but then he raised his rifle and fired a shot into the air, so loud in the silence of the tundra that I thought my eardrum might have burst.

'Shit! Get down!' Don yelled, clearly unaware of where he was or what was going on. But, once he had got up, the noise and the second faceful of snow seemed to have revived him. 'Oh. Jolly good,' he said, taking in his surroundings and raising his own rifle to the sky.

Misha's shot had been a good one and the heavy shape of a goose came tumbling through the air to flomp down in the snow about fifty feet away. Don, obviously, hit nothing. Before long we were all searching the sky through the sights on our rifles and Misha and Dimitri were firing like mad, bringing bird after bird plummeting to the ground in small pools of bright blood. I could see why you need dogs. Tina missed a lot but hit one and the English, naturally, were entirely unsuccessful. I blamed my coat which was seriously impairing my mobility. Also, focussing down the barrel of a gun made me dizzy.

Russians of Dimitri's age got taught to shoot at school. They took them down the range from the age of seven, and at fairs and amusement arcades there are no prizes for the shooting stalls. Everyone hits all the moving targets, which are battered and unrecognisable as the animal shapes they once were, and the stall holder just slaps them back up again, unsmiling. How they ever managed to lose the cold war I can't imagine. They were extremely well prepared. If it had been an actual fight I'm sure they would have cruised to victory.

The icy air around us was now full of the smell of gunpowder, like firework night but with something more acrid about it. The wars I have been to have always been in built-up areas with all the odour of human life to go with the smell of smoking guns. But here, in the pristine atmosphere of the endless tundra, the stench was overpowering. Again I imagined us from above. White nothingness and then a tank, six people with guns, and the specks of bleeding bird.

'Ladno,' Dimitri announced after a series of sharp bangs. 'Vsyo.' And everyone stopped firing. He had decided that that was enough with the shooting for now. Misha plunged off to get the geese we'd shot, OK, they'd shot, wading into the snow and breaking the necks of the ones that weren't dead yet. This was surely a job for a dog?

'Think I got one there, Zanetti,' Don told me proudly.

I patted him on the shoulder. 'Well done, Donald,' I said. 'You can take it home to Ira.'

I had decided against telling him Ira's news. I had enough news of my own and perhaps if he didn't know, just turned up back home with a goose shot by his own fair hand (hey, who was going to shatter his dreams?), she might soften.

'Bastards keep flapping in the wrong direction,' Eden complained, looking very pale now in the dim light.

'Lucky we had the guns to defend ourselves,' I said. 'You never know when one might just dive for you, fangs bared.'

'Exactly,' Eden agreed.

I wasn't cold but I shivered. Dimitri was making a fire with wood he had lashed to the back of the tank in another tarpaulin thing. The tundra does nothing at all to help with one's existential angst. Out here where there is nothing and no one, even in drunken company you are as alone as you could possibly be. No God to look down on you here. People have 'experiences' in places like this. On tiny ships alone at sea, in the desert under the stars. But this is surely different for its complete brutality. There is *nothing* here.

I went and stood by the fire which was burning a bit now. Misha squatted on my tarpaulin, plucking a goose. It was still warm. I know this because it was steaming as he worked. He pulled the feathers out in big handfuls, as quickly as possible since he had taken his gloves off. I was amazed he still had any sensitivity at all in those chapped, calloused fingers. A huge pile of as many as ten or twelve birds lay in a heap by the vast grinding tracks of our vehicle.

Misha hadn't spoken for a very long time. Speaking was not really Misha's forte. Tina was pacing round and round the tank, smoking.

'Come and get warm,' I told her.

'I need a shit,' she said, laughing.

'Oh, God,' I smiled. 'Well. I suppose you'll just have to do one.'

'Yes,' she agreed, and set off pacing again. There were no hiding places here.

'Yo moyo,' Misha shouted, getting up and grabbing a long stick from the firewood. His phrase was a way of swearing without bothering to finish. He had given up with the goose and impaled it quickly on the stick, sending a lot of entrails slopping down into the snow, and put it on the fire. As far as I could see it was going to burn quickly on the outside and stay raw inside. The men were probably too drunk to care.

'Hey, Mish, you missed one,' Dimitri said, pointing to a dying bird quite far away.

Misha was crouching by the fire and wasn't going anywhere. 'Fuck it,' he mumbled, leaving his cigarette between his lips. 'We've got enough.'

Don was still holding his gun, proudly. 'Take a picture of me, Zanetti,' he said, nodding to the camera bag that he'd left hanging off the tank door.

I stomped over to get the camera out, knowing that he was going to shout at me now for half an hour.

'You'll need to change that lens, Zanetti. Look, that one in the black tube. No, not that one. Listen, if you can't even work out which fucking lens to use, you might as well just—'

I interrupted him. 'Oh shit, Don. I'm going to point it at you and press the button,' I said, annoyed.

'OK. But in that case put the flash on and wait for the orange light, and set it on automatic. There's a big red A and if you turn it—'

'I've got it,' I said. 'Don't you want to hold a goose up?'

'Good point,' Don realised, and waddled off to get one. He held it by its feet. 'I think this is the one, actually,' he said.

I nodded and took the photograph. Sometimes, in places like this, it feels odd even to be speaking.

Eden was looking out at the writhing bird in the distance.

'I'll go,' he said, perhaps wanting to participate in the general show of manliness.

'You haven't got the right shoes,' Dimitri told him.

'He says you've got stupid shoes on. You can't,' I translated, helpfully. Don laughed.

I could smell the goose cooking now and was beginning to feel hungry. I assumed we'd be hacking at it with penknives and accompanying it with radishes.

Eden put his gun down and set off towards the goose, already sinking up to his knees after the first few steps. He was going to get very cold. Tina hadn't come back round the tank, so I assumed she'd decided to go for it. Dimitri set off after Eden, his gun slung over his shoulder.

'He's crazy,' he said, tutting and lighting a cigarette as he went. 'Does he know how to kill it?' he asked me, turning back with a twinkle in his eye, claiming possession of me.

'Doubt it,' I said, shaking my head in my big fur hood. 'Very unlikely.'

Misha pulled the goose out of the fire with his bare hands. So, in fact, he perhaps doesn't have any feeling in his fingers. He tore off a leg and held it out to me. No penknife then.

I took it and immediately dropped it. 'Fuck!' I said. 'Hot!'

Not by the time I'd fished it out of the snow, it wasn't. I took a big bite and it was absolutely delicious. Sort of smoky with a crispy skin. Tender and just fatty enough to be filling. 'God, Misha, this is great,' I said.

Misha smiled, for, I think, the first time, and nodded vigorously, taking an enormous bite himself right out of the side of the bird, juice dripping down into his beard. He tore another leg off for Don as he chewed. Don took a long swig of vodka and tucked in, still standing proudly, with his gun strapped round him.

'I could really get used to this,' he said, very pleased with his image of himself as tough guy. Tank, goose killing, fire, vodka. He slapped Misha quite hard on the back to prove that they were cut from the same cloth, hewn from the same rock, all that business. He tossed his bone over his shoulder, wiped

his hands on his trousers and his mouth on his sleeve and
went to get his camera.

'Weird light, this. Going to be tricky,' he said. It must
have been about four o'clock and it was starting to get a bit
darker, I thought, though it was hard to tell. If I was going
to get the midnight train back to Moscow it would be good
to start moving quite soon. I would decide what to do once I
got back to Moscow. Just this thought made me reach out for
Misha's vodka, sitting almost empty at his feet by the fire.

'Can I have a swig?' I asked him and he nodded happily.
Unlike Don, this really was, I saw, Misha's element. As brutal
as he was, as simple and as unforgiving.

'That was gross,' Tina grinned, reappearing.

'Yeah, but look at that,' I told her, pointing over to Misha
who was holding a goose on a charred stick and eating it. She
bounced up to him, leaping towards him like one of those
rugby players from New Zealand doing a squatting, jumping
dance.

'Give us a bite, Uncle,' she said, and sank her teeth into
the other side of the goose, her arse dangerously close to the
fire. How did this sinister wasteland not affect her?

I looked across at Eden and Dimitri, so far away now in
the dimming light. Eden seemed to have fallen and Dimitri
was leaning over, helping him up. Or was he? I took a few
steps out towards them, breathing very quickly. I took a few
more steps and sank a bit, staggering further.

'Hey!' I yelled as loudly as I could.

The others looked round at me but went back to their
goose-related bantering. I am very good in a crisis. I don't
panic until afterwards. I freeze. I can hear my heart and am
aware of all my senses quickening, rushing into overdrive, but
I appear calm and I can function normally, sorting things out,
doing what needs to be done. Then afterwards I take a few

Valium and I have a few vodkas. I had gone into emergency mode now.

Dimitri wasn't helping Eden up. I could just make out the shapes of the two men against the darkening sky, or perhaps just against the shadowy snow. There was no difference here. Eden was lying on his back, protecting himself with his arms. Dimitri, I was almost sure, was pointing, poking his rifle into Eden's chest.

'Hey!' I shouted again, hoping to distract Dimitri, or for something to happen that would prove me wrong.

'Stop screaming, Zanetti, you slag. They'll be back in a minute,' Don shouted over to me, laughing. Tina was sitting on Misha's lap, her features dancing in the firelight. I was quite a long way from them now, couldn't hear their chatter, just the faint impression of it.

I stared at the shapes of the men. My husband, or, rather, the man who had never been my husband. Yelyena's husband and Tina's father. That's who he was, however many pictures of Humphrey Bogart he collects. And Eden, flailing wildly now. The father of my child.

I had been pointlessly dragging my gun with me through the snow, my arm through the sling as though I was carrying a handbag. I lifted it now on to my shoulder and put my fingers on the trigger, getting the men in my sights. These things, I remembered, had special five or ten round magazines. But I hadn't loaded it myself and I couldn't remember how many shots I'd fired at the geese. Not many. Four, I thought. Maybe five. My ring slipped down and knocked against the trigger, a tinkling sound. Irritably I shook my hand and let it fall into the snow, resuming my stance. I saw them, slightly magnified in the scope. Eden wasn't moving now and yet I had not heard a shot. Dimitri appeared to be leaning on the butt of his weapon, maybe pushing the barrel into Eden's chest.

Jealous. It was true. He had always been jealous. Jealous of everyone I knew and spoke to. Jealous even of Yelyena's brother. I suppose I knew. I suppose on some level I knew he was capable of this. Had always known. Otherwise I wouldn't have been so quick to assess this. To recognise the truth. To see what was going on here.

It was hard to keep aim. The coat was slippery and I couldn't get the gun to rest into my shoulder properly. No wonder I'd missed the geese. I had not been concentrating. I shook the coat off my shoulders and was left there, knee deep in snow, my eyelashes frozen and white, my breath crystallising in the air, wearing my leather jacket, jeans, T-shirt and cowboy boots. I raised a hand and pushed my hair out of my face. Since seeing Dimitri again I had lost sight of the woman I had become over the past fifteen years. But now I was back.

My freezing fingers began to tighten on the trigger when Dimitri suddenly spun his gun around and rammed the butt of it into, I wasn't sure, Eden's head, though it may have been his neck or chest. Grotesquely, I then saw the bird, still struggling beside the men.

Now Dimitri took a proper hold on his rifle again and raised it into the air before bringing it down to aim it at Eden's head from less than six inches away. Eden raised his hands to protect himself, I heard Tina cry out behind me, I felt the movement of Don and Misha coming towards me, shouting. But I was focused. I had taken aim. And then I fired.

Chapter 21

I ARRIVED BACK in Moscow on Wednesday morning. Eden lay almost entirely still all the way, clutching at his broken jaw and moaning. Don and I fed him soup, tea and vodka through a straw as his face went deep purple and swelled up so that he could hardly see. The carriage lady who brought tea winced even to look at him.

Tina, who had been restrained, like a wild animal, in the tank back to Vorkuta by Misha's big bear hug, had been left with her grandparents. Misha took her round there in one of the cars and she agreed, pale and shaking, her bright hair ridiculous now against her grief, to stay with them while they got ready to move to Moscow. She didn't speak to me again. Why would she?

While Don and I buried her father, minus half his head, under a white fur coat in the tundra snow she whimpered and moaned, always in Misha's grasp. Dimitri, strangely twisted and stiff, already inhuman, froze quickly though it looked like rigor mortis.

'Bollocks,' Don kept saying while he dug with a spade from the tank. 'Bollocks.' His fingers were raw and red and he looked old, unshaven, against the glow of the moon on the snow. I stroked his back and shushed him. It was only a shallow grave. Nobody was ever going to find him out here. Not ever. Not for thousands of years, until after the climate has changed and someone is sifting through desert sand for ancient bones.

'It's all right,' I said. 'It's going to be all right.'

I might even have been talking to the baby. Maybe.

Misha himself sobbed uncontrollably and, while Don fulfilled his dream of driving a tank, he began to talk.

He talked and talked, over the head of the whimpering Tina who was enveloped in his jacket and arms, choking, her eyes and nose streaming, her insides seeming to be ripped out through her mouth. All the way back to Vorkuta. I noticed that she had gold nail varnish on. Chipped now. I doubted she'd wear all that stuff any more.

'I can't believe he's gone,' Misha began. 'I can't believe I'm free. It's really over!' He kept looking around him nervously as though Dimitri might come back from the dead at any moment. I don't think Tina was in any state to hear him. 'Anastassiya! My Nastyochka. I can tell her he will never hurt her again.'

Everything was falling slowly into place. 'He used to be a friend. I thought we were doing the vodka business together. But then when the others tried to get protection money off us he changed,' Misha mumbled. And it wasn't a surprise really. It had happened to a lot of people. They started out in a small business then things got competitive, violent. You had to protect your interests, get people to help you protect your interests. And there was no choice—be brutal or get out. Dimitri had obviously chosen the former. And he'd made money, consolidated his power, ended up with more and more things to protect, more and more reason to carry on. And I suppose that somewhere along the way your soul ices over.

I smoked one cigarette after the other in an effort to stop my hands shaking. Tomorrow, I thought, I would give up.

Misha stayed behind in Vorkuta too, in one of Dimitri's flats, to bring Tina back eventually and to sort his life out. He wanted his wife, Nastya, and his son Borka to join him up here in the end, he said. He'd be lucky, I thought, but I didn't say it. I could see how he fitted in, but I couldn't imagine him getting a teenaged boy to move from Moscow to Vorkuta. Not in a million years. He hugged me so tight at the train station I thought I might pass out.

'Thank you,' he said as the carriage lady pulled my bag out of the lightly falling snow and the pitch darkness into the warm yellow glow of the train that would take us back to our planet. 'The guy was a cunt.'

Arkady met us on the platform in Moscow along with an ambulance from the Kremlin Hospital. They were going to sort Eden out well enough so that he could fly back to London on the British Airways 16.20 and see a specialist. The paramedic who helped him into the ambulance, not that he really needed it, looked at Eden with a certain distaste. I think the only people she ever saw in that kind of state were fighting drunks. And it was true that Eden had not bathed for four days and probably stank of vodka.

'Have a good flight,' I said. 'I'll send you your stuff.'

Eden winced in pain and held his hand up. 'Good shot, Zanetti,' he said and tried to smile.

'Don't mention it,' I told him, and Don and I got into the *Chronicle*'s Volvo, Don slinging two geese in a sack into the boot. We were exhausted but nearly home.

I looked out of the window at the grey city and all the people bustling about in the slush outside the station, zero degrees suddenly seeming very warm, the big advertising billboards for casinos, mobile phones and lingerie, the crowds pouring in and out of the metro and the choking traffic. And I smiled. It was good to be back.

'So,' Arkady said. 'We should be just about on time.'

'Hello?' I said, leaning forward.

'Prison. We're going to see Jesus. Remember?'

I didn't. There is something about this lurching from one drama to the next (though it's usually other people's dramas not one's own, of course) that helps. You can't dwell too long on one story, one expedition, one traumatic hellhole, because there's always another to go to. It's very Richard and Judy. Straight on to the next thing, however relatively banal. I once watched them go from Holocaust memorial to Botox injections without so much as a flinch. And we were doing it now. The paper wouldn't wait.

'Oh, rank old men's bollocks,' Don exclaimed. 'Not really?'

'Of course I don't remember. I never set this up. Arkady, I have just got back from hell. I need a shower. You don't know what happened up there…'

'And I don't care,' Arkady said, glancing quickly round at me. 'Lyuda set it up, it's now, and it's my job to get you there.'

'OK,' I said, lighting another cigarette. 'OK.'

'Festering leper's testicles,' Don mumbled, swigging at a beer he'd bought on the train. I opened my window, took the can out of his hand and threw it out.

'OK, Don,' I said. 'That's enough. The end. Enough.'

'Whoa,' he said, holding his hands up. 'Easy, Zanetti. Don't get all power crazed on me now.'

I laughed. But I had been abdicating responsibility for everything for long enough. I had some facing up to do.

When the gates of Butyrskaya prison clanged shut behind us I remembered not only this, but that I had my interview at the procurator's office this very afternoon. I was glad they didn't take women at the Butyrka. Don pointed his camera at a group of wardens in khaki having a cigarette outside the barbed wire battlements of the main prison. Our guide, not the clarinet-playing director but a surly deputy, showed us through gate after gate, locking and unlocking with a big bunch of very low tech keys. This story had been Eden's gift and I was grateful. The paper would just die for it. So to speak.

Inside, the building smelt of cabbage and urine. There were wide filthy corridors with big metal doors on either side, tiny peepholes in each and, at the bottom, a cat flap thing for poking food through. There was a roar as we came on to the main corridor, a sexual taunt aimed, I thought, at me. In each cell one man lay on the floor watching through the food flap and reporting to the other twenty men what he'd seen. At the end of the corridor on a windowless white wall was a fifteen foot high crucifix with Christ nailed to it. Christ had been made out of papier mâché and crudely painted with bleeding wounds and wobbly genitalia.

'Craft project,' our guide said. Don knelt in front of the Lamb of God, as though in reverence, but actually to get a better angle for the picture.

'Whoa, nelly,' he said as he snapped.

The deputy director knocked on a cell door with the back of his hand. 'Visitors from England,' he shouted.

He unlocked the door and showed us in. One man with bare feet and a long beard sat hunched on the lower bunk holding a Bible, a beatific smile on his face, like a stoned person or someone who has just had an orgasm. He had a lot of greenish tattoos on his arms. I noticed immediately that he was missing two fingers on his right hand. In front of him, cross-legged and also smiling slightly, were twelve men, their heads bowed. This was a tiny two-man cell, but somehow, in the peace and quiet of it, there seemed to be easily room for everyone.

'That's Briukhanov,' the deputy director said, pointing at the man with the Bible. 'I'll leave you.'

Don's camera was wildly whirring and clicking and he sat on the floor straight away, poking his lens into the faces of the…well, the disciples. What can I say?

'I'm sorry,' said Briukhanov. 'We were reading from the Bible. Come. Sit.' He patted the edge of the bed next to him and I sat down.

'I am the Messiah,' he said. 'And you are?' He looked into my face, open, expectant, kind.

'Faith Zanetti,' I smiled.

'Faith Zanetti.' He turned the unfamiliar language around on his tongue.

'Vera, in Russian,' I told him.

'Ah! Vera. Well, how appropriate,' he said.

He was well spoken but I thought it had to be an act. His tattoos, the scars on his face, the lack of fingers, the fact that he was doing time for armed robbery all spoke of a different kind of background to the one he was putting across.

'As you can see,' he said, putting his hand on mine, 'I have lived amongst men as one of them. My Father spoke to me only once I was truly with the sinners. Here, in Butyrka.'

His hand was uncomfortably warm and I was beginning to feel a bit trance-like. Wished I'd had breakfast. The disciples, I noticed, were all holding hands now, but Jesus had his attention focused on me. He put his other hand on my forehead and I felt all my tension and exhaustion slip away.

'I can see you are troubled,' he said. Well, I thought, isn't everyone? 'I forgive you for what you have done,' he said, and tears started to stream down my face. I shut my eyes and again I saw Dimitri, no more than a boy really, handing me a rose on the steps of the Bolshoi, smiling at me as happy as if he'd seen an angel. 'God forgives you,' Briukhanov said and I murmured, 'Thank you.' I doubted He did though. Maybe He was just trying to be nice.

Jesus still had his hands on me and I felt him draw in a deep breath. 'Look after the child you are carrying. Show her the right way,' he said. I opened my eyes like a shot and shook his hands off.

'What?' I said, trying to stand up and banging my head on the top bunk. 'Ow!'

'What child?' Don asked, standing up too and taking a photograph of me with my hands clutching my head.

'Oh, fuck off, McCaughrean,' I said.

The Messiah was laughing but his eyes were still boring into me like those pictures of Rasputin. 'And tell the father, won't you?' he added.

My arms fell to my sides. 'Yes,' I said. 'I will.'

Don let his camera drop. His eyes were full of tears. 'Hey, congratulations, man,' he said, and threw a hug round me, kissing my cheek.

Now we were all watery-eyed, goddammit. One of the disciples had lit a stick of incense. Maybe that was it.

Don was embracing the spirit of it now and had gone to kneel at Briukhanov's feet, closing his eyes and bowing his head as though he were about to receive communion. Briukhanov touched his forehead. 'You know what to do,' he told Don. 'Go and do it.'

I thought this was a lot less impressive than my prophesy had been but Don seemed pleased. Shaken, I banged on the door to ask the warder to let us out. I had met Jesus and the rest of the story could wait. I'd lift it off Eden.

At home I stood under the shower for twenty minutes. I felt as if no amount of hot water could ever clean me. Very Macbeth. I washed my hair and let the soap run down over my face. The water swirling down the plughole was dark with filth and blood. Mostly Eden's actually, and few geese. The stink of Don's geese on the train had been appalling, but they were his peace offering to Ira and he had gone to give them to her. I never did tell him that she'd booked him into the National.

Coming out, steaming, and wrapping a big white towel around myself, I thought that I was less traumatised than I could have been. I had to do it. I would do it again. It was tragic, and it was a gruesome end to a strange and sinister episode, but I had to save Eden. Some actions barely involve choice. I put my hand on my stomach and went to lie down on the bed, still in my towel. Natasha brought me sweet tea and buttered toast. She was quiet and gentle with me and I felt as though she knew. Maybe with that Russian sixth sense. I picked up a pillow and put it over my face.

'Right,' I thought. 'Right.' It has been long enough. Eden had made his point. What was I going to do? Run around the world chasing wars until I was too old to do it any more? What for? To bring the truth back to the British people? Maybe, but do they really want it or need it? And anyway the papers never print the stories that need to be written. It's all tabloid crap, your slightly racist preconceptions reinforced—from Russia they want spies, vodka, ballet and bears. You know, old KGB files preferably on famous Brits, the alcoholic murder rate, the Bolshoi on the skids, dancing bears still on the streets in Almaty. That kind of thing. Hell, we've written it and you've read it. Was that what I was going to do forever? Did I love Eden? Well, he was an arsehole—but yes. Did I want to have an abortion? Well, in a way—but, no. So...

Smiling to myself and sitting up straight, naked in bed, the towel fallen away, to start my new life I dialled Eden's mobile number.

'Hello?' he groaned, as though his mouth was full of cotton wool.

'It's me. Where are you?' I asked him.

'On the way to the airport,' he said. 'The whole fucking side of my face is anaesthetised.'

'Well, better than if it wasn't,' I offered.

'Yeah,' he agreed.

Should I ask him to turn the car round? To come back and lie in my arms for the news? Would he really be pleased? I mean, it's what he'd been asking for but could he really take it now it was happening? There was only one way to find out.

'I've got news,' I said. 'Really good news.'

'Me too, actually,' he said, slightly annoyingly.

'Oh,' I said. 'OK. You first.'

'No. You first.'

'No. Go on. You're the one with the face falling off.'

'All right. I just got a call from the *FT* and...' He left a long pause. 'Ta-da! They want me to go to China! Can you believe it? China! After all these fucking years of begging and pleading!'

I didn't say anything. I had my hand over my mouth, in fact. Quick rethink.

'Faith? Faithy?'

'That's great,' I said. 'Congratulations. What about the *New Yorker*?'

'Well, it's a twelve piece contract so I can still do it, I hope. Aren't you pleased for me?'

'Yeah. Yes, of course I am. You know I am. Your biggest fan!' I said.

'So? What's your news?'

'Oh, it's nothing. Nothing like that,' I whispered. 'Just… well, Tamsin really likes the "Jesus banged up for GBH" thing.'

'Oh. Great. Good. Have you already been?'

'Yeah. Straight from the station. Listen—I'd better go. Write it up. Safe flight…' I tailed off.

'Thanks. Love you,' Eden told me, and hung up.

Jesus had told me to tell him, but that was before we were in possession of all the facts. And anyway, what did Jesus know?

Chapter 22

THE INTERVIEW AT the procurator's already seems like years ago. I went in that same afternoon that Eden told me he was moving to China. The same day I met Jesus.

I hadn't planned my speech but I was basically relaxed about it. Unreasonably, I suppose. I didn't really have anything new to say. Certainly nothing that would exculpate me. I was guiltier now than I'd ever imagined. But I was sure that they didn't know that and I wasn't about to start confessing to things.

It suited me much better to turn up in my own sodding car with driver as well than it did to be hauled in by Tweedledum and Tweedledee like last time. And it was all taking place in daylight, satisfyingly stripping the experience of the night horrors.

Sergeant Molotova met me at the front desk, bright and cheerful and a lot more friendly than before. I sensed that things were different. We walked along the hideously lit corridor once again and Sergeant Molotova chatted breezily.

'Sakhnov left a note,' she said.

'Really?' I asked, briefly stunned. But then I realised she was talking about Adrian and not about Dimitri. I remembered my bloodstained dress at his flat and a shard of fear shot through me.

'Yes, a suicide note. The usual stuff really, but one thing we couldn't ignore was his insistence that we interview your landlady again. Especially as it was so ballsed up at the time.'

'Zinaida Petrovna?' I asked, amazed.

'Yes, she's still alive. Not only alive, but sitting right here,' Sergeant Molotova said, showing me into the same interview room I'd been in that night, two weeks and a thousand years ago.

And there she was. Zinaida Petrovna. The same pale purple hair, though slightly less of it, bad make-up, big bosom. It's funny the way that people you meet when they are already old don't seem to change much. I had aged dramatically since I'd last seen her, but she looked pretty much exactly the same.

'Zinaida Petrovna,' I said. 'Dobriy dyen. Good day.'

She smiled warily and Sergeant Molotova sat me down and took a seat herself, but didn't switch the interview apparatus on.

'This isn't a formal interview,' she explained. 'We would just like you, Miss Zanetti, to listen to Mrs Dubova's account of the night of the murders and compare it to your own memory. Mrs Dubova has formally retracted her original statement and, in the light of the death of Mr Sakhnov, is now submitting the following evidence.' Funny. I had never known her surname. Sergeant Molotova gestured to Zinaida Petrovna to begin. My old landlady, the very woman who had sewn me into that bloodsoaked dress, spoke her story straight to me, as a kind of apology.

'He was not a nice man,' she began. 'He paid me well for my silence but I can rest easier knowing he's gone.'

It struck me as odd that when she said he was gone she was imagining a grim prison suicide. Though in fact, since I was last here, Dimitri had gone. Or, at least, been dispatched. It was clever of Adrian to write a note. He knew he couldn't escape once Dimitri had made it known that he hadn't been killed in any car crash. But he'd tried to help me, tried to take Dimitri down with him. I knew now, of course, that Adrian had never volunteered to sacrifice himself for me. Dimitri had used him. Punishing him for his pathetic drunken professions of love. Just as he tried to punish Eden. Obviously, he'd promised to look after Adrian's family if he did as he was told. Probably gave himself gangsterish points for honour. And then he'd told Adrian to kill himself. 'Kill yourself or I'll kill them.' Zinaida Petrovna was right. I could rest easier too.

She went on. 'I did something bad. I did something really terrible that night and I wanted to ask your forgiveness. After you left for the party I went into your room and I...' she paused and wiped her eyes. 'I took your chicken. I stole the chicken you'd put in the window. You've probably forgotten...'

'No. No, I haven't,' I said. 'But it's fine.'

'Anyway, I was leaving the room with the chicken and he suddenly switched the lights on. He'd been in there, sitting on a stool in the dark. It really gave me the creeps. He was angry. Wanted to know where you were. Wanted to know where the nice girl next door was. Said everyone was betraying him. I told him I didn't know where she was but I thought her husband was asleep in bed. This shocked him. He started getting really worked up. 'Husband, eh?' he was saying. Then he made me come with him to the caretaker, made me ask Tolik for an axe to chop an old dresser up. He told me what to say. Then he told me to stand guard and he kicked the door to the young couple's room open and he went in and did something...' She seemed almost to choke now. 'I...I don't know what. But when I screamed he ran out of the room, wild, raging, and he slapped me hard across the face. Told me to stay where I was, not let the boy leave or he'd kill me. He made me tell him where you'd gone—I remembered you'd told me you were going to Dom Literatov—and he went out of the house, left me standing there, listening to the boy inside, Leonid, screaming, dying, I thought. I should have helped him, God save me. I should have helped him, but I was terrified. I'm sorry.' She looked at me, imploring.

'It's OK,' I said, as though I was in any position to offer absolution. Hell, the police and ambulance probably wouldn't have come even if she had called.

'While he was gone the girl came in, saw me shivering and sobbing, heard Leonid speaking to himself, quieter now, and she went in and started screaming "Get help! Get help!" and I told her I couldn't and then Dimitri comes back, without you. I suppose he couldn't find you. He's still got the axe. He must have taken it out with him...'

I thought as she spoke that Scott had had a lucky escape that night and I knew now that it was only Misha's presence that had saved him a few weeks later. At the robbery.

'And he starts shouting at her, calling her a whore and a bitch and things I can't say and she's crying and saying you killed my brother and he doesn't believe it's her brother. Never even met him before, apparently. That's young people for you. Don't take family seriously any more. He's laughing now and there was more screaming and then nothing. Then it was quiet. Your Dimitri came out of the room, blood all over him, and I look down and I see that I'm still holding the chicken I took. He takes it from me, puts it down on the floor in the room with the dead people. I'm crying and screaming now and he hits me again, tells me to go home, to call the police in a couple of hours, say I've heard something. I went outside and started to climb up the stairs to my flat, but my legs were like soft cheese and they wouldn't lift me. I sat down and tried to stop myself shaking and that's when you came in. You were singing and stumbling, very drunk. You fell on the stairs and crawled up the last few to your door.

'I wanted to warn you but my voice wouldn't come out. You saw me and waved but I knew you hadn't really seen me properly. You were too drunk. I had to stop you going in and I pulled at you but you carried on, through the open door, and you shook me off, walking into your flat just like nothing was happening. I couldn't go any further and I sat down on the floor against the wall whimpering. I didn't hear him say anything and it was dark in your room, but he led you, standing behind you as though he wasn't there, into the Varanovs' room and switched the light on. I don't know what he wanted you to do but all you could see was the chicken on the floor. You started laughing and shouting about it. "They stole my chicken!" and you picked it up and stared. You hadn't even looked into the room, but Dimitri pushed you forwards, kicking the door fully open. That was the first time I saw the whole scene. I tried not to be sick. I didn't want to attract his attention but I couldn't move. I was paralysed. I think he'd forgotten me, though. Then the awful thing happened. Leonid had been lying on the floor and I could see his leg was cut off, but he started to move. He wasn't dead. He seemed to drag himself up. He was naked, must have been sleeping naked, and he was green, his eyes half shut, not really conscious, I'm sure. He had lost so much blood. Like one of those headless chickens. No, well…' She dabbed at her eyes again, unsure as to whether or not she had made some tasteless joke, but unwilling to drop her mask of remorse. 'And you screamed. You screamed like someone who has seen, well, who has seen what you saw. You lifted the chicken up and you hit him over the head so that he fell back down. He didn't move after that. Not that I saw. And you collapsed. Dimitri, who was clean now, must have cleaned himself while I was outside, before you came back, took you back into your room and shut the door. And that was it. A few hours later I got myself home and I called the police. Said I'd heard something. It was nearly morning.'

Exhausted from her story, Zinaida Petrovna wept properly now and I reached across and put my hand on her doughy damp one. 'It's OK,' I said again. But then I reached up to my own face and felt the silent tears that had fallen there for Yelyena and for Leonid. And all I could think was, 'I was only nineteen.' I wanted to tell them I was sorry. But it was too late now.

Sergeant Molotova had been taking notes like mad, but now she stopped. I suppose they had taped it all already, but she had to take it down again in case it had changed. I knew it wouldn't have done.

'Does that sound about right?' she asked me, smiling, knowing the answer.

'As I told you, I have a lot of memory loss from that night, but it fits in with what I do remember and things that I know about Dimitri and about Yelyena and Leonid. I didn't know then that they were brother and sister. And that Yelyena and Dimitri had a baby, a little girl called Valentina, back in Vorkuta.' But I had known about his jealousy and his Stalinist need for total control at any cost. At any cost at all.

Sergeant Molotova nodded and smiled. It was clear that she hadn't known some of that until recently either. 'You are free to go, Miss Zanetti,' she said. No more Mrs Sakhnova. A lot had come up in the course of her further investigations. Well, I sighed, getting up out of the metal seat with an appropriate air of finality, that was that. I left the procurator's office and stepped out into bright sunshine, the Moskva river glinting under the bridge, Eden now on a plane out of my life and his baby on its way into my life in a big way.

EPILOGUE

IT WAS ONLY six months ago. Amazing. Eden finished his prisons piece and went back to London to get ready for his new posting. And I chose to stay in Moscow, to keep working.

So many things have happened since we got back from Vorkuta. For one thing, Dimitri's lawyers came to tell me that I'd inherited his apartment. Obviously, I signed it straight over to Tina who was already living there anyway with her maternal grandparents, Varvara and Vladimir, and her paternal grandmother, Galina. And her boyfriend, Job. Just like Southfork or something. She'd given her little flat to the maid, Juanita, who brought her ten-year-old son over from Bogota to share it. And today was a very special occasion.

Today I went to the British Embassy. Ira was waiting around on the steps holding the baby and she kissed me on both cheeks and made Donchik hold my hand. 'He's already in there,' she told me, gesturing in towards the location of Donald McCaughrean, her reinstated husband. Goose, it turns out, is Ira's all time favourite thing.

I went down some steps and into a bright little basement room with armchairs arranged in a semicircle and prints of English kings and queens in gilt frames on the walls. There were six or seven people here, most in suits. I sat next to Don and he reached across to squeeze my hand. 'Just kicking off,' he said.

A woman in a green cashmere jumper and black trousers looked at me, smiling and encouraging.

'Would you like to start today?' she asked. With one hand on the arm of my chair and the other on my enormous stomach, I hauled myself to my feet and smiled at the others who were all looking up at me. I paused and hoped tears wouldn't come to my eyes.

'Hello,' I said. 'My name's Faith, and I'm an alcoholic.'